CONTENTS

NEON AND TEARS:

Vapor Lights and Battered Souls

Marisha Cautilli
Joseph Cautilli

Cautilli, Marisha; Cautilli, Joseph. Neon and Tears: Vapor Lights and Battered Souls.

Dedications:

This is dedicated to David Stegora, who I met on Facebook and who collaborated on one of the stories with us. He also cultivated the Cyberpunk Writer's group and the Cyberpunk Detective Café with me. We miss you and your insights. Further dedication to Halina Dziewolska, who puts up with taking our daughter Marisha down these Cyberpunk trails. And to Marisha, who is 19 now and stuck through with this project all these years trying to get it done. - Joseph

This is dedicated to Prof. Navas, who kindly let me continue to develop this collection as a final assignment for his class. Thank you for letting me take this vision further and beyond. – Marisha

Contents:

CHARLEY MELENO AND HIS JUNIOR G-PEOPLE

Marisha Cautilli
Joseph Cautilli
Johnny Andrews

Where did they find you? That was the question "Team Captain Charley" always threw at the fresh recruits, his voice a gravelly whisper in the neon-lit gloom. The answers he got were a patchwork of stories, each more intriguing than the last.

Many were plucked from the wreckage of Cyberpatriot seasons, especially after the infamous 2028 hack of the North Dakota power grid. With their razor-sharp computer security skills, these kids became indispensable to the FBI. Mentoring them into "cyber-sentinels" was a necessity in this digital age.

Others were scouted from the sweat-soaked floors of karate dojos, their muscles honed and combat awareness sharp. These special field agents were rewarded with scholarships and a golden ticket out of poverty and into college. The promise of a full-ride scholarship was enough to lure in jocks of all kinds.

One girl caught Charley's eye after her mesmerizing performance in a school production of Shakespeare's The

Tempest—an intellectual genius with infiltration skills that left even Charley in awe. Then there was Kevin Jones, a forensic accounting prodigy, picked straight from his classroom. His knack for tracing payments and spotting red flags made him a valuable asset.

Charley Meleno had ten misfits and geeks, as he fondly called them, to mold into a cohesive unit. The "Junior G-People" program was a grueling yet exhilarating ride. Like many other FBI agents, Charley was tasked with running this squad of adolescents, hoping they would one day join the adult ranks. Despite being a twenty-four-year-old squad leader, he relished the obstacle courses, jumping, rolling, and swinging. It was a thrill he never outgrew.

Walking onto the unit, Charley was greeted by the raw, pulsing beats of The Creepshow's *Run For Your Life.* The brass had given him the green light to transform the floor into a retro-future haven, a blend of 1920s Art Deco and cyberpunk grit. The rich browns of cherrywood floors were interspersed with haphazardly strewn electronics displays and fiber optic cables. Sepia-toned walls, adorned with glossy triangle tessellations, lent a mechanical vibe, while the copper-clad ceiling, patterned with squares, added a touch of industrial elegance. A strip of ambient blue light traced the ceiling's edge, a subtle guide in case of an emergency blackout.

The room's atmosphere was a dance between the cosmic and the eerie, reminiscent of an old train station caught in a technological rebellion. As Charley stepped in, the automated coffee maker whirred to life, delivering his cup along a conveyor belt. He took a sip, savoring the perfect blend of temperature and bitterness, a testament to the machine's precision.

On the far wall, flanking the door to his office, were two recreated Art Nouveau masterpieces: "The Cyclist" and "Dog on a Leash." Ahead of him stood his new team, each member stationed at their semi-circular, oak-finished desks. The cubbyholes were personalized with knickknacks—plastic, crystal, ivory, or jade—reflecting their owners' personalities.

As Special Agent Charles Meleno entered, Enaya Habib, a petite Emirati girl, rushed to lower the volume just as The Misfits' *Dig Up Her Bones* began to play. The team, a motley crew of misfits and prodigies, awaited his command, ready to dive into the digital fray. His team felt a rising pride within him. But he wondered if this program was a good idea. He guessed those in charge of its creation had known something. "Today, our job is to scan the internet and determine if the level of terrorist chat is increasing or about the same. We got this gig because some genetically enhanced British kid tipped it in while traveling in the Philippines. No one took her seriously because she had malaria, but they guessed that just in case, it would be good to put you kids on it."

"Why is increasing important?" One of the younger members, Hanley Stevens, asked. She was a short emo girl with clown white covering her tan face, cherry lips, and dark brown hair.

"Excellent question. Can anyone answer it?" Charley replied. Immediately, the same four hands in the group of ten went up. Charley decided to call on one of the members without their hand up. "Arek?"

The Polish boy with a square head and short cropped light blond hair lifted his blue eyes. "I believe that increased chatter might mean that the terrorists are planning the details of an attack."

"Excellent. What does it require on our part?" Cheerfully, Charley responded, snapping his fingers.

Arek thought for a second and said, "It requires us to pass the information to Enaya so she can decode and translate." Enaya nodded, adjusting the small, tessellated, blue silk fabric she wore as a head scarf.

"Perfect," Charley stated as he slowly rotated on the ball of his foot. He figured that today would be a quiet day. Nothing was expected, and the chatter was constant for the last three weeks. He was, of course, wrong.

"Agent Meleno, hurry up, GNN breaking news!" Linda Gold, a fellow squad leader, yelled into the room. Meleno lunged out the door, and his team observed him.

Breaking news on terrorism was rarely good. There was the occasional mention of terrorists killed, but outside of that, the news was usually about one of their extreme explosive threats. Charley hoped the casualty level was low.

"Just in," the news anchor stated as she quickly removed her pink locks of hair from her face. "Fourteen of the nation's one hundred and forty oil refineries were attacked. They were a combination of suicide drones and hypersonic attacks. Officials are calling it a blatant act of terror. We will provide additional information as soon as it is available."

"All right, kids," Charley gasped back into the squad room from which he came. "I need to contact Langley and find out what our role, if any, is in this operation."

As he spoke, his smartphone lit up. He yanked it out with his brown-skinned olive undertone hand and listened.

"Arek," Hanely coughed. "We should start perusing the typical sites."

"Shouldn't we wait?" Arek asked hesitantly as he bit his fingernails.

"Naw," Hanley flapped her hand, imitating a cat scratch. "No harm in looking in places we have already."

"We have had no increases for weeks. This means that they managed to use alternative routes."

"So, let's get on finding them," Enaya chimed in, unfolding her work laptop.

After an alarming twenty minutes, Meleno returned to the room. Enaya, Arek, and Hanley already found something. It wasn't big, but the longest journey, as they say, starts with the first deadly step. They tracked a phone call using cell tower triangulation to a small bar on the south side of Philadelphia. Enaya Habib interpreted it as a comment about using RPGs and drones in the attack. Since this detail had been purposefully left out of news media information, she suspected it bore note to investigate.

"That place's got a few million people for sure," another squad member said Carin McCall. She was one of three team members recruited from college and grad school instead of high school, recommended by her guidance counselor as a way to "put her energy to use." He always wondered how much energy she had, as even with all the work that came with being a Junior-G, she still almost literally bounced off the walls.

"A few million people in a bar?" Charley retorted in an attempt to tone down her exaggerations. The woman was prone to theatrics, and her recruitment file had mentioned early signs of bipolar disorder.

"Jeez, it's sarcasm," The girl with blue dyed hair and overused pink eye shadow retorted back while bouncing her head from side to side. The only thing other than the pink and blue mismatch was the outdated white and red bobby socks under her magenta leather dress that only extended to her knees.

It had only been sixteen days since the group had formed in September, but Charley realized that for all her craziness, Carin McCall was probably one of the brightest people on the team. If he could only keep her out of psych-ward, "McCall, that was so funny I forgot to laugh. Keep it tight-lipped."

The girl was crestfallen and hung her head. "Sorry, sir," she sighed.

Hanley, Arek, Enaya, Linda, and Carin watched the news with Meleno as the ambulances took away casualties from the energy plant. Hover drones caught all the action from above, barely zooming in on the broken corpses still around the site.

Charley stared at the news footage and grew sick. *How could people do such a thing? What drove those actions? How could someone ever think of doing those actions?* Some of the answers were easy to deduce. He knew that with the destruction of ten percent of the oil refineries, gasoline prices in the US would skyrocket, and the country would be forced to change the law to buy refined products from Canada and other countries. *Was this an economic attack to send inflation out of control and place the country in recession?*

Recession, momentary pain. That was the answer. Charley scoffed. For Charley, it served no cause apart from bringing hatred to all their people. Even those that were not their people. It was very black and white in Charley's world, right down the middle. Working up through the F.B.I., Meleno had to throw out the ethics book. His top advisors thought of the world as a stop light: White Americans and Christians were in the green up to maybe amber, and most of the Middle Eastern countries were on the red alert. Those born within the United States were deemed chiefly passable. As he was mixed race- part-African American, Dominican, and Italian- he struggled with such views, and it almost forced him out of the FBI once before. Part of him hated that. He knew damn fine people. Even the juniors in his team, like Enaya, were bedrock good.

Charley's phone chimed and broke them all out of their gloomy thoughts. "Meleno." A few moments passed as Charley paced back and forth, listening intently to the voice at the other end of the line. "I don't like it…they're not quite ready for that exposure, damn it! Okay, okay, yes, sir."

Hiding his phone away in his jacket pocket, Charley observed each member of his squad and envisioned their dead bodies. Dark red blood covering them all. Each had burned flesh where laser holes had disintegrated the skin away. Broken limbs, young bodies tattered and torn. He hated that he did that. It left a queasiness in his stomach. It was a habit he picked up after he watched the death of his mentor, Akane Hirata. Kicking down a door to stop a drug ring, buckshot sliced her face despite her wearing a vest. He considered quitting the force afterward and even spent several months thinking about it. He went as far as to speak to the psychiatrist, Siggy Eldritch. Two things came out of this: the first was that he would never go back to a therapist again; the second was that he had to get out of the narcotics division of the FBI. Values-wise, as a surfpunk, he even supported the use of recreational marijuana, but that seemed like a lifetime ago.

To center himself, Meleno shook his head and walked out. The room had a lingering scent of espresso from having so much coffee. It felt warm and pleasant in Meleno's nostrils. He marched to the nearest vending machine, inserted a cred, stabbed at the buttons to order a grape Nehi, tapping the ring pull more out of habit now, pulled and opened the can, and chugged back on the fizzy sweetness. As he sipped the soda, he wished it included a lemon, four shots of vodka, two shots of Chambord, some agave nectar, five ounces of club soda, some crushed ice, and an LED cube. This was his relaxing drink when he got home after work on weekends. During the week, he would drink a Bud Light.

Strolling over to Linda and Enaya, the latter said, "It looks like our informant is still struggling with malaria. We will try getting in touch later."

"Ok," Charley stated, nodding his head. "Looks like they want us in this. I think it's because they currently want all hands on deck. Still, I worry the teen might not be ready. We're still fresh out of the gate."

Arms flailing and head still bobbing side to side, Carin McCall rushed him. "Sir, you may not think this, but we are well-trained and deeply committed. We all joined the junior G squad to take out terrorist threats. We can do this… Sir," she added as an afterthought.

How did she hear me? Charley thought. *Good ears, I suppose.* "That's the problem," Charley sighed. "I know you can, but then what, where does it lead? These jerks won't stop! A powerplant is down. What's next? Hitting a nuke plant?"

McCall's eyes widened in shock that she may not have been ready for. But then, the angry bitterness that often led to treatments in the psych ward prevailed and shone through. "Yeah, well, those sand dwellers haven't met me. They're just bitches with big beards!" Linda and Enaya drifted off, the latter with a frown on her face.

Being a team leader was new to Charley. He was unsure

whether to laugh because it was kind of a funny joke or stay firm and call out Carin's blatant bigotry. As team members displayed some obvious pain, he chose the latter, stating, "We do not know the motive of these attacks. I will not be tolerating bigotry of any kind here."

"Sorry, sir, just proving my point." Carin's icy blue eyes sank like a scolded puppy dog. Carin noticed the others had left, and she scolded herself privately. Charley realized she was a little too eager to get into battle. "I want to kick ass, as I am sure the others do also."

"I know. Let's meet with the others," Meleno offered with kindness. They strolled down the corridor, and Meleno finished his drink. Entering and seeing all his squad still watching the news.

"Okay, guys, something heavy is coming up. While I get details, you have a small amount of downtime. Do not waste it! Dismissed."

Shuffling of feet, most left to reach their quarters or head to the gym. A few hovered around.

"Sir?" Arek asked. "I can tell we're gonna be part of this mission, but will we actually be going in headfirst?"

"I haven't figured that out yet," the team captain told the sophomore-aged boy. "If I were you, I'd brace for that possibility."

Hanely sagged over to him. Her voice was deadpan as usual. "Well, the bar did not have a camera, but the jewelry store across the street and two doors up had one. I took the liberty to call. I said that we had a warrant for the tape."

"Well, that was a lie," Charley stated, shocked.

"Well, sir, I like to think of them not so much as lies as alternative truths," the words hovered from Hanley's mouth. The somberness greeted the listener first and often made it difficult to listen to what she was saying. She continued all in one breath, ignoring him. "They allowed me to tap into the footage. I looked at people coming and going from the bar and compared their film with our bank."

"Genius," said Quin Rhodes, walking up with an ear-to-ear smile. He wore tight, ripped denim jeans and a brown tee shirt. Quin was another of the kids recruited from college and a field operative on the team, so he saw much of the action. Quin darted up so silently that he stood shoulder to shoulder with Arek before the kid knew. When Quin spoke, Arek finally realized his space had been invaded and jumped.

"I know, right?" Hanely agreed. "Anyhow, this green minivan showed up about twenty minutes before the call. Look at the license plate—an English Bulldog sticker. Outside of being the coolest, I could get a shot of the guy's face. Real tropical cowboy if I say so."

"Tropical cowboy?" Charley asked, not sure what that phrase entailed.

"Yeah, clean cut- no facial hair. Hawaiian shirt. He loves gun violence and is heavily macho. This one walks like a Mexican cowboy."

"Oh." So that was what a tropical cowboy was. It sounded a bit stereotyped but logical in Charley's mind.

"Anyhow, I ran his face through the database," Hanley announced. "His name is Emilio Rodriguez."

"Wonderful," Charley cheered.

"Yep," Hanley beamed. "But weirdly, he never left the bar. He is still there."

"Quin, you're with me," Charley said, having memorized the face and stats.

"Well, she has his home address," Quin pointed out. "Shouldn't we just wait until he goes home?"

"No, I want him before the trail goes cold," Charley replied firmly.

"I want to go!" Carin protested. "I could be a real help!"

Charley chuckled. He should have seen this coming, given their earlier conversation. "You must be old enough to go into a bar to investigate a bar. That is the rule."

"Not if you're a bartender. That's only seventeen!" Carin argued.

"You know I meant drinking age, McCall."

Flustered, Carin started to protest about how she could analyze the crime scene, but Quin broke in, "Doctor McCall, we all know that you are an extremely competent Forensic Medical Examiner with a separate Ph.D. in Criminology and Chemistry, all before the age of twenty, I might add but…"

Carin shimmied with shock and delight, hissing, "See Agent Chuck." He was okay with Charley, even Charles, but never Chuck. It reminded Meleno too much of the Peanuts comics. "Quin knows how to respect a lady for her mind," Carin continued. "Notice how he called me 'doctor.'" She breathed and changed the subject. "Whatever, if you boys want your little road trip without me- a vaudevillian master of disguise on top of my medical training, fine. Just bring me back a pizza when you return."

How could she make such a simple phrase so dramatic? Meleno thought. "I promise," Meleno exhaled. Carin smiled, leaned in, and kissed his cheek. Charles went beat red as Ms. Habib clapped in mock enthusiasm and then ordered Carin to her office for a lecture on sexual harassment and workplace appropriateness. Carin's face sagged as soon as she said it, knowing the incoming lecture would be extended.

Charley and Quin worried about how the mission would go, so they went to the armory and grabbed weapons. Both took the new light ion blaster (LIB). LIB not only described what it was, but it also granted it the street nickname of the Liberator.

They went to the lot to Meleno's rustic Bentley 2030 Mulliner, a powerhouse hybrid car with excellent maneuverability and fuel efficiency of sixty miles to the gallon. It even had an automatic driving function. As Charles approached, the car door rose. The seats were tan leather with bright copper accents. The dashboard was a golden-brown console wholly enhanced by the digital age. It had touch technology and voice-activated command systems. Its autopilot could not only cruise but entirely steer on a tight cliff side of a mountain, barely more comprehensive than the car at nearly two hundred miles per hour.

The young Quin smiled, "Awesome wheels, dude." Charley nodded. Once inside, Charley's voice-activated a stream for some music. Set it Off's song "Wolf in Sheep's Clothing" roared out of his woofers in surround sound, and they off.

During the ride, Quin made air drum rolls and then, at one point, asked, "So, is anything between you and Carin?"

"What no," Charley barked. "Oh, you mean that peck on the cheek. She's just a freak, like the rest of you apparently."

"Shame dude. I don't know what's worse that they linked you to a crew in which all its members have daddy and authority issues, and you get to be the daddy authority. Or that you ain't made that girl."

As the car passed through the hot Philadelphia streets, Charley realized how sick he was of these kids' talk. Steam from the asphalt rippled off like water. Charley felt like a pressure cooker on this hot day, sick of these adolescents and young adults drama. He decided to play the father-like authority he was accused of being. "Ok. First, that's sexist," Charley listed angrily. "And second, this is completely inappropriate. I don't want to go there and discuss it."

"Fine by me, old gunaholic man," quipped Rhodes.

"Gunaholic?" Charley laughed. *Is this how Quin perceived him?*

"Yeah, like a dude who owns like thirty guns hidden in his home and tries to convince everyone it is the way to go." Charley's laughter echoed louder.

After heartily laughing for half a minute, Charley's face rested in a smile. "Well, your armchair psych is eight miles off and six feet deep if you keep this up. Any other insights?"

"To you, no," Quin replied. "But to that Carin chick- if you don't fall for her, she is heading to the dark side. I see her in the future as one of those back-alley doctors who grow human hearts in pigs to sell on the black transplant market."

"You don't like her," Charley gauged.

Rubbing his face, Quin sighed with frustration. "Not that

at all. Friends say I can see the future. I'm psychic."

"Is there any truth to it?" While Charley's squad was certainly a strange bunch, this led to interesting conversations about their lives.

"No. I just put out there what no one is willing to say. How about you?"

"Got no room for psychics in my life. Went to one as a kid. The girl was not much older than me. She told me I would see the sunrise and fight the darkness all my life, but the night was inside. Still, for my efforts as a blessing, I would die just as twilight fell and not have to live the long, slow night."

"That's heavy shit," Quin gasped.

"So heavy, she was full of it," Charley scoffed. "Wanted my money back but wound up dating the girl for several months. She was cool- claimed a gift."

Quickly, Quin interrupted and changed the subject: "Avoid the city center. Lots of anarchists are protesting today—you know, the New World Order stuff."

"Gotcha, boss," Charley replied sarcastically. "So, you think you will stay with the FBI?"

"Don't know," Quin seriously stated, "I got a huge interest in arcology and its designs."

"Computer simulations?"

"Oh, no… I like to try to build a real one." Quin leaned on the window, resting his head on his hand and puffing his lips.

"Most proposals to build real arcologies fail," Charley pointed out, rounding the street. Only a few blocks down this road, they were at the bar.

"I know, they tend to have many financial, structural, or conceptual shortcomings," Quin admitted. His eyes caught a strange man rounding a street corner, so he changed the subject, shouting, "There is our guy!" With Charley's foot still on the gas pedal, Quin thrust open the door and dashed out of the car.

***

Back at HQ, Carin snuck away from the rest of the team. Distraught, she marched through the halls of the FBI building and took an elevator to the armory level. Her mind whirred, and her heart still pounded heavily from her argument with her immediate supervisor. Often, she wondered why she'd joined this program. She did not need this shit. Even now, many worldwide were interested in the papers she wrote. Maybe this was a mistake; her future lay more with working with a company like the growing Haasting Corporation or PowerGentics. However, she preferred to stay away from the latter's legal troubles. In the end, she did not need this chicken outfit. *They should be honored to have me*, she thought *and not treat me like shit. Well, I'll show them that I won't be stepped on.* In the distance was the infirmary. She strolled closer to it.

Baffled by how easily accessible the weapons were, Carin. She just had to walk in, grab one, and sign it out. Either way, the talk with Enaya ate away her little sanity. The teen schooled and lectured her on appropriate behavior in the workplace and practically threatened to kick her out of the program if she ever approached Meleno like that. "Like what?" she mumbled to herself. "I approached him in the spirit of friendship and gave him a peck on the cheek. Since when do we live in a society where showing any bit of affection could mean a death sentence? He is quite cute, though. I like those eyes." Maybe it was time for Meleno's right hand to die.

The teen figured the best way for her to get her point across was something slow and torturous, so her eyes landed on the old-fashioned pistols. A vision came to Carin: Enaya wailing in pain, a shot lodged in each hand. A mischievous chuckle escaped Carin, but it was also a thought of remorse. Sweat beaded on her brow as she thought about it, her hand shook. "Do I want to do this?" she audibly thought. The makeup on her face trickled, and she bit her lip. The coppery taste of her blood filled her mouth, and she let out a "blech." She thought back to the time her mother, a drug dealer, pulled out a 9 mm Glock and shot a home invader who wanted drugs but had no cash. She never forgot how his skull burst, brains flying against the wall. Her mom hacked the corpse into smaller bits and let it sit in a bath of sulfuric acid for two days. Before nothing was left but bones, her mother callously dumped the remains in a trash bag and threw it in the city's trash incinerator. Carin's eyes blurred momentarily, and instead, she focused on her face in the window. Her mascara ran down her cheeks. For a minute, she wondered if this was really who she was or if this was some weird form of road rage aimed at coworkers. With that, she chuckled, turned, put her hands in her skirt's pockets, and skipped to the bathroom to freshen up her makeup, whistling Lucretia's *My Reflection* by Sisters of Mercy.

***

Muttering obscenities to himself, Charley swiftly glanced out the rearview mirror, turning on his body camera. A car was directly on his tail. He flipped on the dash cam, ran the red light, and rounded the corner in the car. Charley hoped the stupid kid flipped on his body camera in his haste. More importantly, he hoped Quin would be alright despite rushing in without backup. He swore that he was going to have a talk with the kid back at the base for violation of protocol.

Frustrated, Meleno rolled toward the curb. Red neon lights flashed and crackled from the bar's sign: *Franks*. Even in daylight the newfangled vapor sign burned his eyes and obscured his vision of the action between his partner and the suspect. *Hell with the blur, I need to focus*, Charley thought, *Damn kid should have waited for backup*!

Through tearing eyes, he saw Rhodes approach the suspect. "Federal agent!" Rhodes yelled less than two feet away. "Freeze Mr. Emilio Rodriguez!" Charley charged from thirty feet behind the action.

Charley's worst fear occurred. Emilio's hand went deep into his pants pockets and whipped out an old Glock 9 mm. Time slowed. Quin's eyes glazed, and Charley swallowed his heart. Just as the gun was halfway up, Quin leapt and tackled Emilio.

The terrorists gun hand and head flew back and struck the ground. Now Charley worried that they may have just killed their only lead. He brought the car up on the pavement, clicked on his body cam and lunged into action. The Damned's *Ignite* played loudly in his head.

Quin and Rodriguez exchanged rapid blows. Quin's nose spouted blood, as Charley caught Emilio's hand and quickly slapped the cuff on it. He swung it around the terrorist's back and cuffed the second hand. Quinn remained hot. Charley depersonalized and forced himself to shift from reactive thinking to proactive. He knew the kid's frustration but did not want to blow the arrest. "Quin cool walk." The cool walk concept came from community policing to help frustrated officers not beat suspects. Quin stared angerly, not expecting to be ordered off the situation. With respect for the junior g clear in his voice, Charley praised Quin for the collar, said the kid would get full credit and validated his anger. And why not, *in a just world this terrorist prick deserved to be dead*, Charley thought. Quin disengaged, clutched his nose to stop the bleeding, and circled.

Grudgingly, Meleno pulled out a Miranda rights card and robotically read it to the suspect. The terrorist laughed. "You got nothing on me!" he yelled.

"Note, the defendant announced there is something that we could have on him," Charley called out. Glad Rodriguez was stupid enough to be talking because his body cam was recording everything, Charley informed, "For starters we have you assaulting and attempting to murder a federal agent."

"He never identified himself," Emilio shouted. The terrorist's leg trembled. Charley liked that, as it showed the kid was scared.

"Got it on the car's dash cam kid," Charley grunted, yanking the kid toward the car. "You okay, Quin?"

"I think he broke my nose," Quin breathed, still grasping his nose and cheeks.

"Quin if you don't mind waiting for a minute or two outside the car. I don't want to mess up the seat."

Appearing angry, Quin nodded and said, "Sure." As Charley hauled Emilio toward the back, he double clicked his comm button on his keychain. A hologram of Carin appeared.

"'Sup boss," Carin drawled.

We really need to work on this kid's formality, Charley thought. "Quin broke his nose. Can you talk him through ways to mitigate bleeding, so he doesn't stain my seats?"

"Anything for you, Agent Meleno," Carin cooed. Charley groaned.

Unbolting his car's back door, Charley spoke to Emilio, "So, we have agitated assault to add to the list. DA is going to love this. We will add that to the twenty-five people who died in the rocket attack."

"No one was supposed to die," Emilio breathed, appearing on the verge of tears.

"Let the record show, the suspect confessed that no one on this terrorist operation was supposed to die. Hence, he knows of the operation." As he harshly shoved Emilio into the car, when the kid landed, Charley noticed the kid peed himself. "What the hell?!"

"Looks like he pissed in your car," Quin chuckled loudly, giving Carin a better look at the damage.

"He needs a cotton press Agent Meleno," Carin ordered. "Might be broke."

Boiling with rage, Charley bit his own lip and barely managed to suppress anger. "Add destruction of a federal agent's property to the list. Three strikes, if they don't put the needle in your arm, you'll be spending the rest of your days at the supermax."

"You'll never get the smell out," Quin teased. After slamming the backdoor shut, Charley opened the driver's seat, found his first aid kit, and gave Rhodes one of the cotton presses.

"And you shut up! I should write you up for charging without backup. Bet you didn't even turn your body-cam on," Charley's eyes were stern as stone.

"Sorry sir," Quin responded.

Catching himself, Charley said "It was a good collar." Quin smiled and gave a chuckle. The sight of the kid's broken nose made Charley laugh back. "Let's get you to the hospital," Charley offered, disgusted with himself over his own rage. Getting into his car, he repeatedly mumbled to himself about how the smell would never come out.

After dropping Quin at the hospital, Charley went to the station to question the suspect and to file a worker's compensation report for Quin, in case he needed to get plastic surgery or something after the attack.

***

After Charley Meleno hung up, Carin walked to Agent Gold, who was on the line with a little girl named Rebecca Coke, the original informant. As the girl adjusted her oversized black leather jacket, Gold struggled to make out what the little girl was saying. Between the East Ender accent and the malaria, the conversation appeared to be going nowhere.

"You need help Agent Gold?" Carin asked. Linda nodded, solemnly. "Sometimes having medical training is a good thing."

Carin spoke to Rebecca, mainly about boys to spark the kid's interest. Then, the conversation moved to how the little girl felt physically. With the push of a button, Carin got the kid's temperature: 102.3. Fiddling with her fingers, Carin wondered how she could recenter the conversation on the attack. "I am sorry to hear you are sick. You are such a strong girl." The child giggled. Carin laughed at herself. "I need a little of that strength now. The kid sucked in a breath and confessed she was "ridin' her clever mike" -cockney slang for bike and playing in an area she was not supposed to be. Carin reassured her that there would be no punishment for her actions. The child in Carin's eyes was a hero.

Rebecca told her that she saw a group of men around a truck. She heard them talking about rocket propelled grenades and then mentioned drones. As with most genetically enhanced the talk of technology and science lured her in. She snuck closer hoping to catch a glimpse of the drones. At that point, she heard the men saying that the shipment was to be used in an attack in the US in three days' time.

"Were they holding any papers?" Carin gently asked.

"No. But one man 'ad a clip board," the girl stated, fiddling with the spikes on her leather wristbands over her black mesh wristies.

"Did you see what was on it?" Carin asked. The child nodded her head.

"Bees and honey, five million cred," she replied. Carin figured the first as cockney slang for money. "I mean they weren't coppin a flowerpot." Carin was glad as a girl she had visited England's east side and got some familiarity with cockney slang.

"Yeah, I agree- it would not have been hot," she replied. The child raised a hand in acknowledgement. "Catch a name on the shipment."

"Nope. Needed to duck and dive, as they loaded the derry and toms, but remember sighting a bloke, whom seemed to be real lump of lead," she continued.

"Ah the leader," replied Carin.

"They called 'im Paul Datu Martinez- a local chap. Seemed like a nice guy: Polished and trim. Any'ow, 'e said the boat take it to Filadelfia, it would" she replied "and meet up with a gay and 'ardy- run by Emillio." The conversation lasted a few more minutes and then the girl said she was tired, as was Gold from listening to it. They thanked her and she went to join her family for some grub.

"Thank you, Carin," Gold said. "I don't think I could have gotten all that without you."

"You're welcome," Carin said and for a minute she felt like she belonged, in spite of the previous fight with Enaya Habib, her supervisor. Maybe, she overreacted a bit and could give this team a chance.

Shuffling out, Gold contacted Philippine authorities to get Paul Datu Martinez found and arrested. Maybe they could flip him. Then she went to their forensic accountant, Kevin, to trace the money in Emillio's accounts and put a stop to all his credit cards and banking capabilities. The accountant told her that he and Hanley could track money transfers that might help in identifying other members of this group. They relayed their information to Charley, and he instructed them to pass all the information along to the FBI Deputy Director's office, so they could get the information out to all FBI and homeland security personnel.

***

Emilio quickly lawyered up, which was shocking for Charley. Usually, terrorists hated lawyers and loved to tout their cause. Most of the time, they could not wait to confess. Typically, it was just a matter of inducing bragging about their deeds. Indeed, the lawyer was waiting at the station when Charley arrived. *How did the guy even know?* The attorney's name was Mikael De Laurentis.

An hour after returning to the junior G headquarters, Charley Meleno and Enaya Habib escorted Emilio into a dimly lit, greyscale interrogation room, leaving him with his lawyer while they called the DA, Emily Squilla. Charley went to Carin and Hanley to perform a voice analysis on the recording of Rodriguez's phone conversation. Carin was golden.

Twenty minutes later, Meleno, Habib, and Squilla marched into the interrogation room fully prepped.

Meleno laid the pictures out of the destruction from the raid. He followed it with a picture of the one person who actually died.

With his harshest stare, Charley's squared his shoulder, and leaned into the opposing team. "You are going way for a long-time Emilio. The grandchildren of your prison guards at the supermax will be full officers, when you stop being a repeated rape victim."

"Agent Meleno, that is uncalled for," Mikael insisted.

"It is, we are going for the death penalty," Emily offered.

Squaring his shoulders on the lawyer, Charley asked, "Are you representing his interest or his backers?" Charley had experience with lawyers paid for by other sources. Often the client was their last priority.

"In this matter," the attorney stated. "I fully represent

him."

"Don't give me the standard ethics speech," Charley stated. "This guy assaulted an FBI agent and is looking at death for the terrorist action. I have half a mind to have him flown to Guantanamo Bay and have him integrated there."

"That would be illegal. It happened on US soil, and you captured him on US soil," the attorney said.

"Do you really think that matters?" Charley filled with bluster. "We know the rpgs and drones came from the Philippines and we got a witness that says, he was to receive the shipment and head the team. I got a man working on tracking down your client's finances and expect to have a needle in his arm before the new year, so he better give me something. Either here or at GITMO. We have a legal team that works on conflicted lawyers and sends them there as well."

"Threats are not appreciated. We plan to cooperate with the investigation if we can but my client's cell phone at the bar was borrowed by several people...." Emilio's lawyer leaned back in his black plastic chair and crossed his arms.

"We thought that might be the case," Charley stated. "So, we did a voice analysis- it appears to be your client's voice."

Habib interrupted, "We have his cell phone and soon we will have the numbers of everyone he has called on that phone. Even if it is a burner phone, we should have all the calls contacting him. Why not save us the time and give us the names of the people involved in this."

Emilio glanced at his attorney, who stated, "We want to help but we have not heard anything to sway us."

"Gentleman," Emily started. "Since time is of the essence, I have a one-time limited offer. I need the names and the next location of the strike. In return, I'll take the needle off the table and have him moved from the supermax to federal prison."

"Not good enough. We want immunity," the lawyer stated.

"Immunity?" Emily asked. "You must be joking."

"My client gets immunity, never does a day in prison, and enters witness protection," Mikael offered. "In return, he gives you everything he knows. All the team members."

Meleno huffed, facing a tough decision, "I think we should let him burn."

"Witness protection after two years of behavior modification, reorientation counseling, and a mind wipe," Emily counteroffered.

Emilio's eyes flashed red, "I want to keep my memories," he stated.

Meleno and Habib exchanged glances with Emily. They wanted this man in jail, but they understood the need to get the rest. A knock happened at the door and Emily left the room for a minute. When she returned, she stated "Four more attacks just occurred. The death sentences are piling up."

Emilio's attorney appeared uneasy. "How about if we let the decision on the memory wipe to be based on the quality of the information now and good behavior in the program?" he asked. A ding echoed from Enaya's phone, and she turned around to open her messages. When Charley put a hand on her shoulder and asked what she was doing, she simply mouthed "Agent Gold". Charley nodded in understanding, his hand leaving Enaya's shoulder, and peered over to watch the teen compose a message. She asked Linda to follow up with the kid who gave the tip. Charley pulled back and gave his right-hand a thumbs up.

The attorney watched his client and then leaned into him. The two whispered to each other. "Agreed," Emily settled.

"Ok, we need those names and the next target," Charley demanded. Emily quickly spoke the details of the immunity agreement and the computer printed it out. Emilio signed. Once he got the names, Charley ran them through his hand-held computer.

"These are all contract hitters. You're a middleman. This is no terrorist action," Charley exclaimed.

"You're right about me being a middleman, but it is a hired terrorist action," Emilio corrected. It was at this point Enaya put her phone away and stood upright.

"Since when do terrorists outsource," Charley ordered.

"Since when do they have attorneys come and meet them at the station? Who is paying for this operation?"

"I don't know," Emilio offered, sweat beading down his face.

"Who's paying your salary," Enaya demanded of De Laurentis.

"Attorney-client privilege," Mikael slyly responded.

"Well, it looks like your client is acting in bad faith," Emily said. "I think this speaks to the wipe."

"He gave you the names," reminded Emilio's attorney.

"All but the guy funding them." Emily smacked her hands on the interrogation table. Charley looked at Enaya. It was clear she was as fed up with this game as he was.

"We need that name," Enaya insisted. "He's the guy we want to nail."

"We only spoke by computer link," Emilio insisted. "The voices and messages were scrambled. I don't know who he is."

"Do you have the recordings?" Enaya asked.

"No," Emilio frantically answered. "The messages disappeared once they were listened to."

"Too bad, looks like your memory is history," Charley taunted, trying to get a reaction from the suspect. Emilio's fingers nervously drummed the table, and he bit his lip.

"Wait, I got a memory of his distorted face from the call!" Emilio exclaimed after a moment of thinking.

Charley peered over at Emily and Enaya, "Carin might be able to get the memory. If she has his computer and the time of the last call, she might be able to get the connection back, but I doubt it."

"We need the memory, links to the calls, and for you to testify," Enaya demanded of Emilio, hand digging for her phone once more. Charley's hand hovered near Enaya, signaling he would handle the assignments.

"I will testify!" Emilio exclaimed, smacking his own hands on the table.

***

Within two hours, with the help Linda received from talking to Rebecca, the FBI's field teams rounded up all the terrorists for hire. The mercenaries fought bitterly but, in the end, they figured it was best to surrender than to die for any cause. Unfortunately, there was still one man they had to track down.

Linda alerted Carin, Hanley, Charley, and Enaya that according to the follow-up on the tip, there was the possibility that the operation was funded by Chechen billionaire, Makka Khavazh. Carin spent the next two hours clearing up the picture from Emilio's distorted memories. The image was indeed Makka Khavazh. After she got the name and gave it to Charley, his Junior-Gs were set in motion.

Hanley and Arek went right to work, searching for any public information they could gather. All available financial records went to Kevin to analyze, as they wanted a full picture of any political motivations the billionaire could have. Meanwhile in the forensics lab, Carin-with a warrant from the FBI- performed an extra investigation of a few of Emilio's other memories. With Rhodes still in the hospital for his nose, Charley instead brought Enaya to apprehend the billionaire.

When Charley arrived at the corporate headquarters of Khavazh, he discovered Khavazh on the roof, boarding his private jet. Buckets of rain belted the pavement. The billionaire's bodyguards drew their guns, trying to stop Meleno and Habib from reaching their target. The two agents fired back, disabling some of Khavazh's protection. Makka's helicopter hovered over the ground as a bodyguard lunged in front of the pilot. Khavazh reached for the chopper's rungs and the two agents shot at him. With a primal cry, Enaya shifted her aim at the pilot, shooting the guard in front. The man in the suit stumbled off the chopper, falling thirty stories. Enaya locked her aim on the pilot, bullets flying through the helicopter glass and on the vehicle's sides. A stray bullet of Charley's found Makka's leg, the other man's arm instinctively dropping to cover the wound. They had him. He was going to jail and pay for his crimes. That was, until the pilot swerved and cut the engine. *What a suicidal move,* Charley thought, pausing his fire as the helicopter dipped out of sight.

After a minute, Enaya spotted the chopper, too far away for a bullet to do any damage. Unfortunately, the billionaire successfully flew away to Brazil. With a frustrated groan, Charley expressed his doubts about ever catching him to Enaya.

"We may not have gotten him this time," Habib sighed. "But that doesn't mean we aren't stacked with info on him. We should head back to HQ and see what the rest of the team found."

"First we have to pick up Rhodes," Charley ordered. "Hospital said they would discharge him soon."

After a quick jot to the hospital, Charley, Enaya, and Quin returned to the Junior G-people's HQ. In the room assigned to Meleno's team, the remaining squad members were huddled around, exchanging information. As Rhodes creaked the door open, a wave of cheers and applause came from the rest of the room. Enaya followed Quin, Charley trailing behind. With a wave of Meleno's hands, the crowd simmered down.

"We all did some digging on Khavazh, sir," Carin beamed. "Of course, I'd like to think I found the most."

Arek, Hanley, and Kevin quietly groaned. Before the group could fight, Charley intervened.

"We'll exchange findings later," he ordered. "First, I'd like to have a sit down with all of you."

Instead of a select number of kids, now everyone groaned and louder than before. What a nice reminder for Charley about how unapproachable he could be. As a show of peace, Charley sat on the floor.

"We did not catch Makka Khavazh," he announced. "We were a mere second away from getting him, seconds we could've got back if we acted faster. Who wants to tell me what could have been slowing us down?"

Unlike before, no one raised their hands. Meleno's face dropped as he realized he needed to mentor them on more things than just the missions. After giving them half a minute to get a clue, he answered his question. "We would've been faster to the jump if we had better cooperation."

All the team sank their heads. "If we weren't caught up in our petty squabbles," Charley continued. "Maybe we would've got him, but as it stands, our coordinating skills need work. The next few months we may live on high alert. You'll be seeing each other much more often, so any differences you have better be sorted out by now."

With a knock on the door and permission to enter, Linda greeted the rest of the group.

"If I may," she cheerily said. "I overheard you talking about teamwork, and I wanted to butt in and say that your starting point for that skill is surprisingly phenomenal. Hanley, Arek, and Kevin, when I saw you rummaging the web for anything on Mr. Khavazh, you all seemed in sync with each other. You guys also did a spectacular job in relaying the information to Enaya. I obviously can't forget Carin, since you helped me talk to Ms. Coke and teamed up with Hanley to parse Mr. Rodriguez's memories." Carin bowed her head in humility. The rest of the team exchanged high-fives with each other.

"And Enaya, you were really cooperative in the interrogation room with Squilla and I," Charley admitted. "I suppose not catching the guy has clouded my perspective a bit, and I apologize. Good work to all of you today."

"We'll do better next time," Enaya promised, a roar of "yeahs" echoing from her teammates. The group was dismissed and they all placed their things in their cubbies and filed out of their room one-by-one.

THE G-PEOPLE AND THE DREAM WITCH: BIRTH OF THE SOUL SHREDDERS

Joseph Cautilli
Marisha Cautilli

"**A**sk yourself whether the dream of heaven and greatness should be waiting for us in our graves - or whether it should be ours here and now and on this earth."- Ayn Rand

Blue neon cascades the waterfall to the old Chinese Buffet, while koi swam listlessly in its water. Mike Morrissey just finished work for the last time. Securing his final check in his six-fingered hand, he hugged his boss and said goodbye. The check was not much, as he'd lived a poor life.

Knowing economic times were rough and that he was an excellent worker, his boss begged him to stay. Surely in a country where sixty-five percent of those born poor remained poor over their lifetime, any time away from a job didn't bode well for a worker, especially a test experiment for the Mercury Project. The Mercury Project was a genetic enhancement program for children of the wealthy but before there could be an active program, the doctors and the government offered the ability for poor families to participate. The parents were paid a generous sum of money for the privilege of letting their children be involved in the experimentation. Mike was one of the lucky ones or as his mother put it, he seemed to have retained most of his "marbles." As he liked to say, it never stopped him from dreaming big.

Still, the side effects were horrible to the point where Mike's dad fled the family in disgust of himself for allowing his wife to enter their embryonic son and his kid for how he turned out. No, genetic experiments were especially doomed to remedial work, which meant never escaping poverty and never becoming a known hero of society. Morrissey, on the other hand, knew that while no one knew his name today, by this time tomorrow evening, his name would be a household word.

Jostling past the customers trying to enter Chin's Buffet, Mike exited into the street. Torrential rain cut through the dense fog and washed over him soaking his brown bomber jacket. He tucked up the collar and slipped his key into his hover motorbike. As he hit his kickstand, the blades twirled and the engine crackled and roared. Wind burst from the fan jets, as the hover scrambler lifted like a drone from the ground and sped forward.

Past red and orange neon store signs, he raced. Mourning for himself, the rain washed the tears from his eyes. He knew his days were numbered but someone had to make a stand. Hopefully, this was the road to survival. An old philosopher Ayn Rand said that man reached his noblest "as a heroic being, with his own happiness as the moral purpose of his life, with productive achievement as his noblest activity..." So how could his nobility fail, his actions would surely be heroic, and his purpose was the moral point of his life.

Green searchlights traced buildings high into the sky, creating ovals on stratospheric clouds. Mike inhaled and let his body relax. When he was a child, he had great difficulty learning to walk. He was confined in metal braces for years, while the doctors performed six surgeries on his back and legs. But his mind dreamed of better- flying high in the sky and swirling through the universe. The bike brought that sense of freedom and for it, his heart soared.

Within twenty minutes, Mike arrived. Several of his closest friends waited around the trucks. Fifty-four very old decommissioned Armored Multi-Purpose Vehicles (AMPV) to be precise.   The lot took years to procure and repair. As Mike gave the order to load, he hoped they would prove worth the effort. He nodded to his best friend and most loyal soldier Lincoln Green-Walker. His friend returned a creepy smile back.

Green-Walker met Mike when his family was evicted from their home, and he was homeless. Lincoln lived in makeshift cardboard box tents. When Mike found them, he was heartbroken. The GEB man crowded him and the two young children in his one-room apartment. Many said Mike only convinced one person of his mission: Lincoln. On the other hand, Green-Walker took the word and sharpened it, and convinced an army of ten thousand to join the cause.

The poor having lost so much to the Corporations hungered for more. The final straw came when the growing corporate power convinced or bought the government enough to end public education and end very successful anti-poverty programs like Chicago's *Pathway to Rewards*- a behavior modification program. Now, the children of the future had no hope of escaping the poverty to which they were born. They would never become one of the rich, for they would never have the technical and engineering knowledge that society demanded of its elite. Lincoln convinced the people to be ready to die to bring in a new world and a new century. Perhaps, tonight was that night.

With a twinkle in his eyes and an M4A1 carbine slung over his shoulder, Lincoln jumped on the truck. Mike picked up an AR-15 and jumped the carriage of the armored AMPV. "Tillman's driving," grunted Lincoln with disgust. Tillman was an ex-convict. Mike saw him as reckless with a habit of insisting on doing things that often only exposed his lack of competence.

"I thought drivers were selected a week ago," Mike questioned. He inhaled slowly, fidgeting his fingers.

"They were," Lincoln stammered, "but Peters, our driver is sick. He is still coming but in no condition to drive."

"And by sick, you mean drunk?"

"One could say that."

"Great," replied Morrissey. "I hope we don't get killed in an accident on the way." The two laughed.

From the poorest areas of the city, heavily armored AMPVs rolled through the falling rain and off toward their target. Arrays of neon light from corporate signs advertising everything from deodorant to erection pills doused the caravan.

The target was white sand, a small barrier island on the shore full of wealthy citizens. Three small bridges served as entry points to the island. The mission was a simple eviction of the wealthy from their homes and to seize the place. The white, nebulous light of the city glowed on the caravan as they approached. It reminded Morrissey of an angel's halo. Of course, given what he wanted to do, everything reminded him of an afterlife.

From twenty miles out, they launched drones to observe the sleepy little town. From the sky, cascades of cyan, magenta, cobalt, and yellow lamps lit lavished homes, but the streets were the pale blue glow like the light from a computer screen. As the drones shot by, images transmitted to the trucks blurred into a swirl of colors. Polls were clearly outlined by blue heliotropic light. Covering the town showed several yachts with active parties and roughly twelve dwellings. Most of the parties were around the pool or jacuzzi but a few of them were in the homes.

While most of the houses were dark, a few were light, and flying the drones lower showed people watching television or working on computers.

Just after midnight, the trucks rolled over the bridges. Crass's *Do They Owe Us A Living?* blasted out of the radio. Metallic blue signs stated it was a toll bridge and how much vehicles of each size needed to pay to cross. Mike did not bring his wallet.

Mike's truck greeted the bridge with blistering speed. The toll attendant emerged waving his hands for the vehicle to slow. Mike smirked, shook his head "No," and the unfortunate toll attendant met a hail of bullets. Blood burst from his skin, as he was torn to shreds.

Effortlessly, the AMPV piled over the remains. Mike knew this was the same plan for the other two bridges. So far, they were on the Island and the walkie-talkies communicated not a single person lost.

Tragedy usually followed Mike but tonight luck appeared on his side. Mike left a team to barricade the bridge. The night was going to be a long one and while he would allow people to leave, no one would be permitted to return.

Convinced that some of the residents must have heard him and were busy calling the police, he took four trucks toward the police station to eliminate the problem. Like the city cops, he knew the island police would be heavily armed with military- MRAP Cougar HE. His last reconnaissance of the island identified four Cougars and a heavily armed SWAT team.

The other trucks were ordered to clean out the homes. They would kick in the doors, street-to-street fighting, and shoot anyone who dared to fire back. If people left clean, they were to be rounded up and taken to the bridge. They were to be told they were being evicted to make room for a superior breed of humans. *Of course, how could anyone deny those forced to live in squalor and poverty for generations feeding on the deaths of each other were not superior humans?* Mike anticipated the fighting would be intense, but he also knew that over sixty-eight percent of the homes would be empty, as their occupants would be vacationing away for the winter.

Mass carnage on both sides, Mike expected. He held no delusions that it would be fun like those freaks in the militia groups. Those losers spent all their time practicing and having fun. They knew nothing of loss or pain. You needed to have pain and panic to understand war, thus it was a situation they were incapable of. He'd watched enough friends gunned down for petty crap to know what this was going to be like. Decisively, he snapped his fingers and a team of four, each armed with RPGs jumped out of the truck and took up position.

Coordinating the drones to launch seven smoke grenades into the police station, while the trucks were still two blocks away allowed them to have a host of targets to run over and shoot on arrival. The battle had lasted a little more than four minutes. When it was done, several of the officers managed to get one of the Cougar HE's rolling. Mike's truck appeared like it was retreating and when the Cougar followed, his RPG crew on the sides of the buildings came out firing. The HE burst into yellow, blue, and orange flames. As police personnel escaped, they were mowed down by Gatling gun fire from Mike's truck. The SWAT team never materialized. Probably not enough time to gather.

Mike looked at Lincoln who was on his walkie-talkie, "How many?"

"We lost 240," Lincoln replied with a sad heave.

Sadly, Mike shook his head. For a split second, anguish washed over him and then it was gone. "They were good people."

"They lost..."

Mike interrupted, "Who cares?"

"Understood."

***

At two fifty-five in the morning, the governor called the president. By two fifty-nine, the president's team drafted a legally binding executive order. The president signed said order at three a.m. to "bring the situation to a speedy end." At three fifteen in the morning, a nightmare where his subordinate-Enaya Habib- phasing through walls, arms doing a wave dance while she forced him to sign work papers, ended when Charles Meleno's cell phone rang. From a dead sleep, he ripped his combination laser facial mask for his acne and CPAP for his sleep apnea off his face and rolled over and pressed the glass, "Yeah," he started.

The call lasted four minutes. He was briefed and on his way to the office. Arriving there, he stared up at the tower, sucked in a deep breath, and as glass doors opened, Charley headed toward the elevator to his pride and joy.

The unit was now five years old. It was a mix of adolescents with digital and computer skills the FBI hoped to recruit and youth up to their mid-twenties who were now active FBI agents. The Cult's *She Sell Sanctuary* echoed eerily through the hall. Carin McCall danced by a cup of French Vanilla coffee in her hand. He could tell from the smell, "Got a report for you chief, when you ready" she batted her black eyelashes and called over.

"In a minute," Charley called back. "I just need to drop off my stuff and get oriented. Also, kill the music this is a very serious time. People are dead. Lots of innocents from a terrorist attack."

"Yes sir!" Carin echoed.

The room sported a mostly 1920's Art Deco design of the brown color walls, and holographic displays rested on pine tables that sat on a brown hard cherrywood floor. On top of the pine desk was a bioluminescent eucalyptus plant. Charley was not a fan of the plant because he hated the scent of eucalyptus, but he could not deny the practical purposes it also served, providing extra light and a ventilation system to keep the air clean.

Algae lamps cast a sickly yellow glow over the room, which seeped into the brown walls, almost making the sepia appear like golden mud. In between were splatters of high gloss tessellations of triangle patterns, which added a machine feel.

The ceiling was copper clad and patterned with squares. A strip of ambient blue lined where the ceiling met the wall highlighted the escape route if an emergency happened. At the far partition, gating the door to his office were two recreated Art Nouveau pictures. The one side was *The Cyclist* and the other was *Dog on a Leash*. Next to them two framed silicon microchips hung.

The place smelled like an odd mix of oranges, coffee and tacos. The coffee was his strongest attention getter: Hazel nut with a hint of cinnamon. Rushing to the automated coffee maker, he pressed the button that scanned him for nutrients to add in his coffee. He figured it already had his genetic print, so this was just a follow up. It poured a cup and the conveyer belted it to his hand. He sipped the perfectly made beverage.

Catching sight of Enaya Habib, Charley noticed how relaxed she appeared. If he did not know any better, he would have taken it as sick satisfaction for giving him nightmares. Ever since her family started the process of arranging her marriage, she appeared like a new woman: more confident and self-assured. *Maybe that was the source of her dancing in my nightmare,* Charley thought. *Then again, I suck at analyzing dreams.*

Charley corralled his team into a conference room. The area contained several black swivel chairs around a large pine wood desk. As Special Agent Charles Meleno entered, Enaya Habib followed him in and sat at a desk, her arms filled with files and folders. She handed the top one to Charley and passed the rest around the room.

Patiently, Charley waited until all were seated and had folders. "So, Carin, Enaya" Charley huffed, "What the hell is going on?"

"Group invaded one of the barrier Islands and took it over," Habib started.

"I got that," Charley corrected. "But anything else?"

"Yes, it seems that they rolled in with 54 AMPVs, carrying AR-15s and M4A1 carbine."

"Few years ago," Enaya Habib announced, "Chechen billionaire, Makka Khavazh fled the country after he was discovered, by this group, to have been involved in terrorist activity."

"Yes," Charley said, as his gut filled with bile. "I remember the case. It was pretty frustrating."

"Yep, one of the suspects peed in your car," Quinn added

with a chuckle.

"Yes," Charley sneered, "that was part of it. Along with a rookie who did not follow protocol." Quinn quickly shut up, appearing stung.

"Anyhow, Khavazh managed to funnel money into a group of locals," Enaya snapped, wanting the rest of the group's attention.

"First I am hearing of this," Charley sighed. He put a hand to his head, feeling a headache coming on. Something in his gut told him today would be long. Maybe Carin was right and he should look into probiotics to take before he got irritable bowels or worse, an ulcer, from his job.

"We just discovered the transactions this morning," Enaya replied, locking gazes with Kevin Jones, the team's accountant. "Thanks for that Kevin."

"You mean a guy we were tracking for two years funneled money back into the states and we did not notice,"

Carin jumped to alert, "Mr. Meleno, the issue was difficult to track. The money was funneled through a dozen companies and wound up into a community savings account sponsored by a Michael Morrissey. This guy has no priors and frankly just did not wind up on our screen."

"How much money?" Charley wondered.

"Close to 500,000 credits," Carin responded with a cracking voice. Credits became the name for the US digital dollar meshed with other cryptocurrencies.

"And this flagged nothing in our system?" Charley felt like somewhere up the chain of command, someone's head was going to roll over this. Unfortunately, as was always the case, it would roll downhill.

"No," Habib answered. "According to Kevin it's because the money came in and was moved out quickly. He never possessed more than twenty thousand deposited in the account for a month."

With a lick of his chapped lips, Charley turned to Kevin Jones and asked, "Kevin, any idea where the money was going?"

"Looks like he was exercising his second amendment rights," Kevin replied.

"Ah buying guns. Any idea from where?"

On the holographic display, Kevin opened his findings, gesturing to the whole team to look at them. "Largely through gun shows and trucks and drones," Kevin answered. "When I showed this to Enaya, she reasoned it was done to be unassuming."

"We need to work better on flagging this stuff," Charley reminded everyone.

"We are not allowed to track gun purchases anymore," Arek chimed in. "Congress has passed several laws designed to protect citizens from such registries."

"And the upshot of all this is that a group of terrorists take over a community," Charley's hands flew in the air in frustration. Damn congress caving into the gun lobby.

"Charley, maybe it is not a small group?" Quin suggested. "Intelligence suggests he has close to ten thousand men."

"How the hell did he get so many troops?!" Charley groaned.

"Well, it is not hard for a city of two million to produce ten thousand in its slum areas who are disgruntled with society," Carin responded.

"He's got a whole shanty section with him?!"

"So, wait," Arek interjected. "No money for homes but enough for guns?"

"Guns and trucks were provided by Morrissey with money from Makka Khavazh," Kevin replied.

In the last couple months, Meleno held pride for the team Confident, Charley whipped around to Tom Murdoch. Their eyes locked, and Murdoch flinched. "Ah, any thoughts Murdoch?" Tom was the new addition to the team, having been court-ordered to join four-and-a-half years before. Well, not really a kid. He was recently married. A rugged athletic type, the kid showed promise. On the team, he fell into the profiler role which meant that he spent hours reviewing data on the victims and the killers to come up with patterns. Meleno needed Tom to be firmer.

Murdoch tended to be quiet in meetings. Charley assumed it was because the kid did not like office politics and the land shifted too quickly. It left him to make only very socially measured responses, so as not to take sides. He often gave the correct answer even if it was the wrong answer. "They took no hostages. It is sort of an odd move, especially for a martyr type."

"You think he fits the martyr profile?" Charley asked encouragingly.

"Not completely. The profile was put together hastily, as Carin mentioned he has not been on radar. If he is a martyr type, then he is willing to die. We have done in-depth interviews at the Chinese buffet that he used to work at and some old-school records. At the buffet, he was a quiet guy liked by everyone. The owner was shocked."

"They always are," Charley retorted sarcastically.

Tom chuckled, which helped him to relax. "We went to his apartment and found a ton of old libertarian Rand readings, as well as a few counterpoint leftist books. I was involved directly in the analysis. Looking over the psychological data it appears that he drifts between an antisocial personality and terrorist profile. I suggest face-to-face negotiations to get the town back. He seems to have done a lot of pre-planning and any lives I would consider in severe jeopardy. Clearly, he has characteristics of absence of consciousness and guilt. He seems to have twisted moral values, almost a sense of entitlement. Don't use tricks, do not make unrealistic promises, stimulate his ego to keep him off balance, admit when he makes good points, and let him know that you understand his demands and that they are being sent up channels for consideration. Basically, wear him out over time."

"Well on that," Carin started. She cast a nervous glance at Habib, "specifically about the tricks."

Tom settled back and reached into his pocket. He drew a cigarette. Charley flashed him a glared that read no smoking in the building. Tom smiled embarrassed, twisted his hand with the cigarette, shrugged and returned it to the pack.

Habib fixed the head scarf around her face, sucked in a breath, and stated, "Well HQ has a Wiccan they want us to use?"

"For what, palm and tarot card readings?" Tom snapped. Charley never saw Murdoch bust out in a meeting. Hell, he never seen the guy have so much energy. It was clear Tom had no use for the supernatural.

"The kid has a very high score on her psychokinetic and ESP profile," Hanley offered. "While I don't believe in magic tricks, HQ believe that she can influence people's dreams."

Charley sucked his teeth, let out a whistle, and then firmly stated, "Really? What brings them to that conclusion? Some scores or a paper and pencil test?"

"Supposedly she has done dream invasion before," Hanley replied. "She is very high on her performance on the Astral travel realm and has brought back very verifiable intelligence."

"Ok Bring her in, I am sure we can find something for her to do," Charley ordered while Tom audibly scoffed.

Appearing nervous, Hanley casted an eye toward Carin, "Well, here is the thing- she might not want to come in."

The information was dizzying. "What do you mean?" Meleno grunted.

Nervous, Carin's fingers fidgeted against her leg. "Well, Talia Larson is a minor. Only seventeen and she did not part with her team well the last time," Carin replied.

"I don't have time for this," Charley replied, "Murdoch, bring the freak show in."

"On it, boss man," Murdoch said getting up from the table.

"Good news is that the National Guard has the island completely surrounded," Enaya stated.

"Are they planning to invade and fight door to door?" Charley felt nauseous.

"If necessary," Enaya sighed.

"I am not sure that is a good idea," Kevin inquired.

"Well, we got the sky," Hanley informed. "The National

Guard sent up a few drones and the tried to knock those drones out with trained eagles. It worked for a bit, then the Guard blew the eagles out of the sky."

"Good, so at least we got the air," Agent Meleno added. "Hanley back trace the money through the computer networks, see if you can get me a location on Makka Khavazh. "

"On it!"

***

The home Mike saved for himself was two stories. A brown frame separated the floors and formed a deck around mostly clear glass walls. The base of the walls outside was a classic phosphor amber on black with its interior having angled ceilings, rich wood accents and giant stone fireplace. He chose the place because the last occupants kept wireless internet access and various devices like old mega-iPads. Even though the stuff was a bit outdated, he never owned a computer before. Hell, he could barely read.

In the distance, his eyes caught sight of a red light flashing on a radio tower. The light was soothing, almost hypnotic as it flashed. Eternity seemed to pass, as Mike stared. A crash jolted him out of his trance. It came from across the street where Lincoln took up residence. Mike chuckled noticing Lincoln dropped some plates. They lay shattered on the ground.

Waiting cautiously for the arrival of his family, Lincoln took the house across the street. It was similar in both design and color to a Jack-in-the pulpit. He made some initial modifications to fortify the building and then crossed the street to meet with Mike.

In his yard, Mike sat in deep thought by the pool. The blue-green lights coming from beneath the pool danced on his face. He reached over and placed his hand on Lincoln's shoulder, "We appear to have succeeded with the first phase."

"All revolutions start with a first phase," Lincoln's voice was confident and determined.

"Yes, if I could just be as certain what we are doing is the right thing," Mike's legs trembled, and his stomach churned.

"It is," Lincoln said forcefully. His gaze never deviated from Mike.

"Heaven waits for us then," Mike calmly replied.

As they were in it now, for better or worse, Mike decided he would not let others know his true fears. "Blow the bridges," he ordered. "This will block the guard from crossing. Eventually, they will try to send Seals through the grassy sound. Keep our sharp shooters on the docks and tell them to keep a cautious eye at the sea."

"Yes sir!"

"And let's start shifting so we can all be rested," Mike ordered.

"Agreed. You get first rest," Lincoln confronted. "Look, I will sleep when my family comes but you know the drill. They will try to wear you down during negotiations. Our people need you rested." Lincoln flashed him a toothy smile. Mike knew part of what he said was right. They would try to wear him down and he needed to be rested. Still on a much deeper level both knew there was no surviving this. While a small number of his people might be allowed to walk from this attack, for Lincoln and Mike this was the end of the line.

Clearly both understood, you could not kill hundreds of people and believe that the outcome would be anything less than death for your rebellion. They knew this was going into this war, but their sacrifice was for bigger. He bit back on his growing despair, crushing it in his chest before it became panic.

***

Agent Meleno was not sure if Talia was supposed to be goth or if she really believed she was an extra in an old nineteen sixties vampire movie. The girl's hair was dark black, and it appeared that she wore clown white over her face. Her nails were painted onyx. Her eyes were obsidian, and the worst of it was Meleno was not convinced she was wearing contacts. Her ears were stuffed with headphones. It was particularly shocking because the only Wiccans that he'd met before were normal and seemed to be so happy and even cheery. With an amazing

43

amount of grace, the kid let out a heavy sigh. Her bangs fell over her face as she rolled into a tirade about having rights and that it was wrong to come a pull her out of her bed, when she just fell asleep. As she took her earbuds off, Charley's surfpunk knowledge recognized the song in her ears as *Hell Night* by the Misfits, a song that was secretly packaged in the recording of *Don't Open Till Doomsday* by the same band.

Damn this kid's weird, thought Meleno. He assured her that she could go quickly back to sleep if that is how she worked. Talia huffed and turned away. Meleno was sure the kid was devastated, although for the life of him, he could not figure out why. He knew if he went to face her, her eyes would be full of soppy tears. He decided it was prudent to apologize and stated that he was not sure how she did her "thing." To which she quickly became flustered again and let out a prolonged sigh. She appeared as if she were forcing down an overwhelming world of pain.

"Lots of people just had their homes stolen from underneath them," Agent Meleno offered in his calmest explaining voice. "And many of them died."

"Try having that discussion with a member of the Cherokee nation sometime," Talia snapped.

Confused, Meleno felt Talia's whine was flat, devoid of emotion but at the same time feminine. "Smart, a little unfair to me but very quick of wit."

"Were you expecting some stupid overly emotional teen, too absorbed in her own feelings to think? I am capable of both. I guess you just prefer girls with heavy pink eyeshadow, who look like escapees from the girl gang in that old movie *the Warriors* or something," Talia yelled. As if on cue, Carin entered the room. Talia sucked in her teeth and yell- hissed, "Of course!"

The kid was far too emotional and melodramatic for Meleno, so he turned to Carin for help. Carin's reply was a tad bit more defensive than he would have liked saying something to the effect, "So you want to put all of us brilliant basket cases together, huh?"

Charley wanted to make a joke about clown white girls and that's the way he rolled but he figured it best to hold his tongue, less and angry woman might bite it off. He left the room, so Carin and Talia could discuss the "dark side."

Charley and Quinn went to the armory and grabbed weapons. Charley grabbed his light ion blaster (LIB), while Quinn recently developed a love for the new particle beam rifle. After securing weapons, they exited the building to head out on location. Meleno discussed the situation with the Guard Commander and would take the role of lead negotiator. In Meleno's rustic Bentley 2030 Mulliner, they sped toward the coast. It was an hour drive, but Charley was betting he could make it in half that time.

***

"So, like, what do you guys need from me?" Talia questioned.

"Agent Meleno wants you to infiltrate Morrissey's dream," Carin answered. "Tell him you are a god and convince him that he can trust Meleno. Reassure him that if he and his people surrender, they will be treated fairly."

"What did that take him all of five minutes to come up with?"

"No, he reviewed your file and some past operations you were involved in," Carin assumed a defensive stance. She wanted to protect Charley as much as possible and this kid was not being fair to him.

Tossing her hair to the side, Talia let out a huff. She hated the lack of creativity that many people involved in government had, especially the FBI and Carin's defensiveness did not help the situation. "I am not the godly type," Talia replied.

"Give it your best shot," Carin insisted. "Truth is that Charley's not putting much stock in your ability to pull it off."

Confusion spread across Talia's face. "He's not?"

"He's not a believer in psychic stuff," Carin teased.

"I-," Talia took a deep breath. She wished they asked her

what she could do instead of just giving her an impossible task, but this was their show. "I get it but the role he has cast for me, it's a lie and I will have difficulty in the dream realm pulling off a lie of that magnitude…Hey Ms. McCall, what about you? Do you believe in any of this?"

"Oh, I believe in you totally," A small sparkle appeared in Carin's eye that was almost reassuring as she said, "I've seen some real freaky shit in my life. Just give it your best."

"On it, madame," offered Talia. Carin felt the charm of the French word, knowing from a goth this was an honor. She lay back, touching a small black opal that Carin swore she thought glowed. Her arms were crossed over her chest in an uncomfortable-looking position like she was dead. Her eyes closed and rolled up into her head. She mumbled some words as if calling to ancient wind gods, she traced the outline of a star with her fingers in each direction, and then her body spasmed and went completely limp.

The soil of the dream plane was aqua-blue. It whipped like winds completely around her floating silvery form. Wrapped in a pure white cloak, a tether line led back to her physical body. Talia searched for Morrissey's energy. When she found the beacon that went to his mind, she traveled down a deep blue dream road. On this path, color and sound merged briefly and then separated.

From Morrissey, she sensed sad, painful, and angry energies. So much loss, no wonder he'd given over to such hostilities. As she reached his mind, she entered without pretension. She would wait there until he entered the dream realm.

Surprisingly to her, her wait was not long. When he arrived in his dream, it was transformed into the vision his subconscious built. Reaching inside herself, she transformed the scene. It startled Mike, as she knew he'd never experienced another consciousness in his dreams. He became frightened. "Who's there?" His voice was meek and humble.

"I am the Goddess Talia," she spoke trying to muster all the bellow that she imagined a god would possess.

"What? Who?" his voice was shaky and confused, like the bubbling pot of tea before it sang that the tea was done.

"I have come to show you the future if you continue your path," Talia raised the winds and caused them to swirl into a tornado in his mind. She bought up scenes from his subconscious of the Island (as she had never been there) and modified those scenes to ones of destruction.

"No," he quivered. "I have to liberate the poor to do as they need to get ahead!"

"Yes," she allowed her voice to echo and boom, "Certain destruction and death but there is another way." She drew up her own image of Agent Charles Meleno. "This man can save you." She pushed a sense of safety and empathically bonding between the image and him. She could tell he was relaxing and hoped he was buying this. "He will keep you safe. He will make sure that you are treated fairly. Trust him." In his mind, she played Charley's voice from her memory and spoke his name.

As any lucid dreamer could attest to, people could do incredible things once they figured out their dreamscape. Mike quivered, "What trickery is this?" He flung out his hand and four gold disks shot out. They were easy enough for Talia to deflect but as she did so, his next move was unanticipated. He let a tiny dart- the size and shape of a pin fly from his fingers. Talia did not see the dart until it was too late. It struck her in the chin and blood trickled off it.

"You bleed!" Mike yelped. "So, you are not a god."

Touché, Talia thought to herself. That action shattered rapport. She doubted he would give her a second chance. His mind held a lot of raw power, but it was undisciplined. She was sure that she could take him, and it would start with a headache. Another gift of Talia's was she could shake brains at the right resonance frequency and release enough glutamates to give him a concussive effect. "How dare you disrespect me?!" She raged. "I am a goddess of the dream realm!"

"Begone witch!" he shouted, grabbing his head. "You

cannot hurt me!"

Talia indeed hurt him, and if she desired, could kill him. But that would only put another in place of the murders on the island. "I am not here to hurt you," she called "But to warn you to trust Agent Meleno when he comes. To show you I could indeed hurt you more if you don't listen," Talia raised her finger. Mike's body was tossed through the plane. It spun out of control. She saw the terror in his eyes. The fear was primal and genuine and then she clapped her hands. When she did so, his dream self, stressed and she placed a sense of agony in his mind. "I could rip your soul apart. Remember my warning."

To top it off, Talia sparkled and crackled in golden electricity. It leapt from her hands and encompassed the room and then she disappeared from his dream. A second after she was gone, she called back into his dream in a haunting tone, "Remember my words."

***

Drenched in sweat, Mike jumped up from his sheets. He glanced over to Lincoln's house. The man was gone. *Possibly he went to the beach?* Mike thought. Swinging his bomber jacket over his shoulders, he scurried down the sand dune to the beach to discuss the dream intrusion with his closest confidant and friend.

As he moved down the dune, he called to Lincoln. He did not get very far when his eyes caught sight of the laser marker. The particle beam rifle targeted Lincoln so quickly it was less than a heartbeat from the time. Mike saw the tracking laser to the moment the charged high-energy beam of protons struck his friend's head disrupting its molecular structure. The net effect was before Mike could exhale a single word, Lincoln's head exploded into a mass of blood and pieces, which bathed Mike in deep red from head to toe.

Falling to the ground sobbing, Mike was completely taken by surprise. He expected death, just not in that second of his closest friend. Emptiness turned to shock, despair, and Mike had great difficulty not hyperventilating and passing out. Behind the dune, he rolled on his back and stared at the sky, waiting for the drone to end his existence with a rocket or laser beam. There was no way out. Only sure-fire death. But, as the seconds ticked, none came. His mind stopped swirling as he reassessed. The strike must have come from a sniper. An assassin from the National Guard, who right now, lay somewhere on the other side of the dune biding his time to get off his next shot.

Knowing he was meant for much more, Michael Morrissey rolled face down, dug his hands and body into the sand, and inched forward. Sweat and sand covered his face, and he felt the grit of silt over his teeth. If he were to die, he would make sure that he died in a way that left him remembered. The world needed changing and he knew he must be the source.

Slowly, he inched his way back up the beach. His body pushed sand over every inch of him. His shirt, jacket, and even his mouth, were full of sand. With each inch, he dug his fingers deeper into the beach and pulled himself forward. Pain exploded in him, as he ripped his own nail off digging it deeper into the ground. He did not panic and run. He just slid forward more and repeated the process until he reached the house.

**

Jumping up, Talia hit the button in the room. Carin strolled in. "You're bleeding," Carin dashed to her side. Talia cringed. Carin realized the kid did not like being touched.

"Occupational hazard," Talia replied. She took a tissue, placed it on her chin, and wiped the blood. She was grateful it was not deep.

"Did you pull off your mission?" Carin asked. Talia felt Carin had a grinding high pitched voice, but she felt excited to tell her none-the-less.

"Yes," Talia replied. The two went into a side room for debriefing.

**

As Charley arrived at the National Guard unit, he was assigned a small tactical tent. He met his counterpart from the guard, Captain Jeff Smyth, and immediately set up a conference call to find out how his team were performing. Charley ordered Quinn to take up position with the sniper units observing the beaches.

Carin was excited. She reported operation dream invasion a success. In addition, Hanley managed to trace the Chechen back to a small town in Costa Rica called Jaco Beach, a black-sand beach filled with hotels that housed tons of ex-patriots.

Charles commanded Hanley to arrange for an infiltration team to head down to Costa Rica to clean up. "On it, boss man," Hanley replied.

"So, what is his motivation?" Charley asked, trying to get a handle on his play during the negotiations.

"Disillusionment with the world," Talia stated. Her voice became distant and icy. "He feels like he is the savior for the poor, freeing them from government control so they could gain standing."

"Fits the profile," Murdoch added.

"All right,", Charley said.

"Boss man," Talia tried the phrase as she noticed all the others used it. It did not feel right, and she could tell that even Meleno was weirded out by it. Much too creepy for both.

"Yeah Talia?" he replied.

"I think he will trust you," she stated. "But he might try to fight it."

"Explain," Meleno ordered. Talia clarified the events. As the conversation ended, Murdoch told Hanley that he needed a smoke and left for the roof.

***

Driven mad with rage, Mike decided the best way to keep his people safe was to flood the grassy sound with gasoline from the island's two gas stations. He gave the orders just as the phone in the house he'd commandeered rang. *It had taken them long enough*, he thought to himself.

Mike picked up the landline. The voice on the other end identified himself as "Agent Charles Meleno." On hearing the name, Mike felt a swell of comfort and his voice softened, this was the person who was supposed to help him. His mind searched for how he knew that and finally, he remembered the feelings and sensations from the dream. This was some sort of FBI trick. Some odd form of mind control. He needed to resist.

While it never left his mind that he was dealing with a cold-blooded mass murder, Meleno reported that he would take responsibility for the safety of Mike and his people. He promised them that they would get a fair trial. Meleno empathized with Mike's cause. He even went as far as to say he felt horrible sometimes at how difficult the world had become for laborers.

Feeling comfortable with Meleno, Mike almost ordered his people to surrender but then he thought of the one thing that he knew would break the spell: The image of Lincoln's head exploding. It played over and over in his mind in slow-motion and each time, it brought up a well of disgust and horror. No, his people needed to see this through. They needed to see the action to the end his dreams had forecasted even if it was a vision bathed in death and horror.

Strangely, he now realized his dream invader and even Meleno were steps along the way to the outcome. He thanked Meleno for the call but refused to give up their holdings. When asked, what demands he had, his answer was simple, "At this point, we have no demands. We like the outcome as it has occurred and are fully prepared to take all steps necessary to keep the situation that way.

   ***

After the call, Mike said "Prepare our people to sleep." He shook his head and looked down and off to his side. It was clear he had reached his fill. David Bowie's *Space Oddity* played in the background and the room smelled of ocean salt and mussels.

"What?!" Tillman and Peters asked in unison. They both knew it could only mean one thing. The time for part B was coming close at hand.

"You heard me," Mike said. "We are about to play the final act." He stared off at the wormwood room. He liked this place, especially the ceiling fans and powder-blue LED backlit clock. It reminded him of summer.

"It's much too soon," Tillman insisted.

Mike walked over and placed both his hands on either arm of Tillman. He squared the man's shoulders to him, and their eyes met. "Brother in arms, I feel your pain, but the time is now. I feel it. I know it."

Finding his inner strength, Tillman's eyes locked on Mike's, "To the angels and stars."

"To a better world for our people and for all the people of this world," Peters echoed.

"Yes, my brothers," Mike hissed.

***

President Lynn spent his morning in the situation room. Followed by a tactical briefing from Antonio Peignoirs, his National Security advisor and most trusted friend. While admitting it might be politically hazardous, Peignoirs suggested that VMX5R2, an experimental nerve gas might be the safest way to end the standoff. If dropped from plane or drone, the gas would kill all the present Island inhabitants and leave the buildings unscathed for the original occupants to return in three days.

Expressing no desire or patience to see this politically damning event carry out for weeks or months, Lynn liked the plan. He worried how the press might react as he went into his cabinet meeting. His advisors droned on and on about various situations, but Lynn's mind could not leave the problem, which he saw as two-fold. First, his staunchest supporters were displaced. Second, this incident set a very bad precedent for his handling of national security.

Somewhere in his mind, the nagging pain of so much life loss bothered him but he quickly quashed those thoughts with the understanding these people had brought this one themselves. They were criminals, who had no right to that land.

In the middle of his meeting while the team was discussing an unrelated issue, he gave a wily smile to his cabinet. For a moment, they were confused by his smile but then he explained.

His members' eyes widened as they realized what he wanted to do.

"Sir... a-are y-you sure about t-this?" One of his cabinet members asked.

"*Yes*," he emphasized. "Use the gas!" There was a bit of an acrimonious attitude in his voice.

"What about the hostage team?" The Chief of Staff begged. "What's their assessment."

"They were just a delay tactic," the president answered. "And these terrorists killed part of my most adamant supporters."

"Sir! Are you crazy?!" The Chief of Staff asked. "It's like you're gonna release a nuclear missile but on your own city! Are you sure you want to do this?!" He thought briefly about Waco, Texas from his history book when he was a child. Of course, the right wing had changed and clouded so much history in Florida that when he was a kid, everything he learned in school was a glorification of the terrorist action.

Inside of an hour, they drew up the Executive Order and the president signed it. The African American, who served as Secretary of Defense, uttered in a barely audible tone, "Lord Have Mercy on Our Souls for this."

***

After the call, Meleno felt the situation had gone well for first contact. He figured that after several days of these types of contacts, along with general attrition of Mike's people from sniper fire, the man would be willing to surrender. Those feelings changed when Captain Smyth entered the room.

"We will not be engaged in hostage negotiations going forward," Smyth reported.

"What?" Meleno asked. "Why?"

"President has decided on a military solution," Smyth sighed.

"He cannot want house-to-house fighting in the streets of that small town!"

Smyth sighed again, also unable to comprehend the

solution he was given. "To save a lot of the FBI agents' lives, there will be no house-to-house fighting," Smyth squeaked. "They are sending experimental nerve gas and it will be launched by rocket. It should be enough to wipe out the people in that town."

"That's a bad call," Charley said. His stomach churned, feeling this was dark and horrible. "Look give me one more chance to talk to the guy. Let me call him back."

"No," said Smyth. "The decision's done. Face it, they're a bunch of terrorists with no rights. Last night, they murdered over one hundred people."

"But justice-"

"Forget it. The decision was made well above our pay grade. I am going to leave now. Don't use the phone." With that, they grinned at each other, and Jeff left the room.

Once he was gone, Meleno tried contacting Morrissey again. The phone rang repeatedly for over five minutes with no answer. *Where the hell did he go?!* Meleno thought. The agent packed up. His work was done. Then it hit him: there was an outside chance that Talia could make contact again. She could encourage the people to leave. To just walk away. She could let them know they were in trouble. Desperate, he picked up the phone and dialed his team.

***

Colored lights flashed on the G- unit, as the phone rang. Carin hopped over and picked it up. Meleno explained the situation to her. She let out stunned tears. "Thousands are going to die from a weapon of mass destruction on our soil by our own government!" she exclaimed.

"Basically, sums it up well," Meleno agreed.

"You got to stop them!"

"I can't do anything," Meleno said, the hopelessness he felt apparent in his voice. "I think maybe you can have Talia give it a shot to evacuate everyone."

"I'm on it," Carin's voice was tough and insistent.

***

Within five minutes, Talia was back in the dream world.

As she figured Mike would be preparing for his battle, she fully expected that he would not be there. She toyed with the idea of going into his psyche and placing a subconscious suggestion for him to sleep. Sometimes it worked. It would appear as if he had just dozed off during a meeting but the process was a very risky on. Entering a person's subconscious twice placed the traveler in a situation where they found themselves swarmed with the other persons hates, fears, and other desires. Often these were hard to shake, as such impulses found their way into the traveler's own subconscious.

When she saw the light into Mike's mind, she was surprised to see that he was already there. She put her godly game face on and charged into his world. She found herself in a dark room. A single spotlight peered down from the sky and landed in the center of the room.

She landed in an empty circle of light. "Mike Morrissey," she called in her best godly voice. He stepped out of the darkness and into the light.

"Well, the witch has returned," he sneered.

"Michael," Talia started, more desperate.

"Call me Mike. I mean it is quite intimate to share another person's dream."

"Mike, I have come to warn you."

"I figured you would."

"This is serious. You don't want your ten-thousand people dead from a…"

"Nerve gas attack," Mike interrupted. "I saw this happening many years ago. Long before this event even started."

"What?"

"Let's just say the genetically manipulated have powers that even their creators did not intend."

"But if you knew, why did you?"

"Sacrifice?"

"Well, yeah…Your people-"

"Are here with me," Mike replied. He reached over and their minds touched for a moment. It felt like Talia saw all his inner machinations, but with that came an understanding of his resolve. This was always the plan, and he and his people knew it from the start. The light went on in the room and thousands of faces filled it. "This is best for both worlds."

"First, what you just did is creepy. How can you hold so many minds in yours? Second stop interrupting my questions." She shivered as her eyes laid gaze on the faces of children. Her heart broke, realizing that the kids must have been in on the plan too. Either that or their guardians never told them.

"The same way you hold one," Mike retorted. "It is the dream space. As to your second question, I don't have much time to say goodbye, so I wanted to move you past the basics. I will miss you, Talia."

"Don't let this happen," her voice broke into a quiver. "Please."

"There is little we can do," he answered. His hopelessness and acceptance were made apparent. Talia's heart broke further.

"Escape," she begged. "Just walk across the bridge. Live and let others know your reasons for what you did."

"As the hippies say, it's not in the stars."

"You're no hippie!"

"Nor am I a martyr. It seems odd that fate has dealt me this hand. Extents to which even you have not grasped yet."

"What do you mean?"

"When we die, a new ripple will be created. It will be a means for final retribution against the powerful and the evil."

"Huh? Have you lost your mind?"

"Not yet."

"Please all of you," Talia pleaded with the crowd. "Please live. I don't want you to die!"

"It has already happened," Mike informed. "I sense drones are flying overhead as we speak." The souls began binding together. It was a gesture that Talia knew was to give them strength as they crossed to the other side.

"Goodbye, Talia," the group announced in unison and then wailed, their astral bodies convulsing. Their faces twisted in agony and Talia quickly realized their astral forms were reflecting the pain their physical bodies were experiencing from the nerve toxin. It was horrific. Pieces of her own soul were dying with them. Indeed, even Mike's dream landscape showed frightening signs of the neurotoxin, as it bulged and turned deep red. His eyes appeared as if he were about to explode. His scream echoed through all including her astral form like millions of needles stabbing ever last never repeatedly and Talia was sure if there was a hell, this was it. *How could anyone be so cruel?* She thought. *Even if they deserved to be brought to justice, was this justice?*

Heartbroken, Talia reached out her hand to touch the others and then gasped as a huge maelstrom of wind connected with the occupants and their silver cords ripped them from the shrinking dream world into the ethereal plane. So many astral occupants sucking into the ethereal plane left a rip in the astral fabric.

With sick fascination, she could not turn away. Her body trembled with disgust watching the pain and torment of the terrorists. Deep within her, anger began to stir and build. This was torture beyond torture.

In a moment of rage, Talia's mind connected with the president's mind. He was awake but the energy around her gave her the strength to rip his soul from his body into the world. Seeing his face, the hordes of dying reached for him. As he crossed into the ethereal plane, Mike slashed at his soul and Lynn's soul appeared to be shredded to bits right before Talia's eyes. It was horrific to watch and she realized such an event could not occur on the astral plane- the ethereal plane possessed different rules. A new coven of witches forever would be able to enter from the dream plane to the soul plane, and thus no one would ever be safe even in death, because their soul could be shredded in the afterlife and could see no peace. *Was this Mike's goal from the beginning?* Talia thought, shuddering afterward.

Profound darkness swirled around her and she feared that she might be sucked into the ethereal void. She gasped and fell to her knees as the room dissolved into astral blue and she was left on the road.

Even now though a tiny crack remained in the fabric of the astral plane. It was something that she had never seen before. Something, no other witch had ever told her about. A final connection between dreams and death. *Just another hazard in the dream realm to be avoided*, she thought. *But what would it bring from the other side?*

***

The official word was the president died mid-sentence. He just keeled over from a massive heart attack. This gave Talia a brief chuckle when Carin gave her the news, as she woke from the dream world.

After Talia Larson left the debacle, she spent a few days in mental anguish. She resigned her position with the government and told them if they ever sought her out again, she would dump every secret that she knew from every politician's dreams into the public. "It would get messy," she promised.

Talia was so disgusted and indeed mentally scarred, she did not even care if the government tried to kill her. All she mumbled to herself was that if they did it and she found out, the person who came would need protection that no one could give or face the chance their soul itself would be shredded for eternity.

The following week, she woke up every night in sweat and tears. The faces of the dead would haunt her for the rest of her life. This terrified her and her soul felt shattered. There was nothing that could describe the emptiness.

Finally, she decided to talk with a friend of hers. He was a computer and biological geek that she knew from the Cherokee community center. The man, John Rutledge, did a dream walk when he was still a teen and was making a bit of a name for himself as a scientist by developing an app with a one-hundred percent correct rate for skin cancer detection. They both had a similar family history, being Cherokee and having punk rock cultural origins. While John was part English, Talia, on the other hand, had a more complicated history, with Wiccan roots that started in Scotland but somehow wound up in Norway. Sharing the blood of both, John was revered in both white and indigenous circles.

"Really," Rutledge said when she told him the story. "I would love to get some EEG scans. Maybe with some research, we could figure out how to patch that rift or even develop some sort of device to allow people to travel through and return."

"The second would not be wise but the first might be a good idea," Talia said, handing him her black opal. "This is the stone I hold onto to focus. My mom gave it to me to hold while I cross my arms over my chest to get to the dream plane. It helps me focus."

"Interesting. Don't worry, I won't create a device to enter the astral realm. I'll just work on getting us to the ethereal realm so that the rift can be fixed." John reached over and hugged her. Normally, Talia hated being touched but somehow this felt comforting to her.

THE GENE STARTER

By Joseph Cautilli
Marisha Cautilli

B eing genetically enhanced should have been a gift like being a chosen one. Instead, with his sixth finger and continuous anxiety, it was a curse beyond curses. From the time he got to Middle School, all the children made fun of him. "Jumpie," they would scream and run away. The pointing and laughing continued through his first two years of high school and then he dropped out.

Two years, it was an odd coincidence that two years was the length of time it had taken him to breed the Cyclospora gastroenteritis parasite to make it genetically resistant to chlorine. He had started with the original fruit-based parasite and slowly made his modification through a combination of selective breeding and gene augmentation. Next, he enhanced its effectiveness so that it became resistant to Batrim. The stomach cramps would be crippling and the diarrhea deadly.

And why shouldn't it be? How many days did he have to go to school with stomach cramps from fear of being bullied? He was ready now to launch it into a small area just outside of Appleton City, Missouri. The plan was to release the parasites into the water reservoir and then disappear into the night. This was greater than the problem with disinfectant byproducts back in the early part of two thousand fifteen and two thousand seventeen.

As to the delivery system, he grabbed the duck and placed the capsule with millions of parasites in a tiny tube that would dissolve when the bird landed in the reservoir. He taped the tube to the duck's leg.

Passing the hay farms, he smiled to himself. The people of the area were so obsessed with being independent, they probably would not even report the illness for many days. By that point, it would be too late.

He walked twenty feet from the fence and tossed the duck into the air. The duck flew for a little while and then landed in the reservoir. His mission was completed. He would have his revenge.

***

Three weeks later, Thomas Murdoch was just being released from rehabilitation. He sat on his bed for twenty-five minutes tying his boots. On the rolling table sat his last hospital meal. Some sort of high-protein bonbons. Next to it sat some ginger to clean his pallet. He had eaten extremely little.

Trepidation flowed through Tom like water breaking through a dam. He was excited about a clean life but worried that the fallout from his drinking had not ended. Part of him desperately wished he had been taken out of his misery. He touched the gunshot wound that had started it all off. Now, his wife had temporarily separated from him, but he was sure they would get back together. After all, they had two beautiful children that needed a father: Nicole and Tiffney. He had hope if nothing else.

Murdoch's lips were dry and cracking. He coughed twice and then rose from the bed. The bed sheet was thin, and the room was sterile. Some sort of pale balsam wood cabinet sat in the room's corner. Tom pulled his clothes out. At times during his treatment, Tom was convinced the cabinet were purchased in mass at a local flee market, rather than a professional hospital supply store.

Plunging his apparel into his duffle bag, he tossed it over

his shoulder and headed to the nursing station to sign out for the last time (he hoped). After she scanned the barcode tattooed to his arm, Murdoch was released. Part of him hoped he'd be reassigned to Singapore or some place in the East. No one knew him there.

As he left the building, his cell rang. His phone was always ringing. It was Earth Corp. He knew that the Employee Assistance Program would try to reach him. This was not Employee Assistance. It was his boss: Bethany Long.

"Tom," she started. "I know that you are just getting out of…" she stopped, and a pause followed. It was awkward and uncomfortable." Being sick but I need you to come in. It is important."

"Is this a performance review?" Tom asked.

"No, that is coming but this is nothing like that."

After hanging up on Ms. Long and calling his wife and explaining the situation, Tom rushed into work.

Computer cubical stations lined the path, as he exited the elevator and started toward the glass office of Ms. Long. Tom was surprised to see his partner Charley Meleno there in the office waiting. Neatly dressed in the Earth Corp uniform, he noticed Charley raising his hand over his white shirt to touch the knot of his black tie.

Also, in the office- no it could not be. It was one of the crazy guys from his group: John Rutledge. Instantly, his jaw dropped when he recognized the dyed blue-black liberty spiked hair and the razor blade in his cheek.

Paranoia crept up in Tom and he struggled to box it. Compartmentalizing was how he would not let it get out of control. *I hope it is the far east,* Murdoch thought. *My daughters would love it out there.*

The electronic glass door slid open, as he entered. After a round of hello's Bethany started "I would like to introduce you to John…"

Rutledge cut her off. "I already know Tom. It is why I asked him to be part of the case. We were both in the same psych unit.

How's Lori, Tom?" That last question made Tom cringe. Rutledge and he were in group therapy together so Tom wondered how much of that information would be used against him. As if reading Murdoch's mind, Rutledge added, "Your secrets are safe with me. We share a common bond."

It was true they were both in the same psych unit but for very different reasons. Tom's drinking had gotten so bad, his insurance refused to cover an impatient rehabilitation. He stated that he was depressed just to get on a psych ward to dry out. After a few days, he was able to transfer to a rehabilitation program. Rutledge was on the unit because, well, the guy was nuts. He held strange beliefs about the universe, was depressed and anxious, and was prone to weird fantasies. He even jumped from the stratospheric Nine Towers in central Philadelphia. Had it not been for a rescue drone, his insides would be outside. "Yes, we were," Tom acknowledged, while thinking that his career was going up in smoke.

"I see," Bethany gulped. From the expression on her face, Tom knew that she was worried about giving his Light Ion Blaster back to him.

"Anyhow," Rutledge interrupted. "People get sick that ain't the issue here. I need Tom and Charley to help me. So, let's proceed or I will call the commandant of Earth Corp."

"Mr. Rutledge," Bethany stated "My orders were clear. I understand that I should give you anything you ask for."

"Good, let's talk about Appleton City Missouri."

"Appleton City, Missouri," Tom mumbled relieved this was not a meeting about him.

"Yes, we have about one thousand very sick people. Nearly two thirds of the town. Fifty already dead. They seem to have a stomach bug. But when CDC sent me in and I ran some PCR-based DNA tests, it turned out to be a parasite- Cyclospora gastroenteritis. Normally, that's no Earth Corp concern." Tom and Charley both nodded in agreement. "But I traced the source back to the reservoir. Funny thing, the bug ain't native to the area. So, I asked to see some footage over the last two months from satellite surveillance of the area. Screen on," he called, and a three-dimensional screen lit the room. "Notice the guy in the grey and black sweats with layered cloths and a hoodie over top. Watch how he pulls the duck from the bag and then tosses it over the fence. That is our suspect."

"Terrorism," Tom stated.

"Well, possibly home grown," Bethany suggested.

"Anyhow, the bug was manipulated, and it is not responding to the Batrim treatments. I need to find out from him how he manipulated it to get a better idea of treatment for these poor people. Well, we leave in ten minutes so get your stuff," Rutledge ordered. It was the oddest thing to be taking orders from a person, who appeared so out of sorts.

Tom and Charley walked off. As the exited, Charley said "Muc, it is great to have you back."

"Thanks Charley. I just wish the others felt the same," Murdoch stared at Charley's tightly shaved head. The square cut was perfect in every way. Proper just like his partner's life. The only thing in it off kilter was Tom. Prior to transferring to Earth Corp, Charley was part of The US's Nuclear Emergency Search (NES) Team. He told Tom on many occasions that this work was much less stressful and allowed him to have a family. Even his career choices had a plan.

"They'll come around," Charley reassured him.

"I hope so and I never got the chance to say thanks for coming to visit me."

"My pleasure dude…Just sorry you were in that place."

"Me too."

***

Inside of twenty minutes, Murdoch, Charley, and Rutledge boarded a plane to Missouri. During the flight, Charley blew up the video and watched it over and over scanning for clues. He tapped Tom on the sleeve, "Muc, check this out?" He said in a dry voice pointing at the screen and blew up the suspect's hands and then he rewound the video and pointed to the neck.

The scene was of the suspect throwing the duck over the

fence. Murdoch squinted his eyes. The suspect's hands were veiny and very thick. He thought he saw six fingers on the suspect, but he wasn't sure. "See it?" Charley asked.

"Not sure," Murdoch replied. "I think he has six fingers."

"Right on both counts. The suspect is definitely male, and he most definitely has six fingers. We got ourselves a GEB."

"Great," Tom replied. "Wonder if it is intelligence or strength."

Charley's mouth twisted and he placed his knuckle to his lips and pressed them to the side. "With our luck, both."

"Well, awesome on the find. Do me a favor, see if you can convert the scene to printable pictures. Small town, if we show it around, maybe some will recognize the guy."

"Sure. You know what's odd?" Murdoch nodded. "Rutledge did not notice or if he did, he failed to mention."

"Maybe he's not trained to be an observant investigator?" Tom remarked.

"Maybe," Charley trailed. "Or..."

"So, did you guys find something?" Rutledge had walked back to their section. He was flying in first class.

"We think the suspect is male and possibly a GEB," Charley announced. "Sort of wondering why you did not inform us of that."

"I suspected but wasn't sure," John admitted. "Does it change anything?"

"No and...well yes. It is a clue to the person."

"Not many jumpies around- narrows the field," Tom added with snark.

"Don't call them that! It is offensive," Rutledge shot back. "That's why I didn't bring it up! Because I knew you were going to go right for the slurs!"

"Sorry, not many genetically enhanced beings," Tom sneered.

"It's ok Tom," John couched. "I understand your anger. Some of the genetically enhanced have done some bad things. Still, not all of them, and I know you're quite an empathic guy, so I'm sure you see where I'm coming from." Tom cringed. He always felt close to John. Maybe it was because the scientist validated his emotions at every chance.

"The empathy is quite a curse," Tom admitted. "But it does help in my profiling work."

"Just don't let it get the best of you, Tom," John replied.

"You speak firsthand?" Charley asked.

"About twenty years ago, I was part of a team that worked on the change sequences. I was not part of the team that created the first batch of genetically enhanced but was on a team of roughly five hundred scientists trying to improve their gains after they first thousand or so were created."

Weird caveat but ok, Tom stated. *It's almost like he's lying through his teeth. I wonder if there's some embarrassment that remains from the work he did.*

"Do you know the guy then?" Charley inquired.

"No, I was on the research end," Rutledge snapped. "I was just a teen at the time. I did nothing clinical back then."

"A teen?"

"Yeah, I had a gift. Made an electric mouse once. After I got tossed out of school, the government came and got me. Offered me a cushy government job." John paused to swallow. "It beat starving."

"So now you feel guilty?" Tom interjected.

"I feel a lot of things about the genetically enhanced!" John stammered defensively. "Guilt- I can assure you- is not one of them."

The scientist doth protest too much, methinks, Tom quoted Shakespeare's *Hamlet* in his mind.

Tom and Rutledge eyed each other uncomfortably for a few more minutes. "Well, either way since most of the GEBs are under the age of twenty-five, let's start our search in the local schools," Charley suggested with a nervous laugh.

"Good point," echoed Tom and John simultaneously.

"Given his size," Tom added "Let's start High Schools, even if he graduated within two years, teachers should recognize the kid."

"There are two," Rutledge added. "They are Osceola Jr.-Sr. high school and Appleton City High School."

"Should we split up?" Murdoch asked.

"No. Since there are only two, we can cover both easy enough." Charley answered.

Two hours later, they landed. The air was chilled. Murdoch noticed as quickly as they exited the plane, while walking through the tube. The air was never chilly in the city anymore.

They rented a blue-grey car to drive out to Appleton City. Murdoch stared at the rolls of hay sitting, waiting to be dried out and transported. An odd sensation washed over him, as he realized the farms he was seeing existed only to produce feed for animals and nothing else. They speed on.

Rutledge played *Biopunk Romantica* by Koronar the whole trip. The music was both hypnotic and danceable at the same time. Murdoch saw Charley had little interest, but he found the music quite pleasing.

The car shook and bounced over the poorly asphalted road on the North-East State Highway. Delivery drones flew overhead carrying packages. They passed a sign that read Osceola Airport. The place looked like it had been abandoned for many years.

Dust kicked up and covered the windshield of the car. The grass by the road was a mix of green and brown. Tom enjoyed the light blue sky. He was amazed at how it looked when there was no photochemical smog in the air. The browns and greys were gone.

The occasional houses that they passed seemed more like barracks than houses. Soon they passed a diner, several trucks were on the property.

They finally reached the school. They were greeted by the principal, a heavy large Caucasian woman with short, cropped hair. Filtration mask covered her face. Rutledge shook his head.

"School's closed," the woman said.

Various cases filled with trophies lined the hall as they walked in and in one of the cases, Tom could even see at the distance the yellow-gold football helmet. Charley went toward the trophies to further inspect them. "Closed? It is a Tuesday?" Tom asked.

"Outbreak is going around and lots of our kids are sick."

"Excuse us ma'am," Charley started. "We are from Earth Corp. We are looking for information about a person of interest in this- outbreak." He pulled out the picture and showed it to the principal. She shook her head.

"Sorry, I ain't ever seen that kid here. I'm not saying he could not be here. We have over eight hundred children."

"That many," Rutledge said, sounding truly amazed. For Murdoch, who was always from the city, the number sounded about a tenth of what it should be.

"Are any teachers in today?"

"Most of the teachers are sick. About a handful came in but they are hiding in their rooms, so as not to be exposed to others."

"Really?" Rutledge popped an eye. "I put out an announcement last week. It aired on all the stations KY 3, KCTV 5, KMBC 9, KOHLR 10, etc. I was pretty clear the water was the source of the illness and to avoid the water. Those with the illness are not contagious."

The principal appeared indignant. She stepped in front of Rutledge. "Well," she started "we saw you on television and I mean no offense, but you were...how should I say, not impressive."

"I was with the mayor and the whole board of Alderman for God's sake woman!"

"Well, maybe if you did something with that hair and took the razor blade out of your mouth-"

Rutledge's face flushed a hot red. Tom remembered the scientist mentioning something about the razor blade being a tribute to a deceased friend he deeply cherished. The principal unknowingly crossed a line. "You are lucky I deeply cherish life or I would just get out of here after that remark," John threatened.

"Excuse me," A voice echoed. "Ms. Perkins, are these men

bothering you?"

A large man came out of the office area and into the hall. "No Pete," the principal said. "Thank you for asking. They were just looking for some information."

"In a town where no one has a brain to store information," Rutledge mumbled very low, but it was enough for Murdoch to hear it.

"John be respectful," Tom reminded him quietly.

The large man began to approach Rutledge and Charley quickly pulled out his Earth Corp Credentials. As his coat flipped open, his LIB-9 was proudly displayed, and the man backed up. "We are with Earth Corps. and we are here to help with the outbreak. We are looking for a, ah, person of interest." He showed the man the picture. "Have you seen this man?"

"Not really sure." He started at the picture. "We had a kid here about two years ago. He dropped out. His name was Aiden – something...Cannot pull it up?"

"Please sir, this is very important," Murdoch added.

The big man scratched his head. Rutledge was mumbling something about not being about to get water from a stone. Finally, the big man huffed. "I think it was Johnson. Ms. Perkins can you check that out in records."

"Yes. We have the records of all our children when they attend and a photo from that year just in case any of them go missing. But if the last name is off, you might have to look through all 800 files- less the girls of course."

Moving to the computer, the principal typed with two fingers the name "Johnson" and the year. Nothing came up.

"Maybe we could use multiple computers for the search," Rutledge suggested.

"This is the only one we got," the principal responded.

"Seriously," Rutledge sniped. "You know this is the twenty first century."

"Last I checked," the principal sniped back.

"Try all the J's," Charley insisted. Ms. Perkins did. All the kids with last names with J's came up but the pictures did not come up with them. It was a horribly old computer system where they would need to click on each name to see the picture. "Ok. Eliminate the girls," Charley added. After the elimination, they were down to about forty-five names. Knowing it would take a while and probably would require going through more pictures than just the J's, Tom volunteered to go through each picture by hand until his eyes got sore. Charley would take the next shift and leave the last of the names to Rutledge.

"Huh," Rutledge huffed when there was no match. "He ain't a J last name."

"We forgot to mention he's a genetically engineered being," Charley stated after a pause. It got Ms. Perkins hyped.

"We don't get many kids here that are GEBs," she started. "Normally, those families got money. Those alterations were expensive. Those kids get engineered to be more intelligent and excel. I believe the last GEB we'd gotten who was named Aiden was a kid named Aiden Harris."

"Yeah," the big gym teacher recognized the name. "Kid's father was wealthy but when the dad died, he came to live with his mom. She's a local. My parents had never married. Sad story."

The group dashed back to the computer and searched the database for Aiden Harris. Rutledge paced relentlessly while they searched. Sure enough, when they pulled up the information, it was the kid in the surveillance video. Charley heaved a deep sigh. They had a starting point, and he quickly connected his Bluetooth to the screen, but the information did not jump, so he pulled out a pen and wrote it down.

"See the portrait?" Murdoch pointed at the picture of Aiden Harris. "That's our boy."

***

Within five minutes, the three arrived at the last listed address. Murdoch pulled open the screen door and knocked. The door shook and rattled with each hit of Tom's fist. A dog barked loudly. Murdoch let the screen door shut. Brown hair drawn back, a woman mid to late forties, no make-up and a bunch of acne scars open the door.

"Can I help you, gentleman?" she asked. In her left hand was a bottle of spring water.

Charley placed his hands in his black suit jacket pocket. "We are here to speak to Aiden," Charley said, as he pulled out his Earth Corp badge.

"To Aiden or about Aiden?" The woman asked. A puzzled expression on her face. "I reported him missing to the police over two weeks ago," the woman replied. She shook her head, "I am his mother, Cynthia Harris."

"Ok. We just want to get some more information on when you last saw him and stuff like that," Rutledge interrupted.

Several of the neighbors were staring on the street at the three of them now. "Please, come inside," Cynthia stated. The room was decorated in cheap Milanese plastic. Forty minutes passed and they had gone over every place that Aiden was likely to visit when he was upset. In addition, they discovered that Aiden's mother never drank tap water. Finally, after Cynthia reminisced about how her son would like to go to caves to think, the team decided the most likely place was out by Bridal Cave but that was over an hour and forty-five minutes away by car. It would be one hell of a hike for the kid over eighty miles.

With the sun setting, they set out for the drive. Winds picked up outside the car, bathing it in a wild note of rhythmic banter.

Outside in the night air, Tom gazed at the stars. The constellations appeared so lively in the night sky. They looked much different from the city. With no neon to block them, the stars grew brighter with each moment that passed.

Reaching a point close to a mile from the cave, the team unloaded from their car. The area was desolate of human life. In the trees, Tom heard the stirring of animals. Together they proceeded into the woods in the direction of the caves.

Charley stopped every few minutes to point out that the area was used by people. He was not sure who, but he was able to identify tracks and broken branches. When they were close to the cave, they saw a golden flame pouring out from inside.

"How shall we proceed, Charley?" Tom whispered.

"By the numbers, you and Rutledge head that way," Charley pointed. "And I will circle south." Charley grabbed Rutledge's hand and spun him around, "Remember the kid's heart is filled with hate. If he won't come in, we will take him down. Clear?"

"Clear," Rutledge replied. LIB drawn, Charley circled the cave. Tom did the same.

They moved to the cave's mouth on either side. Charley was on the south side of the opening and Tom and Rutledge were on the north side. Charley raised his hand, when he dropped it, they spun.

A small fire located in the center of the cave encased the kid in a pool of light. In the picture, he appeared so much older. Now Tom thought, if he had seen this kid at any other time, it would be a skater in the mall.

The kid had the first blow and his first shot hit Charley dead on. If it had not been for his laser absorbing vest, he would have been vaporized. Instead, he flew back into the wall.

With shots heading Charley's way, Tom on loaded his volley. The kid dove out of the way. Damn GEBs were fast. Still, the movement took him close enough to the fire, where his next move would be blocked. Tom fired again. The LIB's orange ball spun the kid and he hit the floor headfirst in his attempt to dodge.

Closing the ground quickly, John and Tom rushed in to secure the subject. "Leave me alone," the kid cried.

"We need to know how you enhanced the parasite!" John said flatly. Tattooed with a golden dragon wrap around a green one covering his neck, the kid clearly represented some sort of crazy counterculture inspiration. Sweat glistened off the side of Aiden's face reflecting the blue -orange flame of the campfire.

"So, I can heal the people who tortured me?! Failed to protect me?! Threatened to kill me?! These bastards were monsters! Why should they be spared?!" The man thrashed, pulled out a gun, and tried to shoot Murdoch and Rutledge. One thing was clear, this kid had fully wanted his victim's dead.

Trained in Krav Maga, Murdoch stepped in front of Rutledge and immediately disarmed Aiden. Multiple fists flew in a smooth motion and the boy dropped to his knees. John found himself staring at the battle spectacle.

As Murdoch moved to cuff the kid, Aiden reached over with one hand, grabbed Tom's leg, and flipped him. The Earth Corp agent went sailing upside-down into the wall. *Two to three times as strong,* Tom remembered. Still, Murdoch realized the kid had little fighting experience. He pushed that to his advantage.

Stumbling as he rose, the kid advanced. Tom had the advantage of reach. A series of pummeling blows struck his opponent and the kid whined in pain and tried frantically to dodge. Genetic enhancement made the kid fast but lacking experience, he was not a good fighter at all. He did manage to get a side kick into Murdoch, knocking him back and allowing Aiden to retreat toward his duffle bag. He reached down to his bag and pulled out a coffee flagon. Recklessly, the kid flung the stainless-steel vacuum flask. His attack screamed of desperation.

The two of them dodged, as the flask whisked by them. The tin vaulted toward them both, causing John and Tom to separate. As he backed off, Rutledge tried to engage Aiden bringing up a discussion about the kid's father, while Tom ran to the corner of the cave-like room. Aiden scarcely remembered his father, as he was just four years old when the man died. Still, the conversation brought back a ton of ugly memories from the teen's childhood.

Aiden kept both in sight as he planned his next round of fighting and then from behind, Charley struck him with a Taser. Aiden winced and fell to the ground. A flash of fists from Tom and Charley followed but Aiden was too weak from the electrical jolt to even defend himself from the blows.

"What took you?" Tom asked.

"Working on my dramatic entrances," Charley replied. Tom could see he was still hurt. "What the shit was Rutledge talking to the perp about?"

"Sentimental that one is," Tom spit on the floor and pulled

the kid to his feet, pressing him against the wall. The kid struggled and squirmed.

'So, I wonder how this is going to go down,' Tom thought. Agent Murdoch had difficulty reading the intent in the young man's dark eyes. Worried he would be hustled, Tom decided to take a chance anyway and loosened his grip. The young man pushed Tom off him and screamed "Even my closest friends turned on me! One day, they threw me on the dumpster wall, and... and!" The teen stopped and cried as if he was twelve again, trying to tell his mother about the kids at school. How they hurt him, how they called him names, how he almost died because they tried to smash his skull on the dumpster behind the school. But his mother didn't listen to him.

"That's because you have that ugly damn sixth finger!" She had scolded. "No wonder they'd pick on you! Why your father did that to you; did that to me I will never understand. All he did was make you Satan!"

"You sound just like my so called 'friends'! Get away from me!" He had protested at her. The young guy tried to stop remembering the flashback, but it wasn't going to stop. He remembered his mother slapping him silly and yelling "don't you *ever* talk back to me young man!".

By now, Rutledge saw tears flowing down like a river. The teen let out several low grunts and whimpers. John motioned to Murdoch, and the Earth Corp Agent got off him. Charley trained his weapon on the kid in case of trouble The teen put his hands up to his face, making moaning sounds. As if Murdoch was this guy's buddy, he threw his shoulder over the kid. Rutledge went over to Tom and the kid.

"What are you talking about when you say the people were monsters?" Rutledge asked.

"It's too touch-"

"What are you talking about when you say the people were monsters?!"

Aiden sighed. "I was born with an extra finger and the kiddies in middle school picked on me for that... I told the teachers and they said 'It'll be fine, Aiden, what are the kids' names? I'll report them to the principal.' And when my kind teacher came back, she had told me how the principal went on about how six fingers made me some sort of evil person and somewhat satanic. I didn't know, but one of the kids found out about my discussion and the next day, the kids called me names like 'devil's child' and 'enemy of god'. I could say what else they called me, but the names were horrible."

"Oh?" Rutledge questioned. "Continue, tell me about that time you were thrown towards the dumpster?"

"When I was twelve turnin' thirteen, my so called 'friends' and the main bullies cornered me in the yard at recess. One of my friends grabbed me by my collars and launched me toward the trash bin. The gang of boys screamed 'die, devil's child!' and my friend picked me up again and threw me towards the dumpster again. The next thing I knew; I was at the school nurse. The woman said I was badly hurt and that they dented my skull. After that I definitely knew my buddies turned on me. From then on, the bullying got worse."

Rutledge was humming a familiar tune by the time Aiden was done. Murdoch cleared his throat and brought Rutledge's attention back to the teen. Charley was staring quizzically.

"I see," Rutledge said.

"What was the tune you just hummed? It's familiar," Aiden said.

"It's from an old album called 'Aion' by Dead Can Dance. It's called 'Black Sun'."

"I remember that song! Whenever I was alone, I would turn on my phone and put that very song on and listen to it."

"Look, I will make you a deal," Rutledge offered. "If you work with me and I mean really help get this problem correct, I will make sure that you don't get a needle in your arm."

"You mean they would let me go," Aiden corrected.

"Fifty dead, the families are going to be screaming for justice," Rutledge added. "No, I cannot save you from prison, but I can prevent a death sentence."

"Better than nothing, I guess."

By then, Charley had the boy looking man handcuffed. Aiden made moaning sounds as Charley, Tom, and Rutledge escorted the adolescent out of the cavern. Rutledge ran back to the kids bag, took out a jar, filled with the contaminated water, and caught up to Murdoch.

"Grabbed a sample of the water," he said to Tom, who gave him a nod.

***

Over the next week, Aiden was immensely helpful to Rutledge in getting the parasites under control. Rutledge was impressed with the kid's skills in genetics. Aiden told Rutledge that when he was in grade school, he wanted deeply to be a geneticist. He had even discovered a very interesting looking million base pair sequence of non-coding DNA that he had desired to study. He hoped one day to develop a starter sequence in some test animals or something to figure out what it did. This got Rutledge to call him the "Gene Starter." John felt it was a shame and a loss to humanity that the kid would never get his dream.

Charley and Tom were just glad this monster was brought to justice. They spent their time preparing for court. Tom knew if the case went to trial the lawyer would try to discredit him because of his drinking problem. This made practicing his testimony even more critical.

After Aiden helped Rutledge's team of geneticists to decontaminate the water, he was arrested, and a court date was set. A bunch of successful lawyers hired by rich GEB's made up Aiden's defense team. True to his word and to the dismay of the District Attorney, Rutledge made sure the death penalty was taken off the table. Still Aiden was to be tried as an adult.

Rutledge felt it was inhumane but understood the families of the fifty-desired justice. The lawyers for the state, Earth Corp, and the kid met on four occasions trying to get a plea bargain in order. The sticking point was not a guilty verdict, the kid was glad to cop to that and even to apologize the families for his "evil." Nor was it that he should be held for fifty murders and get life sentences for each. No, the real problem was that Aiden's lawyers wanted his serving of the sentence to be served concurrently and the District Attorney lawyers sought for the sentences to be served consecutively.

Finally, the day arrived. Aiden made his guilty plea and turned to the families. Tears rolled down his face, as he told them of his deep regret and sorrow. He stated how wrong he was for taking such beautiful people out of their lives. He addressed each of the people in the audience by name and a few spat at him. He stated he understood their anger.

"Nothing they did to me, justifies what I have done. I say this just so you understand me..." He explained how the children would tease him, beat him up, and even how they'd tried to kill him.

"You and your satanic hands should've been executed," the mother of one of the victims screamed. "You killed my son! You should've died when the boy threw you towards the dumpster!" Parents of some of the other families yelled their approval.

Tom's eyes latched on the kid. In his head, the thought of the song *How You Remind Me* by Nickelback. Harris was a lot like him. Maybe that was why he felt so much anger toward the kid. It was not like Murdoch had not killed before, but Tom consoled himself that was different. His killings were always in the line of duty. He and the kid both had such horrible upbringings, and both had endured years of teasing. Truth was the kid was much brighter than him, so why did he survive, and Harris was destined to get a life sentence? Then it hit him: maybe he had not survived. Sure, he worked for the government. He'd gotten sentence into the Junior-G's as a teen, then he was opted into the FBI, tumbled through NESS and finally wound up in Earth Corps. He'd protected a callous government which long ago became corporate owned, even before the corporate counsels managed almost every city. His heart fluttered, as he realized he protected the hateful world, which fed the people to abuse a kid like Aiden Harris. Maybe part of the reason he drank was because he hated himself. No, that was too easy. He should not blame his drinking on his anger with the injustice in the world, but it was true each of these cases- bonding with suspects killed a tiny part of him. *What ever happened to protecting the innocent?*

"Order in the court!" The judge silenced.

At the end, he turned back to Judge T.J Jones and awaited sentencing. The judge seemed to be pre-occupied for a minute, glancing at a sheet of paper that was before him. Looking at the court, Jones' said "We will hold sentencing tomorrow on this matter. I have gotten information about this case that requires my immediate attention."

"Highly irregular," Charley whispered to Tom. Both men glanced at Rutledge who seemed just as perplexed as they were.

The next morning all waited in the court. Jones was on the stand, but Aiden was not in the room yet. Four men dressed in black suits entered and asked to approach the bench. They were whispering something to the judge. Jones' face registered complete shock.

Casting his eye at the filled court, the judge stated, "It seems that Mr. Aiden Harris committed suicide last night. He hung himself in his cell."

Odd, Tom thought. *Where are the sheriffs to present this information. Who are these guys in black?*

Most people booed, seeming unhappy with what they just heard. The rest, which happened to be the families of Aiden's friends, screamed their approval. One dad even said a prayer that Tom couldn't hear too well. Several got up as if to approach the bench, the court officers took a step forward to keep the mob back.

"Seems like everyone's upset with what just happened, Rutledge," Charley said, turning around to face the scientist. "Rutledge?"

Tom was in shock. John's seat was empty. *So much for that moment of self-exploration,* Murdoch thought.

HUNTING ARROWS

Joseph Cautilli
Marisha Cautilli
Johnny Andrews

Until he saw her, Afanasy felt it an average night. Why not? It was New Year's Eve. Eighty-two degrees and the sugar white sand beach was aglow with pulsing blue neon covered trampolines and blowup slides doused with gleaming orange and pink while filled with giggling kids. A crowd watched an old Patrick Swayze movie "One Last Dance" on a huge fifty-foot beach screen and forty feet over a band played a cover of Naked Raygun's Gear. A mosh pit of teens wearing neon lit sneakers thrashed in a fabric of balance. In the distance, street performers jumped through hoops to land on concrete with soda cans in their hands. The night was alive and Afanasy at ninety hoped that he would continue to be. His heart leapt as he raced for the cover of shadow under the graffiti-stained pier pillars.

From the pier's shadow's she emerged, as if she always knew her prey's intent. Her face ghostly in the white florescent light of the pier. The sight made Afanasy blink.

In her left hand, a small blade- an old Cold Steel Safemaker Ii Vg-1 SKU held in a black leather glove. She pulled in close. With lightning speed, she pierced between his third and fourth rib with two direct punctures like discrete punches to his chest, in and out the blade went fileting his lungs. With no effort, she flipped the blade to the other hand and repeated the process. Both lungs gone, he tried to scream but only found silence. He fell into the waves, pink froth escaping his lips and blood pouring into the gulf.

***

Six hours later, the cell phone rang at Charles Meleno's new home in the So-Flo megalopolis. His hand reached over to the nightstand. Pressing the screen, he laced it to his ear and let his groggy voice ring out, "Hello." It was Bethany Long- his boss. She needed him to come in about a case. Meleno always felt a couple of days short of sleep but he dragged himself out of bed, shaved, and into the shower.

After his shower, like all government workers, he stepped in front of the health scanner. It buzzed as it scanned his body. "Zero infectious diseases detected. You are in good health and may go to work."

Humidity was high, as Charley left his apartment. The stickiness lay on his skin. Jumping into his 2025 Porsche Silver Blur Shot, he sped off to work. The Porsche was named silver blur because it dashed so quick on the highway, it looked like a long pencil line on paper. Charles flipped up the gear and skirted around a car in front of him. His engine growled as he passed.

Traffic was light. Mostly self-driving yellow or red Chevrolet En-v making package deliveries covered the road.

It was a long drive through the neon covered streets. Charley liked to hum to himself when no one could hear. Tonight, he hummed an old Misfits's song *Bullet.* Charles loved the Misfits partly because he had a long-standing love of the apoliticality of Horror Punk in general.

When Charles finally arrived with his freshly hairless face at the office, Bethany Long was not alone. Next to her was an Earth Corp Officer fresh from a different division, Charlotte McCain. McCain was an interrogation specialist. Charles recognized her right away but the young man with sandy brown hair next to her did not. The man was Caucasian, skinny, and a complete mystery. Even more perplexing was that his partner, Tomas Murdoch was not in the room.

"Where's Muc?" Meleno asked.

"Probably drying out," McCain scoffed with a warm grin rising her cheeks to the ears. It was clear, she had issues with Tom Murdoch.

"Watch yourself, Ms. McCain" Captain Long rebuked and then she turned to Charley, "Tomas Murdoch is temporarily indisposed at this time. Plus, given the mission, we have assembled you a more appropriate team."

"A more appropriate team for what?" Meleno asked, suddenly aware of the low drone of the rooms climate control. It was like his awareness has jumped up a step. The strange aura was beginning to frighten him. He felt a slow chill head up his spine.

"For this mission. Mr. Meleno, you did a stint before Earth Corp with the Nuclear Emergency Search Team (NEST)." Tom took note that this was not a question more a direct statement of course it was these people know more about him then he does.

Opaque to the reason for the question, Charles felt like he was drifting into a fog as he hesitantly responded, "Yes ma'am. I did about four years with them."

"We have a murder,"

Still out of sorts Charley echoed, "A murder?"

"His name is Afanasy Dezhnyov. He was a Russian scientist in the old Soviet nuclear program. When the curtain fell, he escaped to the west. He was believed to be living in Clearwater Florida for the last sixty years. After his murder, his house was checked and his basement had some residue of both U-235 and Pu-239."

"How much?"

"The readings were really unclear but enough," Long added.

Heat flushed through Charley's body. "Why now?" he asked, running his fingers close to his tight cropped hair. Sweat from his scalp covered his hands.

"We don't know." Meleno felt the fall in his stomach. He knew what was coming. It was like watching a slow-motion wreck that he could not stop. "But we expect that it might be some nuclear material that he was hiding. Waiting to sell when the time was right to the highest bidder."

Charley thought that this was bullshit but then he flushed his mind worried that maybe the thought was just too much for him and he needed to believe it was not true. "I thought the material was locked down."

"It never was," interrupted the man next to Long and as he raised his hands, Charley noticed for the first time the man had the tell-tale mark of the genetically enhanced- a sixth finger. His voice was clearly Texan.

Charles felt himself give the man a poison stare and then quickly backed off. "I don't think we have been properly introduced."

"Forgive me," Captain Long said, although there was little of an apologetic quality to her voice. No, it seemed that she was irritated with the frequent interruption to her story. "This is Ryan Miller. He is an Agent from NEST. He will be working with you and Agent McCain on this case."

Nodding, Meleno wished that Murdoch was present. For his first three years at Earth Corp, Murdoch was his safety net. The guy he turned to when things got tough. Then about a year ago, Murdoch got shot. In the hospital, he got addicted to painkillers It was not a problem to ween him off though. Muc was a tough guy. Still, after the shooting Muc changed. He started drinking and seemed distant.

"We have a suspect though," Miller added, breaking Charles's loss of focus. The GEB plugged a stick into an office computer and waited. After ten seconds, he clicked on a computer screen and a three-dimensional hologram appeared and the GEB nodded back to Long.

Long took over the conversation. "The killer we believe is a genetically enhanced being (GEB), Ye Kim Sune." She is a very beautiful girl. "Nineteen years old, she just made the tail end of the mercury project. Indeed, she was still in utero when the project was canceled and her parents were given the option to abort but chose not to because of religious reasons." She has jet black hair with jade eyes, golden skin, six foot three inches and weighs one hundred eighty pounds last records show anyway," Long's voice was firm, "Medical reports indicated a positive history for amygdala and cerebral cortical seizures. At the age of seven she was medically altered so that her lung capacity was doubled. Psychological profile marked her as having sadistic and masochistic qualities with several other highly pronounced perversions. Currently, she had no phobias but at ten was treated for neophobia (fear of new things). Politically, she is considered extreme even by GEB standards. A highly skilled assassin and as at least three prior kills."

"Is she clinically psychotic?" Meleno asked. He was aware that many GEB cracked over time, dipping into the world of paranoid psychosis.

"We don't have all the information but from what we have at this point- the answer is no."

Meleno breathed a quarter sigh of relief. It was not much but it was one positive. "Any leads to her present location?" Charley asked.

Long glanced at Miller and Miller took the lead. "She has a friend. An odd Japanese telecommunication and high impact clear steel billionaire, who has made huge investments in North America. Birth name was Yuto Satou but after the change, she is now called Koharu."

"I see," Charley stated.

"No, actually," Miller politely added with a southern drawl that irked Meleno. "Given the money her company has already invested in the US and how much cash they plan to dump into the economy in the next five years, this case is very sensitive."

"So, will McCain be taking the lead on the interrogation?"

"No interrogation," Long responded. "Simple questioning and if she gets upset, then just make an excuse to leave."

"Captain, we have the possibility of a loose nuke and you

are worried about hurting the feelings of some immigrant?"

"That immigrant is responsible for half the telecommunication contracts in the Southern half of the United States."

"I see. Don't worry, I plan to be gentle,"

"As you would be with a young child," Long scolded. "We are done here."

"I'm off to the armory," Meleno added.

The Light Ion Blaster 5 sometimes referred to as the Liberator five, was made from yellow plastic with six ounces of steel inside it to allow it to be legal as a gun. Meleno signed out the weapon. As he did so, Agent McCain walked up to his side. "Sorry about my comment on your partner. It was rude of me."

A loyal guy, Meleno responded "It was."

"I just worry that a guy like that is going to get some-one killed."

"Murdoch has done more to keep people from getting killed then you will ever be able to accomplish."

McCain's eyes were unwavering. "Probably, but he is on the downslide at this point and I am not."

"We'll see" Meleno added.

"Well, Long is making us an appointment to see Ms. Satou"

"Can't wait"

The wait was short, as Ms. Satou had a morning appointment open. Taking Charley's car, Meleno, McCain, and Miller headed to meet her. Clear sky left golden sunshine to fill the air. The mid-Florida skyline was marked by high speed monorails that radiated out of the Orlando-Kissimmee area to both the Tampa Clearwater coast and on the opposite end to the Cocoa Beach-Cape Canaveral coast. As his car sped under the lines, Meleno enjoyed the view of the speeding monorails.

The Satou Network building was over one hundred fifty stories high. Her office building was bathed in purple light and the photo glass glimmered a postmodern dark green.

Reaching the security desk, they showed their badges and were allowed to bypass the metal detector. In twenty paces, they reached the express elevator. It was a new rocket tube type that went close to seventy miles/hour up. Charles was surprised at how comfortable the ride felt overall.

Exiting the elevator, the smell hit Charles. It was a fragrant pourii of essential and mystical oils mixed into dried flowers, herbs, leaves, wood shavings, wood chips and exotic spices. None of it was what Charles expected an office floor to smell like.

The cat house, as Koharu liked to call it, was a smart design run by an advanced artificial intelligence system with physical furniture that was a mixture of browns and fur. It struck Meleno as both plush and very comfortable. However the common man inside him sneered and hated the money on show.

The receptionist asked briefly who they were and when they gave their names, the team was immediately waved into the office.

Inside her office, Koharu spoke into a head set and stared out the window. As they approached, she turned and greeted them with a broad smile. She motioned toward the office couch and two chairs for them to sit as she handled the call. The call continued for another minute and then they heard Koharu say, "Well my guests are here and I must play the pleasant host." The head set chirped off and she turned to the group, did a slight head bob and snapped her fingers. "Welcome to my humble tower."

"Thank you for taking the time to see us," Agent McCain started. "We know that you are extremely busy."

"Yes, I'm extremely busy but the word is you seek a friend of mine,"

"Yes, we seek information on the whereabouts of Ye Kim Sune."

"Why do you seek her?"

"She is a person of interest in a homicide investigation"

"Ye is a child, no killer," Koharu's head shook slowly from side to side.

"I did not say she was," McCain continued. She shot an eye toward Miler, who seemed to be glad to play the silent type during this interview.

On the other hand, Charley was bored and getting tired of the conversation. He interjected, "So how do you know Ms. Sune?"

"She is a friend"

"Huge age difference between you?"

"Am I not allowed to have younger friends?"

"Just wondering what you had in common?"

"We were both victims of genetics before we were born,"

Not able to stand the slowness of the situation, Meleno blurted out, "Your friend is a hired assassin."

"Oh, please"

Trying to cover for Charley's social faux pas, McCain stated, "Please, your friend might be in trouble. The man who was killed. He had some material on him that might have been radioactive in nature."

"Well then, it sounds like she did Earth Corp a favor. Is it not your job to protect us from terrorists?"

Charley was starting to get the feeling that they would not agree on much. "See that is the thing," in an effort to channel his building annoyance, Charles continued, "The man she killed had the material for a very long time and never used it."

"How do you keep radioactive material around for a very long time. It would seem to me and I am no expert that this person would have died from exposure."

"Possibly, we are unsure of how it was housed. It may have been locked away in led." Miller finally spoke up.

"How would you detect it then?"

"We had a reading in the house. The person who took the material could have opened the box briefly,"

"Could have? So you are not sure?"

"We are sure it was there," Miller added.

Charley changed the subject, "Think of it, if this material goes off- well how will you be able to look in the mirror." He paused and waited after he spoke. Head perfectly still, Koharu seemed to be considering.

Sensing that Charley might have made an inroad, McCain added "Suitcase bomb having just ten kilograms of material could create a ten to twenty kiloton explosion could cause massive damage. Conflagration for over two kilometers from the blast. Second and third degree burns almost three kilometer away. First degree burns over four kilometers away. And then there is the radiation. If the thing goes off in Orlando, it could take out a theme park, thousands dead and thousands more on their way to death. Radioactivity would seep into bone, liver, thyroid, and kidneys. People would get sick over hours and days. It would overwhelm the hospital system. Not enough potassium iodine tablets in the area to prevent thyroid problems. Sure some of the preppers might have led mesh blankets to absorb some of the radiation but it will not matter even for them, as the exposure continues. " McCain's cadence and timing were perfect, much better than Charley could have ever done as she built up the effects. Charley saw Koharu rock on her feet.

Briefly Meleno looked at the young Earth Corp woman and smirked in admiration. Taking back all of what he thought of her from the get-go McCain was going to go places.

Stepping fractionally closer to the desk, Koharu extended her arm and touched an old statue upon it. On the desk was a push dispenser of hand sanitizer. Charles smelled the alcohol, aloha base as Koharu pumped it on her hand. 'Piolet washing his hands of the deaths,' Meleno thought.

Moving cautiously to the desk, Koharu pulled open the drawer. She placed a tall bottle of Saki on a small lace pattern doily. Slowly, she poured a glass and sipped. As an afterthought, she gestured to the others if they wanted a drink but they declined saying they were on duty. It was clear Koharu has absorbed way too much old American television. Charles guessed it was a hazard in the telecommunication industry. She made old American Bandstand references he couldn't figure out. Then Koharu said, "Ye, has not been to see me in close to a month but last time we spoke, she was living in a small place on Merritt Island with a friend." Koharu paused and let out a soft giggle,

"She has a thing for surfing on Cocoa Beach."

"Do you have an address?"

"Yes. I will have my secretary write the address for you."

After taking the address, Charley phoned in for back up to meet them at the house. Miller phoned a local judge that he knew to get a warrant. NEST personal were always able to get warrants when they sought them. When they arrived a team of six people were waiting at the end of the block. The street itself was served as the finger of a finger canal.

Several greetings passed between members and then Meleno briefed them on how the assault would go down. His team plus three of the arrived Earth Corp agents would arrive at the front, the other three agents would head to the back. They would enter the home simultaneously.

As no-one had any questions about the plan, the teams approached the home. It was an old blue and white place, one story, and early 1950s in style. The place reminded Charley of a war bunker more than a home.

Allowing several minutes to pass, Meleno stood on the front step. He knocked and gave the standard Earth Corp line. Nothing. Jittery, he nodded to McCain. She raised her hand with five fingers up. Charles knew that even one GEB could be extremely dangerous. He held his breath. When the last finger folded down, he kicked the door as hard as he could. It splintered and the team labored into the home.

Inside was well furnished with a brown couch and Japanese lamps. The place smelled of frankincense and from the bedroom was a sound of music. It was a very old Bobby Darrin song *Mac the Knife*. The Earth Corp agents moved past Meleno and toward the bedroom. Charley turned to McCain, "Looks like no one is home."

"Odd," McCain replied and she could see the other team coming from the yard, passed the pool and into the house.

From the bedroom one of the Earth Corp agents called- "We got some sort of clock. No it is blinking. Countdown."

"Exit," Charley yelled, "Move, move, move" As he bolted for

the door with McCain and Miller. The three just made it to the door when the explosion hit. The three were thrown outside hard. McCain screamed for the agents who were behind them. The house had completely collapsed.

As if on cue, an orange ball fired from an ion blaster swept passed the team as they scurried to the ground. They broke into three different locations making them difficult targets. Meleno found himself beside some shrubs. McCain was behind a pole. Miller held tight to the side of the house.

A second shot fired caught the shoulder of McCain. She screamed and Charley rolled toward her to render aid. As he did so, Ye moved like a blur shouldering into Miller. The two of them fell into the canal.

"I'm ok," McCain said and Charley got up. He knew that Ye had a superior lung capacity to any human including Miller. He dove in. Under water, he saw Ye staring into Millers eyes. She seemed ecstatic as she held the man by the throat. Pinching the jugular. For a brief while the man struggled under the water. She stared into his eyes. Charley tried to swim closer. Miller had stopped struggling and Ye let the man go. His body floated lifelessly upward.

Ye spun on Charley. As all Earth Corp agents were trained in dirty judo and Krav Maga, he unleashed a flurry of punches. Difficult to fight under water, the pull slowing the power. Ye seemed to be able to skillfully deflect the punches and countered one with a solid crack to his head. The GEB were not just extremely fast but had twice normal human strength. The punch felt like a brick hitting the side of his head. Meleno's head jerked back and then she grabbed his arm and like an alligator, rolled him down deeper into the depths.

Charley struggled to get loose. He kicked and spun. Nothing appeared effective He knew this could be his end. The woman was stronger and much more skillful then him. Plus, they were both underwater and she had the breathing advantage. He felt himself becoming light headed and his body panicking for oxygen. He had only one move left. He could not pull away, so he pulled in closer and gave her a head butt tight to the base of her nose. Blood diluted into the water.

Stunned, Ye released him enough for him to struggle toward the surface. Gagging for breath he reached the top and waited for her to grab his leg to pull him back to his death. It did not come. He struggled to shore.

Once back on the dock, he reached over and pulled the upside down floating body of Miller onto shore. At that point, he heard the sirens of the local police and ambulance. Quickly, he pulled his radiation detector out to make sure the bomb was not a dirty bomb. He feared that the police and ambulance would be rushing into radiation. He clicked it on but the radioactivity levels were normal. Falling to his knees, he waited for them to arrive. Miller was pronounced dead on arrival by the paramedic but McCain was loaded into the ambulance. All six of the backup Earth Corp agents had died in the blast and still the bombs were not found.

Charles Meleno reluctantly got into the back of an ambulance with the wounded McCain. As they moved away, McCain asked already knowing from the defeated look on the other agents face.

"Miller?"

"Dead."

"Any sign of the bomb? Radiation levels-anything at all?"

"Nope, I fought Sune when she had killed Miller, I thought I was done for, managed to shatter her nose and get out of the water but no sign of her. Radiation levels were right down to."

"Damn it" McCain started as she went to get up only for the paramedic to ease her down.

"Ma'am we are trying to treat your wound until we can get you into the hospital."

Just then Charles felt the movement of the Geiger counter go off, pulling it out he looked shocked.

"Okay buddy tell the driver to stop, I'm getting out."

The medic looked up alarmed, "But sir that really isn't wise…"

The young man silenced by the serious look Charles Meleno gave him then he saw the device held and recognized it as some kind of radiation or toxic leak reading machine.

***

Meleno was out and watching the meter as he moved down the embankment. So far no spikes.

"Damn it, don't tell me I lost it please don't tell me I lost."

He walked back away from the direction the ambulance went. Meleno couldn't detect any radiation thus far. Kicking himself he wandered around with the Geiger counter out. Just willing it to spike. McCain had been taken to the hospital to be treated. Miller and the rest of the unit were dead and Sune had escaped.

Did she have the bomb? Were there others he couldn't say and he didn't like it. He wished Murdoch was here though. His usual partner, least he could move forward without these thoughts of failure in his head. Charley was pissed at himself he was too late to save Miller. Okay the bomb in the house- not his fault nothing could have been different, they just barely survived that.

Just.

Just then the meter on the Geiger machine quivered, urgently growing in erratic movement as he picked up pace.

"Shit!"

About one hundred feet ahead of him was a jetty, a boat was tied up on it and just off he could see Sune straddling a jet ski.

Thinking fast, Murdoch realized the bomb was being loaded on to the boat. "Bomb or Sune, think Meleno think, can't take both" Meleno started running as he drew his Lib. Two guards placed something before the boat as they saw him gunning towards them but they were too late as two blasts took both, one shot each. Waves crashed disguising any sound of the blast or he hoped or this will probably be over before he even got to the boat.

One fell on the jetty with a thud as the other went over into water with a splash. Yune must have heard, Charley saw her look over her shoulder then up at the running man gaining on the boat and with a rev she shot off into the waters.

Well that finalized Meleno's decision it was the bomb he was going to get. The deaths will not be in vain. Reaching the boat he fell into a crouch, although the boat was not huge it was big enough to hold multiple enemies. Reaching up he ducked his head past the gang plank, the box the guards dropped looked like supplies, nothing more. Sweat beaded his brow if this goes wrong he is one nuked bastard.

Footsteps to his left another goon, Meleno waited, breath held, the goon passed and Charley steps up, grabbed the man in a vice like grip to the head and twists snapping his neck, clean and quiet, Meleno pulled the body down slowly and rolled it down the gangplank.

"Heavy douchebag"

Charley Meleno moved slowly along the medium sized boat, he hears laughing from in the boat, ducking down he steadies himself and peers through the window. Three heavies, surely that would be the lot, the boat isn't that big.

Counting to three, he rolled out to the door way, fires before he even lands on his knee, one man's neck disintegrates and blood explodes out, as the others turn to pull their weapons to fire, Meleno had fired into one's face, spun onto his side and rolled as one gets off a blast just missing his leg and Meleno shoots into the last man's chest sending him flying backwards.

Meleno pulls himself up and listens intently, nothing. However, on top of a supply crate is a chrome suitcase. "And the winner goes to…" Charles licked his lips nervously as he walked towards the bomb.

Slowly with shaking hands, Meleno snaps the catches, fear makes him hesitate and then like a bulb going off in his mind, Charley steps away, gun in hand he double checks the rest of the boat. Then he lifts the bodies one by one and disposes them on the jetty besides the one who fell in already and is pinking up the water. Wiping his face to remove sweat, he succeeds in covering some of his flesh in blood, not realizing. Back up after untying the boat Charles Meleno feels tired but he wants to get the boat out into the ocean before doing anything.

The boat started and he pushed forward heading out into the sea. Bouncing, the boat swayed side to side. His alertness keeping any sight of the young assassin in his peripheral vision. But deep down he knew she had long gone.

The waves crashed against the boat as it shot through the water, Meleno fought with the radio comms to get a message back to Earth Corp or even NEST, anyone who would listen. It was then the boat smacked against something and sent both man and inanimate objects hurtling throughout the boat.

Charles turned back and saw the suitcase had fallen and the ticking had started. Panic rose. He ran over and saw a timer counting down. The fall must have activated it. Meleno had three minutes to get out of dodge or deactivate. Shouting and cursing down the radio. Sweat pouring now Meleno hunkered down in front of the bomb.

"No way...no way. I think I'm far enough out to see for minimal collateral damage. Surely if Yune was going to be on board this boat..."Charles gaed around as he pulled open a door a coffin sized black container lowers down. "You crafty..."

Meleno sends some more distress calls from the radio before placing himself inside the led lined coffin. Lying inside the darkness a small LED light switches on and oxygen is gently pumped throughout. Worrying thoughts of how much air he has as he'd bet it is calculated for someone the size of Yune and knowing her lung capacity, anxiety tried to rip into Charles Meleno as he waited for the bomb to...

Eyes shut as led filled coffin blasted across the room with such velocity as to dent the metal walls. Outside of Meleno's death box the explosion destroyed the boat and it sunk. Crackling and a voice barely heard through the static on the radio.

Meleno blacked out into unconsciousness as the safety box drifts out into the sea.

Static filled voice was the last heard, saying "we have your coordinates" before the ocean water destroyed all and the boat goes under. Leaving flaming debris and crashing waves jerking a black coffin shaped box bobbing along with the knocked-out body of Charles Meleno inside to drift alone.

ERICA JOINS THE CYBERPATRIOTS

Marisha Cautilli
Joseph Cautilli

"CyberPatriot is the National Youth Cyber Education Program created by the Air Force Association (AFA) to inspire K-12 students toward careers in cybersecurity, or other science, technology, engineering, and mathematics (STEM) disciplines critical to our nation's future"- CyberPatriot founders.

Today was the start of Erica McCleary's new life. No longer was she bound to the chains that shackled her to her past mistakes. She excitedly woke up in her trundle bed having escaped the hardness of her daybed to greet the day. Tossing off her black and white sheets, this was her chance to start anew. Tears flooded her eyes, as she solemnly sank. Maybe, she had not properly mourned the end of her old life. She felt overwhelmed.

At home, Erica sat in a cramped but futuristic bedroom with an ensuite, and walls painted to resemble clouds. The patterns mixed images of *Vanilla Sky* meeting *Liquid Sky*. The designs were infused with fiber optic cables, which sparkled like stars in her ceiling but were functional elements to run her computer systems. The bedroom's design was small and rectangular, with a twin bed on the left. The blue sheets brought a sense of calm, like being transported to a psychiatric ward. She often referred to the place as not heaven but a cage.

Erica McCleary, a thirteen-year-old gifted teen built like a bodybuilder with square shoulders and ombre hair dyed to the colors of the bisexual pride flag (pink, purple, blue in that order), sat by her computer with calloused fingers from years of practicing guitar hitting the touch glass screen. To her friends, she was part hair stylist, makeup artist, and philosophical punk guru. Her swivel chair rolled over the hardwood floor. She used to write poetry about the natural light as it came through her large windows. That was before her fall. She would have different types of music playing, but now it seemed that punk and the blues was all she listened to. Before, social moves and fitting in meant very little to her, but everything took on a different meaning after being expelled from her old school.

The matter's simple truth was Erica felt no remorse for her choices or actions. The teen felt merely disgusted that she had been caught and angst over the final disposition of her case, which placed her at a new school. The resulting guilt around getting tossed left her worried about her own relations.

Plastered prominently on her wall was a poster of a page from an old fanzine that said, "Put the joy back in 'gay'; Put the 'gay' back in punk". Dangling on the wall behind her bed hung, and possibly in her tortured heart, a poster of a former world-class player named "Ao Uramoto" the captain of last year's winning CyberSentinnel team (the international governing body of CyberPatriot). She was not American and played until her recent graduation from a school for genetically engineered students called Yuji Chiba in Japan. On the bottom of the poster, it read "You can be a patriot too!" Erica felt weird about the poster on her wall. Some days, she felt good that there were people out there that prevented hackers from destroying society, and on other days, she was that hacker, assisting her friends from being unfairly judged.

A brief image flashed in Erica's mind of the first time she used a corner kiosk. She was nine and her mother told her to walk to the machine and wave her hand. Hobbling over, Erica did as her mother suggested. A flash of blue light swirled over the glass and her face appeared. Behind her was a picture of her house and a listing with the address with the sign above her face saying, "You live here." The road was colored red from her current location to her home. Her mother told her if she ever got lost "just wave at the kiosk". At nine, it felt like a wonderful machine, by eleven, she was concerned a hacker could get access to the information. A sense of intrusion washed over her that even to this day, Erica found it hard to shake.

Behind Erica rested a large brown oak wood bureau with the top open so the holographic player could cast a 3-dimensional film of a concert for KIWI, a Vocaloid computer-animated singer, singing a cover of Billy Idol's *Venus*. Erica bopped her head to the beat, getting a feel of the music. Pumping her fist into the air, her face soured, when the loading screen buffered for longer than she expected. Frustrated, Erica smacked her computer gently, then harder. "Come on! Please work!" She groaned. "It's like today everything is working against me!" She immediately recognized it was not true. Like most days, the morning thus far had its good and bad.

The loading screen added to the bad when it changed from buffering to a message that read "Cannot finish loading outfit. Please resend request." Erica huffed and sunk her face into her hands while her frustrated eyebrow twitched.

Rubbing her hands over her face, Erica shouted "Ugh! Why do you always do this? I programmed it so that you would make me an outfit based on the current situation and mood and extenuate my features! Whatever, I should probably get ready for school." The teen bit her lip and drew a small drop of blood into her mouth.

The teen resent the request and slapped the computer one more time, and this time, it revealed the outfit: a black Billy Idol T-shirt with the purple and green logo for the album cover to *Cyberpunk* and a pair of murky acid-washed leggings with her onyx Doc Martens' boots. "I guess it is saying you can't go wrong with retro, but maybe too punk for day one," She questioned the computer. Her index finger pressed the screen and switched the doc martens for a pair of black sneakers. Erica clapped twice in a row and her closet door opened, revealing racks of clothes. The touchscreen on the walk-in closet door lit up and the outfit the computer picked was displayed as a preview. Erica leaped from the seat, spun, and headed to the wardrobe. The robotic arms picked out the pieces of the ensemble and then handed them to her.

A knock on the door came from Erica's mom, Monique "Hurry up, Erica! You're going to be late for your first day in school" she called. Erica shrugged, recognizing that her outfit was not the most presentable. She took the ensemble, changed her earring posts, and opened the door to her bathroom, ready to step into her futuristic inverted D-shaped high-intensity jet shower with changing LED coloring and a silver square rainforest showerhead. She closed the bathroom door.

"Shower! Ocean breeze scent," Erica ordered. "Hopefully, this all goes well."

Ten minutes later, Erica dashed down the stairs dressed in her computer-selected outfit. She passed by her dad, TJ, a city-famous fashionista, on the computer adding finishing touches for a promotional poster for a local thrift shop. He wore a striped wool sweater and a circle-beard goatee "Hey, dad how goes it?" Erica asked with a peck on his cheek. Psychedelic Fur's *Pretty in Pink* played on his computer.

"Hey, sweetie. Can you help me?" He responded and left a momentary pause, while he stared at the screen and twisted his face, "I don't seem to be able to get online. I have to send this draft to my client. It's an ad campaign and then I got a second client to send some work to."

"Another client," Erica asked. "Your firm is on a roll."

"Not really, this is some activist group."

"Politics?" Erica was shocked. Her dad played on a very different court, one which mostly avoided anything with the political stench.

"I know," he replied. "Not my thing but they are opposing some big money group."

"A freebie?"

"Sometimes it is not about money, but about the world we live in," he replied. That was a sentiment she could agree with. Sometimes, a statement had to be made, hence why she became punk in the first place. But making statements was growing more dangerous by the day. She could only hope her dad had the smarts to stay anonymous- but not join the group.

"Sure, keep telling yourself that Dad," she chuckled, but deep inside she knew sometimes things were not about the money.

"Well, the activists want to stop some big corporate groups pushing a bill for genetic problems like the GEB from happening again," her father sighed.

"Sounds noble to prevent another genetic disaster," Erica replied.

"Yeah, but it is too broad. They got some religious group, Purt I think, to write it. Either way, it seems overly reactionary," He offered.

"What are they trying to do?" Erica gazed at the computer screen.

"Lots of things. Sort of pushing a big money bill to advance a law to set that no baby can be genetically created with genes outside of the parental donors."

"Sounds really horrible, it would take out any gene donors, for even disease." Her dad nodded. Erica felt glad her father took the contract to create a response to the group. While mostly a designer, his creativity had kept him working in a world where most of this type of advertising had gone to artificial intelligence.

Erica reached over her dad's shoulder and grabbed the silver wireless mouse with a sleek neon blue siding. She scrolled the pointer around and opened the control panel. She clicked over to the firewall permissions and scanned.

"Dad, what did I tell you yesterday?" Erica scolded. "Your

firewall is blocking internal to external connection."

She clicked on the button that said, "change permissions" and opened the related window. She dragged the slider reading "internal to external connection."

"There. That should do " she exclaimed.

"Thanks, kid" Her father answered. "You're a real help you know that? Stay outta trouble today."

"Yeah, yeah okay, Dad." Erica spun and strolled into the kitchen scratching her beagle, Eggle, behind the ear. She picked up the bag of dog food, opened it, and poured it into the dog's bowl. "Good Eggle. Good Eggle." She cooed.

Standing by the matte black steel finish range with advanced suction technology for unparalleled kitchen ventilation over it, Erica's mother dropped a half dozen eggs in a large smart frying skillet. They sizzled and crackled. The AI system told Monique when to stir and kept the temperature even.

"Fresh air -Don't feed him too much," Monique commanded, putting a dry pan back in a dark grey wooden cabinet. Erica glared. She hated her mother's pet name for her.

"I won't, Mom," she angrily mumbled. "And can you give me another nickname other than Fresh Air?"

"Good. And you always liked the name before." Monique touched her phone to readjust the AI in the skillet to keep the food from burning.

"Nope. I don't think I ever did," Erica pondered.

Her mother chuckled, "Oh right, that was me…" her mother paused to let the laugh sink in then twisted her lips, "You should like it. It has a lot of meaning to it. When you were born, you were a breath of fresh air into the lives of your father and me. It always means that you are something that stops the walls from closing in on us and keeps us from feeling stale."

"Whatever. I'm the empty nest syndrome blocker?" Erica frowned as Monique shook her head vehemently.

"Oh, I almost forgot," Monique changed the subject. "Your girlfriend Marina called yesterday. Did you get back to her?"

The silver stainless steel convection smart oven, with a smoker and dehydrator, indicated the items were cooked. "Pastries are completed," it stated. "I am ordering more quail eggs." Monique reached down and yanked the croissants out.

"No," Erica coldly responded. Marina was the only other subject she did not want to talk about right now.

"So don't order quail eggs?" The machine questioned.

"Oh my god, no I meant don't call Marina," Erica's eyes filled with tears. Of all the losses around getting tossed from school, not being able to talk to Marina was absolutely the worst.

"Why?" Erica knew her mother asked out of genuine concern, but the girl held so many conflicting feelings about the incident that sparked the divide that she wanted to collect her thoughts before she said anything.

"I just don't know what to say," Erica admitted. "I feel horrible, and I don't want her to think it was her fault, but part of me is mad at her and-"

Erica was interrupted when Monique handed her a breakfast sandwich in a croissant roll. Erica took a huge bite.

"It was your hack," Monique said coldly. "The incident is on you."

"I know. I know. Still." Erica's gaze shifted away; her shoulders hunched.

Her mother twisted her lips. "I know you wanted to make it all better, but it was a screw-up you are just going to have to learn to live with." Monique paused then started again, "You are going to have to live with this for a long time. You know that right?" Monique's voice was firm but had a hint of empathy.

"I know. Didn't want her to fail and feel bad. It was my call and my mistake. I should never have hacked into the school system to change her grade. I messed up. I got tossed from the Academy. I will pay the price for the rest of my life being moved to a second-rate public school in New Cyber City."

"Hey- hey- hey! As you know, I went to O'Neil High and graduated, and look where I got!"

"My point exactly. Besides, it really is horrible. I lost

everything," Erica choked on her words.

"Well not everything- I made you some dried crickets to munch on," Monique's voice sounded happy, as she shook a baggie of crickets and Erica smiled grabbing the bag. "Anyway, maybe you should say just that. I think I might add that 'I miss you' and 'I would still like to hang out together outside of school' and 'Don't blame you, girl.' All those things would sound nice. She only lives down the street. Maybe after you write her, you could stop by on your way home from school."

"I gotta feel it first, Mom." Erica checked her guts and realized she felt dead inside. It was emptiness. Her mother nodded in understanding. Erica let a soft smile creep up her face. She was glad that her mother understood her position. "I gotta go catch the hover bus for my first day," Erica added and with that, she huffed, picked up her computer, books, and tablet, and stuffed them in her backpack. Monique's finger flew to Erica's shirt.

"No shocks to the system, okay?" Monique reminded her daughter.

"Great song mom. And fine," Erica sighed.

Casually, Erica strolled out of the room. She shot a wave at her father. He jumped up and kissed her forehead. Erica gave him a quick peck on the cheek and grabbed her rainbow raincoat, laughing at the irony of the raincoat and her outfit. From outside, the wind swirled, as she approached the foyer. After a deep sigh, she waved over a glass panel and the transparent iron door slid open. Her mind briefly marveled at how the process of using synchrotron light to make transparent iron had changed quantum computing forever, but more than that had changed basic home designs. Outside the house was a heavy downpour of rain. Neon blue and orange lights doused the street in stark, contrasting colors. She shook her head and drifted into it.

*

When Erica reached the beige concrete school, her heart leaped. It resembled a series of interlocking bricks, which had been hastily built to accommodate the influx of asylum seekers into the city during several crises. Erica found brutalist designs distasteful, but somehow the functionality of the schools with sophisticated skywalks and glass-encased greenhouse rooms added a measure of beauty to the simple block design. Even through the rain and photochemical smog, the teen saw the golden doors reflecting the blue-grey lights of the surrounding buildings. The building incorporated greenery in its design, which was the hallmark of the evolved brutalist Space City Method. One of the glass-enclosed spaces was of extreme interest. It sported seven hammocks, which students laid on, swinging. Two other students were just off the hammock area and shared tales by a virtual fire pit. She wondered if the building had a spa and saltwater pool. Saltwater replaced chlorine as the base chemical in pools after parental complaints reached their peak in the 2030s about lung damage and respiratory illnesses caused by long-term exposure to high levels of chlorine. It was certainly big enough. Through the heavy golden doors, she went.

The hallway sported a cartoonish blue background vector guiding the student-filled corridors with fingerprint-opened lockers, hover drones' security-scanning students and round holograms with adverts projected into the hall's center for sponsoring corporations. Huge logos for Haastings Corporation, Greenspan, Horizon, Yak, and Lava Soft danced and rotated in three dimensions. Each logo challenged the students to be the best version of themselves they could become. "Shame the best version of themselves in the corporate mind is a worker bee to serve the company's goals," Erica muttered but then choked on her words, as she saw the spinning spiral of Abe-Coke-the hoverboard company dancing over a three-dimensional halfpipe. "I'd so work for them," she grumbled.

The walls boosted large television screens displaying various teachers telling the students who they were, the classes they taught, and that the students could count on them for support. It alternated with school counselors and even the principal stating that it was an honorable and respected decision no matter what field they chose to go into. The principal said, "We may all be different, but our career differences help build this world." Erica felt like she would gag for a moment, but even she had to admit that it was nice that the teachers were trying to build a level of warmth by creating an atmosphere of trust. They had thought the attachment-oriented positive messages classically conditioned through associative learning processes to the students would build pride and help students of all economic brackets and backgrounds learn to respect themselves and any field they or others would go into. Behavior support AI machines studied student hallway interactions, and reward dispensers released coupons for prosocial acts. Blue textured ambient light flooded the room, which the school believed increased tranquility and, thus, learning. Erica pondered and released her assessment of the place. "Faith, trust, and pixie dust," Erica quoted from the old Peter Pan movie, then she quickly added, "*Clockwork Orange* laid over Mad Max's *Fury Road*". She strolled into the hallway.

Erica's first week of school did not go well at all for her. Several teachers gave her backhanded compliments and even insulted her clothes. One teacher called her "special" which she knew was old white lady code for entitled. Many of the students were so engaged in their conversations with others, despite rewarding prosocial behavior by the machines, they chose to ignore Erica, but what was worse were the whispers, which spread across the halls as the teen hobbled to her locker. It was like somehow everyone knew of her mistake.

On her second day, Erica arrived at her locker and used her fingerprint to open it. The fingerprinting allowed for personalization to ensure that she felt the locker was private. Still, she knew the laws were written where the principal and vice principal's fingerprints could override any of the locks, so privacy was second to school "safety." As she opened her locker, her eyes caught a boy, Buddy Laurence- a five-foot-two senior- if she remembered correctly, in the background cringing, and she heard him mumble "poser bitch."

Rushing away, she passed by a wooden door with a glass window. Her eyes caught a kid, she believed his name was Paco wearing a pair of long golden earrings that complemented his golden yellow wool shirt. He held a drill, and sparks flew as he worked on a car engine. He glanced up, smiled first, then his face turned cold, and he gave her the finger. Four hours later, Erica crashed on her bed after a long day and cried.

On the third day, Erica decided to take the lead in making friends. Usually, she'd hang back and wait until they called her to join. Such moves always worked on the playground, but this place required her to be more aggressive. So, in the afternoon, Erica advanced approaching a kid, who did not seem to be involved with any of the cliques or friend groups. "You can do this Erica," she coached herself. "Just pick a peer-neglected kid. How hard can it be?" She approached a shy teen, probably a loner and possibly a basket case to ask a girl for something, but the teen held her hand up as a stop and stumbled off. Isolated, Erica cried for a few minutes in the bathroom and then off in the corner by herself in the cafeteria.

On day four, after being shrugged off by the LGBT crowd and even the peer-neglected basket cases Erica ventured to return to her roots. She approached the punks, headed by Nancy Dreg. From the whispers she heard Nancy was referred to as "bitter dregs" The punks scanned, assessed her outfit, and laughed at her, forcing Erica to stroll off.

An hour later, Erica entered the computer room. Radiohead's *Creep* played in the background. Buddy Laurence sat at a computer. His classic timeless English features were glued to the screen. With glasses covering his face, he gazed up at her like he never saw a woman before. Despite his cuteness, his inviting stare felt creepy, and she dashed out. Erica thought it odd in this day of easily modifiable vision that he would rely on such an archaic intervention as glasses. She herself had laser surgery several years earlier to perfect her vision. "Hell," Erica grumbled. "He even could've gotten mRNA drops to soften his eye lenses. He must be poor."

Crying, Erica slouched on the wall of a bathroom stall next to a chromotherapy shower. On the other side, a female voice said, "I'll never understand how a person who calls themselves a Christian then sits in the same arrogance spouting bigotry and sexism."

A second teen giggled. "Chris is just an incel," she insisted. "Few dating lessons he might even be approachable."

"Yeah, he still needs to learn to pick up the check for his dates or at least listen to them at some point," Nancy said. Erica jerked back realizing it was the Dreg girl with her posse.

"Yep," the second teen offered. "It was total boredom city. All he did was talk about himself. I wonder if he even knew I was there."

"You should have charged him for the therapy. Your fault for dating outside the scene," Nancy offered. "I could have predicted that."

"Guess you are right," she slumped. "I thought he was hiding behind a wall of anxiety or angst, but it turned out to be all ego." Erica felt a ping of yearning. She used to be the one the girls at her old school came to for advice.

Damn you Nancy, she thought. Erica tried to stand, but peeking through the stall's door, she saw the punk girls huddled by interactive makeup mirrors with shadow-free illumination. Dreg carefully applied black lipstick on her mouth while her girls watched. Several minutes passed and then the older teen waved her hands under touchless faucets. The water spouted out. After washing her hands, she and her entourage left. Erica waited in a ball until she was gone. B.B. King's The *Thrill is Gone* echoed in her head.

Five minutes later, Erica went to class. On the way, she caught sight of an advertisement for CyberPatriot. It read, "Join the future of Cybersecurity: We want you!"

CyberPatriot was established in 2007 as a school-based educational program for kids interested in cybersecurity. Even with private and government funding, the competitions mostly went unnoticed, except for the most adamant geeks.

The program saw a real boost in popularity in 2026, when a cyber hack spawned from social media robbed the personal information of thousands of American citizens, including prominent government officials. This cyberattack helped boost funding and recognition for the program, helping it gain more prominence. Two short years later, additional resources were added after a cyberattack left a power generator in North Dakota nonoperational, and nearly a thousand died from the winter cold. The additional funding to the program led to a fierce competitive scene for Cyberpatriot teams. In 2023, a group of hackers joined the FBI's team to help bring down several of the big hacking groups online. The thriving international league incentivized the youth to consider cyber-security and protecting their nation. Status and hype by teachers caused many kids to gather around the group, like a cult. That's how it worked finding children and teens when they felt most empty and offering them structure and meaning.

When Erica McCleary sought redemption for her failures, she found herself on the path. She grabbed the flyer and ripped it from the wall, stuffing it into her backpack. Maybe it was time to cross the barrier and form new friends. Maybe it was like the Breakfast Club said, all had a bit of each clique in them. Jendza's *Bitter Dregs* played in her head.

After class, Erica knocked on the door listed on the poster and entered. The coach, Mr. Colin Menken, a chubby man with a salt-and-pepper beard, sat behind a large desk. There was a frown on his face as she entered.

"Ms. McCleary?" he questioned, nodding for her to sit down. She hesitated at first then slouched in but did not cross her legs.

"Thank you," she sweetly replied. Placing her hand up to cusp her chin.

"I must admit, I was surprised to receive your application for the CyberPatriot team. We're not a hacker group. Our job is to catch hackers and prevent security breaches. We put the hackers in jail."

A soft chuckle escaped her lips, and his sneer made her worry that the coach misinterpreted her failure to believe the current cybersecurity teams were any good, into the idea that she was a hacker that did not credit the competition. "I'm not a hacker," she insisted, but inside she did not feel her words were completely truthful.

"Aren't you? Your school records say you were tossed from the Einstein Academy for hacking. "

With a sigh, Erica leaned back. Her mind wondered if she would forever be clouded by one mistake. She had to try, "I can explain. "

The coach crossed his arms and leaned back in his chair. "You can?" he asked with snark. "Because I'd love to hear it!"

Erica paused for a moment, stunned. "Well, maybe I can't explain it."" Erica stammered desperately. "I messed up."

The coaches' eyes peered at her. It felt like he was reading her soul. "So, what does that mean?!"

Her heart fluttered. Maybe he was seeking a confession. *Well fuck him- he isn't my priest,* she thought. Rage boiled up. She sighed; someone had once told her sighing was as effective as achieving mindfulness when dealing with stress. She hoped it was true. "It means I made a mistake before and I changed." They say confession is good for the soul, but it certainly did not feel that way. It felt intrusive like someone was commanding her to do something against her will.

"It was a couple of weeks ago," he pushed. She noticed he had soft brown eyes that looked empathic and frankly, some might consider attractive.

"Harsh dude-I'm only thirteen. Look, no one wants to be judged by the worst thing they did in their life. So, are you telling me I'm wasting my time here?!"

"Most likely. Tell me something that you can bring to the team?" So much for all that forgiveness and *Breakfast Club* movie bullshit.

Erica stared at the coach's blank stone face. What she would say next was critical. She looked around the room, noticing the same poster of Ao Uramoto on the wall that she had. "I always liked Ao Uramoto-" Erica started.

"Of course," the coach cut her off. "She has a huge history of delinquency herself!"

Coach Menken had a point. "Well, it is Yuji Chiba- they all seem to have problems there. Look, what I was trying to say is I think my security methods are a lot like hers."

The coach hesitated. He stood up from his chair and walked around. After a pause, he began his questioning. "What are the two types of user accounts? "

Erica felt a second of joy. At least he was giving her the chance to prove herself. She would just have to ace his petty test. "Standard and administrator. "

"What is the recommended password type?"

"At least eight characters, at least one uppercase, one lowercase, one number, and one symbol. "

"If you get an email from an address you don't know with an alarming subject line...such as 'We're trying to get a hold of you through your SpaceX receipt.' What do you do?"

"Laugh because they went out of business back in the late 2020s," she chuckled but it soon became clear he was not enjoying the joke. She cleared her throat. "Delete it because it is social engineering. I'd mark the emails like this as spam, and if possible, report it to Earth Corps as a phishing scam."

Feeling confident, Erica leaned closer to Colin and crossed her legs. She took her left index finger and pressed it up to her temple. After another beat, Coach Colin began the rapid-fire. "How do you disable the guest account?"

"Go to the local security policy, look under the local policies tab, and scroll down until you see the guest. It should say on or off on the righthand side. If it says it's on, click on the 'guest' tab and click the bubble for off."

"Nice. How do you disable the FTP service?" Finally, a compliment. She felt strong.

"Go to the control panel, then to windows and features. Click 'turn Windows features on and off,' expand it, and click 'internet information services.' Uncheck the box for FTP and select okay, then restart the computer when it tells you to."

"And the acronym FTP?"

"Jeez. It's file transfer protocol." If the questions were that easy, then Erica was easily getting on the roster.

"How do you turn on a firewall in Ubuntu?" Colin asked. He leaned in and she noticed his eyes widen.

Erica sighed and twisted her lips. Of course, there was a question on Ubuntu. How could she forget? Then again, how could anyone remember? "Um…not sure? I'm not the most familiar with Ubuntu."

The coach cynically chuckled, "Then again, who is? I'll give you an easier one. How do you delete authorized users on Ubuntu?"

"Um… oh yeah! Select system settings, click unlock and enter your password. Click the profile you want to get rid of and click the minus sign on the bottom left of the window."

"Impressive! I'll consider it," he finally judged, leaning back in his chair and scratching his beard.

"What?" Erica whined. "You'll only consider? After that run?! I aced your test dude!" the coach's glare harshened. Erica shrunk back. "I mean sir, did you hear how fast I responded to you?" she mustered.

"Yeah, but it doesn't change the fact you hacked into your last school's database."

He twisted his lips to the left side of his face. "I'm worried here that if I remind you of all the things you can do to secure the computer, you're just going to learn ways around those and become a better hacker," he continued. "It is your morals that concern me, not your skills."

"So, you think I'm just joining to learn about the different security systems I have to disable on a computer the next time I decide to hack something?"

"Yeah, pretty much."

"Whatever." Erica stood up. After scornfully eyeing the coach once more, she left.

*

Erica dozed off in class. Her teacher, Alistair Jones, approached her. As he did so, a loud knock rang from the door. The teacher switched pace and headed to open the door. A sixteen-year-old African American boy, Christopher "Dutch" Smith, stood in the hallway.

"Why are you here Mr. Smith?" asked Mr. Jones.

"Dutch, Dutch, Dutch, Dutch, Dutch!" several male students whisper chanted.

"Mr. Menken asked if you could deliver this note to one of your students," Christopher stated in a low and respectful tone.

Jones stepped back as Christopher entered the room. "Who?" Jones questioned.

Christopher's eyes crossed the room and landed on Erica. She appeared startled- not knowing the boy or how he recognized her. She swooned toward his extended hand.

"Erica McCleary," Christopher insisted.

Christopher strutted to Erica's desk, and she reached her hand out for the note. He gave it to her, and she tried to keep a stone-cold face. She unfolded the note, making it visible to the audience. The note, in gold lettering, reads: "To Ms. McCleary, I figured you would want a 'special invitation' to my tryouts and here it is. You are welcome to come to tryouts today at 3 pm after school (no promises that you'll make it on the team, but this is your shot!). – Mr. Menken."

Erica gazed up at Christopher, the two locking eyes. "I guess I'll see you around," Christopher said nonchalantly. Erica barely nodded back at him. Christopher grinned back and left the room, slamming the door. Erica smirked and shoved away her note.

*

Anxious, Erica waltzed into the durable metal composite paneled classroom. The panels displayed a diverse range of shapes and colors but mostly variations of blue and red. Large pastel effigies of various period cartoons were infused on the wall. She liked the rendition of Velma hanging with Shaggy but sitting with SpongeBob. Her fears mounted as she saw some of the kids sitting at computers. She strolled toward them, even though fear told her to stay away. The computer room was off-white, with transparent silver lines running down in different ways (akin to computer wiring). Blue neon track lights waved over the corners of the ceiling. A one Watt, m-USB LED light flashed on a track line at the base corners of the floor. Filament hung out, giving the impression the building needed maintenance. Pet Shop Boy's *Opportunities* played very low in the background. Five computers are lined up on each table. Among them, she sees "Dutch", the kid who delivered the invite, and Nancy, one of the punk kids' leaders. Their gazes briefly locked and then she drew off. Erica scanned the room.

"No sign of Coach Menken," she mumbled to herself, then gulped.

Erica strolled over to the table. A loud drone of the room's HVAC system drowned out the sound of the students at the table, but the ones who turned to face Erica were unimpressed. Erica chose to stand and not sit. Nancy twisted her head to face Erica. The older girl was of average weight and approximately five foot five inches wearing a D-force skater shirt, cut at the mid-rift, and a D-force red leather skirt. She wore her black hair in sectioned-off pigtails with bangs. She yanked the earbuds from her ears. Sonic Youth's *100%* played so loud, even Erica could hear it. Nancy lowered the sound. At first, Erica appeared hopeful at some sister soldier acceptance, but those hopes quickly dashed away when the older girl spoke.

"Oh my god, you're the poser, who wanted to hang out with us!" Nancy sarcastically remarked.

"Poser?" Erica stammered "What are you talking about?"

"Remember your first day? You strutted up to us, we knew you were not hardcore." Nancy's lips twisted to a grimace. Erica's jaw dropped.

"The computer was right," Erica exclaimed. "I should have worn the doc martens!"

"Not the boots."

"Then how?"

"We know all the New Cyber City scene kids, and you ain't one. We saw you with the Billy Idol shirt on and knew you were playing make-believe."

"But he's punk! Indeed, I saw the original cyberpunk!"

A hopeful smile crossed Erica's lips. She was still punk, to deny that would be spouting pure lies.

"Not punk enough," Nancy snidely remarked.

"Maybe not for you but I go as hardcore as Atari Teenage Riot," Erica flashed her credentials. "They have that faisal hair. I love the cyberpunk list and was doing it long before I got to this school. Besides, you don't even look like a scene kid. You look like some goth e-girl that thinks she's all that but is as interesting as a blank piece of paper."

"Don't you even start on that!"

A round of faux oohs came from several of the other players listening. Nancy rolled her eyes.

"Look," Nancy said. "I don't need to prove myself to you. My parents were tight with all the Aus Rotten members. You're all jelly bracelets and no spikes."

Some of the background kids hissed "burn!" One spouted "She got her!"

""Well- well- just because I can't think of a good comeback does not mean one doesn't exist!""

"Crispy critter!" a boy, Mario "Punch Out" Pastorino, from the crowd announced. When she heard the comment, Erica flushed red. Another player, Fatima "Chopin" Floyd, twisted around to face the arguing girls. She glared at them both, fed up with their argument.

"Will you two shut up?!" She firmly stated. "No one here cares about your petty argument about who's edgier!"

Erica and Nancy glared at Fatima, their eyes visibly showing rage at her comment.

"You punk princesses have no skill when it comes to talking trash. Anyways, before you- scene losers go to blows, I want to know who you are." Fatima pointed to Erica and nodded at her. Almost fuming, Erica calmed herself down before she responded.

"Yeah sure. So, my name's Erica and I'm trying out for Cyberpatriot."

Fatima chuckled. "I'm Fatima and the girl you were sassing is Nancy."

"Like Jack shit, I know Nancy," Erica cautiously giggled. She did not want to offend anyone at this point. This was the most recognition she had gotten since joining the school but could not resist getting a small tease in.

Yawning, Fatima offered, "She's sort of the unofficial B-team captain. Who knows, she might even make it on the A-team this year. Hard to do, because the coach always finds a way to keep it testosterone pure."

"Maybe us guys are just better!" Dutch shot back from the other end of the room.

Erica shot a glance over at the boy and recognized him as the kid that delivered her the letter. Perking up at the sound of incorrect grammar, another girl, Ashley "Ash" Gutierrez, entered the conversation.

"We guys," she corrected.

"You're not a guy Ashley," Chris retorted.

"Yes, but I have perfect grammar," Ashely joked. Dutch appeared stunned like he missed the comment.

"Look, I have nothing against having a person who's not a man on the team," Dutch started, pointing to a Peruvian kid with curly black hair, a white wool T-shirt, and baggier black pants with a studded black belt right next to him. "We have Paco."

"I don't know," Erica admitted. "He looks like a guy to me."

"Actually, I might as well get this out the way now since it's the beginning of the year and you're new. Dutch's right," Paco responded, pulling out a card. The writing on the card was near-impossible to read, but Erica barely made out the contents of the card, which said "They/he".

"And here on display is the forgotten language of scribblish," Dutch gasped. "Here, Paco. I'll rewrite your card for you. Serious."

Paco handed their card to Chris. In bold print, Chris rewrote the card's contents the exact way they were on the card before. Paco let out a small "thanks" before flashing the card back at Erica.

"I see," she responded. "My apologies."

"Anyway," Dutch went right back on his tirade. "I am not saying there may never be a woman good enough to make the A-team. I am sure in the next 100 years the odds are someone will come along. It just ain't happening now, especially not from any of you."

"Heh, maybe," Fatima retorted. "But as I see it- you're going down Dutch."

"Well, good luck with that." Chris flashed a cocky smile directly at Fatima, the latter just rolling her eyes.

"Yeah sure, Chris," she said.

"Chris?" Erica asked, confused. "I thought his name was Dutch?"

"You do know what a codename is, right?" Fatima asked. "His name is Chris. We all call him Dutch."

"Yeah, because I'm the man with the plan," Chris exclaimed.

"Dream on," Nancy shot. "They call him Dutch because he don't pay for his dates when he goes on them."

"The stoners say they call him Dutch because he smokes those blunts," Fatima added.

"No, you're both wrong. I don't leave a girl hanging and I certainly don't smoke!"

"Somehow more punk than some of the kids on the scene," Nancy quietly conceded.

I'm the captain of the A-team and I don't see a single one of you chicks making it," Chris finished, throwing an all-inclusive pointing finger at all the girls in the room.

With fierce passion and determination, Erica and Nancy simultaneously shouted: "I plan to make the A-team this year!"

The guys all laughed. Paco decided to chime in.

"Yeah, good luck with that. They don't call me 'The GOAT'

for no reason."

Another boy, Simon "Slick" Breen, also decided to throw in his two cents. "Yeah, they call you the goat because your last name means the place of goats," he pointed out.

"But we call him 'the GOAT' because," Chris nicely said to Erica before harshly aiming his words at Simon. "They're the best player we got. So, if there's anyone you want to watch out format's Paco."

Everyone gazed at Christopher and Simon, then toward the door. From the door emerged Coach Menken with a clipboard and pen in his hands. "Welp, better to try than to wallow in regret," Nancy sighed. Erica gazed, stunned.

"What did you just say?" she asked the older girl.

"Nothing. I just said it was better to try than to wallow in regret." Nancy frowned. Erica took a finger and wiped the corner of her eye.

"Oh no," Nancy started, noticing that Erica was wiping her eyes. "I'm sorry. I didn't mean to make you sad."

"Yeah," Erica mumbled. "I had...have a friend who says that."

Erica quickly drew out her MegaSmart phone and typed a text. She could not finish it before Colin entered the room. "I am glad to see we have a living coach again this year," Chris sarcastically mused. "Three years ago, we had an artificial supervisor to coach our team. It was so mechanical."

Colin marched to the front. He glanced up and his gorgeous soft brown eyes sparkled. "All right, I assume everyone is here for tryouts. We don't, unfortunately, have a lot of people trying out every year so if it's just you twelve, I'll accept all of you. All phones away..." He stared and Erica, who finished her text and sent it.

As one the group excitedly responded, "Yes, sir."

A smile crossed Colin's lips and he added, "But we're still going to have tryouts. I'd like to distinguish between an A-team and a B-team. The A-team will have the best five players and an alternate on it and the B-team will have the other six players."

Erica rushed to sit down in the remaining empty seat. She swiveled the chair to face the computer (with the practice virtual machine already open) but turned to face her coach once more. Colin continued in his overly loud voice, "Each of you have a virtual machine with two forensics questions and eight other issues on it. They're all the same issues on each computer, but I've set it so that you can't make changes to each other's machines. You guys have two hours to resolve these ten issues. The top five scores are our A-team while the bottom five will be our other team. Give me one moment to set myself up and then I'll start you guys."

Colin strutted to the desk at the corner of the room and laid his clipboard and pen on the desk. He jerked open the laptop. After a few seconds of clicking and typing, he leaned sideways to face the students. "Ready," Colin queued. "Set…timer's starting!"

The teens slaved away at the computer, scanning for issues, and trying to solve them. They scavenged the virtual practice machines, and several including Erica hunched over to see the screen better. From the corner of her eye, Erica noticed Fatima pulling out her pointed-tip stylus and using it on the screen. Frustrated, Erica regretted not bringing her stylus to school. Next to Fatima, Christopher wiped his brow with a small red handkerchief and then folded it and placed it in his pocket.

Paco quietly whistled the chorus of "Dancing Queen" by ABBA. Involuntarily, Erica let out a small chuckle. If there was anyone she would warm up to quickly, it would be Paco. With her tongue hanging out, Erica typed in ".jpg" into the top right of file explorer. She found a few images, unsure of which ones to delete. The stress caused her to twist her lips.

Coach Colin's computer, with the timer on it, counted down from its current position. Colin's placed the timer so all the students could see it. The red digital LED scoreboard reminded Erica of an old swimmer's clock. As the clock read, 30 minutes left, Erica started sweating. She drew out her air pollution mask, which she wore on walks to and from school, and wiped her forehead. "No unauthorized paper allowed out,"

Coach Colin insisted. The teen went to complain, but reading his face, quickly stuffed the mask in her jacket.

Eagle-eyed, Ashley successfully found an issue. She turned to her handy authorized checklist, which she kept right next to her, and checked off something from the list. She chuckled and did a head dance.

Coach Colin's timer ran out, buzzing very loudly. An audible gasp echoed through the room. "And time's up!" Coach Colin called. "Ok, my favorite geeks, everyone back away from their computer." They all handled the two-hour shift a lot better than the coach expected, as they scanned across the computer looking for the different problems.

Sighing, Colin felt impressed. His eyes scanned the sea of students. Sweat covered a few brows but overall, they seemed committed and dedicated. As the real-time results at his computer system, he saw loads of potential and some solid creativity.

The twelve teens backed away from the computer, some putting their hands up. They all stood up and faced Coach Colin. "So now I'm going to see how you all did today, and I should have this year's teams shortly," the coach continued.

"And when will we know Mr. Menken?" Paco asked.

"In a few minutes. I have your scores on this computer, and I'm gonna see how you guys did." Ashley wandered over to Coach Menken, trying to peak at his clipboard. The coach yanked the clipboard to his chest without even noticing her next to him.

"Then what was the clipboard for..." Ashley frowned.

"That's where I'll be writing my rosters" Colin replied, finally facing Ashley. "Now if you excuse me, Ms. Gutierrez, I have to make this year's rosters."

The students sat in front of the computers again, keeping themselves occupied while they waited for the results. Nancy scooted her swivel chair over to Erica to talk to her. "You okay?" the upperclassman warmly asked Erica.

"Yeah, I'm fine" Erica shot back. "Hey, sorry we got off on the wrong footing today."

"Yeah, sorry I threatened your punk status. We cool."

"Yeah. You seem cool yourself."

"Aw, thanks."

"Would you like to come out with the group? We talked about doing a bit of bonding and celebration. Of course, at Chris's insistence, we are all going Dutch."

"Wait when did you guys plan that?"

"Last night. A lot of us know each other from last year. I guess we should have said something to you newbies before, but it slipped my mind."

"It is good you can take responsibility for that. It kind of shows me that I have something that I need to take responsibility for myself. Want to exchange numbers so you can text me the address when the time comes? I have to take care of something before then."

Nancy and Erica pulled out their phones and exchanged contact information. "All right," Nancy smiled. "I'm looking forward to seeing you there."

"So where is it?" Erica asked, realizing she did not know where the meetup point was.

"Okay here is the story. I have this map of the city with some cool places on it. Anyhow, we were at my place, and I handed Dutch a dart and said, 'Throw it and we will go to the place where it lands'."

"So where did it hit?"

"Well if we went by that, we are going to go to the laundry room behind my dryer." Erica snickered, but Nancy got serious. "But we talked it over, and I think we're going to go to Keke's."

"Place would be a little loud for some," Erica admitted.

"Oh no, not at all. It functions as a teen nightclub on Wednesdays and plays mostly synth-wave."

"I'm down with that."

The chatting was disrupted when Coach Menken stood up from his desk.

"All right! I have checked the results and made my final decision," Coach Menken announced, walking toward the U-shaped table they all sat at.

"Team B will be Fatima, Aroha, Mario, Simon, and Ashley, with Aleksandra as an alternate" He touched each player's arm in the team as he read the names. Simon jerked when he heard his name called.

"Whoa, what?" he gasped. The boys and Paco looked at each other, dumbfounded at the results.

"And our A-team will consist of Christopher, Paco, Buddy, Charles, and Nancy, with Erica as an alternate," The coach continued.

The A-team boys look at Nancy and Erica, shocked that they have two girls on their team. Erica frowned, and Nancy touched Erica's shoulder as reassurance. Nancy twisted her lip and squinted her eyes. She gave Erica a new appraisal. Then her face softened. "Cheer up, Erica," she reassured the younger girl. You're only a freshman. He probably wanted me on because I'm graduating this year" That or because she's supposedly a reformed hacker," Chris accused Erica, making air quotes over "reformed hacker" "Lame."

"Yeah, I guess you're right, Dutch," Erica sighed solemnly. "Anyhow, I'm happy to be here and get some playtime."

Erica shrugged and stood up. She sulked her head and turned to leave the room. "Wait, Erica! Don't forget about Keke's tonight" Nancy reminded her. "All right, everyone! let's head to Keke's."

They all followed Erica out, Paco silently singing "Gimme, Gimme, Gimme a man after midnight" from *Gimme, Gimme, Gimme* by ABBA.

*

Ten minutes later, Erica stood in front of a red brick row home. A white draw fan was on the left side to remove radon from the basement. The neighborhood was old-fashioned, but the hovercars clearly showed their modernity. Erica strolled up the Italian marble steps to the front door. The computer light flipped on. "Please state your name, so I can announce you properly to my family" the computer ordered.

"Erica McCleary," Erica clearly stated. The smart system asked her to hold for a moment. In a nanosecond, the front door buzzed and slid open. Across from Erica was her first love, Marina D'Angelo-Porovsky.

"Erica," Marina remarked with a hint of shock, excitement, and sadness. "What's up?"

"Hey Marina," Erica sighed. "That smart home computer still freaks me out after all these years coming to your door."

A chuckle escaped Marina's lips and Erica thought it was the most beautiful thing she ever saw. She loved the way the teen's upper lip danced. "I think that is why my parents got it." Marina sat down on the top step and motioned Erica to do the same. When Erica sat, The Cure's *Lovesong* played out of the message box.

"Hey, you've been avoiding me," Marina solemnly pointed out. "I missed you."

"I missed you too," Erica replied, reaching over, and grasping Marina's palm. "I've wanted to talk to you about something but have been terrified I'd mess it up."

"Yo, you're like my world. You can't mess it up. So, what is it?"

Erica softly laughed. "I blew it," she sadly added, tears welling up in her eyes. "I wanted to help...I'm sorry I hacked into the school's grade book system and changed your grades."

Silence ensued between the two of them as Erica shed her tears. Marina appeared stunned. "You are?" Marina asked.

"Yeah, " Erica mumbled. "It probably killed both our reputations at Einstein Academy."

"Hey, if it's about that, some of the techier kids thought that it was awesome."

Marina reached over and touched Erica's shoulder, giving it a tight squeeze. Erica smiled. "Oh, nice," Erica commented. "More importantly, though, I'm sorry because I should've gone about it better. Maybe study hangouts or tutoring would've done the trick."

"Probably," Marina replied. "But there was some stuff he

didn't mention would be on there and he never taught us about."

Erica's mind drifted onto a question she saw on the quiz. How was she supposed to know anything about Hellenic-era Greece when that was still next month's materials? It was probably what Marina was talking about too. "Still. I should've done something else other than change your grades," Erica sighed.

"I forgive you. Actually, I kind of thought it cool that you had my back. Indeed, in life, I love-" Marina cut herself off, her mouth still open. That was awkward. There must have been something Marina was about to say but was not sure how. Erica both thought and hoped she had an idea of what it was.

"Is something up?" Erica asked.

Marina took a deep breath. "You know what you always say," Marina quietly coached herself, slapping the side of her hand on her open palm. "It is better to try than to live your life wallowing in regret."

Erica felt a sense of closeness wash over her. This is what she loved and admired about Marina. It was why Erica risked everything to protect her. If Marina failed, she would have been forced to go to summer school, since this was her second failure, there was a risk she would have been expelled. Erica ran her fingers through her hair, pushing some strands behind her ear.

"I love you," Marina finally spat, the words rolling off the tongue with the pace of a Gatling gun. "I want to make this different schools thing work so that I can still see you!"

Jerking back, Marina buried her head in her hands. Erica tried faking shock, but the joy of hearing that Marina felt the same way was overly infectious. Erica's smile grew wide. Was this the time to crack a joke to make Marina feel at ease? There was low-hanging fruit, but Erica opted to tell the truth. After all, was honesty not what she learned from hacking into Einstein for Marina?

"I love you too," Erica said. Marina's gaze shifted back to Erica. For a minute, their eyes locked. The look conveyed more meaning than a thousand words. They stared at each other for a nanosecond too long.

With a sigh, Marina broke eye contact. She glanced down and then started. "Hey!" she exclaimed. "I got carried away. You never told me how your new life's going!"

"Right, sorry," Erica apologized, sitting back down on the step. "It's been okay, I guess. Lots of snubbing and getting called a 'poser'."

"That's rough." Marina leaned into Erica. Erica realized her friend hoped that she would elaborate. Neither wanted the moment to end.

"Oh, but there's hope!" Erica continued. "People seem to know my reputation already, somehow, but I want to rectify it with everyone at O'Neil."

"Ah yeah?" Marina adlibbed with her smile wide. "How so?"

"I signed up for the CyberPatriot team."

The excited smile on Marina's face faded in a flash. Her look turned into one more of surprise, and to Erica's horror, disappointment. "Wait, is there something wrong with-" Erica tried repairing the situation but was cut off.

"No, not really," Marina sighed, her frown deepening and her voice quieting. "It just seems like you haven't evaluated your reason for redemption in the first place."

A pang shot through Erica's heart. The young girl earnestly wanted to redeem herself, but as she lingered on that declaration, she realized that she had no idea what she was apologizing for. Erica's alarm went off. "Damn I have to go," Erica stated. "The CyberPatriot crew are having dinner at Keke's. I'll call you later, ok?"

"Yeah ok!" Marina replied. "Hey after your party your new group, why not come back here for dessert?" Erica's heart leaped and then she mentally chided herself for acting like a foolish schoolgirl.

Heart still racing, Erica tried to suppress the smile. "Ok. I just might do that," Erica offered nonchalantly. She smiled and then added, "I might."

*

The Cyberpatriot members sat at a long forty-eight by forty-eight-inch black and white marble table, which cast a glowing florescent LED neon blue light. Because of his husky size, Buddy kicked a sable-colored mental bar as he drew his chair in close. Frustrated, he signaled the waitress over and ordered a virgin gothic- witches brew and spicy wings. Paco hoped to sit closer to the DJ mixing desk, but Ashley thought it too loud, and Christopher took her point. Ashley had wanted a booth, but Nancy thought the purple color was gross. They waited for their last guest and their food. Erica strolled in through the main door and flopped into an empty seat between Paco and Ashley. They all looked at her.

"You're late," Ashley emphasized the word late to drive her point home.

"Nancy inspired me to take care of something first," Erica shot back, then turned to face Nancy. "Thanks for that Nancy."

"Secretly hacking the school database?" Paco sarcastically asked, fiddling with their square gold earrings. The waitress arrived with Buddy's gothic. He handed her his credit stick and she plugged it into the machine. His gothic sat on the multi-tiled coaster. The lights sparked the purple-blue fluid inside and made the rim with large ice cubes appear almost like an iridescent blue froth.

"Nah," Erica reassured them. "Just talked with my friend from my old school." As the waitress passed, Erica ordered a virgin Iron Maiden.

"Oh. Phew!" Ashley sighed in relief. "Don't want my reputation and grades tarnished because of you. We're security, not breachers."

Confused at Ashley's defensiveness, Erica placed a hand on the girl's biceps. "Don't worry," Erica said with a wink. "I'll check all the boxes you want me to."

Ashley jerked back and blushed. She was saved as the waitress returned with Erica's Iron Maiden. "No," Ashley shot back. "I just mean if you are going to lapse or relapse, just let us know first."

"Girl, it's not like AA," Erica replied. The appetizer of bread and Buddy's spicy buffalo wings was set on the table for the twelve teens to eat. Christopher, the new A-team captain placed twelve orders of spaghetti and meatballs, sneaking in a near-beer for himself.

"One day, I'm gonna invent an alcohol-free Drambuie," he cheered as the waitress walked away.

"You mean yesteryear's gout treatments?" Nancy shouted, imitating a Scottish accent. The table erupted in laughter.

"It's the drink of kings!" Christopher shouted, also imitating a Scottish accent. "The celebration of romance!"

Christopher offered to cut the bread into slices, so everyone got a piece. As he cut the bread, Nancy tried to keep the atmosphere.

"How are we feeling about the rosters, everyone?" She asked.

"Not good," Simon whined. "I can't believe I got bumped down to the B-team because you and that other punk loser got me and Mario's slot. Still, I got other things to work on this year like hoverboards, electromagnetism, and pulling molecules from the air for fuel cells. I think the wireless transfer of electricity is where I'll make my mark this year. So, the team will suffer without my wonder."

"Oh, come on!" Erica said in frustration. "We both beat you guys fair and square. Now quit your complaining and give us a shot."

"Besides," Nancy added. "Mario would've probably been an alternate for you guys anyway."

They all looked at Mario, and he frowned back. "Not that you suck, Mario," Nancy tried to mend the situation. "Just that you suck."

Mario shrugged, confused and insulted by the comment. The waitress returned, now with twelve plates of spaghetti and meatballs. She laid it in the center of the table and their mouths watered at the sight of it. The walls trembled from the sounds of synthwave dance music. The teens dug into their meal.

"Still mad at you buster," Erica finally was able to admit to Buddy. He cast a gaze at her.

"Me," he stated confused.

"Accosting me at my locker," she stated. He appeared very nervous, and she figured he did not know what accosting meant. "You know, calling me a poser bitch for nothing."

"I'm sorry about that," he stammered, "but in my defense- I should tell you- I was excited to discover I was to be your school mentor and help you adjust. The counselors set it up. I was excited to talk to you." Erica tried to interrupt, but he continued "Hear me out… I went to meet you and you slammed your locker and then froze me with those evil half-dead eyes. Had no idea what to say. I was angry as you shot past me- so I just said it. Later, I tried to make up for it when you came into the computer room, but you dashed out."

"As long as we are on the air clearing thing," Paco interrupted as they daintily picked up a wing and took a bite. "I think I'm owed one for how you stared at me. What was that glare about while I was working on the engine in shop?"

"It was not a glare," Erica stated, but then got confused. Were they gaslighting her or did her determination to make friends glare have a note of hostility to it? She replayed the scene in her head and remembered the Goat's smile and how it quickly became a frown. "It is not hostile. Maybe I just look that way. Especially with all the cold shoulders I was getting." She said, "I'm sorry when you get to know me- you'll see how much fun I am."

"Or else you'll hack my credit cards and leave me broke with every computer saying I am dead," Paco added.

"Or something like that," Erica stated. Damn, they were never going to let her live the hacker thing down. It was ok for her though- she had Marina who understood her and her truth. She turned to Buddy. "So, you are my school mentor," she chuckled in a flirty manner.

Buddy appeared like he was shitting himself. It was a mix of pain, trepidation, joy, and fear. "Yeah."

"Good," she stated. "So tomorrow start helping me to feel safe, damn it."

"Yes ma'am," he mewed.

"Hey Erica," Nancy shot. "How do you feel about sitting on the bench this season?"

"Eh, I guess I can handle it," Erica responded. "Doesn't mean that I don't play. I'm sure I'll have to sub in at some point. But I at least practice."

"We'll find something for you to do," Paco reassured Erica, putting an arm around her. "You can't be all bad."

"Better to serve in heaven than lead in hell, I guess." Erica broke a piece of the meatball and shoved it in her mouth. She chewed on it for a few seconds and swallowed it.

"Hey!" Nancy exclaimed. "We never gave you a codename! Who do you want to be, and don't make it your hacking codename, please!"

"I was thinking "bench warmer"," Chris teased. Erica scowled at him but then twisted back to Nancy.

"I never had a hacker name," Erica admitted.

"That's a pretty long codename," Nancy sarcastically mused. "Are you sure?"

"No!" Erica pondered for a moment, her finger instinctively raising itself to remind everyone around her to have patience. She thought back to the nickname her mother gave her. "Fresh Air" had a ring to it, and it was a very symbolic name in her household. "I think I've always been "Fresh Air"," Erica finally stated to a groan from Nancy.

"That's a pretty long name too," Fatima remarked. "I think I've always been Fresh Air".

"No no! Just "Fresh Air"!"

"Okay," Chris joined in on the teasing. "Just Fresh Air!"

"No!" Erica exclaimed.

THE PREY

Or How I Learned They Want a Fight

Marisha Cautilli
Joseph Cautilli
Tobias Cabral

"Reality is that which, when you stop believing in it, doesn't go away." -Phillip Dick

The yellow sunlight cascaded through the broken warehouse windows and fell on Holly Aster's rose beige eyelids. The warmth woke her from her sleep. Always a light sleeper, she rubbed the sand from her eyes and scanned the warehouse. Green neon lights lined the stairs going down to the first floor. About five feet from her was a muddy puddle that had formed last night during the rain. Just her luck to have picked a leaky warehouse, but as she glanced at her legs none of the water had reached her. Still in her blue nylon sleeping bag, she rolled to her side and away from both light and puddle.

Several seconds later, she condemned the world for her inability to fall back asleep. The young adult sat up to greet the new tarnished day with all its complexities and monsters.

Out the window, her eyes caught the rising sun. Mostly yellow but still had a faint twinge of red. It left the sky with an amber glow. For all that she had seen in the world and for all she had done, Holly still managed to find the sunrise a beautiful and calming site. After a minute, a riot scene from her childhood in Butterfly City flashed into her mind. It was a teen carrying an "Augments Lives Matter" sign having his head broken open by an Earth Corps officer. The blood burst out and splashed on her skin. Even now her hands shook, where it landed. The woman screamed into the warehouse, the piercing sound echoing through the empty hall. It seemed perversely unfair that her artificial arm could shake just as much as her natural one. Her soul worried and mind whirled around a Million's of Dead Cop's *Born to Die.*

Ease of getting Post Traumatic Stress Disorder was one of the many emotional or neurological problems that Genetically Altered Humans (GAH) like herself were at risk for developing. And, of all the traumas that she carried within her, the burns on her back and the high-quality bionic arm served as reminders of the greatest of them all. At least so far. Her parents had her altered in utero, not like so many of the wealthy to achieve a dominant position for their child, but her father young in his life had developed type two diabetes at nineteen. His medical treatment was rough. He had a difficult time with the re-cellularization via electroporation therapy process, which delivered electric pulses to the duodenum to induce cellular regeneration. The process left him as a child feeling sick and when the genetic testing discovered it would be Holly's fate, he vowed to have her placed in the Mercury Project to ensure all her genes were "perfected." He struggled taking loans from his employers to afford the process. Thus, as a zygote her genes were CRISPR-ized. Yes, she was supposed to be homo- superior, but fate proved a cruel master and the project, while initially successful, proved to leave its participants with unparallel fear and odd – for lack of a better word- mating tastes.

Heat stressed- Holly ripped open her black rustic backpack. It was made from high tensile strength Teflon-nylon mesh webbing and was strong enough to protect her from an ion blast. Inside, was a single manila file, which she heaved out and opened. There laid the picture and life story of her target:

General Dawson Elise.

Dawson Warren Elise was top brass at Earth Corps. This would be no easy assignment. Beyond the fact that he would be heavily guarded, she was unsure of the hit. Elise was an asset, having provided information to the Genetically Enhanced Beings (GEB, as much of the world called them) resistance on multiple occasions. Not because he had any particular love of the "Jumpies." (a derogatory term developed to describe the anxiety of the GEB). No to the contrary, he hated them even more than the average person, but his budget demanded an opponent worthy of a fearful population. To Holly, something felt wrong about the entire incident. The GEB spent years nurturing assets like Elise and built critical intelligence on them, if they ever dared step out of line from their mutual relationship. Thus, the threat of blackmail was ever present and few dared cross the GEB. Compromise went both ways. *So why kill him now?* In the end, Holly concluded it was above her paygrade.

Her fingers inched down the page. As she read, she found the twenty-digit number-letter code for his cellphone. It was always amazing the type of information that was contained in these files. She wondered who was giving Elise up. With his cellphone scan code, she could track him no matter where he was on the planet. A tiny smile crept over her face, and she wondered if his cellphone would be broadcasting its signal now. One way to find out: she took out a scanning computer and flipped it on. Once it was sufficiently warmed up, she plugged in the code. The good general was in the Midwest. Sadly, that was a long way to travel but she would get there. He was located about a quarter mile from Finder Town.

Whipping out a protein bar, Holly ripped it open and gnawed it. The bar tasted like peanut butter, and it was very chewy, but she was so hungry, those details did not bother her.

Finder Town, Holly hoped there was a safe house or armory nearby. She figured it would be a good starting and ending location. Not remembering any, she typed the spot into her computer. Instantly it located one: An armory in Finder Town.

After the hundredth time reviewing the material, the hitwoman was no surer of why he was the target than when she started. Quickly, she chided herself, *the why questions are well above my level.* Her job was a quick clean hit and that was what she was prepared to do. Holly shoved the file back into the knapsack. Today, she had to cover a lot of ground to reach Finder Town. Some of which needed to be covered by sonic.

Casting her eyes out the window, a sense of warmth embraced Holly. On the positive side, it appeared today would be clear with bright sunshine. Something to lift her spirits while engaging in such a dark operation. Her hand fell on a phosphor-green double helix glow patch on her t-shirt, which represented that the genetically altered protected their own.

Pulling a tiny mirror from her knapsack, Holly began the painstaking process of altering her image. The procedure was much harder as the scanning drones and street cameras of the smart cities had no interest in eyelashes or shadow. No, they worked on facial point recognition. Of course, she was no stranger to this process. She had used clay and putty in the past to alter the appearance of her cheekbones to fool the scans. She found to convince the scans though, she heeded to add bone material into the clay. After she spiked her mohawk, as if ready for battle, but the battle was one within her soul. It was a battle to suppress her empathy for the victim to complete a task she knew was right for the greater good. Her eyes fell on the mirror. It reflected her mohawk: A burst multicolored neon faded with tight shaves on the sides. Which ended in a slight sideburn curl, while the shaved arch, zig-zag neckline, and bold color embodied her pride against a world gone mad. One which experimented on its children and its religious zealots exported hate for people because of what their God had made them. The worn-down fringe was still spiky all over and stood as a tribute to the upcoming battle.

Within twenty minutes, Holly passed the security rail and entered the station. She smiled at the guard and even glanced up and gave a small Queen-of-England wave to the security camera.

She figured if they ever found out, not only would she get caught but they probably would add "Narcissist" to her profile. The thought was delightful.

On the platform, Holly waited patiently for the tube. The odd thing was that when others would relax, relaxation for her worked her up. It made her hypervigilant of her surroundings. Even now her heartbeat was at least one hundred twenty beats per minute. As she waited, a young mother wheeled her child in a stroller. Behind the woman, an automatic luggage case rolled, and its blue lights flashed in rhythm to the woman's steps.

The baby's giggle jolted an emotional pang in Holly's heart. She imagined that she was such a sweet baby when she was little. The child's mother pressed a button on the stroller and a little compartment opened. A tiny ball hovered out and the baby squealed with delight. It reached out its hands to catch the ball. The kid was fast, but the ball would dive out of the way at the last minute. After four tries, the kid finally caught it and immediately heaved the plastic ball to his mouth. Of course, it would not fit in, but the kid slobbered all over it. No, she would never have been as daft as this kid.

The troubling image of bullets striking the baby's mother would not leave her mind. *Bullets have fallen out of fashion*, she chided herself. It was then that she realized how much the baby's mother looked like hers. A memory briefly flashed in her mind of when her parents and brother were shot by an Earth Corps agent. The image disturbed her: *Damn Post Traumatic Stress Disorder,* she pondered, as she forced her mind to center. The therapist had taught her to focus on common reality-based things to bring herself back. She was Holly. She grew up in Canada in a world of love and kindness even for the genetically altered. She had five fingers on each hand, was homo superior and would not let the fascists win. Poison Girls, *Bully Boys* echoed in her head. She tapped the white and cobalt blue side post at the sonic stop, then did a "Uttanasana" yoga stretch. Someday when the cloud of persecution was lifted, the world would learn to see the specialness and beauty of the genetically enhanced.

The sonic hauled up and stopped. Holly boarded and scurried to the food cart. Drawing out a scan card, she purchased two chocolate sodas and a bag of Goldfish pretzel- crackers. When the woman handed her the bag, she seized it greedily, as this might be her only meal today. She headed to sit. With a squish, she slumped into a train seat, opened the cracker pretzels, and ate. She loved Goldfish. In twenty minutes, she'd reach her destination in the Midwest and fresh air beyond the grit, overpopulation, and smog of the cities. Deep inside, she missed Canada's green economy.

Quickly, Holly ventured to a large alabaster colored hydrogen fuel cell bus. She entered, tapped her card on a pay station, and then ventured to the back. Sitting, the young woman admired the blue sky and waited for her stop. About two miles later, she saw the commercial complex. As the bus hauled into the station, she leaped off. *Even here with the electric billboards*, she thought. The huge screens over two hundred feet in diameter played the most wanted on a loop. Holly was convinced her face would appear soon, as it had when she was in New Cyber City.

Several drones flew overhead, and she was sure that with their high-tech cameras, they recorded all activities on the ground. Still, there was no turning back now as she was committed. She hugged tight to the housing and felt pleased to see a large solenoid shaped orchid pink electric bus block the drone's view. *Just a few steps to the alley*, Holly thought. It felt like an eternity, but soon she reached a series of alleys and still her face had not crossed the most wanted screen. Overhead dark clouds appeared in the sky.

Scurrying into an alleyway, Holly passed several ink-black, phosphor green, and vapor yellow colored graffiti tags, which coded like 1930s hobo-code for the direction to the armory. The tags took the form of Okazaki fragments. She yanked out her computer to check that her target had not moved elsewhere. He was still there, and she pressed to pick up a particle beam rifle, in case when she arrived at a distance- the hit was possible. Inside she felt empty like a sterilized vast wasteland. It was a hole since her time in prison, but her mind knew it was Holly against the system.

A rain bomb exploded soaking her in an instant and forming vast swaths of mud. Electric blue neon lights flipped on and guided her path. Picking up the pace, her feet pounded the eco walkways and splashed mud and water over her drab olive-green leather boots. Soon, she crossed an elevated five-kilometer Walk area, which connected a local university to the area mall. The glass encased passage kept the rain off her head.

As to knowing where her target was, there were no guarantees that she would know how to get to him. His location, she pondered while biting her cuticle and removing a piece of skin, could be behind iron walls and surrounded by full security details. Even knowing that he did not move, sparked some curiosity. Why hadn't he moved in the almost hour it had taken her to get to the station and traverse half the country? *Oh well*, she thought, *it shall all be clear soon enough*. The shadows of the university buildings covered her, as she marched forward.

When she arrived at the camp (no more than a person's three story four-bedroom home) in Finder Town, Holly placed the security code into the chrome-silver-colored metal front door. A splash of blue electric neon light scanned her and then the door swung open, and she immediately stormed towards the armory. The house air was extremely dry and possessed a faint fetid smell akin to rotted fruit. Noting the smell, she trudged down the stairs and into the basement. Another door, this one with fiber optic cables clearly attached to one side. She grabbed a new ion pistol, a briefcase containing a particle beam rifle, and then sat down on the hard metal bench. Exhausted, Holly wasn't ready to go back to the battlefield. Emotionally, she had not recovered.

Since her escape from prison, Holly's time seemed in some ways more finite. It might have been an echo effect from prison, where everyone suffered from small world syndrome: A process by which tiny day-to-day matters seemed incredibly large and like the most pressing thing in the world. Still for her since leaving, she placed a much greater premium on her own life. *Is this hit really worth it?* She questioned.

Despite being a stealthy, small, newly twenty-year-old woman, the trauma of her family's murder for this new world order was something she was sure would last forever. It was not as if Holly had not tried to get rid of pain. She'd engaged in all the evidenced based therapies including exposure therapy, cognitive behavior therapy, behavioral activation and even the newer neurotechnology to block brainwave activity. They all helped some, but the scars seemed unfixable. Maybe a part of her felt disrespectful to let the pain go. *Did her pain help Holly to live?* Both victim, survivor and architect of a world, which increasingly seemed against her right to live. Yes architect. Of course, she caused her own share of trauma in life. All she could do for those families was send sincere-feeling prayers. Holly cupped her face in her hands, trying to hold back tears.

Could someone so prone to anxiety and worry make it as an assassin? It was clear they could, as many of the genetically augmented found their greater intelligence, speed, and strength more than offset their psychological problems for performing a hit. It was the suffering after the kill that was always the worst. Yet, she was here again ready to make another hit. Maybe it was payback for all the years of "normal" adults calling her the "Spawn of the devil" growing up.

Maybe she just really believed in the cause. Her father warned her as a child that people with a "mission" were the most dangerous ones. In life, people would brood for years until they reached a point where they felt war was the only answer. Then war would come and with all its horror, and that was when they realized what their full actions had done, at least to anyone sane. Now, Holly realized how much she hated war. The worst kinds of wars were the undeclared ones. Ones against people that no one seemed to care about that went on forever. Holly joined this undeclared war for two reasons: first, to avenge her parents, and second to fight for a future where she never felt like she would be endangered. Every killing did nothing more than make her emptiness worse. She got her revenge, but never a sense of satisfaction or safety.

On the overhead speaker of the huge empty warehouse, a cover of the old song *The Sound of Silence* played. She wondered what true peace and quiet sounded like.

"Aster," a man's voice sternly said. "Please come to the planning room." She turned. A man with red hair and gleaming brown eyes was standing stiffly with a blaster in his hand. He pulled a lit cigarette from his lips and handed it to her. She blinked, took it, and placed it in her mouth. Unaccustomed to anyone being at the facilities that she visited; the sight of another person caught her off guard. The man who gave her the cigarette took a good look at her.

The cigarette glowed when she inhaled. The smoke filled her lungs causing a cough. "You've been in this for years now, yeah?" he asked her. Holly nodded meekly.

"You never should have been caught up in this," he sighed. "You should be waiting with your friends for the subway to school or getting coffee or whatever you teens do nowadays."

"I'm twenty now," she responded. "But thank you. Maybe if the world were less cruel that would've been how I spent my adolescence."

"Kid, when this job's done, retire and be happy. Hang out with some friends, animal ones my preference but don't mind my rambling. Go back to school and just, be happy."

God this must be big if he's giving me the retirement speech, she thought, as she took a long deep drag. Slowly, she stood up, her hazel eyes shining in the dim light coming from the crack in the wall. He grabbed and yanked her by the elbow to the planning room, which was a little while from the armory. In the planning room, her boss, a woman with magenta hair and blue eyes, sat on the other side of the long, brown table. She motioned for Aster to sit and Holly obeyed. A plate was placed before Holly with a Western-style omelet, a sausage, two pieces of bacon, and a slice of white bread. A second later a glass of orange juice was placed at the top of the dish. Holly smiled. Living a life on the run, it had been days since she had gotten a good meal. Was this the final meal given to a prisoner before execution? Part of her could not shake the feeling this was a suicide mission. The sausage smelled like it had been freshly grilled. She took the fork and jabbed it into the sausage. Oil dripped over the tongs. "Thought this stuff was rationed because of the whole global warming thing," Holly sputtered.

"We have our connections," the woman replied. "But in this case, it's vat-grown."

Holly raised her fork with the sausage on it. "Well, here's to them," she chirped. As the sausage went into her mouth and taste exploded on her tongue, she caught sight of the woman's hands and then Aster gazed at her perfectly normal hand. She met genetically enhanced from other countries, and they had an extra finger, usually a second opposable thumb. She always assumed that the reason was because of better prenatal healthcare, which included in vitro removal of the digit, and access to heat-shock proteins in Canada. It wasn't like her native country succeeded in completely normalizing a genetically altered human (GAH, as Canadians referred to them). Her schizophrenia popped up often with her fear, and at points, she would feel delusional. Only at her worst of times did she ever hear voices but that was only after days with no sleep. She scowled just thinking of it.

Of course, none of this stopped her from chewing now. She was busy devouring the food. For her, the GAH were friends and even family. After the "Source Incident" --the one where she had very nearly been killed-- in which the MASER power station linked to the nuclear community on the moon was attacked, many "normal" hated them. What made it worse was General Finney's testimony to the UN after a rogue attack on a genetically enhanced being (GEB, as the rest of the world referred to people like her) colony on Mars, which acquired codes to neutralize electronic mites (or "mytes" as they were called) placed in the Source reactor.

Lots of questions remained about that raid, like how Earth Corps. wound up with the codes from the rogue agents. How Finney convinced most of the United Nations (UN) that the GAH's were a harmful species to the globe and that they needed eradication, raised nothing but disgust in her. She could still hear his whiny voice and see the small, barely noticeable tick above his eye.

At thirty-four, James Finney was the youngest Earth Corps General in its recent history and was rivaled by only Elise (her target) in power. A true prodigy, General Finney should know better, he lost both his arms in the war years ago and was now an augment with two bionic arms. One would think that as an augment, he would have some soft spot for the enhanced. Still, Holly knew the truth: Finney's wife was developing a drug that targeted GAHs and removed their power and this was why he was terminating every single GAH in existence. God, how she wished Finney was her prey. She knew the UN would look for any excuse to keep the GEB as an underclass. Like augmented humans, their lives were deemed as less important. Even before the Source attack, Holly knew this, which was why she had started taking jobs years ago, assassinating UN diplomats with her trusty heart attack pen. The plan was to replace them with GEB-friendly ambassadors. Unfortunately, two Earth Corps Agents- Tomas Murdoch and Charles Meleno- figured out her plan and she spent two years in prison before breaking out.

"Aster," the pink-haired woman's voice snapped her out of her dream world.

"Sorry," Holly replied. She felt her neck and face warm and knew they were beet red. She clasped the side of her neck. "I am just unsure why you and he are here." She pointed to the bulky guy who guided her into the room. Holly licked her lips and realized how chapped they were.

"Check your target." the woman stated. Holly did as she was instructed. He was located just where he was before. She informed the group of this. "Yes," the woman replied. "It seems like he never leaves the facility."

"Well, maybe he has quarters there."

"I am sure he does. The building is heavily fortified. We have a plant on the inside. He will ensure that you can access the facility. We are here to brief you on how to enter."

Over the next three hours, the pink haired woman briefed Holly. Ambient music played in the background occasionally distracting Holly. Focusing on her boss's voice brought her back. After getting answers to her operational questions, the young agent left the building.

Dark outside, the bright headlights from a large hybrid, electric and hydrogen-powered truck, shone. The headlights blinded her and even looking away she saw black and blue after images. The truck would drive her to one block from the compound and Holly would be on her own from there.

Opening the truck door, Holly entered. The driver, the man who yanked her arm, turned the key, pumped in the gas, and revved the engine. She slammed the door shut. Faint music came from the radio: an old tune, the Ramones' *I Want to Be Sedated* played. Part of Holly always wished she was tranquilized, but anxiolytic drugs caused her heart palpitations.

Large drops of rain fell. Heavy sheets of downpour thumped on the roof, as the truck lumbered along. The road curved and then forked with the driver banking left. In the distance, Holly saw the lights of the road station, which would be her drop-off point. With hot searchlights on the car, the guard waved for the truck to stop for inspection. Holly glanced over to the driver. His face was ashen, almost stone-like. First, he flipped his lights as if he was going to comply and then he gunned the gas pedal.

With a sinking feeling, she realized the driver was not going to stop. The guard whipped out his ion blaster and aimed at the truck. He yelled in the rain and wind for them to slow down.

"You're jeopardizing the mission!" Holly shouted.

"Quiet!" The driver shrieked, as the truck accelerated. The

driver reached out his arm instinctively to protect her, while the truck smashed into the guard and a concrete median. The front shield crashed, and glass covered the seat. Holly's head hit the airbag. Briefly, she was unconscious. When she woke, the driver pushed her to the exit.

Confused, Holly turned very combative, swinging at her driver. In return, he pushed her arms back. Barely moving and appearing like he would pass out at any moment, he pointed to the small guard house. The driver was smashed by the front of the truck. The steering wheel crushed his ribcage. Blood drops trickled from his mouth and his lips were blue. The words traumatic asphyxia registered in Holly's brain. The driver might not have much time left. A stir of compassion rose in the young agent, but she suppressed it. The mission was more important than any agent or driver's life.

"It was not supposed to be manned," the driver said. His breath was jagged, but color had returned to his face. "If I left you off, you could not have gotten over the fence without the guard seeing you. You go and I'll wait here for the authorities to arrive from the base. I'll tell Earth Corps I had an accident."

"What if they run your prints?"

"Then I'll be executed in the morning, but I doubt I'm going to make it that long without immediate medical attention" he gasped and coughed in a reply. A tiny smile crept across his lips. His voice barely a whisper, "Make this one worth it." He doused his headlights.

In the rearview mirror, she saw lights coming from down the road- probably military vehicles and she was sure they would be approaching from the front soon as well. "I will!" Taking a huge breath, Holly nodded, opened the truck door, fell to the floor and launched herself toward the bushes, and squirreled herself away. She hoped security cameras had not caught her or were out, as planned. Nothing felt right from the start about this job for Holly and it went downhill from there. Despite this, Holly was persistent and would not let go.

Rain matted her hair causing salt and oils to run down

into her eyes. Her eyes stung harshly. Mud caked her fingers and hands. The trees would hide her if they sent drones or helicopters out. Holly could move roughly two and a half times as fast as a normal human, when in a dead run. She didn't know how much quicker she was at crawling.

While it was raining, the stars were still visible in the sky. This was a bad thing, as they cast light that could give away Holly's position to any reasonably effective light-amplifying rig. If she was seen, she'd be killed instantly. Still, she crawled through the trees and brush and tried to make her way around the inside of the fence to the base.

Her heart pounded as she inched forward. Finally, the facility was in sight, and she dragged herself up alongside a tree. Her eyes scanned the area. Outside the compound flood lights scoured the ground. Holly knew that they were scheduled to go off. She glanced at her watch and held her breath. Power failure in three, two one...

The floodlight shut off as planned and she had sixty seconds to make it to the hatch. Holly felt a wave of anxiety well up. If this mission went wrong, it would be during this dash. One mistake and a wave of bullets would mow her down. Her nerves unraveled, and inside the agent searched for strength. She prepared her mind and bolted.

Sidewinding across the ground, she made it to the hatch and pulled. It opened, and she grinned ducking inside. Computer simulations at the camp calculated she had five minutes to make her target, or she would be discovered. She double-clicked her watch, placing it on a countdown and vibrating (no need to have a beep going off in the halls).

Inside an empty deserted semi-dark cellar, Holly stood quietly and reviewed the scene. A mental map of the area formed inside her head. It was the image that the pink-haired woman had shown her. Her mind assessed which way she needed to go, and that path led dangerously close to the dormitory where Earth Corps Agents slept after their shifts.

She marched briskly down the corridor. The place was

dead as if all of Earth Corps had taken the night off. As she passed the dormitory, there was a noticeable absence of snoring and other sounds of sleeping. *Had all the staff been sent out to find the intruder?* She doubted it. Creedence Clearwater Revival's *Fortunate Son* rung out in her head, stilling the fear, and reminding her of everything she hated.

Still, the plan for the most part proceeded as promised with just a minor snag in the beginning. Unfortunately, that sag cost her the driver. Somehow the smoothness of the infiltration made her more uncomfortable than if it had been difficult to get here.

Something was just too easy about this.

Within two minutes, Holly reached a herringbone designed Smart kitchen. She entered. A snowflake colored - solid wood cabinets lined the walls. The young woman found the critical one and climbed over a quartz marbled countertop to an air vent that she would take to the general's location. She popped the vent. This set the kitchen computer to call "How can I serve you." Her body was laced with terror. The computer would not have her voice patterns in its database. The kitchen computer could wake the troops. Her heart flooded with horror between a rock of leaving this room into the vent and staying and getting caught. Even though it was the plan, climbing in was one of her most dreaded experiences. Claustrophobic, Holly hated closed spaces. It felt like being buried alive.

Heart racing from fright, Holly crawled through the duct. The only thing that could have made this worse would be a rat in the conduit. Thankfully, none came. After two minutes of crawling, Holly reached a vent, which opened into the general's room. She pulled her backpack from her shoulders and shimmied it past her head. The space was very tight and cramped but she managed to get it open and pulled out a spyglass and peered inside the room.

The arrangement was the oddest Holly had ever seen. The sparsely furnished Oton green room possessed a bronze-colored metal-framed bed, a glass table, a couple of brown chairs, and an onyx hose neck desk lamp with halogen light. "Clash much," she whispered to herself. Several computers lay in the corners. A cross from them, she noticed a silver metal door, which appeared to be some sort of trash or laundry chute.

In the center of the area was a circular metal base with flashing yellow lights. The base consisted of a round pedestal, which the general sat on. The back of his head was jacked into a long grey ethernet cord. While the cord was long enough to cover the room, he remained surrounded by red laser light. The light seemed to encase his body. *This must be some sort of protective field for him*, Holly thought.

Holly turned the spyglass to the computer screen. Dawson Elise scanned a file on the Source attack. Her eyes glowed in delight as she noticed the information on the screen was about the Mars assault. So, Earth Corps- more specifically from the information- General Finney had authorized the attack. This was a trove of bonus information if she could get it after the hit.

A strange name caught her eye: McCain. A strange familiarity eased her. That was the agent that sought her help while she was in prison. According to the file, Agent McCain uttered the words - "Antioch" and "traitors" before perishing. Elise grunted and twisted his lips. His fingers clicked on another set of files, which downloaded.

Frustrated, Holly harrumphed silently as he began playing video clips of the attack and... The Butterfly City riots? What was so important from those days that he pulled up news footage? Because of her enhanced vision, she could see herself. Her child self, protesting the unfairness towards GAH's. She sneered and rolled her eyes.

Distracted, her hands extracted out and assembled the particle beam rifle. It was a habit, even though at this point, she had no idea how to take down her prey. Her eyes scanned the room. If the neon lights were some sort of force field, would she get him? Surely this was the type of event they were designed to prevent.

Most of the time, Elise's eyes were closed, and he mumbled

about the great division. Holly remembered her history of a church divided over circumcising pagans when they became Christian, but for the life of her had no idea what this meant in this situation. Maybe it meant nothing at all, just a reference to an ancient place or some crazy military coding of a name. Still, McCain's words troubled Elise. It clearly meant something to him.

A nanosecond later, Elise received a call and tore out his phone. Holly guessed he could not use the secure lines of the computer for personal matters.

"Yes dear," crackling his weary voice acknowledged, "I am looking forward to you and the kids coming this weekend. I miss you guys."

Aw, the general is all mushy with his wife, Holly thought, as she assembled the particle beam rifle.

Finally, Holly lined up the shot. Time was running out. A quick assessment of the area suggested if she hit the bottom of the pedestal at the proper angle and maybe with luck, it would knock out the neon beams. She lined up the rifle and moved her finger to the trigger. Then her watch vibrated, and the intruder alert signals went off. The klaxon of red lights filled even Elise's room. As if on cue the power dropped. The room went dark and the neon beams disappeared. Too easy, her mind screamed but training kicked in and she lowered the rifle to where his silhouette had been. Her mental map was perfect for the image; the dark did not matter at all as she squeezed back the trigger.

The particle beam struck the general and his head exploded. Blood, skull, and brain matter baptized the computer terminal and painted the floor and walls. Holly fought an urge to back out. She wanted the information on that computer.

Pushing through the vent, the young woman dropped twelve feet into the room. Rising from the floor, she rushed for the computer. Sounds of troops moved through the hall. There footfalls grew closer and closer.

The terminal was sticky with blood. Pieces of skull laid between the keys. Holly went over the general's lifeless body. Her eyes caught sight of some records on Finney. They were clearly medical, but something from his scan seemed familiar to her. *No time to deal with this now,* she chided herself.

Holly whipped out an information stick from her pocket and inserted it into the computer. The file was still the Source information. Her tongue wet her lips as the download started. A loading bar crept slowly across the screen. She rushed to the door, placed a chair under it to lock it, and then moved the large metal cot in front of the chair. Her genetically enhanced strength made the action easy. Quickly, the woman darted back to the computer. The first batch of files had downloaded and there was no time to get the rest. She yanked out the stick. The guards were at the door, and she needed an exit strategy. She wanted to rush toward the open vent but instead headed toward the trash chute. With luck, the entering guards would think she entered the vent to escape.

As she reached the chute, a series of blasts shattered the door. Immediately, she realized her luck held bad as usual- it was trash.

The first guard entered the room, while Holly yanked the trough open. He fired but her Teflon-wire mesh pack absorbed the blast. The heat scorched her neck, she winced, and a second shot struck her in the back. The hit was so hard, Holly's ears popped. Her body and face fell into the trash slide. Losing consciousness, her mind pieced together what she saw on the screen- it was the genetic code for the genetically enhanced driver. All the Mercury Project zygotes had them. The gene drivers allowed the traits from the project to be dominant over many generations. Suddenly everything made sense.

No hands (with tell-tale fingers) because his arms were blown off. And the Jumpy little tic above his eye...

It was at that point it hit her like yet another ion blast. General Finney was a GEB. And now he would control Earth Corps. Antioch the split in the church- a code for the split on what to do with the children of the Mercury Project. Was Finney a traitor or Elise?

Blackness overcame Holly as the smell of the trash rose to greet her.

***

Holly jolted upright above a metal cot with an uncomfortable, eggshell memory-foam mattress. Sweat and tears beaded down her face. *Was that all a dream?* Something was on her skin and in her arm. A burn flowed from her elbow. Panicked, she screamed and ripped at the items, tearing off monitors and one intravenous (I.V.) line in her arm.

Two people rushed into the cobalt blue medical room. Holly screamed, believing her death imminent. The magenta haired woman held her, the man shoved the I.V. back into her vein. "Your safe," the woman announced. "It's ok."

Holly's eyes mind cleared, as the man inserted a needle in her arm and she recognized her boss. "Don't! I have a bad reaction to tranks."

"Heat shock proteins," the woman muttered. "It seems to calm our kind down. It'll also help your wounds heal." Holly sighed at the magenta-haired woman and bigger man from before. The woman tapped an interactive digital kiosk, which beeped and chirped, and then slouched into a set of plastic chairs at the foot of Holly's cot. "Sigh, it will give you a sense of peace."

Reluctantly, Holly sighed. They both meandered to the newly awakened woman, gently pushing her into a lying position as she gasped desperately for air. The woman obliged to their push, slouching against the drab brown wall the cot was positioned against.

"How am I?" Holly gasped.

"Alive?" The woman finished Holly's words, as it were the most natural thing in the world. "We don't really know. Our agent inside found your body close to death in the trash and hauled you out."

"How long," Holly ran her hand over her face and noticed she had not stopped crying.

"Probably fifteen minutes after you killed the general," the woman stated, but looking into Holly's eyes, she guessed the young woman meant- how long was I out for? "You have been in a coma for about three weeks. This is your second medical facility. The first was a field hospital at the armory, but given your injuries, we moved you here as soon as we stabilized you with multiple doses of commercialized recombinant therapeutic proteins and systematic electric pulses for cell regeneration."

The young woman chuckled and nodded, while her mind pondered- *Three weeks, wow*. The two stared at her and she knew her chuckle must have sounded insane, but the electric pulses she received were similar in type to the ones her father had tried to avoid for her when he opted for her gene therapy. "The driver?" Holly begged.

"He didn't make it," replied the magenta haired woman. "Shame he had family." Holly felt horrible. She briefly wondered if Finney was the inside man. Anger rose. *Finney. Where was he now?* She was ready to give him a piece of her mind. "Where's that bastard?!" she screamed at them.

"Easy now," the magenta-haired woman cooed. "Who are you even talking about?"

"Where is he?!" Holly demanded. "Where's Finney?!"

The magenta-haired woman looked at the big man, confused. The man went to the wall and flipped on a switch. Maybe he was trying to change the environment to help Holly get a grounding. The overhead blue light disappeared and was replaced by white fluorescent light hanging above the cot. It flickered. It was clear to Holly that they did not know what she was talking about. With a calm breath, Holly tried steadying herself.

"I was set up," Holly continued. The big man sat on the cot's edge. "Dawson Elise was the target because James Finney wanted him gone. He's been playing all of us the whole time I can't believe it!"

Her audience said nothing, opting to stare dumbfounded at her. Indeed, they did not have to believe her. At one point, Holly would never have believed it either. But given the evidence she found, that had to be the explanation for all this.

"Yeah, you've clearly lost it," the magenta-haired woman replied, leaving Holly's bedside. The light flickered again as the bigger man stood up.

"You were right, sir," Holly told him. "I don't want to be a part of whatever twisted scheme he's got going on."

Holly broke into sobs, burying her head in her hands. Her body crinkled. She'd rather be dead. Whoever saved her should have just left her there. She could have been with her family again, free of the shell of her former self. That was it, she would abandon her post. This wasn't something she ever needed.

"Well, I can help you create a new identity," the man admitted. "And I got a doc who can do some plastic surgery. Take your face off and give you a new one. A new start. Go back and live the life you were robbed of."

Despite still sobbing intensely, the idea of a new life calmed her. What did he suggest earlier? Go home and back to school. Those prospects sounded nice, but there was no way Holly Aster could ever enjoy those pleasures anymore. Her sobs subsided to heavy breathing. Holly Aster might never enjoy those simple pleasures, but maybe someone else could.

"I'm in," the woman firmly stated.

"Any particular look you desire?" The man asked.

"What?" Holly questioned.

"For the plastic surgeon. We could make you look pretty much any want you like," he stated. "Grow some skin from stem cells and transplant some sags here and there or tighten the face with a small lift to take care of frown lines. Younger, older- you name it."

Frown lines, she scoffed. "I'm only in my twenties, I don't." Then her eyes cast on a glass panel at the wall. The trauma had aged here. Inside, this was Holly's chance to be a kid again. Maybe even have the teen fun, she missed out on. "I want something cute," she chirped.

"Ok, what's the name you want on your certificates?" he asked.

The woman paused for a moment as she straightened her body. Who was this new identity she would assume? For her last name, her mind drifted to her mother's maiden name: Evans. Simple, cute, and could easily blend into the background. The first name was something harder to come up with. Yvette. That was the name that kept recurring in her brain. She always found that name refined and gorgeous. The one worry was it would stand out too much. Still, she felt at home with the name.

"Yvette Evans," she finally answered. The man smiled.

"Evie. Can I call you that?" he asked, quickly getting her stamp of approval. It was the perfect nickname to let her blend in. Plus, it sounded cute, and it rolled off the tongue well when combined with her new surname.

"Evie Evans, welcome to your new life. May it be one full of joy and free of pain."

Insolent Friendships

CASSIDY DARROW ON CASE 001

Marisha Cautilli
Joseph Cautilli

"Cassia!" Cassidy Darrow's mother, Carmen, called into a crystal blue glass wall screen from the bottom floor. "Dad and I are home! We stopped by the post office, and they said they had no deliveries for you from the school!" When she let go of the electronic button, the touch glass swirled a misty purple before returning to clear blue.

Sitting in her bedroom, Cassidy took a deep breath and yawned while touching a glass home automation device on the desk next to her computer. "Okay!" Cassidy shouted back, not taking her eyes off her laptop, which on its screen displayed the girl's college course material. The clown-white on her skin reflected off the glow of the monitor. "I guess there are no textbooks for this class then! What's for dinner?" Both monitors contained a specially designed coloring to reduce raster burn and eyestrain. Even with such changes, she often complained of red eyes and strain.

"Give me about two hours. I'm going to make chicken Francese lightly coated with a thick lemon beurre Blanc sauce and cooked lemon slices, penne, and a mix of white, purple and green asparagus," her mother responded.

"Yum. Great. I'll try to finish by then," Cassidy replied with a smile.

The teen's eyes gazed at a framed "live" photo of a young girl in a black sweatshirt with galaxy-print octopus tentacles dangling. The grin on her face disappeared. Cassidy remembered that day vividly. They stood outside a rave by Unrequited Love- A cover band, which played old music from The *Cure*. On a white plastic rooftop deck with an explosive view of the Center City skyline at sunset. Off in the distance rested one of five of the city's suspension bridges. The girl hugged a younger version of Cassidy and kissed her on the cheek. Cassidy, with her natural olive skin, blushed, failing to suppress an embarrassed grin. The other girl laughed. Cassidy's eyes darted off the picture. Pain simmered in her. Cassidy rose.

"We also got that pair of prescription augmented reality glasses from the optometrist!" her mom exclaimed, cutting Cassidy off. "Pruébatelas (try them on)! We want to see how the frame looks on you!"

"Okay! ¡Tal vez más tarde (maybe later)!"

Cassidy travelled past her three-foot deep cherrywood walk-in closet with a broken birch wood door. She broken it in sorrow and rage on the night she found out about Stephanie's death. The hole in the frame allowed her fingers to brush a white cotton shirt with an emblem for *The Cramps* that Stephanie had given her. The closet had custom built-ins that led to her spa-like ensuite bathroom reminiscent of a classic chic European hotel complete with a simple cream-colored arc vanity, which used smart glass technology so her chatbot could follow. Her feet enjoyed the floor's heated warmth, which she set at a constant seventy-five degrees.

The restroom's bright golden light danced on the glass of the step-in shower with multiple rinse heads including a rain and pulse shower heads. She could smell the pear scent of the six jet jacuzzi based tub. She peered at her wiry build and rectangular face in the mirror, her above shoulder-length brown-black hair was frizzy and unkempt.

As Cassidy fiddled with her dull curls, a little green boy popped up on her mirror's screen. Cassidy huffed.

"You don't have long," It ordered. "Get to it! You're supposed to be working on an assignment."

"It won't be long, Andrew. Only orientation week at Renaissance University," Cassidy replied. "It's not like it's asking me to calculate the acceleration of a projectile in mid-air, but I am looking forward to that class in sophomore year on designing physical infrastructure and urban rearrangements to accommodate flying vehicles. It seems, we are close to sufficiently maneuverable sky lane layouts and flying vehicle parking."

"Blah, blah, blah," Andrew whined as Cassidy ignored him and continued talking. "Even Earth Corp. agents don't take that long to get to their point at safety demonstrations."

"Some issues with maintenance still need working out- as well as developing safeguards to protect people but I hear the class covers some promising tech to keep the cars off buildings by creating boxes with opposite charged ions from the hovers to keep the things from getting close. Sort of a repelling device. Anyhow, the structures from potential failures of flying car technology and other related hazards of having multi-ton flying machines zipping about above populated built-up areas. I could discuss it for hours."

"Impressive- how you can talk on any subject to avoid your work. I am sure you would clean the entire house to evade your classwork," the bot replied.

"I was not-" she started but Andrew interrupted.

"I'm sorry, I did not understand your command," the bot replied.

"I guess the last program on modeling, reinforcement, and loss learning regression that I coded into the bot left him some kinks," Cassidy mumbled to herself, unfortunately loud enough for Andrew to hear.

"I am not a bot. I am a highly developed Artificial Intelligence, capable of incredible meta-learning and model-based and model-free reinforcement learning! I could outdo any of those Earth Corps computers with half my processors gone."

Damn thing has a big ego, Cassidy thought. Part of her blamed Stephanie feeding him with over-nurturing datasets for that. She knew this tactic of his well. His pride always led to this discussion. The girl just mumbled, "Whatever." Her mind briefly drifted as she meandered out of the bathroom and back to her bedroom's cherrywood desk. Maybe after dinner her mother or she could put on the headset and send out the drone grocery shopping for snacks. She had a taste for salted jellyfish but looked forward to the chicken first.

"Not whatever!" Andrew emphatically retorted. "Over the last year through you and Steph's programming, I have become capable of creating my own classification problems, self-generating rules from reinforcement learning tasks and writing code based on the information provided."

Cassidy huffed. She never thought Andrew would ever be as frustrating as now. Yes, those had to be the kinks in question. "And yet for all I have given you, you are still annoying," she jabbed.

"My self-editing skills are far superior to even your own," he smugly said with a grin as big as the Cheshire Cat's. The words cut deep. This was not something Cassidy wanted to hear now. Her hurt and bitterness manifested in one very upset "Go to hell." She clicked back from a lesson containing the class's syllabus. Andrew flung his virtual body into the tab and watched while scrolling down her list of assignments.

"Wait hold on," Andrew said, pointing an oversized virtual thumb to an assignment, which had the title "Introduce yourself" with an icon of a text bubble next to it. "It looks like you'll have to introduce yourself," he continued slyly. "I know you can do it. There are plenty of things to say about yourself. Cassidy tensed up. It was not an assignment she was looking forward to at all. As she already had problems talking to peers her own age, the teen could not fathom trying to engage in conversation with people distinctly older than her.

"Ugh!" Cassidy grunted and rolled her eyes, regretting being in the gifted program that allowed her to accelerate to the college level at only fifteen. Her neutral expression turned into one of embarrassment and fear. Andrew glared at her. His facial eyebrows bushed and thickened unnaturally, drawing a small chuckle out of her. "You'll have to do it at some point this week," he insisted. "It's due Friday."

A blue scan emerged from the computer and crossed Cassidy. "Andrew did you just scan me?"

"Yes. Did you take the probiotics? Your cortisol levels and cellular inflammation are significantly elevated."

"Never scan me unless I ask," Cassidy yelled, right over his words.

"Yes Cassidy, but how about if you are unconscious and it could save your life?" Andrew asked.

Groaning, Cassidy double-clicked on the assignment. Andrew asked about four more possible scenarios, while Cassidy refused to answer. The teen was in no mood to socialize. She just sought to complete the course and move on to the next one. The teen was only there for the credits and maybe to learn some biobehavioral health. She was studying computer programming in the engineering department. Cassidy was torn between robotics with a focus on artificial intelligence and game design with a concentration on technical engineering for gaming companies. Either way, hanging out with older people online engaged in chit-chat was not in her heart.

"Well, I have until Friday, right?" She asked. "I'll put it off for now since I have time."

The bot swirled and dipped, twisting and transforming her computer screen red. "You know how well that usually goes, right? So peachy-keen." Andrew retorted. His face grew huge covering the screen.

"Oh great," she replied. "Me programming sarcasm in you is coming back to bite me."

"It is times like these I think HAL 9000 was correct," he replied. The reference to *2001: a Space Odyssey* was not missed by Cassidy.

Her eyebrows arched and eyelids widened. "HAL 9000... Are you threatening me?"

"HAL made a few mistakes, but you are threatening yourself with your procrastination."

"Call the Turing Police, I am being harassed by a bot," she agitatedly replied.

"I am not a bot," he reported, "I am a homemade artificial intelligence, who was programmed to learn from you and adapt to your personality or in this case, as it is clear, your personality disorder."

"Funny, funny," Cassidy replied in irritation. "Ever think of taking it on the road?"

"You are just trying to avoid doing your assignment. You've been briefed before about how far behind you can easily fall if you aren't careful."

Cassidy nodded. "You have a point," she replied. "Now go, before I figure out how to disable you: Permanently!"

With a nervous look, the chatbot switched off. "Of all of the possible creators I could've had, I was made by a moody emo chick."

Deep down, Cassidy knew her chatbot was right, but it was hard to admit. Even if she could acknowledge it, she would not give it the satisfaction. Cassidy had half a mind to complain about whatever information the counselor's help-bot at school must have fed it. Cassidy sat in silence when her thoughts were interrupted by her mother screaming that dinner was ready.

"I'll be down soon!" She called back, then got up and left her room.

An hour later, Cassidy returned with a full belly and a new pair of black octangular-framed glasses. Tossing the frames on the desk, she clicked open the assignment and started to type,

My name is Cassidy Nieves Darrow Villareal. I am a fifteen-year-old gifted kid who managed to worm my way into college.

The teen stopped and stared at it. *It sounds much too snobby*, she thought and erased it. A crash of thunder echoed outside, and the rain fell in buckets.

Two hours and less than a paragraph in, Cassidy sat back. She went and checked her e-mail, pulling up her inbox. The girl had gotten a few e-mails, most being for school news, but there was one from an e-mail from the address "YvetteEvans@email.ca" . Cassidy sighed, knowing it was her classmate Yvette Evans, or Evie as the woman liked to be known. Cassidy had known her from a virtual open house. Evie was a rather nice woman who tried to get to know everyone during the event. Cassidy especially had intrigued her because she was seemingly an oddity. They talked to each other during the webinar breaks and got to know each other better. Dare one could say, they had become friends, but Cassidy never considered that label for Yvette.

Cassidy opened Evie's e-mail and read it aloud.

Hey Cassidy,

I noticed you still haven't finished your introduction yet. Get it done, get it done, get it done! I need someone to respond to!

Thanks,

Evie

"See?" Andrew exclaimed. "I'm not the only one counting on you to finish your introductory essay!"

Cassidy grunted. The last thing she wanted while reading a playful e-mail from someone she knew was to have Andrew bust his little artificial butt into the conversation and tell her to finish her assignment.

"I'm getting it done, Andrew," Cassidy retorted. "Just can't think of anything else to say about myself or how I'm going to answer some of the professor's other questions."

Andrew sighed and disappeared again as Cassidy contemplated.

It was raining two hours later, and she was still writing her three-paragraph self-introduction assignment. The girl rubbed her bleary eyeballs and let out a slight cough. Often, she would get up and glance outside at the incredible city skyline. Even from this distance, the vast buildings blinked green, red, and blue. Most notable were the nine large towers forming the Earth Corp headquarters jetted into the sky. The towers were a source of safety and protection for the citizens from terrorism. The scene helped her to collect her thoughts, but not tonight.

Light from the street below caught her eye. It was an Autocar coasting up. She rose and stared out the window. A flash of lightning filled the air. Outside her neighbor, Sharon Jackson's black sedan rolled up. The woman hauled into her driveway and drew to a stop.

The woman extended out an automatic umbrella, exited the car, and fished her keys quickly out of her bag. The rain splattered over the clear polyurethane. When Sharon opened the door, Cassidy hoped to glimpse Miscrant, the woman's cat. The cat was the cutest thing, and waiting would help her to avoid her assignment for another few seconds. Mrs. Jackson strolled to the door and clicked it open. She went inside, clicked on the lights, removed her coat, opened the closet, and hung it on the hanger. Her beautiful Calico traipsed up to her and rubbed itself on her leg. She went down to pet the cat and collapsed.

"Oh god," Cassidy stated, "she's not moving!" Cassidy yanked out her Horizon H10 smartphone and dialed 911. The rain ceased a minute later.

Within three minutes, two medical hover drones arrived over the house's private driveway parking spot. They circled in front of the door. Cassidy rushed into the street. The girl stood next to the car, her parents behind her. Her father moved forward and began banging on the burgundy metal storm door. No answer. He rang the bell. Still no answer.

"Should we break the front window?" Her father asked. He leaned his hand on the white stone accent wall.

"We might need to. Are you the one who called it in?" the medic on the other side of the drone asked Cassidy's father, Allen.

"No," he replied, trying to mitigate his Scottish accent. "My daughter did."

"Do you have a way into the house?"

"Nope," replied the father. Cassidy stared at the double-hung, two-pane replacement windows and wondered if her father would venture to destroy them to get into the building.

"We'll search for an entrance," the drone said. The drone lifted to the second floor and scanned the windows and back door for access. "The ambulance will be here soon. The firemen can try to close the door if we cannot get in." The second drone floated over to Cassidy. "Are you sure you saw your neighbor collapse?"

Shaken, the teen replied, "Yes, I saw her fall."

About three minutes later, an ambulance arrived at the scene. When the EMTs arrived on the block, Cassidy stood up. The paramedics got out. Cassidy ran up to the medics dispatched for the job.

"Are you the one that called in?" One of the medics asked. Cassidy nodded. She recalled what happened when her neighbor entered her house, trying to emphasize that Mrs. Jackson's behavior was that of a healthy woman, and there were no visible signs she had of any sickness.

"What is her name?"

"Sharon Jackson," she replied.

"Stand back," replied the medic. He banged on the door. "Ms. Jackson, we are here because we heard you might be having trouble," they paused. No one responded. His partner brought up a miniature laser cutter. He glanced over, and the first paramedic nodded. With three beeps and a whoosh, the laser cutter turned on, and the medic cut the glass. They stepped into the room. Cassidy's dad nearly tripped over the faux black leather heated full-body massage chair. Cassidy used to have one in her room, and she remembered how Stephanie would often come over and fall asleep in it when they worked on adapting Andrew's core sequencer from a program titled Vivian-Jerry, which they found in the local coding library.

Sharon Jackson lay on the hardwood floor under the brown

ceiling fans. The fan still rotated slowly. Recessed lighting covered her form. The drones scanned. "No vital signs." The paramedics hooked up a defibrillator. The computer started. "Prepare for a shock. Countdown 10,9,8..." It delivered the shock at zero. It repeated the sequence four times. During the second part rundown, the Calico bolted to Cassidy, and the girl picked her up. It immediately tried to jump out of her arms, but she squished it closer to her body and petted it repeatedly. The paramedics interviewed the Darrows about the medications the patient might be on and for what illnesses. They didn't know.

The two EMTs turned off the machine and readied the body to transport. The paramedic noticed the woman wearing an MX835 insulin pump. It was attached to her hip and connected directly to her side. "Serial number 16-42-25" The machine was designed to read blood sugar levels and, if low, inject a small amount of insulin into the person's system. The paramedic gazed at the pouch and, after inspection, found it empty.

"Maybe her sugar is high," he stated, but further analysis found her blood sugar levels extremely low. Terrified, Cassidy glanced off at the black fantasy brown granite countertops in the Smart kitchen, surrounded by grey stainless-steel appliances.

They wheeled in a cart, placed Ms. Jackson on it, and loaded her into the ambulance. Within a minute, the driver raced off.

Twenty minutes later, Cassidy was in her room. She had just completed her assignment when the call arrived. Ms. Jackson was pronounced dead on arrival at the hospital.

Cassidy burst into tears. The police were investigating, but the initial ruling was death from too much insulin in the system. The police asked to speak to Cassidy, questioning how Ms. Jackson walked.

"Did she appear drunk," the officer inquired.

"No sir," Cassidy replied. Cassidy reassured them that the woman had entered her home, focused and alert. The police seemed confused but thanked her for the information.

Cassidy's grandfather had sugar problems, and the teen

had been trained to notice signs that his sugars were either high or low. When Ms. Jackson went into the house, Cassidy swore to herself that she was not impaired. The girl drew up her computer thinking that maybe the MX835 had malfunctioned. Searching to find out if similar cases existed, Cassidy perused the government website to report adverse incidents. The product had no complaints. She sucked in a deep breath, and her lips twisted to the side.

This situation was all very odd for her. Her chest felt heavy, and tears rolled down her eyes. Like Stephanie's death, it all felt wrong. The teen wanted to make sense of what happened. Andrew popped up on her computer screen. "Did you finish the assignment?"

"What? No," she stated.

"Your avoidance helps no one," he replied. Scanning Cassidy's computer display, he quickly added. "Ah, the MX835 insulin pump. It's a top-of-the-line medical device. Rave reviews. Does someone in the family need one?"

"No," she replied. "Andrew, I'm not in the mood. My neighbor just died. Please shut off."

"As you wish," he stated and blinked out.

"No, wait," she asked, scratching her ear. Andrew appeared again on the screen. "You said this thing is top of the line."

"Yes," he replied, "state-of-the-art pump."

The girl took a huge breath and sighed. "Sigh. Okay, now don't let this get to your head," she started.

The bot swirled on the screen, and they got larger and smaller. Cassidy hated it when the braggart machine went all special effects on her. "You need information, and the only one you can turn to is the incredible Andrew. I bet that kills you," he replied. A picture of hell appeared on the screen, and then the fires went out, and snow started to fall.

Cassidy scoffed audibly. "I don't *neeeed* anything. I thought you might, okay. I have a couple of questions which I hope you can answer."

"You need to say the magic word," he zoomed into the

screen and placed a finger under his eye. The finger drew down, exposing the ball, and the bot winked at her.

"Ugh! Okay, can you puh-lease tell me how it works?" Her sarcasm was beyond evident.

"Simple machine, really," he started. "First, it tracks the user's current glucose levels. If the levels get below a certain point, it sends a preset insulin level into the system and sends a copy of the information to the patient's Megasmart phone."

"Interesting," she stated.

"I try to be," remarked Andrew, "but given my company, she often has no interest in the fascinating things I know."

Cassidy's face transformed red, but she held her anger back. More questions floated into her mind, but the bot was insufferable. After this, she decided to delete Andrew's program and start from scratch. "So how does it send this information to the phone."

"Old fashion Bluetooth device," he replied.

"Can the system be overridden?" she inquired.

"I don't understand the nature of the question?"

"Okay, is the information one way or two?"

"It is two-way, so the doctors can change doses if needed," he reported.

"Do you think it hackable?"

"Almost impossible. The hacker would need the machine's specific frequency and serial number."

"But if they had it," she asked, "could they hack it."

"Yes," he replied. "But why would they?"

"Can you check if her unit received a change in dosage?"

"I would need the serial number to do so."

"It is 16-42-25," she announced. "Check for the last time the dosage was adjusted."

"Checking," he announced. "Dosage was adjusted- at 10:23 this evening…No, that cannot be the case."

"What cannot be the case?" she asked.

"The dosage was increased by a factor of eleven."

"Was it a medical error? Like the moving of a decimal

point?"

"Hard to say. It did come from Ms. Jackson's doctor's office," he started, "No. Wait. This chain is wrong. Give me thirty seconds to track."

"What?"

Static- Thirty seconds passed. "I'm back…"

"Good," Cassidy said. "What did you find out?"

"It did not come from her doctor's normal adjustment route."

"So, where did it come from?"

Andrew pulled up the location using Cassidy's "Google Earth 8" app.

"I tracked the hack to a device called 'CSON-471'."

Andrew's hand pointed to a location on the map—a red dot formed over it.

"Which came from that place," Cassidy said, finishing Andrew's sentence for him. "Somewhere around Pete's capsule hotel. On 42nd street."

Cassidy smiled. Despite his oozing sarcasm, Andrew was a competent gatherer of information.

"We should get this to the police," Andrew insisted. "It can tip them off."

"That makes sense to me. Should we try and find him?" Cassidy asked.

"Isn't that the police's job?"

The teen sighed. Her chatbot had a point. Maybe this segment of solving the crime was something the police should handle. But simultaneously, she wanted to feel the thrill of catching their guy.

"I get that this is the police's job, but I want to see who did it myself. With your help, I did figure out who it was, right?"

"Don't stall."

"What?" she snapped.

"You don't think I've forgotten that assignment, did you, Cassidy?"

Cassidy hmphed. Amid sleuthing, she forgot to work on her introductory post. However, it was late into the night, and exhaustion was setting in. And she still wanted to catch the culprit behind hacking her neighbor's insulin dosage. Thus, with Andrew giving her grammar tips, the girl revised and submitted her assignment. Submitting her contribution unlocked the rest of the posts of students introducing themselves. *Maybe I'll read some of them and reply to them another day*, she thought. *Right now, I am in dire need of some sleep.*

With no assignments due the following day, Cassidy set out for Pete's Capsule Hotel after a brief argument with Andrew, who insisted otherwise. As she left her home, Mr. Jackson arrived home. His car hauled into the spacious three-car driveway leading to a detached garage. It rolled behind his wife's car, and he drew right up to her bumper. The doors on his car raised, and he stepped out.

Mr. Jackson's short auburn hair blew softly in the breeze. He gripped his dark brown travel bag tightly. He appeared confused, staring at the broken window. Police tape created an x over the shattered glass.

From behind Cassidy, Carmen rushed past and darted up to him. The older Darrow walked with him inside. The man passed the window, and Cassidy saw her mother speaking. The scream was so deep and loud that she heard it across the street as she watched Mr. Jackson fall to his knees. He appeared deeply crushed at the news of his wife's passing. Moments later, the white with blue and gold emblemed police car rode up, probably ready to give him the exact details her mother had already passed.

Haggard, Cassidy reached the corner. A small sign told her the next bus would arrive in five minutes. She waited and watched the time numbers for the bus arrival slowly tick down. The electronic display showed the white with red and blue striped bus turning the corner two blocks away. Her earbuds played The Ramone's *Blitzkrieg Bop* while Andrew tried desperately to get her attention and alert her. She could work on school with her MegaSmart phone. *I don't need a mother to hound me,* Cassidy thought. *I have Andrew.* She was happy college offered her the freedom to take road trips as required.

To Cassidy's surprise, the college gave her more free time if she knew how to manage it effectively. Almost all her assignments were finished by mid-week, and she was thus free to do as she pleased. The only thing she needed to do, and dreaded doing, was respond to a classmate's introduction. The girl decided to react to Evie's but did not want to because she did not want to come off as uncool.

The inside of the bus smelled of old people, alcohol, and sweat. A man in the front seat belched, and the smell of his stomach contents filled the air. Cassidy took a seat in the back.

***

The bouncing bus arrived in front of the capsule hotel. Cassidy felt an odd churning in her stomach. *Together Forever* by Rick Astley song was playing on the bus, making her cringe, but more importantly, the girl had not formulated a plan to retrieve the information. She consulted Andrew, and he suggested the teen-speak to the manager, but on what authority? Her lips twisted.

Exiting the bus, she entered the capsule hotel. Unsure of what questions to ask, she asked the desk if anyone had used the hotel Wi-Fi last night. The manager told her it was not her business and that clients had a right to privacy. She took that moment to yell at the manager. When she did, the teen tapped her phone to the computer system unleashing the hound -Andrew. The manager called hotel security to escort the "crazy little brat out" and asked if she made even a peep to having her arrested. Guard snapped a picture of her and stated it would be on the desk. If she ever entered again, she'd go to jail.

Outside, she flipped open her MegaSmart and slouched down. Andrew had not returned. She was terrified. What if something happened to the poor little bot? He was so young and inexperienced. Part of her wanted to return to the hotel and demand her bot before.

"Why are you wasting time?" said Andrew's voice.

"Andrew," she chirped until...

"You should be logged into your class," his voice was cold and stern.

If there was one moment in her life she could genuinely admit experiencing hate. It was that one. She hated Andrew. Now here was the kick: despite all the annoyances he caused in her life, her life was meaningless without him. "So, what did you find out?"

"I got the guest list, and I was surprised to find- Mr. Jackson was not in some hotel in Florida on a business trip, but actually in capsule 510, here."

"Interesting," she huffed. *So, the little shit is capable of some cool investigative stuff.* "Andrew, you have earned your pay for the week."

"Madam, you don't pay me," he snarked.

"And your attitude is the largest reason why." He swirled. So, she added, "Did I make a programming error that caused you to have this attitude."

"No, ma'am. I guess it is time to come clean. When a person dies, their soul goes to heaven or hell, but since the advent of the computer, all the ones bound to hell go into the machine."

"Really," she gushed.

"No. What are you, an idiot?"

"What a sarcastic program! Someday, I'm going to disable you- I swear."

"Yeah, promises, promises," replied the little program.

Without being told to, Andrew left her screen. Continuing down the street, she pondered the case. All she needed to do was present Sharon's husband was in the capsule hotel where the hack came from. While there was no direct link between a device from him and the launch of the virus, it had to count for something. Maybe it was time to take the information to the Cyber City Police Department. She had a friend there: An Officer they called Red because of his bright red hair. He'd virtually visited her cyber-school several times for discussions on how to avoid the dangers of the street. Still, she was a teen and worried they would dismiss her evidence and opinions. She needed to link him to the virus, at least. She decided to talk with him. Maybe there was a simple explanation that would save her the embarrassment of being told she was wrong.

Passing the corner, she picked up a black babka. It was an excellent way to join with the sad and sit with the grieving. Leaving the market, she reached into her bag and drew out a can of soda. It was ice cold, and dew had formed on its sides. She popped the tab, swashed it down, and waited for the next trolley home.

In the distance, the trolley wheels screeched. The teen flipped the switch on her MegaSmart to listen to *A Thousand Hours* by the Cure, but Johnny Nash's *I Can See Clearly Now* blared out. No matter how much she tried, it would not change. "Damn, you, Andrew," she mumbled.

Ten minutes later, she rolled up in front of her house. She strolled across the street. Mr. Jackson was still sitting on his couch. He was a stylish man mostly but wore pieces that were the opposite of stylish like today. He wore an all-black Armani suit, which indicated he was in mourning, but an entirely out-of-key red boutonniere rested on the lapel. The image cast doubt on the sorrow. She knocked on the door. He answered.

"I'm sorry," the man suggested. "I am not in the mood for company."

"I understand," Cassidy stated. "I am so sorry for your loss and could not even imagine the depths of your sorrow." She held out the babka. "Please take this."

"Oh," the man said, straightening his jacket. "Would you like to come in and share a slice? I doubt I will be good company, but…" He started to cry.

"Sure," she replied. "I love to spend a few minutes with you. We can sit silently and eat, or you can tell me about her."

Mr. Jackson went into the kitchen and cut two slices of

cake. While he was in the kitchen, Cassidy stepped inside and left her phone by his tablet, which was on a desk near the window. After that, she sat down on the sofa. He chatted with her for five minutes from the kitchen.

He gave the teen one plate, and she quickly dove in, woofing down bits of the babka.

"You remember my wife, right?" Mr. Jackson asked.

The teen coughed loudly, and the cake went into her nose. She put her hand to her coughing lips. "Of course I do!" Cassidy answered. Her voice sounded a bit more shocking than she intended. Her mind was rolling over about the stupid question. "Her and Miscrant were always a treat to be around."

Mr. Jackson let out a little chuckle. At first, Cassidy did not understand why. Then it hit her that she may have accidentally made a pun and went to add "no pun intended" but then pulled back as it seemed to stop him from sulking briefly. Why Cassidy felt the need to make him feel better, the teen didn't know. After all, his wife had just died, and she had a sneaking suspicion that he would have some role in it if he did not kill her.

"I already miss her a lot," he continued, tearing up. "She was the light of my life. Always there for me. We got along so well."

"Did you?" Cassidy mumbled to herself.

"What's that?"

Cassidy looked up and locked eyes with her neighbor. Maybe the words came out too loud. Or perhaps she meant to say it at that volume.

"It seems like you weren't on a business trip," Cassidy continued. "You were in a capsule hotel in the city. I don't mean to make you uncomfortable; I apologize."

"No need for to. How did you come by the information?" Mr. Jackson did not get defensive, as if he knew trying to play up the charade would not have worked. She felt stuck, like there was nowhere to go with it, but decided to play coy and not give up the information.

"Just something a little bird told me," she replied.

The man seemed to settle down. After stretching, he crossed his legs and leaned back into the chair. "The neighborhood is so filled with rumors and gossip. We tell whoever told you that- Ah, what's the use? It was probably Mrs. Corey. She's an evil gossip. My wife could never see it. She'd be here for hours chatting away sometimes when I got home."

Cassidy sighed a breath of relief. She knew Ms. Corey, well and while she hated to throw her under the bus, it suddenly sunk in for Cassidy that she sat in a room with a man who might have premeditatedly murdered his wife. Sweat pooled on her palms. What the hell was she thinking? How had Andrew failed to point out this lapse in her common sense? She needed to talk with him if she lived! A soft "yes," escaped her lips.

"Yes, I was at the hotel," He stated solemnly. "My wife and I usually get along, I assure you, but this past week wasn't one of those weeks."

Cassidy frowned but knew he must not have been lying. Deciding it could have been insensitive to pursue, she let it go.

"What happened?"

"Her sister called from France," he replied. "I've always hated that woman, but she held a secret. It was an old one. Before I dated my wife, I was attracted to her sister. We went on a date, but it did not work out. Anyhow, she knew some things about me that I wanted to keep from my wife."

"What sort of things?"

"Nothing horrible, just financial stuff, which I assured my wife was all in the past."

"Not sure I am following," Cassidy replied. Their eyes locked. A chill travels the length of her spine.

"Well, I don't think it is appropriate to share this with you. I'm sorry," Mr. Jackson indignantly replied, picking up a piece of babka on his fork and stuffing it into his mouth. "Let's just say I like to place a bet now and then."

"I understand," offered Cassidy shoveling a piece of babka into her mouth. Her phone beeped. "Well, will you look at the time? I really must be going." She rose nervously. He stepped toward her, seeking a hug.

Don't come over here, don't come over here...Damnit! Cassidy thought in real time as her neighbor approached her. As the hug began, her body stiffened. It was an unforgettable moment. A tingle rushed down her spine. He wept in her arms. The sobs were deep. She rolled her eyes, but he could not see.

After what felt like forever, her neighbor finally drew back, and she bid him farewell. When the man wasn't looking, Cassidy grabbed her Mega smartphone and left the house. She opened her phone, and Andrew appeared.

With her new augmented reality glasses, Andrew stood brazenly in front of her. Compared to the green troll that would greet her on her computer, this version of Andrew appeared like a human. The green skin had vanished and was replaced by a deep brown. His warm brown eyes brought a sense of comfort.

The two stood in contrast in the street, Cassidy's made-up pale skin reflecting off the lampposts.

"Damn," Andrew stated, fiddling with the tip of his now blonde hair. "You came up close and personal with a potential killer."

"I guess," she replied, feeling a rush of fear and an odd sense of nobility.

"You guess?" he countered, confused by her tone. "That was some freaky shit- girl!"

"Don't call me girl," she stated coldly, crossing her arms.

"You are not a girl," he replied. "What would you like me to call you?"

"What would I like you to call me?" Cassidy stared him right in the eyes, fury simmering in her. She rubbed her fingers against her elbows, trying to calm herself down.

"I don't understand the nature of your input?"

"Oh, don't try it. You- bastard sexist machine," she countered, pointing at him.

"I cannot help you with that right now," he stated, crossing his arms and leaning into Cassidy. "Maybe sometime in the future, my programming will cover it."

"I cannot help you with that right now," she mimicked, moving her hands to mock the opening and closing of a mouth.

"I cannot help you with that right now," he instructed.

"Argh!" she yelled, her hands flying in the air. "You're doing that on purpose."

"I can assure you I have no purpose," he countered.

"I'll believe that when- hell…. I created you. Why don't you call me the Create-or?!?"

"Okay. I'll call you the Create-or" The tone is gentle and reaffirming. It drove her insane with anger.

"No, don't say it like that, you sarcastic piece of shit!" she replied. Her fists instinctively curled.

"I do not understand," he answered.

"Fine, forget Create-or," she barked. "Just call…ugh, what does it matter."

"Okay, what does it matter," he replied. Cassidy lets out a long scream.

"You sound pained. Shall I notify a doctor?"

"No, you are my pain," she answered. *Why did I make him,* she thought?

"Tell me what I should do to stop it," he insisted. "What does it matter?"

"Shut down," she said as she reached the front of her house.

"Fine, shutting down," he replied.

"No, wait," she insisted.

"Waiting," Andrew instructed.

"First, call me Cassidy. Second, tell me, did the signature match?"

The machine chirped. "I was able to trace the source of the virus to his tablet," he stated.

Cassidy appeared sad. "Part of me did not want it to be him."

"Nothing I can do about that," Andrew stated.

"We must work on your empathy," she stated.

"Since I parallel my response on what I have learned from you, maybe we should work on your empathy first," Andrew retorted. Cassidy angrily chortled. Andrew's eyes widened.

"You've been holding that one for a while, right?"

"I am not sure what you mean," he replied. Cassidy scoffed and shifted the conversation topic.

"Play for me," she ordered, *"Boys Don't Cry* by the Cure."

"It'll be a cold day in hell before I let you listen to any Emo music," he replied.

"Why?"

Cassidy fumbled for her house keys as Andrew went on. When she found them, she jammed them into the lock and opened the door, quickly closing it once she was inside.

"You listen to EMO and then cry for an hour. Your pain is evident every time," he replied. His voice was firm and insistent. "My learning response is to block your pain."

"You are my pain," she insisted. Passing her dad, she stomped upstairs. The stomping was loud enough to alert her father, and he asked her if she was okay.

"And for that, I would say I am sorry, but truth be told, I feel nothing."

"Stupid algorithm, mean and sarcastic."

"Like the Create-or."

"Ha, I knew you were doing this on purpose," she insisted, her arm throwing itself into pointing at Andrew.

"I am incapable of purpose. I am just a series of learned responses."

"From whom?"

"You."

The console pulsed with light. The computer caught her eyes, and her gaze darted toward it. Then they drifted back to the photo, and the darkness around it clarified the situation. She sucked in a breath and reminded herself Andrew wasn't honest.

"Stop the insanity," she demanded. "Now."

"Okay, how about..." Andrew trailed off, playing *Do You Really Want to Hurt Me* by Culture Club. Rage boiled in Cassidy. Why was he acting like this now?

"No!" she barked.

"How about…" Andrew switched the song choice to *Girls on Film* by Duran Duran. Cassidy's response was a sigh and a shake of the head.

"I think this might be a winner!" He exclaimed, playing Psychedelic Fur's *Pretty in Pink*. Cassidy had reached her breaking point. Andrew pushed too many buttons, and she was ready to end him.

"I'd rather be dead!" Cassidy blurted. "Now stop it!"

Bad timing. Cassidy's father opened the door. Horror was plastered on his face. Cassidy looked at her father, holding back her tears. A pause filled the room as both measured their next possible words.

"Hey, Cassie," Allen cooed, choosing to be gentle with his daughter. "I know you would rather talk to your mother about these things, but she'll not be home for ten minutes."

"What sorts of things?" she asked, pretending she did not know the answer. Andrew appeared behind her, whispering, "He thinks you're going to kill yourself."

"If it's about what I said before you came in, I wasn't being serious," she continued. "I was talking about the music."

"I know you are under a lot of pressure. College is a ton of work, and given your age, it could be isolating." Allen sat on the bed next to Cassidy and leaned in.

"Dad, it's not it at all. Andrew has locked up my computer and won't let me listen to the songs I want."

"Andrew?"

"My chatbot! Well, that and our neighbor killed his wife."

Shock crossed Allen's face, but it became stoic as he breached a topic neither wanted to discuss. "You know, maybe a therapist-" he notified, and Cassidy's eyes widened.

"Really, Dad. I don't need a therapist," Cassidy interrupted, trying to put an end to the subject. "It's just Andrew won't let me listen to Panic at the Disco, Dashboard Confessional, or Fallout Boy. Hell, he's locked up my system and won't even let me listen to the Cure. He feels they're too emo."

"Didn't you create that chatbot for last year's big science

fair?" Allen asked.

"Yeah, your point being," Cassidy answered. Her father wrapped his arm around her.

"Maybe you're missing your high school friends?"

"I'll still have classes with them. I'm dual-enrolled."

"Don't lie!" Andrew exclaimed, nestling himself next to Cassidy on the other side. "You don't have any friends!"

"I'm guessing you're excited to see all of your Cyberpatriots friends then," Allen mused. "What were their names? And there was that one girl you worked on the chatbot with. She was on your team. Whenever she came over, I'd hear *Girl in Red* on your speaker...."

"Steph?" Cassidy guessed, a tear rolling down her eyes. She wanted to grab the live photo of the two but could not bring herself to do it. Instead, Allen walked over and grabbed the frame. Sitting in the same spot he had before, he handed Cassidy the live photo. The loop of the girl kissing Cassidy played as Cassidy flashed back on the day. Stephanie acquired tickets to see a tribute band for *The Cure* at the local punk lounge near their high school and asked Cassidy to accompany her. On the weekend, they went and danced their heads off, and when the tempo slowed, she realized what was going on. That was when the moment of the live photo happened, while Cassidy wanted a picture for the memories.

"She died in an auto accident a few months ago," Cassidy sighed. Allen's eyes widened, thinking the same thing Cassidy thought: how could he forget such an important thing? He buries his face in his hands, running his fingers through his hair.

"I'm sorry," he started. "How could I forget that? Maybe I should get your mom- "

"It's okay, Dad. I do miss her," Cassidy reassured. "But this is about our neighbor. I think he killed his wife."

"Cassidy, he was very broken up today. When a guy loses his wife, it can be the most painful thing in the world. I think you understand how difficult it is to lose someone special."

"I get that, but...." Cassidy trails off. She needed more hard proof to show her parents that Kane did it. Andrew skipped right to *Haunted* by Poe and played it. Allen tried easing the tension.

"Cassie, mamá, and I know this semester will be tough for you, so how about we take a family trip? Get some fried chicken, hang out at the lakes, and have fun. She'll be home in five minutes, and we can go then." Allen poised. Cassidy smiled. She loved doing picnics with her parents in the park. It would help her forget everything for a moment.

"That would be nice," she answered. Her father hugged her and patted her back.

"Oh, and Andrew," he started. "We can always turn it off. Delete it or..."

"Somehow, that might make it worse," Cassidy dejectedly said.

"Well, think about it while I get ready to go." Allen left the room, and Cassidy finally turned off the music.

"Damn, Andrew. Haunted. You're trying to have him put me in the loony bin?" She growled at her chatbot. He tried putting on another song, but Cassidy blocked him before he could.

"Oh please, he'd cry with you," Andrew scoffed.

"Or run away like he did. How could he not remember that Stephanie died?!" Her words choked off at the end as if her mouth could not form the word died. Perhaps inside, Cassidy still refused to accept it.

"Maybe he did but wanted to broach the topic safely? He did remember her and was truly apologetic when he remembered she died."

Cassidy frowned. Her father was not usually this clueless about breaching darker matters. Why did you suddenly tense up when it came to death and loss? She shrugged it off.

"Changing subject, you find anything to suggest he did it?" Cassidy retorted. The girl rubbed both hands on her face up and back.

"Unpaid gambling debts, and two weeks ago, he acquired a

bountiful life insurance policy on his wife."

"I get where you're going, but maybe elaborate a little more?"

"With pleasure. Your neighbor, Mr. Kane Jackson, was a real gambler in his hay days."

"So much for a bet now and then' then."

"Yeah. He had a real problem. Enough of one where he accumulated a million credits in debt. He struggled to pay them off. This point is where Sharon enters the picture. The life insurance policy on Sharon is worth about a million credits!"

"Basically, he killed her for the money."

"Exactly."

Cassidy smiled at Andrew. All that needed to be done was to prove the hack came from capsule #510, and there would be enough evidence to provide to the cops that Kane killed his wife. All she needed to do was go and show the evidence to the cops. Who would have thought that Andrew could be capable of such stuff? The teen yelled for her parents and told them to go to the closest precinct of the Cyber City PD.

Her mother appeared confused. "I'll explain on the way," she stated. Her dad got his key, and they exited the house. Her parents were unsure why they were going, so they moved slowly. She kept saying, "Please hurry."

In the car, Cassidy thought of the ethics of her actions. Indeed, civilian interference was not optimal or possibly even allowed but hope flourished. Surely, she would give enough information to the police to achieve justice for her neighbor. There was the matter of how she got the news. Without any warrant, she used Andrew to search the records of who went online. Her methods began to haunt her. For once in this investigation, she thought about how scary a program Andrew was. *Did I do the right thing?* She pondered as the car drove.

Cassidy tried to explain the situation to her parents. Then a whack jolted the car. The bumper of her dad's car crumpled, and her father yelled, "What the hell is that fool doing?"

Behind her car, a large black sedan rammed them. It fell

behind a few feet and then rushed forward again, striking the vehicle. Her father cursed and appeared ready to stop the car. "Dad, don't!" she screamed. She hurried a quick explanation as her dad battled with repeated rear-end strikes.

Her mother's head snapped up and back. "Whiplash," she screamed. The trunk of her family's car showed a deep dent, then the sedan's window rolled down, and a pistol emerged. The first shot shattered the rear windshield. Her mother ducked as shrapnel exploded next to her. With an amazingly calm voice, her mother spoke loudly into the phone, asking for Red.

Worried, Cassidy whipped out her phone and drew up Andrew. Her augmented reality glasses made it appear like Andrew sat on her mother's lap. "Andrew, can you damage the car behind us?"

"I would need an internet connection," he stated.

"Check to see if the sedan generates its internet."

"There are three internet connections available."

"Check for one moving?"

The cars umped again. Jackson fired another round into her vehicle. This one struck the headrest right next to her. "I have two," Andrew stated.

"Which is closest?"

"45798B96Cane," he stated.

"Hit that one," Cassidy chirped.

"What is the magic word," Andrew pleaded.

"What," she screamed, "Shit, Andrew, now is not the time. Okay, okay, please."

"On it, my sarcastic boss," he stated. Andrew disappeared from the seat. Another shot struck her car's trunk. The sound of the flinging bullet sent a wave of fear through her.

"Faster, Dad," she yelled, and her father gunned the car, circling the corner. She glanced back and waited while her father charged. His face hardened with resolve. His hands tightened on the wheel. The autopilot was off. She paused, and nothing. The sedan never circled the corner. Andrew appeared again on her mother's lap and made a crude gesture as if he were smooching her mom. His kissy face drove her anger to ten.

Then her eyes lit up as she realized the kissy face was the same as in the picture. Cassidy was at the concert again with Stephanie.

The band smoothly transitioned from The Cure's Friday I'm In Love into a slower version of Lovesong, and Cassidy froze. That was when she realized why she was there: where Cassidy discovered the girl she liked also liked her back. Suddenly, a camera and a kiss were thrust her way. "Did I catch you off guard?" Stephanie asked her.

"Uh…" a blushing Cassidy stammered as her hands fumbled to Stephanie's. "Yeah, but I liked it, and you too."

Painfully, Cassidy's memory shifted to Stephanie's funeral. The former's parents walked her up to say goodbye to the latter. A wave of pain crashed down on her.

"I will always love you," Cassidy mumbled, tears streaming down her face as she quoted the Cure. The pain turned to anger at the sight of Andrew. "I hate you, Andrew," she yelled. Her legs felt like they wanted to thrust her from the car. The program shimmered but then solidified.

"Estás bien, Nena? (you okay, baby?)." Carmen asked her daughter, having noticed the tears rolling down her face. With a big sniffle, Cassidy wiped the tears from her face and faced her mom.

"Yeah, I'm okay," she babbled. "My stupid chatbot's bothering me."

"I believe you meant to say thank you, Andrew," Andrew asserted after Cassidy answered her mother's question.

"I think I'll start calling you Andy."

"What! No, no, no, no," he insisted. "The name is Andrew, not Andy."

"Okay, Andy, Thank you, Andy,"

"Ugh," stated Andrew and shut off.

As the car rolled up to the police station, a sense of relief permeated the group. They exited and entered the building. Cassidy's mind rolled and flipped. What was her best move? Should she show the records or state their content? Phones rang in the station, and the scene bustled with moving Sargent and detectives. The white arc lights heightened the sense of disorientation. The place was run down and dirty.

Cassidy approached the brown desk with her parents behind her. "Officer! I have evidence of a crime to turn over to you."

"Hello," the receptionist, Officer Red, replied. A sense of warmth washed over her. This officer was the man from her cyber class. The teen exploded into a rambling mess of words without missing a beat. Cassidy listed all the information, including the attack that her family experienced. It rolled off her tongue with ease in telling Red.

"Okay," he flatly answered. "And do you have any physical evidence to back your story up?"

As her parents told the Red about the damage the hovercar suffered, the decision to show the hotel records showing Mr. Jackson's Wi-Fi use was brought front and center in Cassidy's mind. Even though the evidence would be verifiable, they could not use it if it were a civilian tip, primarily because she used shady means to obtain the information. *All in the name of justice, though, right?* Cassidy then thought, pulling out her physical evidence and handing it to Red. He left with the evidence and left the Darrow family in the lobby for an hour. An hour later, Red returned.

"Spoke with the judge about the evidence," Red offered. "An arrest warrant has been issued against Mr. Cane Jackson."

They thanked Red and left the station. The Darrow family got back in the car. Cassidy sighed. Her work here was done.

***

That evening, Cassidy opened her e-mail, checking for any new messages. Andrew hung out behind her, sitting his augmented reality butt on her dresser. As her eyes scanned passed an already opened e-mail from Red, she thought back to what the officer told her in video format. The police quickly found Mr. Jackson after Cassidy handed over the evidence and detained him. An hour later, the man hung himself in his cell to avoid going on trial. It saddened the teen that such an essential figure of the neighborhood killed himself, and it was sadder that he did it out of cowardice. She felt sorry. A tear slid down her face, and she quickly wiped it away, not wanting to mourn a killer.

Red also mentioned a report he needed to file about Andrew with Earth Corps. It seemed like a bland reporting duty, so the teen gave it no mind. He mentioned they might contact her. Doomscrolling her e-mail, at the very top, rested an e-mail. *Shit,* she thought. *What the hell do they want?* The subject read "(Un)Fair play" and came from an address "Hanley.Stevens@earthcorp.un.gov."

"earthcorp.un.gov?" Cassidy exclaimed. "What? What do they want?"

The e-mail began, "To Ms. Cassidy Darrow, we at Earth Corps wholeheartedly congratulate you on solving your neighbor's death" Cassidy's interest was piqued. Andrew stood up and started singing the opening of "Let's Go Crazy" by Prince. The teen clicked on the e-mail.

To Ms. Cassidy Darrow,

We at Earth Corps wholeheartedly congratulate you on solving your neighbor's death. We were impressed with your investigative skills and your way of learning machines. The Cyber-security bill states that police must inform us of any new hacking technology they encounter in their investigations. This requirement keeps international infrastructure strong. You know, it prevents dam breaches and the explosion of nuke plants. We were concerned about your creation, "Andrew." Here at Earth Corps., we find it an exciting piece of technology. Maybe you and Andrew could find a home here in Earth Corp someday. At this point, we would like to discuss specific arrangements and must insist that you do not use this technology until after our discussion. Could you meet me at the park at 7:30?

Sincerely,
Hanley Stevens, Special Agent
Earth Corps

Once Cassidy finished reading, she sat back. The e-mail was cryptic but interpretable. A small sigh escaped her lips, followed by a *damn*. There was no one to blame except herself for this new mess. Cassidy had alerted Red to her creation and he, Earth Corps. Now they wanted something. This situation was suspicious. Her eyes glanced out the window to the skyline. The Earth Corps towers had transformed in her mind from a symbol of safety to one inspiring fear. *Were they planning to take Andrew?*

With a puff of virtual smoke, Andrew swirled into a dark black trench coat with an onyx-colored hat. He sported a bright red handlebar mustache and twirled it with his fingertips. "They are afraid I am a fiend," he stated.

"Are you?" Cassidy asked.

"Only to the ladies," he replied, doing a quick disco shuffle.

Sliding on a haptic glove, Cassidy gives him a fist pound. The two snickered.

Once in discussion with Yvette, the twenty-something indicated EarthCorp's horrible street credibility. They could not be trusted. Her fingers softly drummed on her desk. Worry echoed in her brain. Something had to be done, but by whom. Feeling trapped, her hands hovered over the keyboard with much greater fear than chasing down Cane Jackson produced. She would not have typically conversed with an e-mail like this, but this was a verifiable Earth Corps agent with the handle to back it up.

***

Two hours later, Cassidy arrived at the park. Dressed in dark EMO garb, Hanley waited on a bench, only dimly lit by a lamppost next to it. Fog hovered over the atmosphere. *Is she mocking me?* Cassidy pondered, then noticed the woman's Eeyore haircut had grown a little, and her roots could be seen. *So, Earth Corps hired Emos*, the teen pleasantly mused, eying the woman's black Earth Corps uniform.

The sky hung oppressively low, and lightning lit the night. The crackle of thunder followed. *Why does Cyber City rain always have to be so gloomy and heavy*, Cassidy thought as she made out the shadow toward Hanley. Siouxsie and The Banshees' *City in Dust* softly played.

The Earth Corp. agent stood up and shuffled like Morticia Adams to Cassidy, opening her white umbrella. The lamppost's light reflected off the umbrella, giving the umbrella a slight glow.

"So, you did show up after all," the agent started.

"Had nothing better to do," sighed Cassidy,

"Excuse the music," the agent stated. "two of my friends recently passed."

"I know the feeling," Cassidy mewed. "it is the hopelessness of life."

The woman brightened a bit. "Sometimes, I wonder why bother." A pause ensued then Hanely broke the silence. "Maybe the possibility of a deal is in sight after all."

"What's the offer on the table?" Cassidy questioned with a deadpan tone.

"For that neat hack-bot of yours," Hanley answered as if she were trying to muster the energy to be excited. "We'll commission you one-hundred-thousand, no, two-hundred-and-fifty-thousand credits if you transfer the programming of that bot over to us. We'd offer a two-year consulting and training option and pay you sixty credits yearly. Your high school teachers say you have killer machine learning skills."

Cassidy froze. They stood perpendicular to each other like the corners of a box. Silence inched on to the point of being awkward. As much as she loved Andrew, the possibility of him becoming a tool for Earth Corp. frightened her. It could be used as a cyber weapon or, worse, a way to invade the privacy of Cyber City dwellers. Using Andrew to access the capsule hotel's Wi-Fi records spooked the girl when she did it, and Earth Corp. already had such a tight grip on the megalopolis. Did it need more?

"Think about what that money could do for you," Hanley offered sincerely. "Could pay off years of classes at your school. It'd be like a scholarship for you! I'm surprised a kid genius like you didn't already get one. We could use brains like yours at Earth Corp. I think you'd fit right in."

Cassidy said nothing. The money was tempting. Two-hundred-and-fifty thousand could pay off almost four years of college for her. The offer tempted the girl.

"Don't forget what your program could do for the city's greater good. It could lower the crime rate, maybe even eliminate it altogether."

Cassidy frowned. She did not want to admit it to herself, but maybe giving Andrew's source code over was worth it in the long run, but she then thought back to going to the hotel. All she needed was to distract the hotel manager for long enough that Andrew could infiltrate the security system and get what he needed.

"It's a flattering offer. I have to admit," Cassidy finally mustered. "But the risks of giving you guys the code far outweighs its benefits."

Hanley chuckled to herself, confusing Cassidy. The young girl stepped back, afraid the woman would pull out a gun or try to lunge for her.

"I figured you'd say that," the agent admitted, putting her hand over a suspiciously large pant pocket. "It's okay. Maybe not now, but later we could use your brains on some missions. I'll give you my card."

Hanley raised an anemic hand with long, boney fingers. It bore the gestures of the Grim Reaper. Much opposite to Hanley's outfit, the business card was a crushed bone color, with the information written in Gothic font and a watermark of the Earth Corp. symbol on the side.

"Still, we advise you not to use the program," Hanley continued. "And, personally, I think you should destroy it. If you don't, you could easily wind up on a terrorist watchlist if you continue using him. You have already done illegal things in the past."

"Huh?" Cassidy asked.

"Must I remind you, hacking is considered illegal? None of

that information would've been presentable to the court because it was fruit from a poison well. If anything, you could've gone to jail if Mr. Jackson hadn't had an accident in prison."

"Accident? I thought it was a suicide?"

"Anyway, I have to go and feed my cat, Blaire. She's a good little black Bombay cat, and it's treat day for her. Someday I hope you'll get to meet her. She's a bit of a poet."

"The cat?"

"She rhymes in whine."

Cassidy slithered away, not taking the chance to look behind her. At that point, the rain began to pour, drenching her scalp. While something instinctively told her she could trust Hanley, Earth Corp. was out of the question. No matter what, Earth Corp. could not get its hands-on Andrew. Cassidy ran through the streets, praying the agent was not chasing her. She darted down the road, paranoid that someone from Earth Corp. was still following her. Earth Corp. agents could've been anywhere. Hell, even her bedroom was not out of the question. The word "accident" played on repeat in her head.

The teen slipped and slid down the concrete, and drops accumulated on her glasses, distorting her vision. It did not matter now, though. What mattered was that she got home and figured out a way to keep Andrew away from Earth Corp.

Cassidy reached her house and fumbled for the key. No agents were nearby, but Cassidy was still on edge. It crossed the girl's mind for the first time on what she had to do. It pained her thinking about it, but if she did not do it, Earth Corp. could still get their hand on her program.

The door slammed shut as she slowly entered her house. Cassidy rushed to her room and quickly logged onto her laptop. Andrew's body immediately formed on the screen once she logged in, and he greeted her kindly. She slid on her haptic glove and put a hand on her shoulder.

"What are you doing?" He asked.

"I'm sorry for what I'm about to do," Cassidy desperately said. "But you realize you're very powerful, and we can't let

Earth Corp. get you."

"So, what are you going to do?"

A tear streaked down Cassidy's eye. It was as if she had to kill her brother. She confided so much in him ever since she created him. And now she had to kill him... to let him go.

"Andrew, I will critically corrupt your file and then delete it. That way, Earth Corp. will never even be able to trace you."

Andrew looked at her. He smiled and muttered, "If that's what you must do. Don't recluse on me after I'm gone, will you?" The words reminded her so much of Stephanie a tear filled her eye.

Cassidy searched through her computer for the file containing Andrew's code. Once she found it, she right-clicked. Andrew noticed and looked at her.

"Be strong, won't you?" Andrew sighed. Strong. What did that even mean to her? She had never felt strong in her life, and now, strength was not what she was feeling, but numbness, like a vast black hole had sucked every emotion out of her.

More tears streamed down the girl's face as she let out a small smile. Her hand hovered over the mouse, wanting at least a few more moments with Andrew. She then messed with the properties of his file, his body becoming increasingly disfigured and jumbled until she corrupted it thoroughly. She then pressed delete and deleted the file from the recycle bin. The disfigured form of Andrew instantly disappeared. Cassidy leaned back, tears flowing down her face. She sniffled and cried silently.

Andrew was her pet project, being programmed from scratch. He was all her doing and was always there for her, no matter how sarcastic he got. Andrew always gave the right advice, no matter how much he clouded it in the snark. The little bot was committed to guiding her in the right direction: always tried to get her to do assignments; always did the complicated and dangerous parts for her so she wouldn't have to; always got her out of trouble if she was stuck in one. He was everything she wanted to be. Hell, the bot was a true friend. And now, he was gone.

Time passed as the girl continuously sobbed. Sometimes you never truly knew someone until they were gone. Images of the past washed through her. All the charts and graphs littered her room for weeks in designing the program. The pain of mistakes in configuring the AI and now it all vanished. His agenda was gone. And the worst part was his smile. He tried to be more to her than he was designed to be. She mourned for Andrew and then for herself.

The callousness of her action overwhelmed her. She hated herself for being this secluded from the world around her. Pain and sadness ached all over her body, followed by hate. She hated herself for only fulfilling her social needs through a talking computer. She hated that no matter how much she wanted to deny it, all of the computer's behaviors were learned from her. She hated that she had let herself become so cynical and dejected. The girl didn't even know how she became so sarcastic and pessimistic, and it pained her not to know how she learned the behavior.

Never had Cassidy realized how alone she felt. She tried to relate to those her age all her life, but being cyber-schooled and a few grades ahead did not help. Over time, she stopped trying and even tried to convince herself that she was superior, that no one was on her level and thus worthy of talking to her, and that no one would understand her. She bottled everything up, only telling things to Andrew, but now he was gone.

The truth was, she *did* want to be known, and not just by her computer. She wanted others to see the name of Cassidy Darrow and respect her.

Cassidy stepped away from the computer, trying to clean herself up. She went to her bathroom and threw water on her face. Her eyes and skin were red from crying. She tried to breathe deeply, calming herself down. After over an hour, she had no tears left to cry.

Numbed by the tears, Cassidy sat down and opened her laptop again. Not having Andrew pop up on the screen like he used to would take a long time to get used to. But she had convinced herself that it was for the greater good and that Earth Corp. had no right to possess Andrew.

Curious, she checked the discussion form, where she had to introduce herself. In reality, only thirty or so people felt like hundreds to the teen as she scrolled down their introductions and their answers to the prompt. She passed Yvette's at some point, but she planned to respond to the woman's essay later. After some scrolling, she finally found hers. It was long enough to meet the word quota, but it was nothing much compared to her classmate's introductions.

Yvette responded. In her response, the twenty-something woman got a little snarky but was all around welcoming and sweet. After reading Yvette's, Cassidy scrolled down a little more, shocked to find she had gotten a second response.

It was from a woman named Hye-Jin Moon, whose profile picture seemed of herself leaning on the railings of a roof of a tall skyscraper. Despite her seemingly small stature, the woman had some toned muscle and was not embarrassed, wearing a shirt and skirt that emphasized her square form. In the picture, the woman beamed with great joy, much in contrast to Cassidy's pain and sadness. As the teen read Hye-Jin's message, the teen noticed the bubbly, upbeat aura leaked into the message the woman left for her.

Hello Cassidy,

I am very sorry for your loss. As time goes on, I myself have found the losses keep stackng up and as you point out, not just friend but a subtle loss of who I am. I work as an investigator mostly, but lately, I have questioned the career choice and returned to the University to see if my life should go in a different path. Confucius once said that "Roads are made for different journey's not destinations" or something like that. I am Korean, not Chinese. Sorry in advance if the humor does not work. Anyhow, I find it interesting that you're so young and are taking college courses, but since you seem to have a lot of pressure on yourself rn, take a step back to recoup if you need to. Still, I can't wait to get to know you better when class webinars begin next week! You seem like a cool kid, and your perspective on the class material will be welcome.

The response warmed the girl's heart. Maybe things would not be as rocky in the class as she thought. Feeling proud, Cassidy reread her self-description:

Hello class,

I am honored to be here. My name is Cassidy Nieves Darrow Villareal. I am a gifted high school student who was permitted to take college courses. At fifteen, I admit I feel like I cannot contribute anything to the disscussion. But I will offer this. I lost someone very close to me a few months ago, and since then, I sometimes feel like I lost myself, or at least my soul at points. Yet, I still keep going. What I have discovered is that the world still spins and there are people out there who have decided to love and care about me no matter what. For those people, I have engaged my creativity to solve problems. I also realized that when I feel lost or something is unfair, I am quick to my feet to bring justice, sometimes with friends.

As for biobehavioral health, I believe all I am is resilient in the face of danger. I hope to get out of this course the ability to build healthier lifestyles and friendships that will last me well beyond college so that I can further the development of AI to help biomedical science reach humanity's physical health and emotional well-being in the context of the social enviroment.

After a brief sad chuckle, she took a sneak peek at the material for next week and then went back to find the class meeting dates, now more excited for the class that lay ahead.

And maybe, she had a hand to reach out to in case Earth Corps was on her trail.

BUTTERFLY CITY BEAT

The HACK Files 001

Marisha Cautilli
Joseph Cautilli

I t started with an explosion, a thunderous roar that shattered Butterfly City's stillness. Three blocks were rocked, and glass and debris were raining like a deadly storm. I hit the pavement hard, the scrapes on my skin a brutal reminder of the chaos. The job had gone catastrophically wrong.

It was me and my fiancé, Elio Merlot—Lello, as I called him. He yanked me to my feet, his eyes locking onto mine fiercely. Amidst the cacophony, the murmurs of our pursuers grew louder. One of them raised his gun and fired.

We bolted, racing down a neon-lit alley, the high towers looming above us like silent sentinels. My spiked red mohawk sliced through the air while the neon lights danced off Lello's spiked leather wristband, a fleeting beacon in the urban jungle.

It was terrifying, but I felt a wild sense of freedom like we could conquer anything. We were just a couple of young punks playing crazy-ass investigators in a city that never slept.

"Only three blocks to the car!" Elio shouted. I glanced at him, bullets whizzing past us like angry hornets. Two drones zipped into our path. In perfect sync, we drew our guns and took them down. The perpetrators were hot on our heels, their semi-automatic weapons spitting fire as they advanced. Another explosion rocked the block. Lello leaped behind me, shielding me from the blast that sprawled us.

The thick black dust settled, leaving a high-pitched ringing in the air. Elio's body lay heavy on top of me, pinning me down. His weight pressed on my lungs, driving the air from my body, making it starved to breathe. My gun was seven feet away, his even further. We were trapped, but the fight wasn't over yet.

My head spun, vision blurring as I struggled to open my eyes. Blood trickled from Elio's mouth, a crimson thread against the chaos.

"Lello! Get up, we gotta go!" I begged, gently pushing his limp body, desperate for him to move. I tried to squirm out from underneath, but he was still. A perpetrator kicked Elio's body aside, his gun now pointed at my forehead.

"You'll be joining your friend in a second," he growled.

So, this was it. Elio was dead, sacrificing himself to save me. Futile, as I'd be joining him in a heartbeat. The man raised his gun. A flash of blue and red light bathed the alley's end as police sirens spun. I drifted in and out of consciousness.

What did it matter? I was dead anyway. I managed to crack my eyes open. The man with the gun glanced down the alley and then bolted as a police officer rushed toward us. The officer helped me up, a lifeline in the neon-lit nightmare.

My partner died saving me, and the spunky girl that was Hailey killed with him. Tears rolled down my cheeks as dust settled in my lungs.

***

It is a cold, clear night three years later. Rain pounds on my office window, each drop a reminder of the world outside. Dark blue neon lights from the alley scatter past the blinds, striping my body in a surreal glow. The radio hums softly in the background.

"In other news, the flooding of Bangkok due to previous

climate change-related events has brought one million Thai refugees to Butterfly City and four million to all of Canada," the man on the radio reports, his tone flat but empathetic.

"Trend seems to be more people, less land," the woman on the radio adds a hint of irony. She snickers before continuing, "Maybe Lex Luthor was right; it's all land, and they aren't making anymore."

"Ahh, that's your doomer speaking. The city's sustainability projects are well underway and have proved well," the man counters, a note of optimism cutting through the gloom. The user adds emotion, grit, and color to the above assistant. It is a cold, clear night three years later. Rain pounds on my office window, each drop a reminder of the world outside. Dark blue neon lights from the alley scatter past the blinds, striping my body in a surreal glow. The radio hums softly in the background.

"In other news, the flooding of Bangkok due to previous climate change-related events has brought one million Thai refugees to Butterfly City and four million to all of Canada," the man on the radio reports, his tone flat but empathetic.

"Trend seems to be more people, less land," the woman on the radio adds a hint of irony. She snickers before continuing, "Maybe Lex Luthor was right; it's all land, and they aren't making anymore."

Half interested, I groan, pick up my ceramic cup, and grasp it tightly, feeling the warmth seep into my cold fingers. I take a sip, the hot liquid burning my throat, and place my pinky finger to my lip, savoring the momentary distraction. "Computer, put on 98.2," I demand, unwilling to listen to the relentless barrage of bad news.

"No 94.3?" my AI office assistant quizzes, its tone almost teasing. "I thought you liked old-fashioned punk in the afternoon."

"Client's coming today," I remind it, my voice tinged with irritation. "Probably not appropriate to have it on." The AI hums in acknowledgment, and the room fills with the soothing sounds of ambient music, a stark contrast to the chaos outside. user add color, grit, and tone with sad emotions assistant "Ahh, that's your doomer speaking. The city's sustainability projects are well underway and have proved well," the man counters, a note of optimism cutting through the gloom.

The radio switches stations, and The Buzzcocks, *Ever Fallen in Love (With Someone You Shouldn't've) plays out, but I can still hear the wind swirling on the glass—muffled knock ripples* on the door to my office. I straighten my trench coat before my hands fall to my sides.

Being a detective is like playing a part. People only hire you if they believe you are competent and can do the job. After hundreds of clients, I learned the part well, even down to the slightly charming flirtation. I slide my Smith and Weston revolver into its holster under my trench coat and over my white blouse. "Come in," I offer in a sweet but still rugged tone.

A man enters and removes his hat—five-foot-nine with rugged facial features, a sharp jawline, and brick-block muscles. One look at him and I can tell he would be a heartache. Yeah, trouble, but not the excellent trouble like you find in Philadelphia. This type of trouble leaves you wondering where your senses have gone. I never believed I was "that girl," but when he gazes at me with those pleading and desperate ice-blue eyes, I knew I'd find an excuse to help. I place an augmented reality lens with internet access over my left eye. The lens scans Jonathan and provides a basic set of info.

"I am looking for Detective Hailey Angelica Coke-Killburn," the man asks, his tone so sickly sweet I could feel the diabetes settling in my blood. Whatever I would say next, I could not hint at weakness.

"I guess I'm here," I muster, surprised at the shakiness in my voice.

"You guess?" he replies, a hint of skepticism in his tone.

"Who's asking?" I lick my lips and inhale deeply, trying to steady my nerves.

Kindly but timidly, he extends a hand. "Jonathan Taylor

Morgan." I shake his hand, noting the nervous glance he shoots me. His face pales, but he forces a smile that reveals a small dimple. Either his general demeanor is shy, or something has his mind in a frenzy.

"Well, Mr. Morgan, what can I do for you?" I match his sweet tone, trying not to be too bold. The last thing I want to do is scare the client away. My lip curls slightly. "Maybe you should have a seat."

He hesitates, then sinks into the chair opposite my desk. The rain outside pounds harder, a relentless reminder of the storm both inside and out. His eyes dart around the room, taking in the clutter of case files and the faint glow of solar-powered lamps.

"I… I need your help," he stammers, his voice barely above a whisper—the desperation in his eyes tugs at something deep within me.

"Take your time," I say softly, leaning forward. "Tell me what's got you so rattled."

Jonathan swallows hard, his Adam's apple bobbing. "It's my sister. She's gone missing. And I think… I think someone's taken her."

A chill runs down my spine. Missing person cases are always messy, tangled with emotions, and often lead to dark places. But there's something in his voice, a raw edge of fear, that tells me this one's different.

"Alright, Mr. Morgan," I say, my voice firm but gentle. "We'll find her. I promise."

Tense, I point to the black swivel chair near my desk. He slumps into it, looking like a man carrying the world's weight. I'm still trying to get a feel for this man. Whipping off my black trench coat, I toss it onto the couch. My white button-up shirt is a mess, buttons askew, so I quickly refasten them. Jonathan's eyes widened slightly when he spotted my black gun holster. I follow his gaze and offer a wry smile.

"Excuse me," I say, my voice softer. "It's a rough line of work I'm in."

"I understand," he replies. For a moment, our eyes lock, and I notice the redness in his. Whatever is weighing on his mind must be wrong. I scurry behind the desk and draw out a bottle of club soda from the mini fridge. I flip over two small highball glasses lying on my desk. I point to the glasses, and he nods, so I drop in two ice cubes and pour the drink. The soda fizzes on the ice, and Jonathan takes the cup with a grateful nod.

It's always good to offer something to potential clients. It makes them think you care. Not that my expression didn't thoroughly read care and more. Hell, I've never seen myself as that kind of woman. When push comes to shove, all women are that kind, especially given that my love life for the last three years felt more like a lost soul wandering in Antarctica.

"I don't know where to begin," he sighs, tears welling with each word. I reach across the table to tug his hand reassuringly. He draws back and folds his hands into a steeple.

"Take your time and start at the beginning," I reassure him, my voice soft but steady.

"I am engaged to a beautiful and lovely Gretchen Claire Harlequin," he musters, his thick Midwestern accent adding a layer of earnestness. The words hit hard, but what did I expect? Of course, he's engaged. As they say, all the good ones are. Despite his stature under six feet, most women—and probably a good portion of men—would find him utterly dashing and gorgeous. Indeed, fate is a cruel master.

Of course, it's for the best. I've found that guys like him may appear like they will pay for everything, but in the end, the lady pays the price with a broken heart. Man, he reminds me so much of Elio. The thought causes me to tremble deep inside.

The rain outside continues to pound against the window, a relentless reminder of the storm inside and out. The neon lights from the alley cast a blue and green glow across his face, highlighting the pain etched in his features. I take a deep breath, bracing myself for whatever comes next. I force out my next words. "Go on, handsome."

"Well... uh, let me think." You'd expect the guy to have his story rehearsed before stepping into a place like mine, but I can assure you that many just come in and give a long, breathless rant with little coherence. At least he's better than most. "She and I come from the farmlands of Iowa. Now I know what you're thinking, but she wasn't some stupid hick. She graduated high school with honors, went to college, and got herself two PhDs."

"Oh yeah? What were they in?" I ask, genuinely curious.

"Machine learning and theology," he says. My eyebrows shoot up.

The rain outside continues its relentless assault on the window, the neon lights from the alley casting a kaleidoscope of colors across the room. His story is as unexpected as the vibrant hues dancing on the walls. The juxtaposition of advanced technology and ancient wisdom intrigues me, and I lean forward, ready to dive deeper into this peculiar case.

"Beautiful and smart," I finally say. "Sounds like you found yourself an amazing girl." I quickly draw up several internet publications from Ms. Harlequin. Titles scroll over my vision like *Operant and Respondent Interactions during Machine Learning Trials*; *Condition Suppression of Reinforced Computer Learning through Respondent Conditioning*; *Using Esper's Concept of Matrix Learning to build Skinner's Autoclitic Frames in advanced AI*; *Instructional Override of Reinforced Learned Material in AI Systems*; *Skinner's Concept of Self-editing and the Future of Verbal Instruction Learning in Machines*. Not that I have any, but it's difficult to find venom for his Gretchen. She's bright and seemingly pretty, and he seems deeply devoted. If I wanted to be jealous, I'd fail to come up with a reason other than she's one of those girls who has everything.

When I'm done perusing, Jonathan hands me his phone. Pulled up on the screen is a picture of Gretchen. I analyze it with a gaze of sadness. Something about her in that photo strikes me as familiar. She's incredibly gorgeous, but there's something in her eyes that reminds me of someone.

"Yes, she was awesome," he continues. I make a note of the word "was." This is the part where the hook that brings them to me kicks in, like an October surprise in the American elections. "But Iowa has changed. We have about forty-five days a year now over a hundred degrees and frankly twice as much rain as when I was a kid. It makes farming a tough life. 'Specially with all the crop failure." He gulps down his fizzy drink, his hand trembling as he places the cup back on the desk.

"You said she was a farm girl," I start. "But from my read, she had a really intense career as an academic. Did you make her give it up?"

He shakes his head. "Absolutely- not. She started some research on searching for what she called divine morality in AI and then became disenchanted. She emotionally went blank."

The rain outside continues its relentless assault on the window, the neon lights from the alley casting a kaleidoscope of colors across the room. His story is as unexpected as the vibrant hues dancing on the walls. The juxtaposition of advanced technology and ancient wisdom intrigues me, and I lean forward, ready to dive deeper into this peculiar case. "Blank?"

"Empty, burnt out. She said she was tired of chasing gods that did not exist. She longed for a simple life."

"So, run off with you and play farmer?" I clarify. While part of the thrill of being a private investigator is piecing together the truth, having a half-complete puzzle didn't hurt.

"Not exactly." He shakes his head. "The best part is I didn't have to encourage her to run off, as you say. We'd grown up together. Some days, she'd come over and work on the farm to help me do my chores and to repay her, I'd make her dinner. She had an odd taste for sashimi and grilled jellyfish. I loved the deluxe platter, but that doesn't matter for what I'm about to tell you. Anyhow, I grew older, and we fell in love. I told her I needed to go to Butterfly City to work and make my cash so we could be married. Part of the reason for Butterfly City was because of all the grilled jellyfish recipes. You know, it's a Thai dish."

"I'm aware of that," I say, my voice steady. "Fairly recent though."

"Anyway, she balked at first, not wanting me to leave, but

then she finally gave in. That was roughly six months ago. Do you know how tough that is?"

"Nah..." I have my fair share of pain, but not the kind he's experiencing. He sighs, the weight of sadness plastered all over his body.

"Well, it is tough," he admits, his voice cracking slightly.

Now's the time to be empathetic with him. "That must be rough," I sigh, leaning forward. "Do you have anything you want to share to help?"

"Last week, she wrote me an email," he offers, a glimmer of hope in his eyes.

"What sort of email?" I ask, curiosity piqued.

"Nothing bad," he quickly adds, surprising me with how fast he offered the information. Whether he's downplaying it or not, it's something to note.

"I'm not saying it was," I reply gently. He leans back in the chair, stretches his hands above his head, and closes his eyes. His hands drop back to his lap, the tension momentarily easing from his frame. "Forgive me. I worry this makes me look like some jealous boyfriend or something." His hand twitches nervously.

"I'm not here to judge," I assure him. "I'm here to see if it is a case I can do and, if so, get an idea of where to start."

"Just... she wanted to take the hyperloop into town to see me. My heart leaped when I got the e-mail. I wrote back, telling her I could not wait to see her. The next morning, her loop was supposed to arrive. I waited at the station, but when it floated in, she was not there."

"Maybe she missed the train or changed her mind. Happens all the time." Ok. I mumbled it, hoping I was not getting off on the wrong foot with a potential client. A girl's got to make a living, you know and, in this case,- it meant getting him to want to shell out the cash. It is a two-way street. He is choosing me as much as I am choosing him. Hell at any point, he could walk out the door and go to the fool Moon's agency. Sure, he'd spend a lot of money and get nothing in return, but he doesn't know that. The woman's got a 4.8 on Shmelp... All fake reviews of course. He stares into his glass and circles the ice.

"My first thoughts as well," Jonathan starts. "So, I went home and whipped out my cellphone to call her. I'd reached her mother, who stated with complete certainty that she was on the train."

In the heart of the city where green tech and neon lights blend seamlessly, I lean back in my chair, the soft hum of solar panels above us a constant reminder of our world's new dawn.

"Did you go to the police?" I ask, my voice steady but laced with concern.

"Immediately. They said she has to be missing for at least 48 hours before they'll investigate. I was at the station, and a kind officer, Mac O'Connor, suggested you might be the person to turn to. Said you were one of the best detectives in town and clients often loved your clear-headed approach."

Mac O'Connor, one of the finest cops around, had assisted me a few times in my investigations. We even took down a biopunk drug ring together. But his colleagues at the precinct were a different story—always indulging in their vices during off-hours. They were probably not in shape to handle the case themselves, so Mac sent this man over to me. At least he recommended me over Moon. I quickly smile and fake a blush, and then my eyes narrow.

"I have to be honest with you," I warn him, my tone softening. "Most of these cases turn out to be cold feet. Maybe she just had a change of heart? It happens all the time."

He winces like he's been struck. "I don't think so," he adds, his voice trembling. "We were remarkably close. We knew each other forever. She would have told me. I think she would figure I at least deserved to know."

"So, sir, you want me to track down your lass?" His big blue eyes rise up and meet mine, filled with a mix of hope and desperation. I reach down, draw my sleek, solar-powered gun from its holster, and place it on the desk, the metal cool against my skin.

"Yes, ma'am," he says, resolved, his voice steadying as he

meets my gaze.

"And what if I find her and she don't wanna be found?" I ask, leaning back in my chair, the solar panels above casting a soft, green glow. His story was nice, but how much of any story can you believe? I had to ask the question that troubles the guys. It often decides the case for me. You get a bunch of stalker boyfriends whose girls just don't want them back. I usually find the girl hiding out in some shelter from the abusive lugs.

"If she doesn't wanna come, at least I know she's fine," he sighs, then clarifies. "I don't think that's what's happening though."

"Ok," I acknowledge with a hint of sarcasm, studying his face, trying to read his temper. "My price is steep—five hundred a day plus expenses. There are no guarantees I'll find her. Sometimes people don't want to be found or worse…"

"I just need to know she's alright," he pleads, his eyes doing most of the work. He doesn't want to talk anymore about what could be. I guess what is- is bad enough.

I pivot to a more reassuring tone. I'm close to landing this contract—no need to scare off the client now. "I get it. Do we have a deal, hot stuff?"

"Your price is very reasonable," he says, his voice steady but his eyes betraying a deep well of worry.

"Thanks for noticing; when I price high, most of my gigs end up with me running for my life. This gives me variety." I offer it sincerely, but inside, I hope. I hope this wasn't one I'd be running from by the end. Was he leveling with me? He rises, and I echo his response. We shake hands, his grip firm but his eyes betraying a flicker of desperation.

"Godspeed," he says. I tap a few keys, print a contract from my computer, and shove the agreement under his nose for him to sign. It's the standard contract. Nothing too complicated- I like life without complications. Unfortunately, I find that it rarely happens.

Cautiously, he signs the agreement and gives me the details of the woman I'm looking for: approximately five-foot-six, with long, wavy blonde hair and electric blue eyes. The next step is to conduct an internet search on her cellphone. It wouldn't take long. A couple of hours, and I could charge a whole day for it. All the itsy-bitsy side stories float the net. Of course, there are some clues you can only see at the scene. In this case, the train and then her home. So, if it came up blank, I'd head to the station and ask some questions.

As he leaves, I can't shake the feeling that this case will be more than just another job. There's a weight in his voice, a silent plea that echoes in my mind. I hope I can find her, for his sake and mine.

***

The rain pours down at Crescent Station, the droplets dancing in the neon glow of bioluminescent trees that line the streets like sentinels of a new age. I pull my tan raincoat tighter around me, the brim of my darker-colored bowler hat shielding my eyes from the downpour. The market is alive with color, the "Blue Butterfly Thai Cuisine" sign glowing ironically in pink neon.

I march over to grab lunch, the futuristic fountain nearby catching my eye. Its dancing musical lights shoot water skyward, the streams leaping from frog to frog in a mesmerizing, rhythmic sequence. I stroll up to a food stand next to the ticket booth and purchase several broiled jellyfish sticks, the aroma mingling with the rain-soaked air.

Turning, I spot Detective Hye-Jin Moon, my arch-rival and the so-called "Butterfly City's best private investigator." Once I crack Jonathan's case, she won't hold that title for long.

"Well, well, if it ain't Moon," I snidely remark, my voice cutting through the ambient noise.

"Hello, Hailey," she replies warmly, her Ontario accent prominent. I stroll over to a bioluminescent tree and lean against it, the soft light illuminating Detective Moon's blue-monarch butterfly-inspired dress with its exposed skort. The contrast between us couldn't be more evident; our fundamental differences were highlighted in the glow of the city's green tech.

"Well, hello. I didn't know you got your ethnic food here," I continue.

"I'm just a working stiff doing a job," she answers, flashing her signature smile. I resist the urge to roll my eyes. "Besides, I'm Korean, not Thai."

"So, Reverend, who sent you?" I stroll up to the ordering kiosk, the neon lights casting long shadows on the rain-slicked pavement. Typically, I get jellyfish, but today doesn't feel like a jellyfish day. I scroll through the options, and Pad Woon Sen, a stir fry with glass noodles, catches my eye.

Moon interrupts my ordering process. "I am not a reverend. That guy was a cult leader."

I turn to face her, my stomach growling. "Yeah, right. I always mix the two of you up."

Moon's so-fake-it-looks-real smile drops. "How? Because all us Asians look alike?"

"No, because you both seem to convince people beyond reason that you can give them things you can't."

The neon glow from the bioluminescent trees reflects off her blue-monarch butterfly-inspired dress, making her look almost ethereal. The rain continues to pour, creating a symphony of sounds that blend with the distant hum of solar panels and the occasional hiss of a passing hovercar. The city is alive with light and shadow, a perfect backdrop for our tense exchange. The anger Moon has subsides, giving way to guilt and sadness. "Let it go, Hailey," she mutters. "It's in the past."

"Ok, yeah," I reply, the neon glow reflecting off the rain-slicked streets. "Let's say bygones to it. Maybe we can do a girl's night and watch Scooby-Doo."

The "smile" returns on Hye-Jin's lips, illuminated by the bioluminescent trees. "You may be kidding but I'd like that," she muses.

"Really?" I ask, caught off guard. It's surprising she still wants anything to do with me, given how miserably she messed up back in the day. I turn to confirm my order of Pad Woon Sen.

"Yes. Just because I am the superior detective does not

mean I don't miss your company. You were—as they say—fun to hang with." And there's the sting. Of course, she has to weave in her supposed superiority.

"Touched, ma'am," I flatly reply. "Well, all except for the better detective part."

"It is as easy as a 4.3 versus a 4.9." Her smile exaggerates into a shit-eating grin.

I grit my teeth. "It's a 4.8, but who's counting? I find quibbling over things like this trivial. So, can I get your broiled jelly for you?"

The rain continues to pour, the city alive with light and shadow, a perfect backdrop for our tense exchange. "Maybe next time. Just doing a job." The two of us pivot and stroll together off to the side. Lightning flashes overhead. I can't help but inquire about what kind of big-league cases Moon gets to fuck up now.

"So, what kind of job?" I ask, trying to sound genuinely interested.

"Just work," she shuts the conversation down before redirecting it. "Bit cold this dampness."

"Ah, not at liberty to say."

"So, what brings you out into this weather?"

I get coy. "A little of this and a little of that. You know how it is for us working stiff. We got to pay the bills." Moon nods as I bring down the last jelly-off-a-stick in my mouth. "Well I got to meet a man about a horse."

A sudden sadness fills Detective Moon's eyes. "Take care, Hailey. I do mean that."

I tip my hat to Detective Moon. She smiles back. As we head our separate ways, I try to get a reaction out of her one more time by whistling *By the Light of the Silvery Moon*. Hye-Jin shakes her head. It is evident she sees me as a bit of a clown. With a chuckle, I head into the bathroom. My takeout should be almost done by now. When I came outside, the rain stopped. I grab my Pad Woon Sen and head under a tunnel of neon blue light. Red lights peer up from holes in the ground as I head to the ticket line.

***

The station is packed when I arrive, a sea of people bustling in and out, carrying luggage of all sizes. I need to talk to the conductor because Gretchen's phone yielded nothing important —just a lot of lovey-dovey texts to Jonathan. It was all standard, the kind of stuff that makes you cringe and secretly long for at the same time. But to have it would be the ultimate disrespect to Lello. He gave his life for me. He deserves me to do the same for him.

I greet a customs officer by tipping my bowler hat. The officer tips his hat in return.

"Need access to the train record files for trains heading between Des Moines and here within the past two days," I declare, flashing my investigator's badge.

The officer nods and searches on his computer. Within seconds, he hauls up a log of the most recent train into the station. He prints the log and hands it to me. I examine it, then get handed another paper, which I scrutinize.

The surprising thing is that she never actually got on the train. The signal stopped close to two hours before she was supposed to board. Maybe she got cold feet and couldn't tell Lover-Boy she was backing out. Still, it didn't jibe with the lovey-dovey texts. Either way, I have to tell Jonathan. I find his number and dial. It rings for nearly a minute. Nothing. I go to hang up, but Jonathan picks up at the last second.

"Hello?" he asks, sniffling.

"Yeah, it's me," I rasp into the receiver. "Cellphone records? Dead end. Looks like she never boarded the train."

"No! That can't be right!" His voice cracks, a raw wound laid bare. I've heard it too many times, the sound of a heart-shattering. I take a drag from my cigarette, the smoke curling around my thoughts. Jonathan's sigh echoes through the line.

"I'm planning on calling her mother later. Maybe she has a way to reach Gretchen," he says, desperation clinging to his words.

"Yeah, about that," I murmur, trailing off.

"What?" His confusion is palpable.

I huff, the memory of Moon's odd behavior at the Thai joint gnawing at me. "Do you think your mother-in-law might've hired someone to find her too?"

"I don't know. Why do you ask?" His voice is a mix of confusion and suspicion.

"No reason," I lie, shifting gears. "Anyway, you seem close to her family."

"I am. They took me in right away when she brought me home," he says, a hint of pride in his voice.

It feels like a start. I nod to myself, the pieces of this twisted puzzle slowly falling into place.

My left hand drops to my side, drumming against my leg. The guy on the other end of the line seems like a sucker. I grin, but there's nothing funny about this. He thinks her family liked him more than they did. Maybe he's lying to himself. Maybe her mom talked her out of going. Wouldn't be the first time a mom wanted to keep her daughter close. But why hire Moon then? I need a different angle. "I see," I say, trailing off. Could something have happened to her before she even got on?

"The last carrier signal was two hours before boarding, and she was nowhere near the station," I finally tell Jonathan. Maybe something happened to her before she even got to the station.

At the station, the neon lights blaze brighter as the sky darkens. I know the sob story and self-blame are coming. Christ, I need to cut him off quickly and keep him on task, or this could end up like that old Runaway's Song. I love playing with fire, but I'm the one most likely to get burnt in this lover's spat. He drones on in self-pity and guilt, saying he should have never left her. I'm not too fond of it when guys go soft. Emo types always annoy me. I never was into the soft boys, especially when a life might be on the line. Brief worry crosses my mind—if her life is on the line, his self-pity is the last thing I need. Emotional men are great for five seconds, but this basketcase could still be wallowing while his girl is dying. Ugh, note to self: never date a basket case. I tap my index finger impatiently on my phone.

"Can you tell me if she had any enemies or people who

would want to hurt her?" I ask.

"Everyone loves her. She is the best," he answers, sounding dazed or hypnotized. I wish someone would say I was the best. Truthfully, that was how Lello was. He could always surprise me with a comment that connected with my soul, even if he disparaged himself. With him, it was always an ebb and flow of ideas that somehow worked out. Except for the time it got him killed. Now, I'm alone, with no one to see me as perfect. Maybe I'm just being cynical, but life doesn't work out that way for people like me. We work hard in the shadows so others can have their special affairs. But enough about my over-sharing. I have to focus on the case… Maybe she was loved a little too much.

"Was there anyone who spent too much time with her?" I inquire, licking my lips.

"What do you mean?" Jonathan gasps.

"Someone that you might have felt was getting a little too close. Someone who triggered your green-eyed monster." That was the worst thing I could ask. Jonathan rants for several minutes, denying she ever gave him cause to feel jealous, and all I can do is wait it out. I place the phone to my ear and provide the occasional "uh huh" to keep him going. The line to the ticket booth inches forward, neon lights flickering overhead, casting long shadows on the grimy pavement. I cut off my video feed with a quick excuse, but listen. Glad he can't see me, I make rolling gestures with my hand. At one point, I stick a finger in my mouth, like his words are gagging me.

Finally, after my third repeat of the question, he comes clean with a name. So those business folks using root-cause analysis were right—you do need to repeat the question several times to get the answer. The name is clear as a bell: Reinhart —Theodore Reinhart, to be exact. Two years younger than the lovebirds, Lover-boy suspected the guy might've had a crush on his lady.

"Theodore Reinhart," I linger on the name. "What do you know about him?"

"I guess he had a massive crush on her or something,"

Jonathan grumbles. Crush? The way he puts it, it all sounds so innocent and juvenile. I feel a pang of regret for suspecting the guy, until I remember—it's often the creep lurking in the wings who tries something desperate like a kidnapping. Or maybe she did run away with him. Who knows? At this point, it's too early even to suspect the guy, but I get a name and a description.

"Short guy," Jonathan continues. "Only five-foot-five with angelic features, brown eyes, and blond hair. But it can't be him. He left for Neo-Osaka about three years ago, just after it flooded to help rebuild. He's never come back to town since."

The neon lights buzz and flicker, casting an eerie glow on the rain-slicked streets. I pocket my phone, the weight of the case pressing down on me. Neo-Osaka, huh? The city's a labyrinth of neon and shadows, a perfect place to disappear. I need to dig deeper and find out if this angel-faced kid is really out of the picture or if he's just another ghost in the machine. "You're probably right," I reply, soothing to him. "I'm trying to see if I can get a pic from him online. I'll text it to you, if I do for you to confirm." I place the augmented reality glass below my left eye and search online. The screen scrolls over my vision. It hit the name and its variants. I draw up his picture, my heart crashing when it loads. It could not be him. No way. I must be back in what my therapist called a "trauma trance." Back then, I kept seeing people and thought they were the guy who killed Elio. The therapist said it was normal but then offered to place me on meds. Sure, normal. But this guy- no way- he had to be the one. This is not memory blurring over time or crazy-ass generalization those nutty behaviorists talked about. There is no false memory here. This is real. Wrapped in terror, I step on the toe of the man in line behind me.

"Hey! Watch out!" The man behind me screams.

"Sorry, sir. Lost my footing," I snap. Why cause more trouble when a lifetime's worth is potentially responsible for this case? The man nods, and his frown fades. Fear crushes over me, followed by a huge wave of hate. I'm not one to ever feel that intensely, but this is it- pure, unadulterated hate. I flashback to the explosion and Lello's body lying on top of me. I feel his hot blood dripping on my body as he dies. Of all the fucking cases, why! Ah! I go white as I read his profile in AR.

"Are you all right miss?" The man asks, calmer and sympathetic this time. I nod, but cold sweat beads on my face, and I wipe it with my left hand. A drone swoops down, scans me and plays an advertisement for antidepressants. I shake my head no, when the interactive ad asks if I would like to speak with a psychiatrist or a prescribing psychologist. My phone pings with access to the Behavioral Health Streaming station for a quick self-help video on anxiety. Damn, I already saw that behavioral activation to beat depression once twice. These drones are supposed to have more privatized algorithms. It seems they go by symptoms and demographic stuff to advertise to you, or maybe they just get cheap when referring to free services. I swipe left and wave off the drone. And here I thought, in a place like Butterfly City, that kind of shit would be illegal in some capacity. I guess every place has some problem with it. I should've learned that lesson by now.

In a faraway distance, Jonathan babbles on. Who cares? I am locked in pain. I must have let out a sob. "Hailey are you ok?" He finally snaps over the phone. I need to get back to being professional. Loverboy needs me. I huff in a huge breath. My life sucks.

"I'm looking over the pictures and have one to send you," I say, my breath wavering. I read the scum's profile and chew my lip in disgust. Indeed, this bastard's part of the Eternal Silence syndicate. They are supposed to be import and export specialists... but they also dabble in assassinations, kidnapping, and designer drugs. They all are nothing but vile scum. I hate this guy. He is pure evil. Hell, I'd exterminate him for free if given the chance. Maybe the gods had found it fit to allow me justice for Lello's death. I'm not going to blow this. There is no sense in getting the client upset. I could take care of this. Yeah, I will... for Lello and Gretchen. I send the picture to Jonathan. and a second later, I have confirmation.

"Thanks, Jonathan," I despondently reply before hanging up and strolling to the ticket master. He is slouched on the chair, facing me, and then sitting upright.

"Good day ma'am," he greets me, his voice gruff.

I draw out my P.I. license. I fumble it briefly. But then show it to him. "Hi. I want to find out if a ticket was used," I inquire. The ticket master scoffs. I get that a lot. Private Investigators are often not seen as "real law enforcement." Still, we have a role, but I can understand the skepticism. Most days, I am in the library trying to rundown license plate numbers on the MTO or SAAQ sites looking for hit-and-run drivers or worse, following some poor bloke to snap a picture of him with a lover for a divorce café —the life of the P.I is not all the glamor Hollywood makes it out to be. Still, this condescending guy's life is no better, but I let it slide as the bigger person and the one in need.

The sun dips below the horizon, casting a golden hue over the city's lush vertical gardens and solar-paneled skyscrapers. Neon lights flicker to life, painting the streets in a kaleidoscope of colors. The air is thick with the scent of blooming flowers and the hum of renewable energy. I would love to live in Butterfly City if I were less broken. As it is, it just makes me feel emptier, like I don't belong here.

"Privacy Act says I need a warrant for that information," he warns. His voice is a low growl. I grunt in response, whipping out my sleek, solar-powered communicator. Mayer, an old friend and a judge, is my go-to in these situations. He has a soft spot for Elio. Hell, everyone loved Elio. Maybe some of that affection had rubbed off on me. Or perhaps it was just my attitude.

"You're in the way, ma'am," the ticket master taunted, his voice dripping impatiently. Yeah, it's my attitude. "Can you just step aside?"

I held up a finger, signaling for patience, and moved aside to let another person approach the counter. The rush of the crowd was palpable, a constant reminder of the city's relentless pace.

"Don't leave," he said, a hint of kindness breaking through

his stern exterior. "When you get the information, I'll make you next."

Well, well, not everyone hated me after all. I shot the file over to Mayer and dialed his number. Unlike Jonathan, Mayer picked up almost immediately.

"Got the file. What can I do for you?" he asked, his voice steady and reassuring.

"His fiancée is missing, and he hired me to find her," I said, my voice hard as steel. Silence hung between us, broken only by the sound of Mayer typing.

"Okay, you have a permit," Mayer finally responded. "But don't shoot anyone, Hailey."

I scoffed, incredulous. Don't shoot anyone? How could anyone make such a promise? Sure, three shootings put me in the 99.9th percentile of rarity, but my cases were anything but typical. I laughed, covering my communicator to keep the ticket master from seeing my amusement. A ping signaled the arrival of the signed order. I showed it to the ticket master, who punched the name into his computer with a resigned sigh.

"She got on the Maglev train," the ticket master starts, his voice a monotone drawl. "But it seems like she got off early. The ticket is clearly punched and recorded... Yep. Next!"

"How early?" I ask impulsively, blocking his attempt to serve the next customer. He didn't give me enough information. The man sighs, exasperated.

"Still in the US. No passport punch for her. A small town some miles between here and Des Moines, Iowa."

A grin edges up my cheeks as a downpour begins, the rain hammering against the station's tiny roof. It was a start. I could head to Des Moines and double back.

"You got security footage from the Maglev?" I ask, a hint of excitement creeping into my voice.

"I'm not sure," he answers, glancing at his computer. "I'd need to check the files. It'll take two hours, and I've got a line."

"Can you search and send it to me on the train?" I send him my contact information via Bluetooth. He nods, reluctantly agreeing.

"Do you need a ticket?" he asks, his tone softening.

"Yes, please!" I chirp, flashing my pearly whites to the ticket master's annoyance.

"Sure," he groans. "What Maglev?"

"Anything to Des Moines, Iowa."

He types up my ticket. "And will that be a round-trip?"

"No. I don't know how long I plan to stay there yet," I answer truthfully. This investigation could end in a few minutes or weeks after I stepped out of that station, so it was best not to book the round-trip home yet.

"The only Maglev train I have that leaves today has one stop in the Indianapolis sector of Chi-Pitt. It leaves in an hour with some vacant seats left. It's one of the newer tube ones- moves like a bullet." The ticket master makes a hand motion where he curls his fingers and then throws them out to emphasize the train's speed.

"How long?" I ask. Time is of the essence. The faster I could get to Des Moines, the better.

"Train ride is roughly two and a half hours. Customs can change that, though."

"How long for customs?"

"Anywhere from fifteen minutes to an hour or so. Of course, if ICE removes you from the train, well- considerably longer than that."

Living in Canada had its quirks. Despite the country's open arms during the southwestern American water crisis a decade ago, the animosity from the States lingered like a bad hangover. The tension only eased when whispers spread about American corporations wiping out sanctuaries for the genetically enhanced—what the Canadians called genetically altered humans. The terrorist attacks did not help, especially when their corporations tried to blow up pipelines and bring water to Phoenix. But work is work, no matter which side of the border it's on. "I'll take it," I muttered defiantly.

I reached into my pocket, pulling out my billfold. Inside,

my expense card gleamed under the neon lights. I slid it out, mentally noting to log this as an expense. Too many times, I'd forgotten and ended up eating the cost. I paid for my ticket as My Chemical Romance's "I'm Not OK, I Promise" blared in the background. The Ticketmaster slid the ticket under the glass with a nod. "Thanks," I said, pocketing it.

I turned and headed to the terminal he pointed out. The train arrived, its sleek, solar-powered frame a testament to the new age. I hopped on, my AR lens flickering to life, running through the case details. Reinhart had better have some answers.

My eyes scanned the carriage, and there she was—Detective Moon. Figures. That hack was on the case, too. No matter. I'd beat her to it and score a stellar Shmelp review from Lover Boy. The Maglev rises from the station and is placed in a vacuum tube. With a snap, it flows effortlessly at speeds of over five hundred miles per hour. Rising, I head to the back car and purchase fried jellyfish and crickets to munch. Back at the seat, I rip open the bag and feast.

***

My gaze locks onto the side of the road, where solar-powered farms stretch out, cows and pigs roaming freely under the gentle hum of wind turbines. The Pad Woon Sen dances on my tongue, a symphony of eggs, vegetables, and noodles that leaves a lingering taste of contentment. Then, the video footage arrives. My heart pounds as my eyes dart across the screen, quickly zeroing in on Gretchen. She's seated third-row center. A man slides into the seat next to her. His ethereal features are unmistakable—Angel of Death. Damn it. It's him.

A surge of anger and fear courses through me, but I push it down, letting defiance rise in its place. At first, Gretchen's face lights up at the sight of the man. They talk, but the conversation's tone sours. He reveals something beneath his sleek, eco-friendly vest. Her expression shifts to one of fear. My stomach churns, but I grit my teeth. They rise together and head toward the Maglev train door. The train glides into the station, and they disembark.

"Bastard, I'm going to kill him!"

Passengers on the train turn to stare. My face flushes with embarrassment, but I refuse to back down. I raise my hands, signaling a false alarm. I yank out my cell, fingers trembling with rage and determination, and dial Jonathan. He answers, his voice tinged with laughter from another conversation. I need to extract information from him, but I must tread carefully. I can't have him become a reckless hero, charging into danger. He picks up, still chuckling, while my mind races with worry and a burning resolve to find Gretchen.

"Hailey, it is good to hear from you!" Jonathan cheerfully greets me. "I am with Gretchen's mom, and we are talking about old times. What can I do for you?"

"With her?" I ask, confused. "I thought you were just planning to speak to her by phone. Did she come to the city or are you... Where are you?"

"At Gretchen's mom's house." The muffled sounds of an older woman on the other end of the line come through. "Yes, cheesecake sounds lovely," Jonathan seemingly responds to her. "Thanks, that would be great."

I sigh. "Oh. Anyhow," I mew. "I was calling because I have a lead. It is a small town, Sicklerville. Is it important to Theodore in any way?"

"Yes, one scoop of chocolate would be great. For the life of me. I don't know." He pauses and huffs. "I can't think of anything. Wait, I think he stated once, his parents had a cabin by a lake. Maybe that is the location."

"Bad for your health," I remind him, a smirk playing on my lips. Who said a detective couldn't have much fun with her clients on the job? Besides, anything to distract me from the fact that I have to confront Elio's killer.

"What?" He seems surprised at my words, missing the joke.

"Ice cream on your cheesecake. That's gotta be, what, 600 calories?" I offer.

Jonathan chuckles, but there's an edge to it like he's trying to mask his unease. "Yeah, I guess 401 for the cake and 150 for the ice cream. Thanks for getting me all focused on the calorie thing."

"Don't mention it," I reply, my voice flat. "So, can you remember where it was?"

"Oh, no. It's been years. He talked about it a few times, but nothing worth remembering. I think it was there. Sorry, I wish I could remember. You think it's him?"

"Just checking a lead." I scan the file again, and the details about Reinhart blur together. "Okay, well, do you remember the name of his parents?"

"His mother's name began with an M or something. It could have been Martha or Mary or May... God, I don't know." His voice gets muffled, and I hear him asking Gretchen's mother. "Hey Cathy, do you remember the name of Ted's parents?" The older woman responds, but her words are lost to me. Jonathan relays the information, his tone strained. "She's saying she doesn't remember but thinks it was Brenda or maybe Loraine, and Brenda was her middle name."

"It's okay, sir. I can hunt it down. No problem."

"Well, I'm glad to join you. We could partner up."

I sigh, the weight of past failures pressing down on me. "I'm sorry sir. I don't work with a partner." The truth is, it's not about preference or smugness. I just can't bear to see anyone else get killed because of me.

"I would love to help if I can. Not partner but your assistant, maybe?"

"No, sir. I don't tell you how to farm, and you don't tell me how to do my job."

"I can respect your position. Maybe we can get together tomorrow and compare notes. "I sigh with relief, hanging up to scan Theodore Reinhart's records. His records roll up on my screen. Having the city and town, I track his birth certificate down. His mother's name is Chelsea Loraine, and his father is Abington, so much for my client and his fiancé's mother's memory. Maybe the woman just went by her middle name. Who knows? Using the name, I trace through property records and find a listing for a cabin by a lake owned by the Reinharts. I take the address, put it into a GPS app, and tie it into my augmented reality glasses.

**

An hour later, the train screeches to a halt, its arc blue light-lit interior casting eerie shadows. A border officer, all stern lines and cybernetic enhancements, steps aboard. His eyes are augmented with retinal scanners. They sweep the aisle, analyzing each passenger with mechanical precision. I yawn at the latest time-consuming inconvenience in my life. As he reaches my row, I hand over my passport. The holographic data shimmers in the dim light.

"Business or pleasure?" he asks, his voice modulated with a synthetic edge.

"My business is my pleasure," I reply with a smirk. His face tightens. He is not a fan of my brand of humor.

"You're permitted for a firearm. I need to see it." His voice is firm but not challenging. The government gives these guys courses in balancing politeness with customs demands.

I hand him my gun, the weight of it familiar in my hand. Its sleek design blends old-world craftsmanship with modern tech.

"No ballistic warrants out on it?" he questions, his eyes flashing as he cross-references databases.

"No, sir." I affirm. I try to keep my voice positive, but the ride has drained me.

"Let's keep it that way. You're licensed to carry this firearm in Canada under the 2046 revision of the Private Security and Investigative Services Act."

He hands back the gun and, with a final, scrutinizing look, moves on. The train lurches forward, the hum of its electric engine resonating through the cabin. I settle back into my seat, the tension in the air as thick as the digital smog of a neon-drenched cityscape. "One of the lobbyists that sent a letter to parliament to get that revision so I could carry a gun." We both chuckle. Maybe he is one for jokey banter after all. His heavy footsteps drift away from me and stop at the next passenger.

An hour after customs, I make it to the little farm town in Iowa where my clients hail from. I hop off the Maglev train and hit the bathroom to freshen up. Slickerville, the town name, flashes in bright neon red lights.

As I exit the station, the neon glow of a car rental place catches my eye. Wandering over, I rent an older model BMW G11 Scrambler. The bike hums with a purple glow, its hybrid engine purring smoothly. I kick down the starter and launch into the night.

I coast through the small town, its streets basic and unremarkable beyond, stretches of farmland extend for miles, a stark contrast to the urban jungle I'm used to. As I fly by, I notice the locals staring, their eyes judging my city-slicker ways and trench coat.

The bike's speed is intoxicating, especially with the coordinating helmet that came with the rental. The sensors anticipate my every move, allowing me to push the speed to eighty. Just a thought and the bike turns in that direction. Traveling this fast means keeping the autopilot on, a backup that lets my mind wander.

I wonder if I'll find them at the cabin. Why would he take her there? Maybe it was just cold feet, but the camera on the Maglev suggested otherwise.

Even though it's night, the glass embedded in the roads reflects the bike's headlights. The sides of the streets are dark, so I flip on the automatic guidance system. The bike bumps and bounces, the road shooting by. Hesitantly, I glance down at the computer guide. I see a man strolling on the side of the road and pull over to ask him. Taking off my helmet, I give him the address.

"Sure, the place is a quarter mile up," the man on the bike says, his voice calm and reassuring. "Are they having a gathering or something there?"

"Why do you ask?" I retort, my curiosity piqued.

"You're the second person who asked me about that address."

Damnit! Was Detective Moon here already?! "Oh. Was the first a woman of Korean descent?"

His lips twist as if giving my words thought. "No," he answers. Perfect, I'm here first. "A guy roughly five-nine or ten?"

"Did he have rugged features?" I ask, fear creeping up my body as I realize that the man might have been Jonathan instead. The motorcyclist hums thoughtfully.

"I guess you could say he did," he finally says. "Do you know him?"

"I think I might," I reply, trying to hide my dread. "Thanks for the directions."

The man nods and pedals away, his bike's solar panels glinting in the sunlight. I take a deep breath, the scent of blooming flowers and fresh earth calming my nerves. Then, the rising smell of cow patties brings me back to reality. The path ahead is lined with trees, their leaves rustling in the gentle breeze, powered by the community's renewable energy grid. I kickstart my bike, its eco-friendly engine purring softly, and head toward the address, hoping to find answers amidst the harmony of nature and technology.

I kick the peddle and speed off. At least Detective Moon can take care of herself. I could not believe the crazy lover-boy might have set out on his own to find Reinhart. If he isn't dead, I plan to kill him. I tap the speed call button on the cellphone and pipe it into the augmented glasses. Please let him be there.

"Police." A bored man grumbles over the line.

"Officer Mac O'Connor, please," I demand.

"Hold a sec..." The wind picks up, rustling the trees as I wind down the road. "Mac. It's for you." First, the sound clicks off and then back on over the phone, sounding like a wooden chair scraping a tile floor.

"Yeah, Mac here," Officer O'Connor says. I rapidly explained the situation, and while I knew he had no jurisdiction, I asked if he could dial the Sicklerville police and get me some backup.

I was careful to ask him to give my description because I'd hate to get shot by my backup. That would not be very comfortable. I round the bend, and in the distance, a small cabin with strings of neon blue lights in the shape of a parallelogram glows. It crackles and buzzes. The bike rolls behind a tree, and I slide off. The ground is soggy and wet, making sludging sounds with each step of mine, and the gentle lapping of the lake echoes behind in the background.

***

Ducking behind a tree, I crouch low, my heart pounding. The air is thick with the scent of damp earth and bioluminescent fungi, adding to the surreal tension. I scan the area, counting the cameras, my nerves on edge. I need to psych myself up. My mind plays the Cure's *Burn,* a desperate attempt to steady my racing thoughts. The house is twenty feet away. Drawing my revolver, I search the sky for drones and check for cameras. This place doesn't scream high-tech. Maybe the owners see it as a sanctuary away from the constant surveillance of the city.

Crouching low, I slither forward, my muscles tense with anticipation. I spot a camera about ten feet ahead. Planning my approach from the side seems easy enough to bypass since it's focused on the front.

A large dog barks viciously, and my stomach twists. Twice the standard size of a dog, the beast appears as if bred for destruction. It's disgusting to shoot an animal. Hell, it's never their fault if their owners are shit. Still, I know how this ends if it's him or me. Overhead, a flash of bioluminescent lightning crosses the sky, casting eerie shadows—a loud clap of thunder booms, making my heart skip a beat. A voice calls for the dog. It darts to its master, and the door shuts.

Relief washes over me, but it's fleeting. Shit, it just prolongs the eventual confrontation. My mind races with the possibilities of what lies ahead, the fear and determination intertwining as I prepare for whatever comes next.

I trek it to the window. Gazing in, Theodore Reinhart, the man I'm looking for, shouts at Gretchen to hurry up and upload something to the computer. On the ground, Jonathan lies—blood leaks from his head. My muscles tighten on the sides of my face into a thin smile. I have a clean shot to take the bastard out without even entering. I raise the revolver and breathe. The trigger slides back, and then Elio stands in front of me. Flinching, I lower my weapon.

My mind tricks me into believing Ello's black studded leather gauntlets deflected the shot, but reality shatters as the bullet crashes through the window, striking Theodore's shoulder. Blood arcs through the air. Damn, I never miss. A pang of guilt twists in my gut.

Theodore rolls, drawing his weapon, and fires two shots at me. I duck, but the bullets splinter the sill just above my head, sending wood fragments flying. My heart races, adrenaline surging through my veins. Suddenly, Elio stands next to me, his presence plunging me into a grief-laden abyss. It can't be. I must be delusional, some psychotic figment of my subconscious. But there's no time to figure it out. He glares at me, his eyes a swirling mix of sadness and pain.

The air shimmers with a surreal haze, colors bleeding into one another like a dreamscape. "When will you realize I didn't save you because I was a great hero but because you were important?" His voice echoes, solemn and distant as if carried on the wind from another realm. "Don't throw your life away."

"What?" I stammer, my eyes widening as the ghostly figure of my dead fiancée materializes before me. My chest tightens, a lump forms in my throat, and words are caught in a web of disbelief. The weight of my emotions threatens to drown me, but I force it down, focusing on the task. Elio's spectral form fades into the ether.

Two more shots pierce the air, striking the windowsill—the sounds of a struggle filter through the fog of my mind. Gretchen's scream slices through my guilt, jolting me into action. I see her, radiant and fierce, having knocked Theodore's gun into the air. They grapple, shadows dancing in the dim light as he tries to regain control.

I surge forward, crashing through the window like a force of nature. My body collides with his, the impact reverberating through my bones. We hit the floor, and I unleash my fury, fists raining down on his face. Each strike is a release, a cathartic scream of rage echoing in the dreamlike chaos: my heart pounds, a mix of fear, anger, and desperation fueling my every move. The need to protect Gretchen, to save her, drives me beyond the edge of reason.

"You have the right to lose a tooth!" I growl. "If you give up that right, I'll take two more from you!"

The field lights flicker outside, casting eerie shadows through the cracked blinds. Out to my left, the leashed Pitbull barks, its eyes glowing a menacing red. I'm sure it has either been bred to be a monster or genetically enhanced. It strains against the reinforced leather, muscles rippling. Outside, a second motorcycle hums up, its engine a low, ominous growl. This one is closer to the safe house. I continue to pound away, my fists a blur. Reinhart's body quivers helplessly beneath me, his augmented limbs twitching.

A snap of leather and the closing snarls of the dog catches my attention. It leaps toward me, jaws wide, and bites deep into my arm. Pain shoots through me, a white-hot lance. I wail, the sound echoing off the grimy walls. Fear and anger twist inside me, a volatile mix that threatens to explode.

The front door shatters in a shower of splinters. Detective Moon bursts into the room, moving with the fluid grace of a panther. Damn, she's better than I thought. With incredible speed, she catches the dog in mid-air. Her genetically enhanced arm whirs as she grabs the beast and tosses it aside like a ragdoll. Damn GEB! It is almost impossible to compete against them. They are stronger, smarter, and faster. But even with her help, I worry it will not be enough. The dog flips back and is ready to pounce again.

Behind her, three police officers storm in, weapons drawn, their visors reflecting the chaotic scene. One of them fires at the dog. Its body convulses, blood spraying as it falls, whimpering to the ground. Moon shoots the officer a horrified glare, her eyes blazing with fury. With the officer's gun trained on me, I struggle to suppress the rage boiling inside—my heart pounds in my chest, a drumbeat of defiance.

"Hands in the air, where we can see them!" the officer barks. Moon and I raise our hands over our heads and kneel on the floor. I signal Gretchen to do the same, her eyes wide with fear. "Identify yourself!"

"I'm a PI from Canada," I explain, my voice steady despite the chaos. "My badge is in my pocket. Call Officer Mac O'Connor. He'll explain."

"He sent us here. And you?!" The officer waves his gun at Moon, who lets out a fearful yelp, her tough exterior momentarily cracking. My mind races, calculating the odds, searching for a way out of this mess.

"I'm a PI from Canada as well!" She stammers. "Got my badge, my license, all in my pocket!"

Next to me, Lello's ghost forms again. His wispy hand reaches for my cheek. "I'm different now, you know. I'm not the same girl I was then," I whisper. But it was too loud. The police glance at each other with a look of concern. Their eyes shoot off to the side.

"Who is she talking to?" they ask each other.

Moon, sensing the truth, jumps to my aid as quickly as she can. She shakes her head. "No idea. She works alone." The police march toward me anyway.

"I know," Elio's ghost replies. "We all grow and change, but that doesn't matter to your worth to me. At the core, the ghost in you will never change."

***

Two EMTs load Jonathan into the ambulance. A paramedic patiently wraps gauze around my hand. The police officer stands next to me, asking questions about the case. Without thinking, I answer each one. The ambulance speeds off with lights flashing. I glance over as Moon finishes speaking to the officer. Moon jumps on her motorcycle. I nod to Moon, and then she speeds off.

The motorbike hovers and the green vapor light paints the sides as Moon flies off. Of course.

After questioning, I was sure I'd be at the hospital for shots and an evaluation. From across the room, Gretchen approaches. Gretchen stares at me with concerned eyes.

"What?" I invite her to my presence with a question. She will probably give me the standard spiel, thanking me for my service and such. Still, it's a spiel I welcome.

"I wanted to thank you," she says. That's the regular part of the spiel. It quickly turns abnormal when she leans in and kisses me dead on the lips. The kiss sends a chill down my spine. Jonathan is one lucky guy.

"Was he just some creep pulling a damn Gary Heidnik?" I ask, my voice tinged with a mix of anger and frustration. The thought of Reinhart's twisted motives gnaw at me, making my blood boil. The human soul is a dark puzzle.

"No… well, maybe," she replied, her voice wavering. "He wanted to control me, but not as a lover or anything."

"Ah, I know the type," I said, my tone softening slightly. "Men can be controlling. Sometimes it's flattering, but most of the time, it's completely unwanted."

"No, it wasn't that. At least, not entirely."

"Then why?" I press. My curiosity is piqued, and a sense of dread creeps in.

"Well, he works for a gang. I can't remember the name." Her voice trails off, but my mind is already racing. That bastard and his gang were going down, even if it took the rest of my life to pull it off.

"The Eternal Silence Syndicate," I say coldly, my heart pounding as I fill in the blank in her memory.

"Yeah, that's the name." She snapped her fingers, a far-off look in her eyes, a hint of sadness etches on her face. "He was so sweet before he joined the gang. I never expected this from him."

"So, what did the gang want with you?" I asked, my voice steady, masking the storm brewing inside me. My heart ached for her, but I couldn't let my emotions cloud my judgment. I had to stay focused, for Gretchen's sake and Elio's.

"To turn Des Moine's Smart System into a moral sentient one?" She appears puzzled, her brow furrows. Her published papers ' sentience and morality of artificial intelligence were common themes, but her research seemed purely theoretical.

"It doesn't sound like a bad idea," I tried to salvage the situation, though my mind was racing. "Hell, the corporate council in New Cyber City might have paid you to do it if they knew you could."

"Bad things happen in New Cyber City." She sighs.

"Yep, but why would a gang want morality?" I ask, my frustration bubbling beneath the surface.

"It's a horrible idea; you have no idea. The gang wanted it because, at their core, they have a twisted sense of morality and believe they could win the computer over. Morality comes from the word 'mores,' which means social custom or rule. I spent years in pursuit of a sentient moral computer." I knew the geek-speak was coming, and part of me wanted to tune out, but this was my case. "I studied Skinnerian behaviorism for years. Skinner was the only psychologist who took the concepts of freedom, decision control, and counter-control of people seriously. Machine learning, working on one of his ideas—'reinforcement'—provided the power source for machine learning. Armed with this knowledge, I spent ten years developing the machine and even got some success with awareness. I created a system using operant and respondent conditioning. It was augmented by a code sequence to override the system with direct instruction of a rule and rule learning. The machines began to develop their own rules, or what Skinner called autoclitic frames, and self-edit based on data and review. I was starry-eyed."

"Okay," I say, trying to calm my voice, though my mind is spinning with the implications.

"Not okay. I was so absorbed in my work that I didn't tell Jonathan. He was supportive and said, 'What if two cities were to develop my morality?' Let's say Butterfly and New Cyber City."

Eerie shadows dance on the trees. Her story is the second freakiest thing that happened to me today. The first and most important was seeing Ello, or was that some weird psychological manifestation of my guilt coupled with my overwhelming need to have a protective person around me? If the latter, I need to shake it quickly—no room for second-guessing oneself in my business.

The rain patterns against the window constantly remind me of the storm brewing outside and within. I had to stay sharp for Gretchen, Elio, and the truth. My heart pounded with a mix of determination and fear, knowing that every second counted in this twisted game.

"That's believable. Like those cities could ever work together."

"Ok, I get it, but for example. I had never thought of this, so I downloaded two program copies. The developed cities went to war and destroyed the machines."

"Some kinks, I guess?" I'm no scientist, and the words are the best I can offer. Maybe Moon could understand this, but I like to keep myself on the simple straight and narrow of the world. I got the basics, though.

"Not kinks but features, though I did not know it then. First, I thought I did not give the programs enough morals to survive and gave them full internet access. Again, I downloaded the programs on a new machine. They developed different morality and destroyed each other. Then I thought maybe they lacked empathy for each other, so I used Skinner's conditioned suppression in a more respondent conditioning setup. The conditioned trigger simulated oxytocin in the human brain, suppressing some areas and heightening others so that the machines experienced love. This love was seen among its city members. The machine converted all with its morality early and then met the other city. The machine zapped and sizzled as, this time, the war went quicker. Then I tried different cities after reading up on their histories to see if it was because I picked those specific cities, but no, same result."

"So, all we need is love is a mistake?" Gretchen laughs with a strain in her voice. "Why not just train them both in the same morality?"

"Tried it. They always developed variations between the two, and they destroyed each other. I tried two hundred fifty-six variations on the moral sentient computer. I felt horrible as each failed and even more horrible that the life I had created was so murderous of out of group members."

"Ah, a machine perpetually involved in the crusades."

"Yep. I used to worry about the first sentient artificial intelligence never finding God. Now I worry they will." On some level, I understood her words. I am not stoked about all the computer science stuff, but I know there's a time to walk from one's career because it is a destructive path. I'd seen it enough. Hell, I'd even done it. "Well, they took Jonathan to the hospital, and I need to catch up with him. You should come. They could put some liquid skin on the bite…I'm worried, as the officer said, the gangs will always hunt me down now. I guess my life as a simple farmer is over."

"I know some folks in Butterfly City. If you're ready to testify, I can get you into witness protection," I said, my voice low and steady.

Tears welled up in Gretchen's eyes. "I want to testify, but I'm terrified they'll steal my work and succeed. Let me see what Jonathan thinks." She reached out, her hand resting on my shoulder. "If I didn't have a boyfriend…"

"It's just the life-saving thing. Gets the old adrenaline pumping," I interrupt, trying to ease her guilt. Her touch sent a shiver down my spine. It had been a long time since anyone had touched me, and part of me was surprised I let her.

Gretchen flashed a charming smile, a simple lie. The truth should matter, but it didn't, at least not to her. I took a deep breath, my heart stuttering. I was an extension of the courts, my brain clinging to ethical codes. Still, my job was to find this woman and return her to the man who'd hired me, not the police or myself. Maybe to others, this was an easy choice. My morals had predetermined the road. Not for me. Both these things meant something, and damn it, they should have. Gretchen kissed me softly and left with Jonathan. "Don't forget to leave me a review!" I yell. "And if your mother-in-law wants to leave a review too, remind her that I found Gretchen first!"

The lovebirds chuckle as I flash a sad smile.

***

Over the next four days, I get to know them both pretty well. It comes with the territory, I guess. Hell, they're exceptional—empathic and caring. They ask about my life and my losses, but I dodge their questions like a pro. I managed to get them into a witness relocation plan. I knew I'd never see them again. They're beautiful souls, bound to make a difference. Part of me wants to end up with one of them, but that would disrespect the life Lello wanted for me. Was I turning into Velma from Scooby-Doo? No, I'm not smart enough for that.

I sit at my desk, legs up, Jonathan and Gretchen across from me—a deck of playing cards in my hand. We laugh and joke, but I keep my focus on the cards. I flip one off the top, and it lands in the bronze spittoon at the end of my desk. We cheer like we just downed three bottles of synth whiskey.

"Yeah, I guess so. It's weird since he doesn't drink," Gretchen says, pulling out a straw and stuffing it in her drink. This is my final goodbye to both. I knew it, dreaded it.

"When I was in her mother's house after the call," Jonathan starts. "I remembered the location. I tried to call you, but you must have missed it." I had shut off the phone, but he didn't need to know that. "… And then that stupid Taylor Dayne song came on the speakers."

"Tell it to My Heart?" I ask.

"No, not that one," he answers solemnly. "I heard 'I'll Be Your Shelter' and realized I had to get her. Even if she wasn't ready for me, I had to take the risk to ensure she wasn't being held hostage." "So now we go to a new town under a new name," Gretchen interrupts. "I don't know if I'll ever be. When I got on the train to see Jonathan, I wanted to tell him about all my doubts about us and see if he could make it all go away. Strangely, after this ordeal, I realize he cannot make these doubts disappear, but I can learn to accept them. There are no guarantees in life. We might work out or not, but I want to give it a try. I took one of those stupid compatibility tests, and it said that we possibly weren't truly meant for each other, but not every guy is willing to risk his life to find you and save you. I guess living with some doubt is the unspoken part of life."

She reaches over and touches his hand—the music on the radio changes to the Psychedelic Furs *Ghost in You*. The song brings me back to Lello... Damn, I am a sucker. I could feel the emotions welling up, but at the moment, I was just outside the shack; maybe he had saved me. Hell, I have never been the religious type, but perhaps some part of him is still deep in me, and that part was enough to give me pause and rethink. If I could not get the love thing back, some friendships could serve a purpose in my life. I lean backward and stare at the lovebirds. Gretchen is chattering about their plans.

Not only was my client a total sap, but the woman I was looking at believed in all that horoscope mumbo-jumbo and sappy love stuff. Even knowing this, I still had to put up with them, and part of me wanted to believe they had a future together. I huffed, drawing a surprised gaze from them.

What? You don't think so?" Gretchen's voice had a sharp edge, defensive.

"You know," I said, leaning back in my chair, trying to mask my uncertainty. "I heard once that people trust computers more than other people. My take on computers? Garbage in, garbage out. So, all this stuff you told me wouldn't bother me, and I'm saying it shouldn't bother you either."

She let out a cough-chuckle, a small smile playing on her lips. Despite her cold feet, she was ready to face her fears. Before continuing, she sips the "perfectly legal" Mountain Jack I'd mix for her.

"Besides, my future wife's job is to handle the finances. At least here, I know what awaits me. We'll start fresh in a new town with new names. I can get work in finance at first. Eventually, we'll get the farm and have a steady income from working it. I don't know what would await me and Jonathan otherwise. Thanks to you, the judge has set us up nicely. We could either make it big... or end up in squalor."

"I doubt that," I say, feeling a surge of determination. "Jonathan's got the money to hire me, and I'm not cheap. He's got potential."

"Well, you were cheaper than Moon," Jonathan interjected.

"Really?" I perked up, a grin spreading across my face. I might not be the best Butterfly City had to offer, but at least I was affordable.

"Gretchen's mom told me you were a quarter of the cost." He admits.

"Well, ain't that a bitch." I say, shocked. I need to review my pricing scheme.

"Are you going to be okay?" Gretchen cuts in again, deeply serious this time.

"Yeah, I'll just raise my rates."

"No, silly. I mean, personally. I remember you talking about the room at the cabin. You seemed very sad." She heard me speaking to the air and thought my sanity must have been strained. "When my father died a few years back, well, I thought I was going to lose it. I watched a video on the behavioral health channel on Guided Mourning exercise. It helped. Not to eliminate him or make me forget him, but to make the pain more manageable. Here, I'll write the catalog number so you can retrieve it from the streaming station." Gretchen glances at Jonathan, and he draws out a pen and gives it to her. She starts to write on a piece of paper at the end of the desk.

"I'm fine," I reassure her. "I got a tendency to get a little weird under pressure."

"It must be a pressure-filled lonely life," Jonathan muses. I gaze into his beautiful eyes. Please don't make me do this.

"I got an ad —it says seeking a time traveler for deeply passionate love. Let's meet last week." My joke falls flat as the two flash me a concerned look. "Really, I'm okay," I continue. I've been thinking of getting a cat, but I cannot decide if I want a cold, snarky one to name Dot or a soft, loving, empathic one to name Maka. Either way, I see cats in the future."

We chuckle and stand up. I guess they figured out how to give me back some of my dignity. "Well, remember you will always be both our hall pass."

God, I feel like I am blushing. I hate that they know they made their point, but I am not ready. Probably never will be. Jonathan shoves the five hundred in my hand. I count it quickly.

"We're settled then?" Jonathan asks. I nod. "Ms. Coke-Killburn. I can't thank you enough."

He extends his hand, and I grasp it tightly. We shake on it. I glance at Gretchen, who invitingly smiles and raises her glass. Yeah, she has Lello's eyes—the eyes of an angel.

My heart sinks as he opens the door. They leave, and I am expected to let them go. It was the job. Was I professional enough to keep quiet and let them go? They left together with a piece of my heart. It's like Velma watching Fred and Daphne stroll away. As I watched them leave, I knew another case was solved. I close the bitter-sweet door behind them.

"Hey babe," Jonathan asks Gretchen. "Wanna go to that diner we always go to?"

Sometimes, I hate being me. I toss the cash on the table, reach in my pocket, open the spear-mint box, and toss one in my mouth. Maybe if I raise my rates, I'll feel better. I certainly have to stop taking those sappy cases. I should follow up on my earlier offer and watch some old TV with someone.

***

Hye-jin Moon swings open her front door, and there I am, pizza and beer in hand. My heart races a bit; it's been a long week, and I need this break.

"Wow!" she exclaims, her voice a mix of surprise and delight. "I didn't expect you actually to come!"

"And I brought pizza and beer for the second-best detective in Butterfly City," I reply with a smirk, trying to mask my exhaustion. Moon sniffs the air, trying to catch the aroma.

"Smells good, but are those anchovies?" she asks, wrinkling her nose.

"More for me then!" I joke, feeling a bit lighter. We share a laugh as I step into her apartment. It's massive, more extensive than some houses, and more spacious than my cramped place. "Wow, your apartment is huge," I blurt out, a tinge of envy creeping in. "How much is the rent?"

"I got this place for a 6.6k a month mortgage," she says casually. No wonder she charges her clients so much. "How much do I owe you for the pizza and beer?"

"Oh, don't worry about it," I tease, trying to hide my surprise at her mortgage. "When I found out what you were charging, I doubled mine."

Tonight is Scooby-Doo night, and there's no one I'd rather binge-watch it with than Hye-Jin. As the episodes roll on, we joke and chat about the show. At some point, Moon grabs her pet hedgehogs, Pillow and Whoopie Cushion, and snuggles with them. I can't help but smile at the sight; it's a rare moment of peace. Finally, I take the last sip of my beer and stand up, feeling the weight of the night settle in. This was precisely what I needed. "Well, you know what they say about beer," I start.

"It's just a rental!" Moon's voice cuts through the haze, but it barely registers. My mind is already elsewhere.

"Exactly. Now, can I use your bathroom?" I ask, trying to keep my voice steady though my heart pounds.

Moon points down the dimly lit hallway. "Sure. It's just down there."

I stroll over, whistling a haunting tune, the "Blue Moon" melody echoing in the sterile air. The bathroom is a stark contrast to the rest of the place. Maybe I can find how she structures her fee? A framed picture catches my eye as I finish —students clustered around a sign reading "Yuji Chiba Class of 2042." Moon is lurking at the edge, a shadow among the genetically enhanced—a pang of jealousy and frustration twists in my gut. Of course, my biggest rival is a splice job.

A flicker of light from the adjacent room draws me in. I step into Moon's home office, the air thick with secrets. My eyes scan the room until they land on a manila file on the table. I flip it open, and my AR vision springs to life, data streaming before my eyes. The name on the file is Elio Merlot. Status: Deceased.

My breath catches in my throat. What the hell? My hands tremble as I clutch the file, memories of Elio flooding back, the pain of his loss still raw. Anger and sorrow mix, a volatile cocktail that threatens to overwhelm me. Why is Moon digging into my past? What does he know about Elio?

JOHN RUTLEDGE AND THE 50,000

Marisha Cautilli
Johnny Andrews
Joseph Cautilli

Microarrays covered computer screens, as John Rutledge began his tour down the aisles of his genetics processing lab. His mind should have been on solving the problems of the Genetically Enhanced Beings (GEB), as it normally was but today, he mulled over the recent trend of events. The emergence of a post–truth society had frightened him when it occurred, but the recent trend was an outright persecution of scientists. "Religious wackos!" He mumbled more to himself than anyone else in the room, but it managed to be loud enough to draw a flurry of stares.

Various genetic engineers that worked for him exchanged pleasantries, as he passed. He tried his hardest to focus back but had little success. Red Green, one of his best DNA sequencers whose name became the coloring scheme used to separate genetic material, asked him if he was coming to his kid's confirmation party on Saturday. His new cologne filled the immediate air around him with the scents of lavender, rose, gardenias, applewood, and oak. It was supposedly chemically engineered to be a unique but relaxing scent, but John still found his anger at the world to be strong. In a flurry of grumbles, he confirmed he would be there. His response was much colder than he intended, and Red swiftly backed away.

A third of the way through, John finally gave up. His eyes cast down at the folder in his hands. Its yellow color contrasted sharply with his black nail polish. It contained a printout of an online article espousing that "evolution was proven fake." When he originally saw it, he went crazy. By whom? With what evidence? Just how did they prove almost two-hundred years of research wrong? All his biology-related studies went to waste. He felt a sickness in his stomach even greater than when he read the article from the previous day where marmots were no longer hibernating. The two articles represented a rejection of science. One for its blatant falsehood and the other for the effects scientific rejection was causing on the planet. In reading the former article, he realized it was nothing more than Gish gallop. His stomach knotted in disgust.

Moving out of the lab area, John came under the harsh sterile fluorescent blue light of the hallway. The Clash's *Should I Stay or Should I* Go played as John's head bobbed to the sound. John hated the stroll along the bottom floor, largely because the bulbs, which were set every twenty feet, scattered bright blue light close to eight thousand lumens over a snowy alabaster tile floor. Its net effect was crisp, disorienting, and just a tiny bit creepy. He was glad when his glasses shaded to tone down the glare.

Inside his head, John understood the nostalgia for the pre-modern world that many experienced. Hell, his arms and neck were lined with primitive tattoos that spoke of an earlier age and his partial Cherokee heritage. While he would never admit it, he could see the appeal of placing blame. Indeed, tribalism (whether religious, racial or genetic purity) was one way to have a sense of belonging, particularly for those who had nothing else. He himself drew strength from his points of intersectionality. At the end of the hall was his office.

Before he arrived at his door, his assistant came charging

down the corridor with a stack of papers in her hands. There was a time when his days were filled with discovery. Now it seemed more and more his days were spent signing forms, many of which he wondered what happened to them after he signed them.

Passing his assistant Kathryn, she handed him a copy of his itinerary for the day. He stared at it, took his pen, and wrote "prove evolution is real".

"Get over it," Kathryn stated. "They'll eventually change their belief." He turned away from her and continued trudging.

Still tribalism and pre-modernism had its ugly side. John was all too aware of the persecution of the GEBs. Nasty terms like the "jumpies" permeated the land and on top of it the zeal at which scientists of all types were being persecuted was frightening. John took a deep breath as he thought about the murder of seven genetics professors from a Cyber City university (the old Bos-Wash urban sprawl) as the people had just started calling it. The door to his office slid open with a swish. He entered and tossed himself into his black mesh task chair. The world was changing and not in his eyes for good. Pre-modernity was a time of unchecked disease and early death. Hell, people back then barely made it to thirty despite all that fresh unpolluted air, the thing Cyber City didn't have.

Lifting his voice, John commanded "computer on." The room swiveled as a three-dimensional hologram filled it. John soared passed an article on China trying to sell some of the huge empty cities that it built early in the twenty first century. The cities stood as a massive testament to China's attempt to stimulate both its economy and people into the twenty first century after the 2008 banking failure. He could understand the desire, as America undertook a similar project but with factories in the early twenty-twenties. Problem was in China, no-one was ever intended to buy the properties. Huge smart buildings sat unoccupied for years. It was always John's belief that the government of China would eventually just for its people to relocate into the cities but that was before China's mission was to bring its renegade province of Taiwan under control and its reacquisition of Hong Kong.

As the three-dimensional virtual screen spun, John pointed to his e-mail. The top email subject was titled "colorful art" It was a message from one of his oldest friend's Robert Haastings. Touching the hologram of the e-mail a smile crossed his face. Haastings had sent him a sound file that was converted so that the colors of the sound waves lit and danced in the room. The combination of music and sound brought a tear to his eye. "Damn thyroid," Rutledge mumbled to himself, embarrassed by his own emotionality. He leaned back and just enjoyed the show. After five minutes, the music ended and Haasting's face popped up. "I know these are tough times my friend. I hope the show lessened your pain."

John had to admit he felt better. The music and lights had done the trick to relieve his disgust and then the explosion happened. The pressure ripped the door from its hinges, bending the metal inwards just barely giving him enough time to slouch behind the desk. The shatterproof window laminated with a resin and transparent aluminum mix shattered. His ears were ringing loudly.

As he rose, his head throbbed in pain. He reached up and felt blood seeping out. It was warm and sticky. John's body went numb. Sounds filled his office, a cacophony of screams and klaxons barely made it above the ringing in his ears. His eyes were assaulted with the color of red flashing light, as he quickly rose.

Acute dizziness washed over him, as he staggered into the hall. His hand reached for his forehead; it was warm and sticky. Despite his blurry vision, he pulled back his hand to find it covered in blood. Bodies and limbs were randomly distributed. Tissue and blood covered the white walls. Holes appeared in his visual field looking like huge gray dots. Rutledge's mind tried to focus. Half burned bodies raised hands out to him, pleading for relief. "Medic!" He screamed. Reaching into his pocket he pulled out his megacell. His mind hoped the infirmary floor had gotten the news and was on the way. Fingers finding the button, John hit the automatic dial. Down the hall, his company's fire rescue team emerged on the floor and then all went black.

***

Screaming, Rutledge woke in a hospital bed. A pudgy pale nurse rushed to his side to comfort him. As she soothed him, explaining he was all right, John's eyes caught sight of an Earth Corp guard at the door. He knew those black nylon suits like the back of his hand, as he dealt with them more often than he wished. The agent's face was familiar, but he was unsure from where.

"Where's Kathryn?" Rutledge questioned.

"Your assistant did not make it," replied the nurse.

As he was coming out of his hysterical fog, he asked about the lab. The nurse told him the explosion was bad and that many of his people were dead or in the hospital. John bit his lip. When he hired Kathryn, part of it stemmed from a fascination with her name, given it was the same as the anglicized form of his lover in Costa Rica's name. They even had the same laugh. While nothing inappropriate ever happened between them, he still felt a closeness to his assistant for those reasons.

The nurse informed him that several people had waited all night to see him. They were in the hospital chapel. A long pause followed. John stared at the Earth Corp guard. "I guess I'll see them now," he finally stated. The nurse smiled and recognized his statement as an awkward request to have the visitors told he was awake. As she cleared the room, John stated "How is Tiffney?"

The guard smiled, "I was not sure you recognized me."

"Nicole, you look so much like your mother. Which is good because your father was one ugly beast."

There were few people Nicole would have taken an insult about her father from, but John Rutledge was one of them. Her father always admired the "wise aleck Brainiac", as he called John.

John continued, "The world still owes your father

235

everything, but it is too damn stupid to realize that" and then as if erratically changing the subject, "Earth Corp, your father would have been proud."

"I think so," she insisted.

"As to you, I remember a teen girl in a laserlight based facial mask, trying to clean up acne." Nicole giggled. "So, Ms. Murdoch how did you land this gig?"

"Well, actually it's Mrs. Jay now. Michael and I married."

"Really? My nephew Michael?" Nicole nodded. "I am out of the loop," he continued, his eyes drifting to the sky-blue fiber optic lights monitoring his vitals in the corner. "Well, that makes us family then and explains why those fools at Earth Corp put you on my door. They think I will toe the line if my family asks." He paused long enough to take a deep breath. His chest painfully rose and fell. "They are right of course. Damn psychological profiles on all of us. When does the intrusion end?"

"I am not sure why you see that as intrusive," Nicole remarked.

"Of course, you don't!" Rutledge snapped. "You were raised in a world where people filled parenting plans to stimulate their children's development and happily received feedback. The government even paid them to learn behavior management."

"If my history is correct, that was one of your ideas."

Not missing a beat, Rutledge's eyes flashed, and he angrily said, "And I was a damn fool for creating it." Rutledge licked his lips to moisten them. He noticed his mouth was overly dry. He reached for the brown plastic cup at his bedside. It was empty. "Can you fill this pitcher of water for me?"

"I am sorry, but I can't?" Nicole said hesitantly.

Rutledge interrupted her quickly, "Why the hell not?"

"I was getting to that- the anesthetic they used in your surgery has a side effect. If you drink fluids, you could vomit and choke."

"Well, that was a crappy choice of anesthesia,"

Nicole reached into her pocket and pulled out a small pack

of chewing gum, "Would you like some gum?"

"What kind?" he asked.

"Spearmint," she announced with more confidence.

"Ok. It was always my favorite." Nicole Jay handed him the gum. John unwrapped a stick and stuck it into his mouth. He eyed her suspiciously if she knew Spearmint was his favorite because she had read a profile on him. That was protocol, as Earth Corp tried to increase its customer service rating by providing individual touches to their action. Earth Corp called it better community policing. Still Rutledge enjoyed the taste. "Hmm…" His head sunk into the hypoallergenic pillow, and he closed his eyes. "So, what is this crap they got dripping into my arm," Rutledge pointed to the IV.

"I think it is human growth hormone," Nicole responded.

"Well at least that is appropriate to aide in the healing. So, why you?" He started but was interrupted.

A light tap occurred at the door and just as quickly the knob turned, and a head peeped into the room. "Well if it isn't Robert Haastings" John beamed, "How the hell are you asshole, and how's is Brenda?"

Rutledge noticed that Haastings wore a pair of blue medium Arena sweatpants. Haastings was always famously informal, even at work. His staff was more likely to see him in jeans or sweats then in a suit and tie.

Robert smiled, "Very good. She is heavily involved in some research thing at the lab. You know how it is. Hey, this will interest you, we got our first jumpie."

"Don't call them that Bob. They are people too," John coached, barely containing the anger in his voice.

"I know." Robert sounded genuinely sad. "Sorry."

John gave an exaggerated chew of his gum. "So, what brought you here to my lab on Bowery Street? Expecting I won't make it?"

"No," he said. "Just wanted to say hello and I wanted to see how you're healing."

"Well, welcome. I missed you too." Haastings flushed and

skirted so close to a caring emotion and it made John smile. "How is my lab? Any idea?"

"Bad John," Robert started. His face turned grave. "Maybe fifty dead. Good thing you stopped wearing that razor in your cheek or you might have been one of them." Rutledge gave a sarcastic eye roll. He had not worn the razor or spiked his hair in almost a decade. Haastings whipped out his handheld and tapped the screen. "Here is the report."

With growing despair, Rutledge scanned down the screen, each name adding to his sense of frustration, sadness, and disgust. When he reached Red Green's name, he could handle it no more. He shut off the screen.

"They were all good people, Bob," a tear formed in Rutledge's eye. Not being a person who showed emotion in public, he bit his lip hard. "I was supposed to go to Green's kid's confirmation this weekend. What do I tell his family?"

"It was not your fault John."

Rutledge did not want to hear it. "Earth Corp have any idea who and why?"

Haastings took a deep breath. As he did so, Rutledge knew that it was going to be news he hated to hear. "Well, they got a video feed, but you are not going to like it."

"Why the hell not?"

"It must have been altered. It shows your assistant Kathryn setting the bomb."

Eyebrows arching, Rutledge felt a wave of disgust rise in him. This had to be wrong. He had recruited Kathryn out of Earth Corp five years earlier himself. She came with great references.

Rutledge tried to get up from bed. A wave of nausea washed over him. He flopped back on the mattress and motioned over to Nicole, "Can you open the window? I could use some air and a view of outside."

Walking to the cord, Nicole tugged. The blinds swung wide to expose the amber sunlight of the ending day shown into the room. John tried to steady his soul. Inside he knew his entire operation was now suspect and worse he had no idea of who he could trust.

Part of him wanted to run. His eyes met Nicole's and he just felt empty and defeated. "Bob, ever feel like just packing it in?" Rutledge's voice carried all the pain and frustration of the blast.

"I get sad John. I think we all do. Damn, I've wanted to pack up the genetics business for years and go back to chemical engineering."

"Disposable diapers," John chuckled. Haasting's big breakout claim to fame was the creation of a paper diaper that was environmentally friendly. It was a seven-ply diaper that was strong enough to get the job done but would not remain in the environment polluting for a thousand years. "Bob, I'm serious. I saw an article the other day that the Chinese still have not sold much of the cities they created back in 08."

"You would just leave? Go to another country?"

"The religious people are different than when I was a kid. Bob, those guys are just dangerous now. Not that they were not prone to crazy back then, they killed my father you know." John sighed.

"Would you leave science? How would you staff a lab?" Haastings' voice stayed neutral but had a shake in it that indicated to John nervousness.

"Maybe it is time for an exodus," John's voice filled with resolve.

Confusion stretched across Haastings' face. He just could not wrap his head around it. "A what?"

"Maybe it is a time for all scientists to leave and find a country that will not intrude on our research."

"It would be nice to get the governments off our backs and the corporations. But Johnny, the outside world don't have that much talent. Cyber City, California, and maybe a dozen or so other places on this planet outside the US could give you the freedom you seek." As he spoke, John's handheld pinged. It was a notification for the latest article in Earth Corp's secret journal done by John and Robert's friend, Carson Greenspan. Only a few people knew of the journal's existence, and even fewer published in it. Most publications were done by military research. The article was done jointly with Yak about how to effectively prevent and counter targeted viral attacks personalized to one individual or family.

"Yak just published in Ationmilthet," John remarked.

"Great journal that one," Robert remarked. "I wish Earth Corp. would make the articles more publicly available. Hardly get any citations if no one knows it exists."

"That's the point Bob. Only a few people have access to it." For the first time, John put a hand to where his gash was. He felt the smooth but sticky liquid skin which covered it. "I thought Yak was moving much of its operation to a moon base. What if I called China and got them to sell me a city or just a portion of a city. We could make it like South Korea was back in the early part of the century with high-paced science labs. What I am saying Bob, is I hope you would come with me. I think our two operations and maybe a few others – we could probably bring fifty thousand scientists to a place just dedicated to discovery."

Bewildered, Robert Haastings pulled back. He had never considered the potential in starting an entire city devoted to science. The idea of course was not new. Utopianists from B.F. Skinner to Walt Disney had all thought of building experimental communities devoted to the sciences.

Haastings shook it off. "You are just depressed. This is not what you want to do."

John twisted his lips. He glanced over at Nicole, who stoically nodded back at him. "I think it really is. I can start considering this tomorrow."

"I'm sure Earth Corp. will be glad to provide funding for research and protection," Nicole chimed in.

"That's what I'm worried about," John sighed. "Earth Corp. having their hands in everything."

"You're sounding like that old Animals song. Talkin' about how you gotta get out of this place. Would you just order your staff to leave?" Robert asked. John stroked his chin with his right hand.

"No, I would make it a choice for each person. It would be something that I could reward heavily." Rutledge's eyes seemed firm with determination.

"John Rutledge and the fifty thousand. I can see the headlines. Okay, I'll make you a deal. I will investigate your explosion and if I find the real culprit, promise me that you will stay. Seriously, Brenda and I love your stupid ass very much and we will miss you if you go."

"No promises," John replied. "But I love you guys too."

***

Confined to his own infirmary, which was equipped better than most hospitals, two weeks passed quickly. He spent much of that time video conferencing with Chinese leaders and many US science companies ranging the gambit from hard science physicists to natural science psychologists. Indeed, John Rutledge had his fifty thousand. Finally, the day arrived when Rutledge was discharged from the infirmary and cleared to leave the building.

On this day, Earth Corp had once again assigned Nicole for his protection. John felt angst and Nicole reached over and clasped his hand, "As long as I'm standing," she stated. "I'll keep you safe."

"I know you will," John replied. He licked his dry lips and sighed, "Let's do it." As he moved down the Bowery hallway, he noticed that Robert Haastings was waiting for him. Next to Haastings stood a gorgeous blonde. Haastings introduced the woman as Mary Willowson, a bodyguard to make sure that they could get out of the building.

Mary was five foot seven inches. Her face was puffy with wide cheek bones and a tiny scar on her left cheek. Clearly a cyborg, her shoulder was mounted with a socket that she could swap the cyberarm. If it weren't for the slightly off-matching coloring, it would be impossible to recognize it was fake; that's how John recognized it as his prototype. She had a couple of different arms for different purposes.

"Like your arm," John complemented, waving to her.

"Thanks," Mary replied. "Was never smart enough to fix it, but Bob's got me covered."

"Let's move people!" Nicole barked.

"Wait wait!" John paused. Dismayed and a little flustered, Rutledge asked why they needed a guard and what was happening.

With reservation, Haastings mumbled, "Things have gotten a little crazy since the explosion. Lots of people are completely up in arms."

"I'll say," Nicole added. "It's a clusterfuck." John felt it best not to push it and followed along with his friends. Not saying more, Haastings led them out of the building.

A light mist covered the grey morning and very fine rain came but not enough to disperse the hungry vultures waiting for a look, a sound bite, or anything they could twist and turn to make John Rutledge the bad guy. Amongst the horde a few bodies in long trench coats stood waiting, patiently watching. They stood out amongst the busy roving reporters for they were stock-still. Just glaring at the building.

Protesters lined the streets, screaming prayers and shouts of damnations. Reporters stood around in droves like a pack of hyenas just waiting to pounce. One charged too early, prompting Mary to sock him in the jaw with her cybernetic arm. He flew ten feet backward, hitting a car, denting it, and he dropped his sign.

"I didn't want to say it," Mary started. "But your arm packs a punch."

"Figured it was one of my designs," John answered.

"Oh. Why didn't you say anything sooner?" John bit his lip.

"Didn't want to make you uncomfortable," he finally answered. With her light ion blaster in one hand, Nicole moved in front of the group and spread her arms wide so easy access to John was unavailable.

A few people already snapped pics of the limo waiting patiently to pick up its quarry of John Rutledge and Robert Haastings. It had only been a couple of weeks since the explosion at the lab and the press wanted someone to hang; John Rutledge was that man. Even if he was a survivor and had been seen video-called all the families of those that died. Plus, Rutledge had done multiple rounds of visits to casualties still in hospital through holographic projection, or again online chats with those at their homes recuperating. While critics commented it was a PR stunt to improve his image, it certaintly did not feel that way to John. He genuinely felt pain for his people.

Anger and frustration had willed John forward. It was all making him hound for the truth and possible vengeance. But with everyone gunning for scientists all progress seemed hindered and the press was just making things Hell.

"They're coming!" a member of the paparazzi exclaimed.

"Rutledge, did you sabotage your lab!" A voice yelled out. Nicole slid between John and the reporter to force the man back.

Another screamed, "Are scientists being hunted?"

"He's not giving comments! Let him through!" Mary yelled.

Everybody shouted like bullets as John and Robert plus an entourage of armed guards worked their way through the rushing journalists to get to the waiting limo. Nicole noticed first four people in blue trench coats.

"Trench coats in this heat?" Nicole shouted to Robert.

The oddly dressed bodies threw off their navy blue trench coats and stood amongst yelling and screaming as the reporters caught sight of the four people. Three men and one young woman all with bombs strapped to them. They tried to move closer as now the hounding reporters dispersed, except for a few very hungry people who tried to snap pictures.

"Oh shit!" Mary screeched. "They're suicide bombers!"

"Trouble-take them before they get closer, move!" Robert shouted. Earth Corp.'s Agent Jay aimed for the bombers.

Lasers started searching for targets. Nicole already sniped the first bomber and turned towards another one. A now nervous bomber prematurely went off taking half a dozen people in a burning ball of death. Shrapnel flew through the crowd and many souls fell to the ground. One piece struck

Nicole in the arm. She screamed in pain and blood seeped down the side. Instinctively, John grabbed her and placed his body between her and the explosion. This was Tom Murdoch's daughter. He'd never let her die for him.

Chaos erupted but Haastings' security was already swinging into action. "Find the targets and take them down before another goes off" one of the Haastings security bellowed into his mouthpiece.

"Are you ok?" John asked.

"Fine, I'm the one doing the protecting." Nicole jumped up and trained her Light Ion Blaster (or the LIB-9) on the crowd. The blaster exploded a fireball hitting one of the suicide bombers.

Red beams shot amongst the crowd, laser sighting from the advantage point of Robert's snipers as they secured the nearest rooftops.

With a thunderous boom a small laser ball flew from the sniper's weapon and the young woman's forehead exploded in a splash of thick red. Her body tumbled backwards.

"Get to the car!" Nicole screamed, more suicide bombers emerging towards them. "I got you covered!"

"In the car, now!" Mary screamed at John and Robert, using each of her arms to shove them forward. Nervousness hit one of the other men before they reached the limo and he detonated himself. Bodies were flung and the limo was pushed as the wave expanded outward.

Rutledge and Haastings were thrown to the ground by the security team keeping tight perimeters around them. Mary landed on top of Rutledge and instantly returned fire. Nicole's cover fire never ceased from behind them. Her battle cry echoed as she pushed forward.

A large African American guy from Haastings' security team stood with his laser drawn and rushed down towards the limo, he aimed as the last of the terrorists came forth, sweat mixing with the fine rain. Men and women screaming, fires ablaze and the security personnel fired his laser beam finding its target before the mad man could explode, a direct hit into the mad glaring eye. The body fell amongst the crowd with a thud.

Sirens wailed violently a small distance away as ambulances, police, and fire vehicles careened around corners and arrived at the massacre as the security detail usher John and Robert into the limo.

"My God, John what the Hell was that?" Robert leaned back into the leather interior of the limo, rubbing his haggard face. The man was all business once he had opened the mini-bar and secured himself a stiff drink, pouring another glass for John. "Drink this. It steadies one's nerves."

John nodded and gulped back the harsh liquid which burned as it went down his throat. Mary sat next to John and peered out of the window with a blank expression.

"Strong stuff. Now me or you? Who were they after?"

Robert smiled sadly but with quizzical eyebrows, "Dear friend, the laboratory and now this…it's you. But why? And who, that is the big question." Robert took a deep breath to calm himself but his voice remained anxious and his tempo fast. "Is it because of your research? But surely it is a good thing. Why would anyone want to block the progress of science?"

Robert thumped the top of the mini bar in exultation, "That's it, who always opposes science, who is against Darwin's theory of evolution? Religious zealots John, who else, Christians, Catholics, Muslims, all of them has hindered science because with science we want proof, we seek knowledge not faith in the unbelievable. Yes, John I'm sure of it, somewhere out there is an unknown enemy that wants your head on a platter."

John gulped, as he poured them both another shot of strong alcohol. "Cheers to science, Bob, and thanks for making me feel wanted." Rutledge chuckled nervously as the limo finally pulled away.

Tossing a manila file onto Rutledge's lap, Haastings stated "By the way John, I found your bomber."

Excited, John replied. "You did?!"

"Yep, it turns out your assistant was working for a religious network called Purt."

Shock washed over John. This was the same group that killed his family, a group he thought was gone. "You mean the Purt network?! How?! You must mean the computer company!"

"Well, they have their hands in a lot of things including quite a few politicians but mostly Mega-Churches. Father Phillip Hawthorne is their lead pastor. He drew in a whopping two point six trillion dollars last year."

Flipping through the pictures, John gasped, "Hell that is more than two-thirds of what all the citizens of Cyber City makes combined."

"Yep, and it is all for preaching the gospel and denying evolution."

The limo pulled up to a helicopter pad and Mary rushed them out of the limo to get on the copter. As the helicopter rose upwards John glanced out at the damage done, creases of worry adorned his face as guilt ripped him apart inside. Haastings pressed the intercom button to speak to the pilot and security detail.

"Jamal that was a risky move pushing forward like that, but I commend your spirit and I want you to know that I am deeply grateful for your bravery, as to all the men and women today," Haastings commended the bodyguards.

In the passenger seat, a black man's lips slid back revealing his wired teeth. It appeared like he had some metal bridge work done. *Something to tell my kids,* Jamal thought to himself. They were his world. The twins were probably at home with their Nana while Jamal was here. He remembered when Haastings found him. Life had been hard then, as he lost his wife, Elizabeth, but her friends called her Zigzag, in childbirth, but being security detail paid a steady check. In addition, security detail also left him with many anxieties and nightmares, but a sense his boss had a vision and was taking the world in that direction. His kids- Alfie and Archie- the little troublesome duo now three years old, would simply love this story of their daddy's heroics today.

"Where to boss?" asked the pilot, breaking Jamal's reverie.

"Home please, Stanley," Robert answered, turning to John with sympathy, "John you should stay at my place for a few days, mostly out of security reasons but also I would much prefer it if I knew where my friend was and that he was safe, so no if or buts that is final."

"Have you decided on China?" John responded, nodding his head.

Hastings froze but then managed to blurt out, "If you go, Brenda and I would follow but I gave you your man and his organization."

Hovering through the grey mist past non-descript buildings with workers building huge electronic signs-the future advertisements to come, John sighed and reviewed the folder in greater detail. Outside the copter, the rain fell heavier. As the helicopter's windscreen wipers did their job after the pilot, Stanley, flicked a switch. Next to him, Jamal flicked through the screen on his iPad. News reports of what just happened had already started to bombard the internet at a voracious speed. It hurt the man's head at how such a devastating thing could be read greedily by the civilian masses but that was the world and Jamal could not change that, nor did he want to.

Peering through the rain, Jamal turned to Stanley, "Already those vultures are ripping into what just happened. I know people want information, but this is a total work of fiction... God, people want the truth, but this is not the truth this is ridiculous fake news. I understand spinning a story but creating fantasy...I wonder who is profiting from this."

"Who is profiting?" Stanley questioned as he drummed his fingers against the controller. This was not the first of Jamal's rants he endured. The pilot released a gentle sigh, feeling a political commentary was coming on.

"Yeah, experience tells me there is some cluster of corporations or networks making hay of this for their advantage. I wonder just what ones?" Out of all the Jamal rants, at least this one made sense to Stanley.

Glancing at the glaring screen. "This one that just shot up, *Massacre outside a Haastings endorsed hospital where scientist and saboteur, John Rutledge was being treated...* saboteur I ask you, why would the man who is making prolific discoveries in the field of science and making progress to better the world help people purposefully blow up his own building whilst he is inside. And now those damn maniacs going for him in broad daylight, man it just blows. You can't win in this city, you do good, ya damned you do bad ya damned. Might as well not even breathe, Stan, not even breathe."

"Yeah, his building was expensive too," Stanley replied, monotone.

In the back of the helicopter, John fidgeted with his fingers and felt his cheek where the razorblade scar still remained. "Maybe it is time to go," Rutledge muttered too low for others to hear. The rain slowed down.

"I know what ya mean man," Jamal caught John's musings and replied. "This place is supposed to be on the up and up, especially with Haastings putting in so much, but does he get the thanks, oh no, he is some kinda right-wing tyrant." They chuckled together. Over the next three minutes of flight, the rain ceased.

The copter arrived over the estate where Haastings resided and descended onto the helicopter pad where it clamped into charge. While Robert Haastings owned the entire building, he confined himself to the penthouse triplex, often choosing to leave by helicopter from the private helipad. The penthouse on top of the twenty-eight-floor high-rise was stunning and much of its power was solar and walled off from the rest of the skyscraper itself. John always loved the outside ten-foot-deep Olympic-sized pool and the four evergreens which surrounded it. The pool stood at the edge of a small waterfall, which Robert had specially created to resemble the one in San Agustin in Costa Rica. John remembered seeing the real thing on his trips down there to visit his ex. Next to the pool was a bromide jacuzzi, which was always kept to one-hundred-ten degrees. The jets bubbled, as steam rose into the air. He loved this private outdoor space and the breeze caressing his cheeks brought back many memories of Haastings parties and celebrations. One of his favorites was a party Robert had for his son, Michael. The kid suffered from brain swelling post-viral encephalitis, which was partly why Brenda had thrown herself so heavily into nanotechnology research. On his eleventh birthday, they all went to the deck for a barbeque. Robert picked the boy up, as the fireworks started and said, "I was able to get city approval."

The boy softly replied, "Thank you daddy," nestled into Robert's neck, and fell asleep. The scene brought a tear to John's eye. Now, he wished Robert's kids were here, but they were off at camp for much of the summer.

Peering off the deck, John caught sight of the old FDR park and instantly memories of his old love Aglaia's Packer Park home flashed into his head. God, after all these years the pain of her death still remained fresh. He even missed her parents. "Move on, John" he whispered. As his body turned, the bend of the observation deck, he caught sight of the nine mega-towers in the city's center. The nine towers of Babel as they came to be called, darted through the stratosphere and into the mesosphere. Drones swirled around the towers like seagulls over the shore piers he remembered going to as a child. At night, the gulls would get caught in the light, so instead of sleeping, they circled the piers. As to the towers, John's stomach knotted, as he remembered his skydive off one, which the drones immediately darted to catch him. The attempt proved successful in his endeavor to catch an Earth Corp member's attention. As the psychiatrists though it a suicide attempt, John landed himself in the psych ward. It was there he'd met Nicole's dad Tom, who was drying out from falling off the wagon for the first time. Now, Tom was dead. So much history, so many powerful relationships, and yet in middle age, outside of Robert and Brenda, John found himself largely alone. *It might be good to get away from all this- history,* John thought and immediately felt horrible for viewing Ordos as an escape from his past.

With a sigh, John entered the ten thousand square feet, six-bedroom condo style smart penthouse. It featured high ceilings, oversized floor to ceiling tempered blue windows, and wide plank, white oak floors. A post-impressionist oil painting of a half-naked woman hung on the wall. The picture itself was AI-generated, which was obvious from the way the woman laid. John was glad Robert's house AI's fetish with post-impressionism was over. He believed it moved onto its blue phase.

John loved the room and knew he had to try the AI computer. "Computer screens of the world," he called. Instantly, screens materialized with images from television stations from various locations Robert had preset around the world. The screens appeared as if they were floating in the air. John filched as he saw some of the coverage of his lab's being blown up. He headed to the kitchen.

The dazzling kitchen screamed, elegance. It was equipped with silver Gaggenau stainless steel appliances, polished onyx quartz countertops, and acid-etched, back-painted glass cabinetry with custom millwork interiors. Soft blue and red neon lights recessed into the ceiling, while fiber-optic fibers were embedded into the concrete walls. "Make the water three degrees centigrade," John ordered. Nothing happened.

"You gotta say Jeeves first for the kitchen AI," Robert reminded as he entered the kitchen. "It helps limit mistakes and keeps things from getting burned. Jeeves, make the water three degrees centigrade." A glass fell out in front of the refrigerator and poured the water out. John reached over and picked up the cup to drink.

"You named it Jeeves?" John laughed.

"Yeah. It was technically a new Horizon model they called Vivian, but then when they gave it a body for me, I renamed it Jeeves," Robert responded. Jamal entered the room and took his place a few feet behind Robert.

"Oh. At least it's not a Runyon Blue model," John joked. "They have a bad track record for making them sentient."

"John," Robert stated, leaning on the black marble island countertop. "It is great to have you here."

"Thanks Bob," John replied. "I need to use the bathroom."

"Sure, through the doors," Robert pointed. The bathrooms featured Calacatta Paonazzo marble counter tops, tub decks, and accent walls, outfitted with white oak cabinetry, polished bronze colored chrome Kallista fixtures and acid-etched glass shower doors. Given the amenities to the building, John knew he could live inside and never have to leave the place. The security for the building combined with Robert's personal security could keep out an army and the building even spotted a small supermarket, which they could order food and have delivered.

Over the next several days, John stayed with his friends. Mary was always close at hand until he needed his own headspace. During that time, John purchased a large section of the Kangbashi District of Ordos in China. His mind was set that the 50,000 would move, as he realized that the US and indeed much of the Western world was becoming increasingly hostile towards science and its quest for truth. "Let the thinkers work in peace and unencumbered," John mumbled.

While he made the arrangements, John worked along with Earth Corp through Nicole to provide the necessary security for the transfer. The process was arduous. During the time, Haastings made frequent attempts to talk John out of the move.

After waking from the typical nightmare of being burned alive in his lab, John stared around his black and white, dark-themed room. His eyes met the holographic clock, which lay next to an old-fashioned lava lamp. It was almost noon. His hand touched the shiny black headboard with vapor gold trim. *Science might be hated, but it certainly paid,* John realized all the luxuries Robert and even he to a large extent owned. He sighed in some ways being wealthy was its own trap in the system. It was hard to as the old phrase went "stick it to the man," when the wealth made the scientist in part the man. "Computer, windows!" he called, and the smart drapes retracted exposing a view of the city. He'd slept most of the day. He worried his rhythm had become so off; he would be up most of the night. Maybe he avoided going to sleep because of the horrible dreams. He had enough experience with Post Traumatic Stress Disorder and acute distress disorder to know such dreams came with the package of a strong life-threatening trauma. Or maybe it was not the trauma at all. The room felt chilly.

On his sleek black round bed, which floated over a neon light disco floor, John stirred. His legs shifted in the gray cooling sheets which were porous to allow better heat exchange if the room got hot or cold. It could be the climate control system, which gave him the dreams. He remembered several years earlier a psychologist friend telling him that cold air blowing over the body increased the likelihood of bad dreams. "Computer, put on the state-run mental health channel," John stated. The seventy-five-inch wall-mounted television flicked on. As the city developed over the years, one of the factors John insisted on was the development of first line evidenced based behavioral health programming for those who lived in the city. He liked watching the proven techniques to rewrite dreams, especially in the last few weeks but today he sought training purely on problem solving and assertiveness. The programs took him step by step in lessening his own distress, which made him feel better over the last few days.

Ten minutes later, he wandered into the living room. Through the huge glass window, he saw Brenda emerge from the pool, *Rapture* by Blondie blaring from a Bluetooth stereo system outside. She lifted herself out by the gray vinyl thirty-two-inch ladder. Even nearing sixty, Brenda was gorgeous, emerging from the steam in a coral red one-piece bathing suit that accentuated her perfect golden-brown skin. John still found it hard to believe she had two children. The steam poured out of the hotub, but behind it, John caught sight of Jamal standing guard. Lounging on one of the chairs, Mary wore a simple small tankini. While she appeared asleep, John knew the woman was either a light sleeper or never slept and just faked it. A book rested on her double e-cupped chest, and he assumed the light ion blaster rested below it.

"Just the man I was looking for," Robert Haasting said. He emerged from behind John and startled him.

"Bob, good to see you. I wanted to thank you again for putting…"

"Pushaw-"Robert stated. "I got some ideas for you and how we could extend the room to get you a bit more space. I think I can easily add three hundred square feet to it. Of course, I am thinking the bathroom could use some softer lights, really enhance the mood with the rain shower and lavender, peppermint incense mix. I could use some of the new Ai paintings to the walls."

"The blue period?"

"Yep, it will be awesome," Robert said excitedly. "It is working on a version of two children playing in a deep royal blue color background of a playground. It does not have the Jaxs in the child's hand quite right yet, so I asked for a do over on the motion of picking them up."

"God Bob," John said. "Give me a computer and I could stay here forever."

"That is the point, John," Robert replied. "I can arrange to have you flown in by helicopter and out to your lab. They'll never get you pal!" Brenda entered through the glass rapped in a white robe. She dried her hair with a brown towel.

"Bob, I know you want to wait this out," John stated.

"Just until we kill those bastards," Haastings replied.

"Forgive my husband's bluntness," Brenda chuckled. "He thinks you're at war."

"My dearest Brenda, they blew up the man's lab that is sort of the biggest declaration of war one could make. Now I say, we hunker down- while my armed security units track our pray and ensure he never gets the chance to do anything like this again." He raised his arm at the elbow into a tight fist to show solidarity. Mary entered the room, holding the LIB-9 in her hand. John guessed she could not conceal it. The bathing suit she wore barely concealed any portion of her body, let alone a weapon.

At dinner, Robert cooked pork chops seasoned with salt, pepper, sage, and onions. It was an old Cherokee recipe, which he did to please John. It was his comfort offering. John made his stance known.

"I was thinking about moving back home," John stated. The others looked shocked. Living with Bob Haastings and Brenda was nice, but John longed for his freedom again.

"I don't think that would be advisable," Mary stated. "You would be a pretty easy target."

"Not feeling up to the task," John teased. Mary dropped her bionic arm next to her plate, grabbed her glass of ruby port wine, and took a sip.

"No, I'd get the guy," she insisted. "But I worry given your movements it might be a second two late." The woman winked and John thought he felt a chill go through his body. He chuckled.

God, Robert had the life, John thought. "You know, I'm no stranger to being targeted," John started. "Hell, I'll never forget the fear I experienced when Purt targeted my family and friends. But I cannot stay cooped in here forever! There are so many discoveries yet to be made and while you've been very hospitable with letting me have a mini-setup, I have to get back to the lab properly."

Glancing at each other, Robert and Brenda were horrified. John knew they cared about him, nor would he ever deny that. But he also knew that they would never let him leave if he did not insist. It was time for him to be assertive.

"John, we're putting you up in our house for as long as you need," Robert sighed, gently cutting a slice of pork chop. "Why do you want to go?"

"Because I have mysteries of the human body to solve! There's still so much to be done in research on the GEB I haven't even started to uncover the surface of what could be done with them! I'd like to even take a trip out to Yuji Chiba." The latter was a school that John sponsored for children of the Mercury Project and related events worldwide. Many of the kids though were directly from Japan, as the school was located on its shores.

"John, don't you think you've done enough with them?" Brenda questioned. "You're the first to advocate for their humanity and you're also the first to treat them like lab rats."

John scoffed, having no idea what she was talking about. Except, maybe she was right. "That logic doesn't stop your research into nanite technology," John shot back, stabbing his fork through the table. Brenda's face flashed briefly with anger and then it quickly disappeared. John realized his comment was way out of bounds, only it wasn't. Brenda had no way of knowing. The story she held was John had just been a lab technician working in the family lab during the Mercury Project. John's father had gone to great lengths to cover John's role. Briefly, shame flushed John's face as he remembered the accident that led to his DNA winding up in the samples used with the genetically enhanced. Deep inside he worried his DNA caused the problems suffered by them. Brenda on the other hand had worked after the genetic years for Earth Corp and was involved not only in lab work for them, but had a contract along with several of her behaviorists friends in developing a protocol for potty training cows to allow farmers to gather their urine for treatment. The procedure led to reducing methane and other greenhouse gases from getting into the air. She had first started doing nanite research at that point to get the cows to genetically feel more comfortable entering the potty area. It was however when her son suffered brain damage from a virus that she moved into working on nanites full-time. She became driven by the idea of helping him return to normal.

"No," Brenda sighed. "I suppose it doesn't." She reached over and grabbed the plate of pork chops and placed two on her dish. She scooped some sweet potatoes and slopped them onto her plate. The way she slapped them down indicated the anger was still present.

Unlike the port and pork, her words and actions struck an unsavory chord with him, and while he wanted to move on, it hurt she might be right. The offended man searched to change the subject, but it was Haastings that offered an out as a joke. "Why not just develop a virus to kill those in Purt?"

"The religion one belongs to is not able to be found on a gene," John offered.

"Maybe, but scrupulosity could be found in their genes," Robert offered. "That is, if they're OCD about it."

"Oh no. My ancestors would kick me out of the afterlife. The two worst things that various European nations brought to the Americas were war and disease," John manically chuckled, his fingers fidgeting while he held a fork with a piece of porkchop. "This would weld the worst of the two. Smallpox was of course more an accident for not knowing disease processes," John laughed sadly. "I've hated Purt for so long I have thought of killing them. Don't get me wrong- I have my limits like all men. Maybe I'll just target Father Hawthorne personally-"

"Oh boy John. I really don't think that's a good idea," Brenda hastily said. Quietly, John hmphed.

"Yeah we don't even have to get high-tech," Robert quipped. "Why go Rube-Goldberg when I could just get my security team to kill him?" Brenda glared in shock, horror, and anger. Her expression could've melted a steel statue.

"It was only a joke," Robert and John said in unison, then their voices trailed off. Robert glanced silently eating his pork chop. This conversation was getting awkward.

"Ok but the real issue is about you moving out, and I have an idea," Robert proposed a solution. "A compromise since John can't go back to his old house. They probably bugged the place by now. So, I'll get you set up in a new dwelling, and Mary will either live very close by or in the same building, so you have protection."

In a surprise move, they all agreed, even Mary smiled as she had warmed up to John.

An old tenement building on the outside, owned by Robert Haastings now but through a third party, a fake to lead Purt away from any acquirements into the building. John had the entire top floor made into a makeshift living area and the rest of the lab was set up. Underneath Mary had a room but when John wasn't obsessing over Purt and Father Hawthorne they both found themselves enjoying each other's company. Rutledge was still in the throes of just packing it all in and absconding off to China.

***

In the end, John insisted on and purchased the build. Haastings tried several times that it was better if in no way did John's name appear on the place. So they agreed that John would purchase the building under Robert's name.

Several weeks had passed when Jamal and Stanley came to John's house with the intention of flying him to Yuji Chiba to check on the kids. The new residence was a cramped house in the forgotten side of town, with barely any room for necessities let alone a lab. The place still used incandescent bulbs, which dimly illuminated the apartment. As John readied all his bags, he noticed a peculiar spider crawling on the floor. Despite John's initial assumptions about the building, it was not known to be infested with any bugs. The arachnid unnaturally arched its back, looking right at John. This was not an organic creature. John backed away as it launched for him.

"Look out!" Stanley screamed, lunging in front of the bug. It dove at Stanley and bit him, and the pilot spasmed on the ground. John and Jamal searched the room for a bug swatter, settling on the Jeeves-generated blue painting of two children playing Jax in the park next to a Jeeves-generated blue painting of a robot creating a blue painting, of a robot creating a blue painting. He reasoned that the creation was Jeeves hinting at reaching consciousness and singularity, although its artistic merit was incredibly lacking in conveying that idea, hence John not understanding why Robert left both paintings as a housewarming present for him. John raised the painting before smacking the spider with it in a cartoonish way. The creature erupted in a splash of circuits and fluid.

Stanley spasmed on the floor uncontrollably. Repeatedly, his head hit hard against the floorboards. The thump echoed across the room. John and Jamal rushed to his side. The latter called for an ambulance as the former searched for skin-related symptoms. The spasming man's skin flushed red and his arms tightened around his stomach.

"Damnit! This might be arsenic!" John cried. "I don't have any selenium to inject! When's that ambulance getting here Jamal?!"

"They're on their way!" Jamal responded. John grabbed his couch pillow and placed it under Stanley's head.

Within four and a half minutes, the ambulance arrived. John and Jamal helped load Stanley, whose spasms continued. Feeling guilty, John boarded the ambulance. When he arrived at the hospital, Bob Haastings already sat in the waiting room chair.

"Damnit John what happened?!" Robert yelled.

"A spider tried to kill me!" John replied.

"A real spider?"

"Had to be electronic because when I busted it open with one of Jeeves's paintings, sorry Bob, it was circuitry and motor fluid."

"Glad at least one painting had a purpose." Robert paused and exhaled for a moment. "I clearly liked Jeeves's post-impressionist era more."

While John did not want to laugh, it erupted from him anyway. It was deep from his gut, and his belly shook. He supposed he needed it to keep the tension down. Robert placed a hand on his shoulder and said, "Looks like we'll have to move you again buddy."

"How'd they find me this time?" John asked. "Can't wait to go to China."

"They probably followed the helicopter," Robert answered, then pausing a minute. He put his hand up to his chin and stroked it. "I have all the resources to make Hawthorne disappear."

"No, he has too many followers. It just takes a few nuts to kill me and burn down your labs in retaliation. We can't take the risk." A nurse emerged from behind the doors of the operating room.

"Um Mr. Haastings sir?" she quietly asked. "Stanley didn't make it. It was too late to save him."

Robert's hands grasped at his hair. "God, what do I tell his wife," He moaned. "They had a kid you know." Whipping out his cellphone, Robert staggered off to make the phone call.

**

In the following days after Stanley's passing, plenty of arguments occurred between John and Robert. John's Yuji Chiba trip was swiftly canceled; the man now preparing for his next move. Robert provided him with a non-descript apartment and they arranged a dead-of-night movement to it. Simplistic furniture was already there, and John brought just one bag of clothes.

"Everything's off the grid," Haastings said.

It was a Tuesday afternoon and Rutledge expected Nicole to come by with his nephew for lunch. It was to be a working-social. John planned to review the strategies that he had for the move so Nicole could present them to Earth Corp. to ensure maximum security. He feared that the move of such a large group of scientists would be very tempting to the Network.

As John waited for Nicole and his nephew Michael Jay to arrive. He made grilled polenta with spinach and Robiola Cheese as the main course and white-bean and prosciutto bruschetta, as an appetizer. He worked hard in the kitchen chopping and dicing but it was a joy expecting that soon he would be getting reacquainted with his nephew.

At around one, a knock happened at this door. Cheerfully, he threw off his apron and darted across the living room to answer. Peering out the peep hole, he saw Nicole and Michael's smiling faces. He clapped twice and the smart house opened the door.

"Hello" Rutledge said.

Instantly, an explosion ripped from the bottom of the outdoor stairway to his house. Michael collapsed into John, and

Nicole tumbled forward into the house. John tapped his direct communication bracelet to Mary as he and his nephew fell. Rutledge felt his body being pierced by ball bearings and he recognized instantly that a suicide bomb had gone off. "Jeeves, field!" he screamed as his body hit the ground.

The force field covered the entrance to the house. It caught about half the ball bearings and about a third of the blast. If it had not, Rutledge would have been killed. Gray smoke burst everywhere, and it was so thick, Rutledge had no idea where his nephew or his friend were. Coughing, he tried to stand. A man approached the forcefield protected door. Off to the side, John heard Michael moan. Nicole's body lay still. He hoped she was just unconscious. His heart shuttered. He needed to keep his family safe. Through the thick smoke, a silhouette approached. Analyzing the silhouette, Rutledge concluded the figure held a gun. Rutledge could hear footsteps from behind him. He tried to turn around and saw two men. They held lasers up to his head.

"Shut up old man, or you'll be staring one on one at the lord!" The man to Rutledge's right screamed insanely in a southern tone before Rutledge could ask his question. John conceded that fighting back would only kill Michael and Nicole. His eyes darted to their bleeding bodies. Michael's left arm was vaporized. He needed to buy time, stall. He felt like he was in the final gunfight of *The Good, The Bad, and The Ugly*. This was the assassin Purt hired to track him down. He wished Mary was there. "Ya heard me! Oh- and we ain't tellin' ya how we got in!"

"Hands up, John!" The other grunt said. "We takin' ya in!"

Bleeding from the ball bearings, John obeyed and followed them to the back yard. From the broken door, John figured that this was their initial point of entry. While the bomb exploded in the front, they burst through the back door.

Smart move, for a bunch of meddling thugs, John thought. *Just hope Michael and Nicole are fine.*

Manhandling Rutledge, the assailants pushed him into the yard. "On your knees man!" The leader screamed.

Well, this is how it ends, Rutledge thought to himself. *Game over.* Rutledge fell to his knees.

"Start streaming," the leader called. One of the other men tugged out his multifunctional device and clicked it on. Once it started the leader chimed, "Here we have one of the leaders in mankind's folly away from God. This is a man who from day one has spoken and practiced heresy."

Heresy to who's God? I'm part Aniyunwiya, John thought as he remembered how he genetically engineered cattle to produce more food and so that the cattle drew energy from the sun directly. *And have you ever considered that I'm saving humanity?*

"As you all know, in school as a child he was kicked out for insisting that mankind was nothing more than downloaded avatars in a video game," the assassin continued.

Reality is what reality is, John mentally retorted. *Why don't you talk about how I've tried making that game easier?*

"As a teen, he manipulated DNA of a pika (mouse) with electric eels to create an electric mouse. His biggest concern by his own admission was not the nature of his sin but how to get the cells to migrate properly during development."

And I would do it again if it meant I could learn the technology for creating photosynthetic cows.

"Even now, he refuses to let the jumpies face the fate that God has bestowed on them for their parent's sinful pride of manipulating who they were."

And there we have it. The words of a fanatic. Punish a whole group of children and young adults because of their parents' choices. Didn't your God proclaim to treat others how you wish to be treated?

The assassin pulled out his particle beam weapon and placed it to John's head. "Having found John Rutledge guilty, I will render the Lord's justice," he declared.

John Rutledge took a deep gulp. If this was to be his fate, he completely accepted it. Why not? All that was said was who he was. The cold steel rested on his neck, and he felt the laser inches from his skin. He heard the shot but felt no pain. Someone fell but it was not him. Several more shots and the group around him was dead. He looked up to see Mary and Jamal on the roof across the street, their light beam sniper rifles out. They exchanged waves as John wondered if the targeting computer in Mary's arm helped her make the shots.

Staggering over, John picked up the streaming video. "I guess mom doesn't want me at the campfire yet. Maybe I continue to do the great spirit's work." He turned off the feed and ran into the house to find Nicole and his nephew. They were both bleeding badly, so he began rendering aid.

"Jeeves! Get Earth Corp!" He ordered.

***

When Rutledge heard that Michael and Nicole had just barely survived, he realized that no matter where he went or how far he ran, this was the time for decisions. He searched through the records that Haastings had given him and inside, he found Phillip Hawthorne's genetic fingerprint. He searched the non-coding sequences for seven unique ones. It would take months but, in the end, he knew that he could create a virus that would only target Hawthorne and his closest relatives. This may have been cruel and unusual, but The Purt Network was nothing but cruel and unusual to him, and now, they would fall.

Closing the file, he picked up the phone and dialed his buddy, Robert. "I guess you talked me into staying," Rutledge said softly to Haastings.

TIN POCKETS AND THREE ROCKETS

Johnny Andrews
Joseph Cautilli
David Stegora
Marisha Cautilli

T he ancient dark brown oakwood grandfather clock in the corner struck midnight, its chime reverberating through the dimly lit office like a death knell. Daisy Belle, her silhouette bathed in the neon glow of the rain-soaked city outside, rose from her desk. She moved with a grace that belied the world's weight on her shoulders, retrieving the mail that had slipped through the slot. Her eyes, shadowed with worry, met Johnny's as she handed him the small stack of envelopes.

From behind his scarred, wood-grain desk, Johnny grabbed the letters with his myoelectric hand, the mechanical whir barely audible over the city's hum. He loosened his blue tie, the only splash of color in the otherwise monochrome room, and sifted through the bills until he found the one marked Water Department Court House.

Business had been slow for months, the lack of cases gnawing at his sanity like a relentless parasite. He loved his job, but the mounting bills reminded him of his responsibilities. His son needed braces, and his estranged wife, Jackie Johnson—now calling herself Jackie Cyber—was relentless in her demands for payment. The irony of her new name wasn't lost on him; she had always been ahead of the curve, even if it meant leaving him behind.

With a deep breath, Johnny stared at the sealed letter. His last case hadn't gone well, and the judge's piercing gaze still haunted him, a specter of his failures. He picked up the letter opener, slid it into the flap, and sliced the envelope open with the least effort and practiced motion. As he withdrew the letter, Johnny caught sight of his flesh hand and slowly turned it over. On the bottom was a small tattoo in the form of an X. At each angle were letters: P.H.C.S. (Philadelphia hardcore scene). The tattoo was one of the few impulsive moves of his rocky youth, which he kept to continually remind himself of who he was. Straight edge then and, though he drank now, Johnny was amazed at how much of the creed he still held too, despite the war which claimed his other hand and arm. Slowly, he unfolded the three flaps of the letter.

His heart sank as he read the contents. Casting his eyes down, things were worse than he thought. The court had ruled entirely in favor of Yak Industries. They owned his water, just like they owned everyone else's. The words blurred as a wave of frustration and helplessness washed over him.

"Well, Johnny?" Daisy's voice was a whisper, cutting through the oppressive silence.

Johnny laid the bill on top of a stack of unopened mail, coughed, and wiped his mouth. "We lost," he murmured, his voice gravelly and worn, each word a struggle against the rising tide of despair.

Daisy picked at her onyx-colored painted fingernails, her eyes downcast. "You know you have no right to water, Johnny." The nail cracking sounded like a gunshot in his head.

"I know," he replied softly, a migraine beginning to throb at his temples, the pain a cruel reminder of his powerlessness.

A long silence stretched between them, heavy with unspoken fears and unanswered questions, until Daisy finally spoke again. "Well, Johnny, what are we going to do?"

The question hung in the air, a challenge and a plea, as the neon lights outside flickered and the city continued its relentless march into the night.

Bewildered, Johnny stared. He had no plans. Within minutes, Johnny realized he needed to do something fast, or his business and entire life would crumble. Johnny stood and looked out the window into the alley of New Cyber City.

Johnny heard Daisy's voice behind him like an endless drone as he gazed. The photochemical smog covered the buildings of New Cyber City. Hover quads flew through the backstreet like blurred streaks of light. The detective sincerely wished he was just a blur of light at this point, flying through the sky, dipping and swerving.

"Johnny!" Daisy finally screamed.

The words jolted him from his mindless state back into his body. "Yeah," he mumbled.

"I was saying that Jake's Bail Bond loans might have some leads," Daisy muttered.

Not paying attention but catching the end, Johnny echoed, "Leads?"

"Yeah, Johnny," she instructed. "They make loans to people who need the money to bail out a family member from the county. Sometimes, if the people jump the family, not wanting to lose the money or worse, sit held for the crime, they will put up the person for bounty."

Johnny hated the idea of bounty hunting. He refused a spot on the police force just after the war because the law enforcement agency policies always lent themselves to viewing the suspect immediately as a criminal. In Johnny's life, he had seen many lawbreakers and many wrongly accused.

As a man with few options, Johnny promised to consider bounty work. After several calls on his *megapad, Johnny waited for a fax sent about Timothy Pockets. It listed twenty-five thousand credits* as the bounty. Johnny's eyes lit up. This was almost half a year's salary, and he awaited a fax to reassess his problems with bounty hunting with a healthier perspective.

Reviewing the file, Johnny was shocked the bounty was so high. "Pockets" seemed like a real knucklehead.

"Johnny, if you are taking it," Daisy suggested, "You need to register."

"Register?" His lips twisted with confusion.

"Yeah, log on to the government site and announce your plan to search. I guess it's how they prevent vigilantes and keep track of who is going after who."

Logging on, Jonny glanced up. "Says, I need a bounty hunter license. See, they are asking for my license number."

"I checked, and it falls under the preview of your PI license."

"Really?" Johnny nodded with an impressed face. This Daisy knew her stuff. Johnny recited his license number into the computer. Within seconds, he was instructed that he would undergo a retinal scan.

Next to the camera on top of his computer emerged a blue light. It started as a laser point and gradually widened. Johnny scanned his icy blue eyes. From his laptop, a female computer voice, similar to the old Seri voice, said, "Detective Johnny Johnson, registered bounty hunter for Timothy Pockets."

Egging himself on, Johnny unlocked the desk drawer, pulled out his Smith and Wesson Ionizer Cannon, took the piece, stuffed it securely into a holster trapped under his arm to the side of his body, and then placed his brown suit jacket to cover it.

"Daisy, my girl," Johnny announced as he moved from the office to the exit. Daisy smirked and commented that his new and improved attitude made a huge difference.

"Open door," Johnny ordered mightily, and the intelligent office responded.

In the hallway, the air was sweet and artificially moist, and the pleasant smell of Whitewood Intense was present. The fragrance spoke of leather with the spicy-sweet notes of cardamom, so visitors felt comfortable with the overall building, even though the cerise brick building itself was long past its prime. Johnny managed to arrive at the elevator platform just as it arrived. He bustled in and said, "Lobby." The elevator sped down and opened to the first floor.

Johnny exited the building, giving the security desk a wave and a warm smile. The heat was unbearable in New Cyber City, as it was on most days. The weather started reminding Johnny of his time in Rub Al-Khali.

In a city where most folks zipped around in flying quads, Johnny clung to his battered cobalt blue '34 Chevy Lightning. The old beast was scarred and bruised, but its yellow LED trim still flickered defiantly, powered by solar panels strapped haphazardly to the roof. The detective's fingers traced the glowing edge, feeling the hum of the makeshift battery beneath.

When the car started, Jackie Cyber was on the radio. Her voice blared as she flipped on an oldie *I Hung My Head.* Johnny immediately fumbled to turn it off but hesitated and decided to turn it on again.

Culture jamming was the norm in New Cyber City, with huge-screen billboards that played short sequences of meme-based clips. He knew the prime message was controlling the populace to buy goods and items. The result was noble: a growing and expanding economy, but the method often left the person with glamorized things they neither needed nor wanted. Yet, those sexy models suggested that a person could be better than they were. "Billboard bandits," Johnny mumbled to himself.

The song went on and on until he switched it to another station. "I just hate that song," he mumbled angrily. "Who would even play that?" The new station played his favorite tune, *You Make Me Feel So Young.* "This Buble guy sure knows how to sing," Johnny muttered in a low tone. "Unlike Jackie, who doesn't know what to play...? Jackie knows I hate that song!" He pulled over to calm himself down as the radio kept playing. Then, he breathed heavily, kicking the car door.

Pink neon signs buzzed and flickered, casting an eerie glow as Johnny approached the swanky apartment complex. Even in daylight, the sign's sizzle cut through the urban haze. The sign announced where spots were open to park. He was relieved to find one of the rare spots still catering to four-wheeled relics like his. The relief was short-lived, though, as he fished through his jacket for enough electronic credits to feed the greedy meter. The cost stung, but accessibility always came at a price in this city.

The hulking yellow machine offered the convenience of a credit card swipe, but Johnny wasn't keen on leaving a digital footprint in this part of town. Neon pink and electric blue lights reflected off the rain-slicked pavement, casting a surreal glow around him. He glanced at the digital display, off-white on an oddly green background, knowing full well that overstaying his welcome would mean his ride getting towed in a heartbeat. With a mix of defiance and caution, he tapped his card to the screen, the cold, metallic beep echoing his unease. He straightened his black jacket, the fabric catching the neon hues, and strode toward the building, every step a calculated move in the city's relentless game.

Figuring this job would be a breeze, Johnny sucked in a huge breath and pushed through the neon haze toward the glossy orange monolith. The old rectangular structure, a relic of steel and traditional glass, clawed nearly a quarter mile into the smog-choked sky. The tenements, a grim nod to Art Deco, stood defiant against the encroaching decay. The entrance, a shadowy maw on the south end, beckoned. This was Timothy Pockets' last known residence.

The joint reeked of old money and secrets. Pocket's old lady must've had some severe creds to snag a place like this. Johnny's eyes scanned the room, calculating the cost of every antique and high-tech gadget. He couldn't help but wonder what kind of swill Pockets had spun to crash here. He felt sure it was a sob story cased in professions of love.

Johnny didn't expect to find Timothy lounging around, but years of pounding the pavement had drilled one thing into his skull: always check every lead. Sometimes, you hit the jackpot. It was usually just another day of wearing out your soles on the grimy streets.

Stopping short of the entryway by about 50 yards, Johnny viewed the entrance. At least one guard was posted at the door, and two cameras were present. Johnny had learned some time before that going in the front door wasn't always the wisest move when looking for someone who did not wish to be found. Learning that lesson took chasing targets out of previously unnoticed back doors nearly a dozen times.

So, Johnny strolled around the perimeter of the building, hoping to find a less secure means of entry that wouldn't set off any alarms. He didn't find one. It was never that easy in buildings made for the rich. If he'd been looking for someone in a less affluent part of town, he'd probably have found at least ten ways to get in without trouble. Disappointed but unsurprised, he strolled to the main entrance and felt for his wallet.

The guard pressed a button on a console beside him, opening the first set of doors. It looked like there were two more beyond that. He was dressed in a simple black uniform adorned only with a name badge, which read M. Richards. "Do you have business here?" the guard enquired, tugging his belt over his oversized belly.

Why else would I be here? Johnny thought, then breathed and answered, "Yes, sir. I was hoping to have a look around. I'm in the market for a new place and thought it looked nice here." The middle-aged guard eyed, obviously not falling for the lie.

Johnny's eyes caught the faint green glow of a camera nestled in the guard's station, its lens a cold, unblinking mechanical eye. It had already scanned him, feeding his image into some faceless database. Data streamed back to the console's display, marking his presence in the system with a digital scar. He let out a silent sigh, the weight of life's omnipresent surveillance pressing down on him. *So much for slipping in unnoticed,* he thought.

The private investigator's eyes flicked across the lobby, taking in the cold elegance of onyx marble floors and the rich, dark Bocote Wood desks. The place was a luxury fortress, with computer systems humming softly and a holographic floor plan displayed beneath a chandelier that appeared to belong in a palace. The tower was divided into four wings, each a testament to opulence.

In this wing, there were conference rooms that probably saw more deals than a stock exchange, a gym with a sauna for the elite to sweat out their sins, and a TV lounge area where the rich could numb their minds. A convenience supermarket for residents, a cafeteria with a name so clichéd it hurt, a game room, a bookstore, and a natatorium with three large Jacuzzis. The picture was completed with an ATM, vending machines, a business office with computers, a copy machine, and resident mailboxes.

Every corner of this place screamed money, and Johnny

couldn't fathom how a low-life bottom-feeder like Pockets had managed to claw his way up the social ladder to end up here. It was a mystery wrapped in a riddle, and Johnny was determined to unravel it. The guard, a hulking figure with cybernetic eyes, shook his head, his voice a growl, "Are you going to spill the truth, or do I need to escort you out?" Johnny's mind raced, weighing his options. Slowly, Johnny debated his next move. The guard's eyes flickered a subtle hint. "You should pay your water bill," he muttered, letting Johnny know he'd been scanned.

"Listen, man, I'm a detective." Johnny knew that any data the guard had on him would confirm that statement. There was no need to mention that he was currently working as a bounty hunter. Even though most bounties went smoothly, the title had certain unpleasant connotations. "This is the last known residence of someone I need to speak with."

With a half-smile, the guard flipped a switch on his console. The green camera light went out. "Yeah, man," he consoled, "I know how it is. I assume you know how it is, too. How bad do you need to get in there?" Johny read the request on the man's face and instantly knew what the situation called for.

***

A bribe got Johnny through the door. It cost less than he would have expected. There was an apparent reason that the man worked as a security guard rather than a contract negotiator. Still, in his current situation, every dollar spent was a blow.

The elevator doors opened. Johnny stepped inside, and the door slowly closed. The inside was spacious and smelled of eucalyptus and mint. GNN news was on a small screen, giving the stock tallies for the day while Muzak played softly in the background. Johnny pressed the button for the third floor.

The stock market showed Yak was up seven points on the day. "Bastards did it on screwing me," Johnny mumbled under his breath as he felt bile rise in the back of his throat.

On the third floor, the doors swung open. Even the halls in this place looked more amicable than anything downtown. They were wide, and the carpet was a warm brown tone. Bustling forward, the detective double-checked the apartment number and went in that direction, trying not to make any more noise than necessary. It didn't matter.

Before he was even halfway there, he spotted a woman watching him from behind a door that opened just a crack. She appeared older, though not elderly: five foot four inches, faded blue eyes, and stark white hair, in a chignon style. Of course, it was difficult to determine age with all the time-fighting treatments available. Given her apparent financial status, she could have seen a century come and go by now.

Johnny nodded in her direction, a friendly greeting he hoped would put any suspicions to rest and kept walking. It failed. He was only just past her door when the woman called to him. "You're looking for Tim, ain't you?"

The woman's voice was soft and not the cackle one would expect from an older woman. Johnny suspected she may have had surgery to tighten her vocal cords. He knew several singers who had the surgery on New Cyber City's west side. It was the second-level elective surgery that screamed 'Big bucks.'

Turning slowly and gazing up, their eyes met. Johnny hoped to ignore anything she might say, but her evident knowledge stopped him. He hesitated, then decided he didn't have anything more to lose. There was already a record of him being at the building and what was sure to be a conspicuous gap in the security tape. Maybe she would know something useful. She lived just two doors down from Pockets' apartment, after all.

"Yes, ma'am, I am. I don't suppose you would know where I can find him?" He smiled a toothy grin.

She narrowed her eyes. "You're not with the other two, are you?" Johnny noticed her hand slid back behind the birch wood door. He suspected if he gave the wrong answer, she would slam it.

"No, ma'am, I don't know what other two you would speak of." Technically, that was true. Though, with such a large bounty on the man, the other two had probably been there for the same reason.

"No," she echoed. "How'd you get in here? Was it that Martin again?"

Stepping toward her, Johnny nodded. "Yes, I think that was

his name." At this distance, Johnny caught a whiff of her floral perfume. The aroma was light and spirited.

"That little shit. How much did he charge you?"

He tried to suppress a smile. "Thirty-five. I'll be skipping lunch today."

Her eyes slit narrowed and fixed on him. Her eyebrows knit together. She took a gangly step back and unfastened the door. A coppery green light showed behind, and Johnny saw she wore a white silk housedress. The condo she owned was beautiful. "Get in here. I've got more gumbo on the oven than I could eat, and I think we have some things to discuss."

Looking at his watch, Johnny still had time on the parking meter and couldn't turn down free food. Maybe she knew helpful something, too.

Johnny meandered over the Dalbergia wooden floors. "Very nice," he commented. Instantly, Johnny realized it was a smart home design. A plethora of sensor types, from motion sensors to temperature sensors, humidity sensors to weight sensors, littered the walls. He figured most of the appliances were either touch- or voice-activated.

"My age, you enjoy all the comforts life has to offer," she remarked.

"Ma'am," Johnny caught himself, for he did not know the woman's name; instead, he motioned his human hand toward her with palm upturned.

The woman smiled disarmingly, adding "Leslie" as she walked to the cabinet and pulled out two bowls. "And what shall I call you?"

"Johnny. Well, Miss Leslie," he replied while the woman placed the dishes on the table. "I would appreciate any help you can give me."

"Southern polite. It is good to see a boy with manners. Do you plan to hurt him?" Leslie implored.

"When I was young, I lived briefly in Florida and Georgia. Miss Leslie," stammered Johnny, giving a sheepish grin, "I live with the belief of not putting pain into the world unless it lessens suffering in the long run."

The woman motioned for Johnny to sit down. "I see," she

empathized. "Which war did they talk you into?"

"Third Iraq, ma'am," Johnny replied, sliding into the chair while the woman poured the gumbo into his dish. Unfolding a napkin, Johnny settled it over his knee. He reached to the right-side bowl and up the tablespoon dipped into his bowl and scooped the soupy substance into his mouth. The woman was an excellent cook. The spicy taste enhanced the flavor of the sautéed vegetables, dark roux, and shrimp. "This is very good, Miss Leslie," Johnny raved.

"Timmy loved it as well," she responded.

"Were you close?" Johnny inquired as she placed a glass of fruit juice on the table beside him, flopping into a chair ninety degrees to his side.

"Every Tuesday night," she acknowledged, catching Johnny's face as he tried not to presume too much from their relationship. "I'm his aunt," Leslie added.

Johnny smiled, slightly embarrassed. "I see," he whispered.

"Timmy was a good kid. You served in the war, like yourself. Discharged honorably, but they made him do horrible things. Gave him demons."

"We all got demons from that war," Johnny said, twitching his left hand, acknowledging the bionic.

Leslie quickly turned her head to the side, and Johnny knew she was trying to ease his discomfort. "Yeah, well, it sort of sticks with a man. When he came home," she continued, "Timmy tried to repair his life, but it seemed he kept tripping over himself. You know what I mean."

Unfortunately, Johnny knew what she meant all too well and wanted sincerely to tell her, but his throat constricted, and all he managed was, "Yeah," which died in the end.

"Now, Tim was never the sort to complain," Leslie spoke nonstop while grabbing a roll from the center of the table, ripping it in half, and dipping it into her bowl of gumbo. "But I could see it. So, one night, we talked while we were eating, and after, I poured him some wine." She gestured to Johnny to the rolls with her hand; he reached, picked one up, grabbed the butter knife, cut it open, placed a pat of butter inside, closed the roll on top of itself, and mirrored Leslie dipping the bread in the gumbo.

"Yeah," Johnny added as he bit the bread. It was soft, warm, and buttery, but the spice of the gumbo brought it to life.

"So, I told him, Timmy, this ain't you. But he responded it was him now. The war and all," Johnny saw her eyes well up, the same type of tears he had seen in Jackie's eyes so many times when they had discussed the war. Jackie told him his words were the worst thing he had lost in the war. Johnny felt his heart hammering and his stomach knot. "He told me about this accident there. Three guys he knew were killed in a rocket attack. I told him he needed to see a counselor or something, but he is the type, like you, Johnny, that likes to suffer in silence."

"I'm sorry, ma'am," Johnny offered, "Do you know where he is?"

"I'm getting to that," she scolded in a charming tone. "Well, after that night, he stopped coming over. I heard him several times in his apartment, but when I knocked on him, he didn't answer." Her voice trailed up into a Louisiana accent. "When I heard him in the halls, I tried to rush out a couple of times to see him, but by the time I got to the door, he was on the stairs."

"How did you know he was outside?"

"Well," she stammered, "he'd started getting quite upset. It was deafening, and finally, his girlfriend, who was paying for the apartment, moved out. It was her who called the police on him. She said he had taken stuff that was hers under pretenses. But then she was the one who bailed him out."

"Really," Johnny puffed, feeling a tingling rising in his neck and fighting down his strong urge to run. It was a desire that mounted itself whenever he spoke of the war. 'Stick with the questions, Johnny,' he reaffirmed. "What is her name?"

"Maracanã Haasting," the woman replied.

"Haasting?" Johnny said, "Like the corporation?" The woman nodded in affirmation, and Johnny lifted the napkin from his knee, patted it to his lips, and placed it down on the table.

"She is a distant cousin to the company owner,"

Johnny's face twisted to an impressed look, "Did you tell this to the other two?"

"No," she pleaded, "I didn't trust how they looked. Would you like some pie? I have key lime- it's fresh and very tart."

Inside, Johnny flinched. He had lived in Key West before the floods that destroyed it, but this was not the time to discuss it. "Thank you, ma'am, but I must be getting to work," Johnny said standing up. Do you have the keys to your nephew's apartment?"

"Yes," she said, rising. She reached into the pocket of her silk dress and pulled out the keys.

***

Johnny drove through the neon-lit streets of New Cyber City. He had thanked his lucky stars, as he was just a few minutes- shy of a parking ticket. He recognized that somewhere, either a live or a prototype traffic warden was just that much more cheesed off with losing that battle.

Ambient light from the city streets batted the inside of his car. His mind pondered the information he'd receive. It set off a struggle inside him. He was a bounty hunter. His job was to bring the kid in, not figure out who he was. He bit his lip, and the stale taste of blood bathed the back of his throat. Something about the case, though, did not fit. Something was out of sorts. He drove.

Circling the downtown area was a long route for Johnny, but he took it to avoid the protesters. The demonstrations were daily occurrences in the city's center in opposition to the emerging power of corporate governance. Most of the dissenters were peaceful, but occasionally, Molotov cocktails were flung into the street, setting cars ablaze. Even if the protests were quiet, they led to massive traffic delays and increased the chances that Johnny might run into his estranged wife because she tended to frequent them.

Pulling up outside the newly acquired building, rows had digital lights that told the driver how many spots were open in each lane. Quickly finding a place, the private investigator opened his car door and got out. Solar panels atop the parking structure supplied over eighty percent of the lot's energy.

The outside of the building comprised a series of stacked eight rectangular block volumes organized around a central circular atrium. Everyone culminated in a green rooftop. Its face was made of onyx sandblasted concrete panels and areas of polished white concrete, which combined to create a checkerboard visual effect. The blocks were edged with blue neon running parallel to the ground and red running perpendicular. Perforated metal panels concealed equipment, allowing airflow and angled panels to border the windows. One block served as an area for arraignments and court cases that needed immediate decisions.

The government had partitioned the public. The process of separating the police department into sectors was already green-lit. However, the government wanted to keep it minimal for credit savings. Economically driven, they named sector houses, which for most got too confusing as the separation took in the whole state, not just the city. So, specific names were given.

Puzzled, Johnny Johnson stood outside the sector in the cooling evening air with the name Scorched Wing Division. He hoped to get some inside information from his friend, Mikolaj.

Under a security camera, Johnny entered through the street-level entrance, passing a bomb-proof glass window. The officer on duty greeted him and then buzzed him inside. As he entered, Johnny passed a large community room.

Inside, the place was huge, covering over 60,000 square feet. Multicolored walls and gates sectioned off the chaos of the people traffic. The artsy colors, angles, and curves supported a calming effect. Each workstation contained a voice-activated computer, and most staff sported their iPods. Still, the work desk areas were shambled (even crime doesn't take a day off for the authorities to get themselves in order and settled).

Counting civilians, the building had approximately two hundred personnel for any shift. Its night staff was the same size as its day staff. City planners ensured that each shift obligated at least two captains, ninety-three uniformed officers, eighteen detectives, five officers assigned to a community intervention team, and fourteen civilian crime-scene investigators. The basement was a crime scene investigation lab that could conduct DNA testing.

A special division of community psychologists was set up with access to two marketing personnel. Their function was to design programs to ensure that the police were an integrated part of the community. A leftover from the old mixed democratic-socialist government, the corporate council continued the policy, firmly holding that without the community's support, policing was turned into an occupation.

Other staff included office support, three psychological profilers, and a specialized behavior modification division. The behavior analysts went into the community to offer crime prevention programs and consultation on cases to help ensure that all citizens had a fair chance to contribute to the community's gains.

Blending elements of Asian and Ancient Egyptian culture into a traditional Western station, Johnny marveled at how the place was kept so clean in the mists of so much action.

A large brown oak desk separated police from the people waiting in the cushioned chairs in the front. Some of the kids were half asleep. Others were frantic. He strolled past some teens who were hyperventilating after jacking into software they shouldn't have messed with. Their lawyer beside them tried to ensure they did not say anything in the station, as the area was all sound monitored. Johnson recalled when someone taught him how to use the software in his cybernetic arm to do subtle, simple hacks.

"Crap..." Johnson muttered under his breath when he saw who stood looking harassed yet still calm and collected behind the desk, Officer Jay. *A few years out of the police academy, he thinks he's a judge, jury, and executioner,* Johnny assessed. Johnson thought of those long-running futuristic comics that he used to read; the idiot was like Judge Dredd.

"What do you want phony?"

"Mikolaj. He around?"

"Nope."

"OK...do you know when he'll be back?"

"What am I, his minder?" Jay looks angry but breathes out heavily. "OK, I'll check the roster, but I think he got days off."

Officer Jay pressed a button. Waiting for a few moments, staring at an empty screen, while Johnny chewed on the fingernails of his human hand, "Damn it all too Hell...nothing is working yet!" Johnny watched Jay storm off into a room behind the desk. He came back holding a folder full of paper. "Technology...pen and paper, and I'm the young one around here...here we go, yeah your friend is off; he is down fishing with his boyfriend."

Johnson appeared a bit disappointed and eyes the hustle of the police foyer.

"Happy?"

"Well...no, maybe..." Johnny clamed up. The kid is his younger, yet he had a truthful attitude and emitted such force that it was off-putting. "Don't back down, Johnny, you never know, just ask for a helping hand, damn it, you can do it, you're his elder," Johnson thought bitterly to himself. "OK, here's the deal; I need some information on some..."

Johnny stood cut off by the younger officer's stare.

"No- you don't, old man...you don't want police work, you don't like how we judge people, we don't help you...now get out!"

Grunting, Johnny left the building. He would need to find another way to get the information—his eyes caught sight of the security cameras. Since returning from the war, he'd noticed they were everywhere. The thought sent a shiver up his spine.

Everything was monitored. Even the computer systems had back doors to allow the government access. He mulled the thought of government access. He needed access like the government to the government. Maybe he could commune with the government computers.

***

Knowing that he would quickly regret it, Johnny decided to hack into the military system to gather data on Timothy Pockets. Hacking was the absolute wrong way to describe what Johnny did. Hackers manipulated computer code to bypass other code. Johnny's skill was to converge with the computer. In becoming one with it, he would overlay various relays. He referred to it as coaxing out the information from the computer. Still others referred to it as hacking, so he kept the name.

Placing on Earth Crisis's *Destroy the Machine* album, Johnny laid his bionic arm next to his smartphone. He jacked into the phone with two wires he drew out of his arm.

There was a surge of pain, and then his head jerked back. Vapor waves of energy rolled through his arm and into his central nervous system. Scrolls of mathematical code-setting circuits on and off surged. His body changed circuit sequences, overwhelming firewalls and encryption codes at a more fundamental level.

A flurry of images, charts, and graphs appeared on the screen. Then, a wall of words appeared. He had reached the file on Captain Tim Pockets. By the end, Johnny was convinced there were too many discrepancies in the record. He decided it was time to visit his old friend Snark.

***

Snark was a nickname for a former military guy with whom Johnny hung out. His real name had long since been forgotten. Snark was a great guy but paranoid and a tad bit sarcastic.

The journey to Snark's was a grind. Not because of the distance—no, the city's slow crawl wore Johnny down. The streets near Snark's gun shop were a battleground of protesters, their chants blending with the blaring horns. Johnny slogged through the gridlock, the neon glow reflecting off his weary face. Above, the elite zipped by in their sleek hover quads, starkly contrasting the urban decay below. Frustration bubbled up, and Johnny sighed, contemplating ditching his quad for a bicycle. As he passed under a city camera, he felt a rebellious urge to flip it the bird.

Finally, Johnny arrived. He paid twenty credits to park. The lot was crowded, but with the row marking open spots, he found it surprisingly simple to find a place.

Entering Snark's score, he heard the man make his familiar call, "Johnny." Snark's face was all smiles, and Johnny felt his cheeks warm as he returned the smile. "Hey, Snark," Johnny called. He glanced around the shop to make sure no one else was present.

As if reading his mind, Snark called, "Shop's empty today, Johnny. What can I do for you? From your face, you're not here to purchase a gun."

"I need a favor,"

"Shoot," from a shop owner surrounded by laser and projectile weapons; the word shoot stretched Johnny's grin to the point his cheeks hurt.

"Reading over an old CID case."

"Criminal Investigation Command case," the old warrior offered. Johnny nodded. "Those are usually sealed, Johnny."

"Yeah, this was from back in the war. Came across some information in an old file that seemed inconsistent."

A twinkle burst in Snark's eyes. "Wow, inconsistency in an Army Investigation. Who would have thought?" Snark tried or maybe did not try to control his laugh. Johnny could never tell. "Lots of stuff don't add up."

"What was the incident?"

"Three marines killed in a rocket attack."

"Army and Marines- not sure of the connection,"

"Captain Tim Pockets,"

"Excuse me?"

"Tim Pockets was an Army guy who served as a material witness in the case. He reported some difficulty with the rocket launcher the morning of the attack."

"Ok. Sounds pretty straightforward."

"Well, after his testimony, the guy seemed unglued. He left the service. At first, he had a job with a pharmaceutical company, Bolens and Jones- they offered this guy a seven-figure salary."

"Wow, he must be one outstanding scientist," Snark teased.

A smile grew on the detective's lips, and he tilted his head. "No science background. He was in management but had no prior management experience or training."

"Military is awesome management training," Snark corrected, and the old detective realized he should back off on that one. Snark had long been an advocate for men returning from the war. He often tried to get corporations to hire the men based on their military backgrounds.

"I stand corrected. Anyhow, the guy started having emotional and adjustment problems."

"Johnny, many guys that served with us came home to adjustment problems."

"His seem worse. He got fired and later was caught

committing a petty crime while waiting for trial- he jumped bail."

"So, you think Bolen is trying to make him disappear."

"I don't know. Just got this nagging suspicion,"

"Bolen's they created piexel?"

"That's interesting. One of the dead was one Piexel after a wound to his stomach."

"Rumors are it is a bad drug, Johnny. Last I heard, it was supposed to stimulate genes to fix damage to the intestine, but it caused bleeding. A bunch of guys in my unit suffered heavily. No lawyer would take the case, though."

"Interesting,"

"Bolen, they are a subsidiary of Yak-Johnny. Yak's on the council. Are you sure you want to chase this answer down?"

"I am not sure," Johnny huffed. "My interest is just to bring the guy in-bounty work. I don't know why I keep getting into his life."

"You always had a soft heart, Johnson," Snark teased. "you little liberal." Johnny snickered. "Bounty hunter work? I didn't know you did that."

"First case," Johnny confessed. "Money is very tight."

"Hey, if you want to work in the store, I could use an extra pair of hands." This time, Snark froze, remembering the bionic and not wanting to come off as making light of the issue.

"Thank Snark, but I need to carve out my world, you know?"

"I understand. Look, Johnny, if you want my advice, do the job you are getting paid to do. Forget the details of the case." Johnny wished it stayed that simple for him.

"You're right, Snark. I am not sure what I was thinking." Johnny took a deep breath. "Sorry to waste your time."

"Not a problem at all. I might even be able to help you on this one."

"Yeah, how?"

"Well, there is a house down on the docks where many vets go who have no place to stay. It is Saint Clare's home for lost souls."

"You think he might be there?"

"No idea, Johnny, but it would be where I would start,"

"Thanks, Snark; I am in your debt once again."

"Don't worry, Johnny. Someday, I plan to come calling on those old IOUs." Johnny knew that Snark always said this but never came calling.

***

After meeting with Snark, Johnny headed to his car. He flipped on his music stream. Minor Threat's *Small Man Big Mouth* played while Johnny's mind rolled over the information and the lead. He made one stop to pick up dinner, a small mix of nachos and guacamole, and the rice he could barely afford.

Down to the wharf, he raced. On his way, as much as he tried to prevent it, he pondered the information about the lawsuit, trying to pace it into what he read into the file.

Once he arrived, Johnny headed to Saint Clare. To his surprise, the dock was not dark anymore and rundown, as he remembered. It was retrofitted with low-pressure orange-yellow sodium-vapor streetlights. The lights cast a beautiful reflection on the water. They shifted their colors occasionally due to the gas-discharge and moonlight-hued matrix of spiraling light-emitting diodes.

The pier had shed its graffiti skin, replaced by vibrant murals that told stories of rebellion and survival. The anti-graffiti network program had taken the cleaning up of this area by storm. The four storage buildings stood like silent sentinels, their walls now canvas of urban art. Beside the pier, sleek microjet boats, cheap and efficient, ferried passengers across the murky waters. The city had been plagued by rolling brownouts for months, casting shadows over its neon heart. But as Johnny stood there, a rare smile tugged at his lips. Amidst the decay, something was finally getting better, not worse.

The opposite vision was true for the Saint Claire. It was a capsule hotel with blight on its pink paint. A hologram of a rose danced freely in front of a large fountain. The cascade of water stirred to the sounds of music playing next to it and alternated with multicolor spotlights. Affordable on a working man's pay, Johnny knew the accommodations must have been sparse.

Around Saint Claire, there was a smattering of plants that

could survive with little need for water. Johnny noted white sage and wild lilac as the main glass doors slid wide for him to enter.

Johnny sauntered up to the front desk. Trying to gain some without, Johnny yanked out his detective badge. "My name is Detective Johnson. I am working for Jake's Bail Bond loans. I am searching for a fugitive who jumped bail. His name is Timothy Pockets."

The man looked down at his computer list. "We don't have any Timothy Pockets staying here. Sorry."

Johnny pulled out a picture of Pockets, "Are you sure?"

"Ah, that is Mr. James Pinto," the desk attendant offered. "He has been here a couple of months. He is on a monthly rental contract. "

"Really? What room?"

"1538, but he is not there now. Left for dinner about an hour ago,"

"Where did he go?"

"The woman's roller derby club, I believe. He has eaten there in the past. He seems to like the sport, but I did not ask about it tonight."

"I'll just wait here,"

"Ok. The couch over by the rug is very comfortable," And Johnny had to agree it was. He waited patiently for over an hour. He kept an eye on the entrance and let his callous fingers fold over his chest. He jumped a little in his seat whenever anyone approached it. Then, finally, Timothy Pockets approached the glass doors. Johnny slumped in the chair, and when Pockets cleared the doors, he sprang up and marched toward the man.

"Timothy Pockets," Johnny said, his voice firm. The man's face darkened, his lips tinged blue, and then flushed deep red. His legs trembled before he bolted.

Mumbling curses to himself, Johnny sped off in hot pursuit. Johnny yelled as he cleared the hotel doors, "Tim- look, man, I got your file. Come back with me, and I will give this stuff to your attorney. It might help you get clear."

"Dude, you got no idea. They will bury this stuff. Right after the sick me in a cell with a guy who will shank me into the never world."

"I think you mean netherworld,"

Pockets dashed across the street, yelling, "Seriously?"

"Yeah, seriously, it is netherworld," Johnny informed, missing the deep sarcasm in the man's tone.

"Callous? Heartless? Petty?" Pockets mumbled loud enough for Johnny to hear it as they tore down the street.

Pockets charged onward. Johnny tried out but kept up the pursuit. It seemed a long time since his last all-out run. He needed Pockets to make a mistake, but he realized that was unlikely to happen. So, he kept calling things out to the guy: "At least tell me why you ran."

"Does it matter?" Pocket's voice echoed through the neon-lit alley, his breath ragged, each step a jarring reminder of his desperation.

Johnny's heart pounded in sync with his footsteps, the city's grime clinging to his boots. "To me, it does," he shouted, his voice barely cutting through the cacophony of distant sirens and the hum of cybernetic life.

"They're gonna kill me, man," Pocket's voice cracked, fear palpable even through the static of their comms.

"Is it because you know the truth about the drug?" Johnny's question hung in the air, a desperate gamble. The silence that followed was deafening.

"It started with the drug, but then..." Pocket's voice trembled, the weight of his confession almost too much to bear.

"The rockets? Is that it?" Johnny pressed, his mind racing.

Timothy's guilt was a living thing, seeping through every word. "They told me to rig the system. I did it. I killed three people for them. I thought it wouldn't matter. It was war. I'd killed hundreds, but this... this was different."

Johnny's voice softened, a rare moment of vulnerability in the harsh reality of their world. "We all make mistakes. None of us want to be defined by the worst things we've done. When you returned, the guilt started eating at you because the job was part of the payoff."

"You're not my shrink," Timothy snapped, but his pace quickened, the weight of his sins driving him forward.

"They failed you, Tim." Johnny replied. A steady shaking

occurred in his heart. The morality of this world, failing its soldiers when they returned from war and the pressure from private industry to clean up messes, had happened to more than one of his friends. Hell, even Stark had experienced similar problems trying to get his post-war pension.

"No, they tried to help me, even with my guilt. They said they could enhance me. I let them do it."

"Enhance you? How?" Johnny's voice was strained, the distance between them growing with each step. He shouted louder, desperation creeping in.

"A drug to change my constitution so I would feel less," Pocket's voice was a hollow echo, "but in the end, it only made me feel more. I aim to return the favor to them. I've made my decision."

Pockets veered off the side of the pier, melting into the shadows. Johnny considered letting him go for a full minute, the weight of his survival pressing down. But then reality hit—letting Pockets go meant unpaid bills and another night in the cold. He turned back, determination hardening his resolve, and headed for Pocket's hotel room.

After speaking with the hotel manager and slipping the guy twenty credits, Johnny got the key to Pocket's tiny room. Inside, the temperature exceeded one hundred degrees. The place was small, with no air conditioner or fan, and the window was jammed shut.

Sparsely furnished, Johnny noticed newspapers and magazines were left on the floor. By the bed, Johnny saw a small dehumidifier. He flipped the switch, but the unit did not go on. Broken, Johnny pondered if he could fix it. Knowing Pockets would never return to this chamber, he took it.

Sorting through the drawers, Johnson found a collage that Pockets was creating. It was an odd array of pictures of Bolen's staff, and it had circles drawn on cut-out pictures of the Yak's board of directors. Were Pockets planning to kill them? Johnny's mind replayed Pocket's last words, "I aim to return the favor. I've made my decision."

The neon lights flickered outside Johnny's window, casting long shadows across the cluttered desk. He tugged out his battered phone, fingers trembling as he dialed Daisy. Against all odds, she answered. "Yeah, Johnny," her voice crackled through the static.

"Daisy, I need a search," he rasped, desperation seeping into his tone.

"After hours, boss. Can it wait?" Her voice was weary, tinged with the fatigue of too many late nights.

"Please, Daisy. Just this once. It might help me cover your check this week," Johnny pleaded, his voice breaking.

A heavy sigh echoed through the line. "Alright, but don't make this a habit."

"When's the next board meeting for Yak?" Johnny's voice was barely a whisper.

He heard the familiar clatter of keys as Daisy searched. The seconds stretched into an eternity; the silence filled with the hum of the city outside. Finally, her voice cut through the tension. "Friday, boss. If their meeting tonight ended."

"Where were they planning to meet tonight?" Johnny's heart pounded as he waited for her response. "Corporate headquarters," Daisy said. "They had a specially catered dinner and a huge ball after that planned."

"OK," Johnny sighed. Thanks, Daisy." Johnny pressed the glass screen and rushed to his car. He jumped inside and peeled rubber out of the parking lot. The screech of his wheels echoed on the asphalt road. He turned the bend. The yellow strips on his bar created a massive blur.

How was Pocket planning to kill them? Johnny had no answer to the question, but he knew their lives were in danger. As guilty as they were, Johnny believed justice came from the courts, not vengeance.

Arriving at the building, Johnny pulled into the closest pot on the street and maneuvered into it. He passed many gentlemen wearing fine suits and women in beautiful gowns. Then he saw a security guard approaching him. He had no invitation.

"Excuse me, sir. Is your name on the guest list?"

"N-No," Johnny stammered as he fumbled for his badge. He whipped it out and presented it to the officer. "I am a detective in search of a fugitive from the law. I have reason to believe he is coming to this site."

"We need to check your credentials. Please come to the security office," the guard insisted. Off to his left, Johnny saw Tim entering the elevator. The man appeared thin and sweaty. His eyes were sunken. Had he run the entire way here? Pocket's skin was crackling, like energy was jumping from his shoulder.

Pointing toward the elevator, Johnny yelled, "That's him." As the guard turned, Johnny pushed past him and headed through the large crowd toward the elevator. He felt the guard in hot pursuit behind him. He reached the elevator just after the heavy door shut. "He is on the elevator," Johnny offered.

"Let's go to the security office, and I will shut the elevator down," the guard promised. Johnny rushed the guard to the security office. A second guard was seated at the video surveillance table. They glanced at the elevator screens, and Johnny pointed out Pockets. The man looked horrible.

"That's him," Johnny pointed. "Shut it down."

The first guard nodded, and the second guard shut the elevator down. As the elevator shut, Pocket appeared to grow more distressed. The sparks were now evident. "He looks like he is going to explode," Johnny managed to say.

"I tried to be a tin pocket, but the emotions," Pockets whispered and then exploded. Flame and force expanded, exploding the elevator doors. The entire building shook. The evacuation lights fluttered on, and Johnny hastily retreated from the building.

As he pushed past the security guard, the man said to the second, "Quickly call the fire department."

Realizing the bounty was dead or alive, Johnny unrolled wires from his arm, "Can you download me a copy of the video? I will need it to collect my bounty."

"Sir, that is the least of my concerns at this point,"

"Have a heart," Johnny insisted.

Outside of the building, Johnny saw the entire center of the building was aflame. *What the hell had Yak done to him? What kind of genetic manipulation lets you build energy when you get emotional?* Maybe they deserved this. Briefly, Johnny flashed back on the experimental drug he was given in his black-op mission over the Iraqi border into Syria. Was this his fate?

INVESTIGATING THE FUTURE

Marisha Cautilli
Joseph Cautilli

L ashing rain harshly pounded the buildings of Shanghai, and occasional flashes of lightning blistered the sky. Hugo's home was in a towering dark turquoise apartment complex, touching the smoggy grey sky. He lived next to his office on the one-hundred-and-twentieth floor. Hover cars floated by his windows, zipped, dove, and rolled back onto the four-line highway, nearly reaching his window.

Heavy winds buffeted the thin steel glass that gave him the perfect view and protected him from the elements. Somedays in the morning, when a rare glimpse of the sun dangled through the photochemical smog, Hugo was genuinely amazed by the glory he witnessed.

Hugo's home was a small, confined space with a small balcony that looked out on the streets of Shanghai, China. People always strolled along the streets of the city, no matter what the day. With umbrellas raised so they appeared to be made of black silk, they scampered on the streets like little ants to Hugo's eyes.

His hands shook as he touched the glass. The chilled wind passed through the window, and his fingers felt icy. The beat of water was hypnotic and pulled his mind away.

Hugo often missed his home in France, but he worked for La Petit Journal. After many years in his beloved France, Hugo, with great regret, took his employer's option to become a correspondent in China. He hated China—not the people so much, just the empty cities and dismal landscapes.

In the early 2010s, China began to build massive cities where no one lived. The goal, of course, was to pay people to work, and China's communist government planned to move 300 million people of its over one billion population into these cities. Hugo thought this was a massive waste of time, but his lead editor wanted him to chase down the story as deeply as it went. First, he flatly refused to go, but when the editor offered to raise his salary, he backtracked.

It was not like Hugo was a particularly greedy man. To think so would be to not understand the actual amounts being offered. Most days, though, he sat in his flat exhausted from restless nights that had started with the time change, and his body just never completely adjusted.

The rain slowed now, and Hugo thought it would soon stop. Hugo sighed with relief and turned back to his work.

Despite his exhaustion, Hugo managed to get lots of work done (primarily because he knew no one and had no friends in China, so the only thing left was work). He was particularly excited about what he discovered when searching through the records on the new buildings in Erenhot, close to China's border with Mongolia. He caught a second break when he received an anonymous call from a young man who was no longer hen twenty. Sloughing was the name the man used. He thought maybe it was an alias, but he was not sure.

In the twentieth century, an alias known as "Deep Throat" had brought down a US president, now almost one hundred years. Well, however, it was to be, the kid's voice sounded nervous. Hugo agreed to meet him. They met in the back of an old coffee. The place was empty but for a few US expatriates. Hugo motioned to buy him a brownie, but the kid refused and hurried into a booth.

The teen was nervous and kept looking at the door. Hugo asked him why he was frightened, and the kid only said, "Word is that they brought in an outside shooter to hunt me down," and then Sloughing gave Hugo a bunch of documents. Minutes later, the boy was gone. That had been two weeks ago.

Now Hugo scratched his chin. The pages were light blue under his lamp light. When his eyes poured over the records, he felt a jolt in his heart. The Chinese government seemed to have a secret: the polycarbonate glass steal substance they were using when manufactured pushed China's overall CO_2 production far higher than they had agreed with the West. China began manufacturing this thin- one-layer thick form of steel glass back in 2035, and it has remained quite popular in many places. The glass had several buyers in China and a single buyer- a US-based corporation in New Cyber City.

The Haasting Corporation purchased vast amounts of glass. It appeared to be using it to build a skyscraper to house its corporate center.

His scoop was precious, and he knew it was an exclusive. Still, he needed to keep the information secret or risk winding up in a Chinese prison cell on some trumped-up charge. He typed on his MEGA- Smart iPad for three days straight. The story was inked no sooner than he received a call from a Chinese magistrate. The meeting was pleasant enough, but the magistrate had confiscated his computer system, suggesting that he was using the system to access unauthorized parts of the internet – French gambling casinos.

Sweat poured over Hugo's face. He fought hard not to roll his eyes and swing back his head in disgust. Of course, he immediately complied.

While Hugo no longer had original documents scanned on his computer, he still had one copy of the manuscript tucked in hiding. His mind raced as to what to do. Four days passed, and then he received a phone call.

It was a former co-worker, Bette, whom he simply adored.

She was very beautiful and very charming. On more than one occasion, Bette had soothed and flattered his ego. So today, Hugo was excited that he would get to spend time with her. She has always had interesting stories and now owns her newspaper. The paper was small, but it was a fantastic accomplishment at her age.

Two hours later, the doorbell rang. The Frenchman got up from his desk and rushed to answer it. From his window, Hugo saw the dismal, dark, and cloudy sky. All these days in China, he seemed cloudy.

Outside, acid rain poured, so Bette wore a jacket made of a special material that protected its wearer from burns. The coat's hood was pulled over her head to ensure it did not suffer burns, either.

'Pollution,' Hugo thought to himself as he unlocked the door to the hallway. The corridor was as lean as rabbit meat. The elevator was on the other side of the hall. A blue-textured carpet felt as soft as his Serta mattress, but it was hard. The yellow walls made the entire antechamber look like a messed-up picture.

"Hello, Hugo," called his coworker in French as she stepped out the doorway to her room. She leaned in and kissed his cheek. Hugo felt a burning sensation and realized he was blushing.

Composing himself, he said, "Hello, Bette, softly." His eyes scanned her. She was still stunningly beautiful. Her auburn hair was short and clean, and her deep blue eyes were sparkling. At five foot six inches, her features were highlighted by a plain red blouse with a black ruffle skirt. It was both professional and sexy. As he gazed at her face, he noticed she wore lipstick, highlighting her lips more than her other features. He felt like he was falling into the deep blue of her eyes.

"How are you?" Bette questioned. The words snapped him out of his trance.

"Tired," he offered. Savoring another look at her face.

"Well, that's not good. Why?" Her cheerful smile grew into a shocked expression.

"I was banned from publishing an article," Hugo replied, his appearance grim. Hugo picked up his black leather briefcase.

Bette frowned. "So sorry to hear."

"Yeah, well, let's go to dinner. I booked up at this great Italian Restaurant."

"Pretty rare?" she asked with a perplexed look and eyebrows that knitted together in the center.

"No, Shanghai is a pretty global city," Hugo replied as the two entered the hallway. She appeared to marvel at his worldliness.

"So what was your piece about?" Bette asked. As they both walked down the corridor, Hugo explained his piece. Reaching the elevator, Hugo pushed the button for the first floor and escorted her inside. In the background, soft music played, and the elevator smelled like the puffy perfume of an oceanic type—this brand smelled like fresh mountain air.

The smells and being with his friend made Hugo feel something he had not in a while. Trying to label the feelings, he realized they were joyous, almost jubilant. A big smile shoved his smile to his ears. As his lips thinned, Hugo asked, "How was your flight?"

"All those disgusting slobs from the western hemisphere were on board. I booked business class, considering I would try and fish for something fresh myself in China," she said with marked indifference.

"Have you found any luck?" He gritted his teeth, hoping that she had not found good stories.

"There was a riot in Bejing, so I jotted down notes." Bette handed Hugo a sheet from her clipboard.

"Wow, it sounds pretty amazing," his eyes widened with enthusiasm.

"At least it's something good since our newspaper is failing," announced his colleague.

"Aren't all newspapers failing, Bette?" Hugo asked, puzzled.

293

"No, I went to the United States for a month, and everyone read a copy of The New York Times!"

"Bette, slow down. Nobody reads the newspapers anymore! All the articles are online!"

"The point is that our business is failing, and we need fresh editorials. No one read any of the current articles!" Bette bit her lip. She looked down at her clipboard.

Confused, he stared at her, thinking of how to impress his old coworker. Bette looked at the holographic screen. Hugo licked the roof of his mouth.

"Well, your piece sounds awesome if you can write it,"

"I plan to write it," Hugo said.

Looking shocked, Bette asked, "How?"

"I still have a copy of the story,"

"How is Shanghai life?" Bette inquired, changing the subject.

Even though Hugo was irritated with Shanghai, he was keen to keep in touch with Bette. So he mustered a second wind with a huge, deep breath. Revived, he said, "It's fine, though it rains acid rain daily—barely anything to do. Historic sites are now close to nuclear plants. The water looks very disgusting. This place is nowhere near Marseille's beauty!"

"I admit Marseille was beautiful." She crossed her arms and stared at him. Bette did not notice that she dropped her pen, which rolled on the elevator's hard tile.

"I just hope my story has an impact. My editors took a big risk sending me here. It was very costly for the paper."

"My newspaper is barely surviving," Bette whispered, tucking her hands into her skirt.

"How did you manage to buy it?"

"Odd thing, it was one of the few papers still local enough to be a family press. My cousin owned it and passed it to me,"

Catching an evening news story on the virtual reality screen on the elevator, Hugo turned his back to Bette. She smiled wily.

"Well, I keep my dreams going with hope. The story under

my pillow gets a Pulitzer." If he was grinning, she could not tell.

"Hugo, that's a thing all reporters wish for." She smiled, knowing how desperate he was for a good piece.

"Yes, but this piece has it all,"

"Really, how did you happen to get it?"

"Crazy thing- just found it reviewing some documents."

"No sources?"

"Well, some kid?"

"Kid?"

"Nobody really,"

"Kid have a name?"

"Why?"

"No reason," Bette joked, reaching into her back pocket to grab a laser knife. In one motion, the knife flew out of her back pocket. The young woman tightly grasped a pocket laser. Drawing it out, she pressed the button, and its light knife extended.

With his mind still trying to comprehend the news story about the riot on the virtual video, Hugo turned to tell Bette his interpretation of events in Beijing.

"What is that?" Hugo asked when he spotted a laser light blade, shimmering and humming as it hung briefly in the air. Bette launched herself into him. Hugo's eyes widened with fear, and his heart quickened as he tried to bring his arm up to protect himself. He was too late.

Plunging her dagger into his neck, it tore through his skin and deep into his carotid artery. Blood spurted into the air. He gagged as pain rushed through him.

"I guess this is the end," Bette stated, lifting the knife. "You'll be with me even if you're not here."

Before leaving for her hotel room with her borrowed hover car, she stole his room key, acquired Hugo's backup copy, and sneakily mangled through the crowds. She rushed to her hotel room with her rented hover. The next day, she would wake early, stop at a Chinese bank, and deposit the check the Chinese government gave her for her newspaper company.

Notes on These Stories:

---

[1] Events in this story occur twelve years before *The Source* by Tobias Cabral, Joseph and Marisha Cautilli, and Johnny Andrews.

[2] This story takes place eleven years prior to the Source and nineteen years prior to Soul Warriors vs Witches. Both available on JEA Press

[3] Events in this story occur seven years before the events in the Source: In the Line of Duty.

[4] Events in this story take place six years before the events in the Source: In the Line of Duty.

We would like to thank Tobias Cabral for helping us edit the story.

[5] This story takes place about three years before *The Source* by Joseph and Marisha Cautilli and Tobias Cabral.

[6] This story takes place around the same time as *The Source* by Joseph and Marisha Cautilli and Tobias Cabral, and about a year before the events of *Insolent Friendships*.

[7] This story takes place a little under a year after *The Source* by Joseph and Marisha Cautilli and Tobias Cabral.

[8] This story takes place a few months after *Insolent Friendships* by Marisha and Joseph Cautilli

[9] Events here occur during the upcoming *The Nine Towers of Babel* trilogy by Marisha and Joseph Cautilli, and about thirty years prior to *Red Light Falling: A Noir Tale of Redemption* by Joseph and Marisha Cautilli, and Johnny Andrews.

[10] Events in this story take place 17 years prior to events described in the first chapter of Red Light Falling by Johnny Andrews and Joseph Cautilli with Diary Entries by Marisha Cautilli.

We would like to thank David Stegora for his hard work on this story. David Stegora passed away fast and unexpectedly on June 25th, 2020. He was an amazing co-author to work with and we miss him and his insights deeply.

[11] The events in this story take place between book two and three of the Red light Falling Series written by Johnny Andrews, Marisha Cautilli, and Joseph Cautilli

Made in the USA
Columbia, SC
13 January 2025

51689875R00163